Journey back to an age of seductive dan... and scandalous love as na... unter draws you into the hea...

THE SEDUCER

Daniel St. John: Charismatic and mysterious, this dangerously seductive man has survived a treacherous revolution; a master of the arts of war and intrigue, he knows the secrets of winning a woman's heart . . . and body.

THE SAINT

Vergil Duclairc: This dashing nobleman leads a dangerous double life; beneath his perfect composure and self-control is a sensual master whose mere touch can tempt a woman to the wildest abandon.

THE CHARMER

Adrian Burchard: This virile aristocrat is used to having women at his command; darkly handsome, sensuous, magnetic, he lives in a world of mysteries and secrets . . . a man dangerous to love, impossible to resist.

THE SINNER

Dante Duclairc: A daring and reckless libertine, he's as infamously charming as the devil himself, and his sensuous temptation promises the kind of fall into earthly paradise every woman dreams of taking.

THE ROMANTIC

Julian Hampton: Like a knight of old, his smoldering reserve conceals a sensual undercurrent of passion and poetry that sweeps every woman before him—but his love is reserved for only one.

Fighters, protectors, lovers, they live in a dazzling world of glittering ballrooms and sinful gaming halls, in a time of heart-stopping duels and soul-searing passion.

These are their stories . . . .

THE SINNER

"Packed with sensuality and foreboding undertones, this book boasts rich historical details and characters possessing unusual depth and vitality, traits that propel it beyond the standard historical romance fare." —*Publishers Weekly*

"Sensual, intriguing, and absorbing, prolific Hunter scores again." —*Booklist*

"There are books you finish with a sigh because they are so rich, so tender, so near to the heart that they will stay with you for a long, long time. Madeline Hunter's historical romance, *The Sinner,* is such a book." —*Oakland Press*

THE CHARMER

"With its rich historical texture, steamy love scenes and indelible protagonists, this book embodies the best of the genre." —*Publishers Weekly* (starred review)

"In yet another excellent offering from Hunter, her intriguing characters elicit both fascination and sympathy." —*Booklist*

THE SAINT

"[An] amusing, witty, and intriguing account of how love helps, not hinders, the achievement of dreams." —*Booklist*

THE SEDUCER

"Hunter . . . sweeps both her readers and her characters up in the embrace of history. Lush in detail and thrumming with sensuality, this offering will thrill those looking for a tale as rich and satisfying as a multi-course gourmet meal." —*Publishers Weekly*

"*The Seducer* is a well-crafted novel . . . characteristically intense and frankly sexual." —*Contra Costa Times*

"[An] intriguing and redemptive tale." —*Booklist*

"Angst and passion battle it out in this very sensual story." —*Oakland Press*

Also by Madeline Hunter

THE SINS OF LORD EASTERBROOK

SECRETS OF SURRENDER

LESSONS OF DESIRE

THE RULES OF SEDUCTION

BY ARRANGEMENT

BY POSSESSION

BY DESIGN

LADY OF SIN

LORD OF SIN

THE PROTECTOR

LORD OF A THOUSAND NIGHTS

STEALING HEAVEN

THE SEDUCER

THE SAINT

THE CHARMER

THE SINNER

the ROMANTIC

Madeline Hunter

BANTAM BOOKS

THE ROMANTIC
A Bantam Book / November 2004

Published by Bantam Dell
A Division of Random House, Inc.
New York, New York

Cover art by Alan Ayers

ISBN 978-0-553-58729-6

Manufactured in the United States of America
Published simultaneously in Canada

OPM 10 9 8 7

I had decided to dedicate this novel to my editor, Wendy McCurdy, even before I wrote the first chapter. After ten books, it was past time to acknowledge the critical role she has had in my career.

As it turns out, this is the perfect book in which to thank her for her advice, support, and friendship.

One reason is because her editorial skills helped improve this story in important ways, and make it better than it might have been.

She already knows the other reason.

the ROMANTIC

chapter I

For a bachelor, there is no more dangerous person in the world than a happily married woman.

To such a female, an unattached man of position and property is a rough stone sticking out of life's wall. The more blissful her own union, the more convinced she becomes that the bachelor stone wants smoothing. She is sure it would be a much happier stone if it were as neatly chiseled and mortared as her husband.

So it was that Julian Hampton found himself seated beside the talkative widow, Mrs. Morrison, when he attended the Viscountess Laclere's banquet.

He made no special note of the way the viscountess watched the progress of their conversation, but he did not miss it either.

"Your occupation must be fascinating, Mr. Hampton," the comely widow said, when her very detailed description of her summer holiday in Brighton waned.

"Being a solicitor is very dull employment, in reality."

Actually it wasn't, but the Mrs. Morrisons of the world would never understand why.

She laughed and her eyes sparkled. She turned so that her glowing face was fully visible. "I cannot believe that anything you occupy yourself with is dull, Mr. Hampton."

"I assure you that I am a thoroughly unremarkable man. I bore myself so much that I can barely stay awake."

"Well, you do not bore me," she said with a meaningful smile.

He speculated on why the viscountess had chosen to throw at him this golden-haired young lady of little wit, submissive grace, and dull loquaciousness. Since he had not pursued the more compelling women trotted out thus far, the viscountess and her friends had probably concluded he did not want interesting companionship in his home.

Since Lady Laclere had opened her circle to a woman she probably did not overly favor, and just for his benefit, he dutifully gave Mrs. Morrison serious consideration. She was more than attractive enough, and he suspected she would be pleasant to have in bed. She had a respectable fortune, and lovely breasts partly revealed by her décolleté. Her manner indicated that she would be the sort of earnestly accommodating wife whom men were supposed to want. She would be a perfect prospect for a man seeking to secure domestic tranquility.

Regretfully, he was not such a man.

He lobbed a question about her young son. She took up the topic with the enthusiasm any good mother would show. While most of his mind listened to tales of the boy's antics and brilliance, a renegade corner of it composed a letter to the Viscountess Laclere.

> My dear Lady Laclere,
>
> I greatly appreciate the concern that you show for my future happiness. The parade of eligible females whom you have arranged for me to inspect these last few months has been impressive in its variety. I am touched, nay, I am moved, by your thoughtfulness. I must regretfully inform you, however, that your quest is in vain, as is that of the Duchess of Everdon, and the more subtle efforts of Mrs. St. John. I will not marry. Therefore, I respectfully request to be released from the social yoke that you have placed on me.
>
> Your servant—

"My, she can certainly converse with the best of them, can't she?"

The low, throaty voice intruded on his letter before he could add his signature. It came on a hush of breath from the woman sitting to his right.

Señora Perez. Another married woman, and dangerous in her own way. One quite different from the viscountess.

Señora Perez was the wife of Raoul Perez, a diplomat from the young country of Venezuela who lived in London to promote his people's economic interests. They were present at this banquet because it was being hosted by the Viscount Laclere to celebrate the recent passage of the bill that abolished slavery throughout the British Empire, an event of momentous symbolism for all people in the Americas.

Julian had tried to ignore the fact that this married woman had intimated since their meeting that she found rough stones on smooth walls appealing and challenging.

He let the comment pass, but soon it was time to pay this other lady attention, as the conversation shifted to the right.

"Your English is exceptional, considering you only recently joined your husband here in London," he said.

"I have been studying your language and customs for years. I told Raoul that I would not come until I could make him proud, and not fumble like a peasant at parties such as this."

"You have succeeded admirably."

While she explained her studies, that mutinous corner of his mind wandered. He saw the bright colors and sharp contrasts of her land in his head. *Crystal blue waters stretched along ivory beaches. Pirate ships bobbed in the surf as daring men hauled booty to shore, and chestnut-skinned women watched, clothed in reds and oranges and blues. An argument broke out over some gold, and swords were drawn, and metal clashed and storms blew in and the ocean churned in sublime fury and—*

"You are not a man much given to social intercourse, are you, Mr. Hampton?" Her throaty voice carried a Spanish tinge, and nuances of other, more primitive cultures. Her dark eyes flashed humor at him, and her skin, the color of shelled almonds, appeared very exotic in her very British blue dinner dress.

"I regret that I was not blessed with the natural ease in such situations that many others enjoy."

"That is not true. I watched you in the drawing room. It is not lack of ease. You do not care for it. No doubt you know that your reserve is often misunderstood, but you do not care about that, either."

"Is it misunderstood? I would have thought it not worthy of notice at all."

"Men think you are proud, and just as dull as you claim."

"Perhaps they are correct on both counts."

"Women, however... well, women wonder what is in that head of yours, and what lurks under that armor of indifference, and what you think as you watch our human comedy play out on life's stage."

She exuded a carnality that no man could ignore, no matter what his armor. She wore her own lack of reserve like a flag, in the way of her more expressive culture.

"Is that what you wonder, madame?"

"Yes."

"Would it please you if I confide it all? Reveal the truth? Admit the contemplations that emerge in my silence?"

"I would love to know."

He cocked his head conspiratorially. "I think about..."

"Yes?" she encouraged.

"I think about what I will have for supper the next evening."

She leveled her dark eyes on him. "I consider it a great triumph that you deign even to tease me. I understand men such as you very well. Your reserve is more like that of my people than your own, you see. The silence smolders. I think with time that you would indeed reveal all, however. With the right incentive."

She let him know what incentive she meant. Her leg pressed his beneath the table.

Julian took a sip of wine and gazed through the flickering candles at Lady Laclere.

My dearest Viscountess,

Your hospitality at the banquet overwhelmed me. It is rare for a man to leave his home of an evening, and find himself within hours sitting with a prospective wife of handsome fortune and sweet demeanor on one side, and with a potential mistress of indubitable sensuality on the other. The opportunities which you have afforded me are truly generous. Unfortunately, a life of tedium waits with one woman, and an angry husband demanding satisfaction with the other. Therefore, I think it best to retreat from either pursuit and must, with some pain, refuse both gifts.

My sincere gratitude for the honor of the invitation, etc., etc.

Julian Hampton

That night, back in his house on Russell Square, Julian sat down at his writing desk to compose another letter. This time he used pen and ink.

The events of the evening caused the words to flow in a rush of scratches. It was an outpouring to relieve an agitation of the spirit that needed release before it provoked bitterness and resentment.

My incomparable beloved,

Seven months you have been gone, and I fear you will never return. I await your brief, infrequent letters like a boy, desperate for any small indication

> that you remember I exist, hoping for evidence that you tire of that foreign land where you now live. I read your missives a hundred times for the slightest intimation that you will be coming home. The part of my mind that does nothing but wait grows daily, and soon nothing will be left to attend to life's duties. One word, my love, just one word; that is all I seek. One word to let me know that you will not stay away forever, and that I will at least have your presence and friendship in my life, even if I can never have your passion and your love.

The last phrase came much more slowly. The admission was essential to write, however. He had sworn to himself half a lifetime ago to have no illusions where this woman was concerned.

He did not bother with his signature. Calmer now, oddly so, he gazed down at the letter for a long while, then carefully folded it.

Opening a desk drawer, he glanced at a thick stack of similarly folded papers. Some contained letters like this, written to ease a brooding restlessness or explosive fury. Others held poems or stories in which love thrived in worlds much kinder to deep sentiment than this unromantic, practical Britain. The ones at the bottom, the oldest ones, already showed changes in the color of the ink as a hallmark of their age.

It had been a very long time since he had added anything to this drawer. Why tonight? Why had this mood gripped him as that dinner party wound its way through the dark hours?

Maybe it had been those two women. He normally

did not mind that he could not accept what each offered, but tonight, as the evening wore on, he had minded very much. He resented like hell that playing the besotted lover was a role he could no longer pull off. For years he had pretended he could, but eventually the dishonesty of feigning the expected affection had disgusted him.

So it probably had something to do with the women. Each was tempting in her own way. Too tempting, in the case of Señora Perez. He had spent the night in a state of mild but aggravating arousal, and that had only fed the storm rising in him. Tomorrow he would deal with that part of the tempest in the efficient, soulless way he chose now, with a professional woman who did not want love and revelations.

He looked at the letter resting between his fingers. A cold resolve entered him. He would burn it, and the others. Destroy them all, and marry Mrs. Morrison and have an affair with Señora Perez and live a normal life. He was too old to be writing letters and poems that were never sent.

He gazed at the pile of papers, then to the low flames in the fireplace.

"Sir."

Julian barely heard the salutation and hardly felt the nudge.

He emerged out of a dream in which he was doing scandalous things to the sweet widow Mrs. Morrison. Since she had been talking all through it, he was not entirely sorry to have the fantasy interrupted.

"Sir, I regret to wake you, but she will not leave." His valet's face hung over his own, doleful in its distress, hovering like a ghost's in the night lamp's glow.

"Batkin, what the hell are you talking about?"

"I only heard the rapping on the door because my chamber is over the street and my window is open and I do not sleep well. There it was, this sound. Not even loud. Well, I stuck my head out and there was this person at the door, and I went down and it was a woman, a lady, and now she is inside and won't leave."

Julian sat up and his valet came into fuller view. Despite being dragged from his bed, Batkin looked pressed and perfect, but then if a valet could not get presentable quickly, who could?

"What is her name?"

"She will not tell me. She only insists that she must speak with you at once."

"Does she have an accent?" He did not think that Señora Perez would come here in the dead of night with so little encouragement, but one never knew. Considering that his body was taking time to recover from that dream, a ruthless part of him hoped she had been so bold.

"No, her voice is that of an English lady. Her hat has a veil that obscures her face, so I am at a loss to describe her. She does claim that she is one of your clients."

Julian swung his body and sat on the bed's edge. He doubted any client had business so vital it could not wait until morning, but if this one would not leave he had no choice except to meet with her.

"Put her in the library. I will dress and be down."

A half hour later he descended to the library, both annoyed and intrigued by the mystery of this invasion.

The lady in question sat on the divan facing the fireplace, with only her hat visible when he entered. He could see only the crown of the green millinery and its fluff of blue feathers and the edges of the blue netting hung from the brim.

But he knew who it was.

The night's earlier restlessness returned, only now as a glorious tumult of euphoria.

The Countess of Glasbury had returned to England. Penelope had come home.

Contrasting emotions assaulted Penelope as she sat in the library.

The strongest reactions, the ones that felt so good that it seemed her soul exhaled a long-held breath, were those of relief and safety. She might have emerged at port after a dangerous sea voyage.

Beneath that peace, however, lurked a distinct awkwardness, and a growing concern that Mr. Hampton would be shocked by her presence in his house.

She could not ignore that she had intruded on a man's abode in the dead of the night. It was a scandalous thing to do. After all, Mr. Hampton may be her confidante and adviser, but he was unmarried.

She had never seen where he lived before. He had moved to this large house five years ago, but he did not entertain and she had never entered it, just as she had never seen the rooms he kept prior to buying this handsome home.

Tonight that struck her as odd. After all, she had known him since they were little more than children. He was a good friend of her brothers, and the family solicitor, and was usually present at their parties. But his private life remained a mystery, just as he was in many ways an enigma.

A large watercolor on the left wall caught her attention. Despite the low lighting, she recognized it as a study by Turner. This wash of hazy, romantic brushwork was even looser and more amorphous than his oils.

It was not the kind of painting that one would expect Mr. Hampton to favor. His crystalline reserve implied that he would prefer clearer, more classical works. Yet she had always sensed that other things lurked in him, and this watercolor appeared to confirm that. She had always suspected that with Julian Hampton the waters not only ran deeply, but they also carried unseen currents. The potentially dangerous lure of those depths had always made her slightly uncomfortable with him.

There were other little touches that fascinated her. Some Turkish pillows and a long narrow painting that looked Chinese. Had Mr. Hampton chosen those items himself, or had his friends, Adrian Burchard and Daniel St. John, who had traveled to those exotic lands, given them as gifts?

The library distracted her enough that she was startled to realize she was no longer alone. She sensed a vital presence, as if an invisible power began affecting the air.

Her spirit reacted in the oddest way, as it had for years with this counselor and friend. Indescribable calm washed through her, but other emotions pricked her instincts, too. Happiness. Fear. Melancholy. There was also that unsettling something that had no name but which placed her at a vaguely breathless disadvantage.

She turned her body on the divan to look to the door. He stood there, tall and dark and strongly lean, dressed as if he had just returned from a dinner party even though she suspected she had woken him from his sleep.

It had been a long time since she took specific note of how handsome he was, but she did tonight. Perhaps that was because she had not seen him in half a year. His dark hair and smoldering eyes and crisp features created a very romantic image. Her dear friend Diane St. John had once said he looked as if he would speak in poetry, should he ever deign to speak at all.

His expression was both curious and stern. She realized that the veil still obscured her identity. Balancing her hip against the divan's back cushion, she folded the veil back from her face.

"Countess."

The greeting did not even carry a tinge of surprise. It acknowledged her presence and welcomed her as if they had arranged this meeting.

He came forward. Still twisted on the divan, half kneeling, she extended her hand. He bowed to kiss it. She could feel his warm lips through her glove. Little sparkles danced up her arm.

"I apologize for intruding at this hour, Mr. Hampton. I know that it was a reckless thing to do, but events have left me no choice and I did not know where else to go, or whom to consult."

He was not a man who smiled easily, but he did so now. It was a nice smile, rather dazzling in its subdued, masculine way. It was a wonder he did not use it more with women, considering the girlish flutters it inspired.

"I would have been wounded if you had even considered turning elsewhere." He made a little twirling gesture with his finger to suggest she should right herself on the divan. As she did he walked around it and sat in a comfortable, heavily upholstered, wine-colored chair that he angled to face her.

Those keen eyes slowly took her in. "I have sent for tea, but you appear so distraught I wonder if something more fortifying is in order."

A liquid much more fortifying than tea would have been welcome an hour ago, but she did not need it now and said so.

His long look made her awkwardness spike. She wondered what conclusions he was drawing with his inspection. That she was showing her age? That she wasn't very pretty at all? He had not seen her in half a year either, and no doubt was noticing such things anew just as she had.

"I did not realize you had returned to England." His voice had a wonderful timbre. It always had. Even as a girl she had loved hearing it. "Laclere said nothing."

"My brother does not know I am here. No one in my family does. I have only been back several days and have been staying at Mivert's Hotel. I thought I could hide there while I contemplated what to do, but I was wrong. I am fairly sure that I was recognized today despite the veil. That is why I came to see you tonight. Once it is known I am back in England, I fear my situation will become perilous." She heard her own voice, not at all calm like his.

His lids lowered in a way that she recognized. The mind that had protected her better than any sword was sharpening itself to meet the challenge.

"Since you risked both our reputations and your own

independence visiting me like this, I assume you are in great need of aid, madame. Tell me what has happened."

Fear and frustration branched inside her. So did guilt, that she was so helpless that she had indeed risked his reputation for her own need.

"Glasbury is trying to abduct me. After all these years, he wants me back and is demanding that I give him his heir."

chapter 2

The valet brought them tea. Penelope felt abashed for being such a nuisance that the poor man had been reduced to such duties. Once all had been set out, Mr. Hampton dismissed him.

Which meant they could speak freely and would not be overheard or interrupted. They were alone.

Again the awkwardness pressed on her. It was foolish, really. As one of his clients, she had conducted many conversations in private with Mr. Hampton.

Yet this privacy was subtly different. The chamber and mood held an intimacy that both lured and confused her. She did not completely feel like a client seeking advice, but instead too much like a woman boldly visiting a man at night. Her awareness of their situation created a peculiar little simmer inside her.

Nothing in his manner encouraged that sensation. This was not a man who wore his opinions on his face. If he was as constantly conscious as she of how improper this was, he would never let her know.

"The earl wrote to me in Naples while my brother and Bianca were still there," she said. "Perhaps Vergil mentioned that to you."

"In passing. He did not give that as your reason for remaining there after he and Lady Laclere returned."

"What reason did he give?"

"He indicated that you found the society there more amiable for a woman in your circumstances."

She felt her face blushing.

That was a gentle way to put it. She suspected that her brother Vergil, the Viscount Laclere, had alluded to the men who hovered around her in Naples, offering fun and flattery.

"Was it more to your liking?" He asked the question casually but his gaze met hers quite directly.

"Yes."

"Then why have you returned?"

"I came to believe that the earl sent men for me. I felt I was being followed. I did not think it was safe to remain there."

He absorbed that, thoughtfully. "What was in the letters he wrote to you there?"

"The first two came early in my visit. They were his typical nasty notes, with threats to cut off my support if I did anything to bring disrepute to his name."

"And the others?"

"One more came, right before we were to sail for home. It was different. He demanded my return to our marriage. He said the law was on his side and he could force me to come back if I did not see reason. He said that he wanted the heir I owed him." It rushed out, every word of it just as repulsive as the man who wrote it.

Mr. Hampton leaned forward, his forearms resting on his knees so that his body angled toward her. For a moment she thought that he would reach over and touch her in a gesture of reassurance. He had done that once before, at another private meeting, when she was so distraught that her composure had left her.

To her astonishment he did reach out. He did not touch her arm, however. His hand covered hers where it lay balled on her knee. He gave a reassuring squeeze before he broke the contact.

Her body reacted as if he had not let go. The warm press of that palm and firm grasp of those fingers continued, invisibly.

"I wish that you had written and told me this."

"You said he would never dare such a thing," she said, a little resentfully. "You said he had too much to lose."

"And he does."

"It is very obvious that he is willing to call your bluff about exposing what I know."

"It was no bluff, and he knew it."

"Then he is so desperate for an heir that he is willing to take the scorn and scandal." The restlessness of the last few weeks returned. She got up and paced away to the windows. "So I remained in Naples, thinking I would be safe there. Then, a month ago I began to sense that I was being watched. Followed. I noticed a man, Neapolitan or Arab, always in the background when I went out."

"Could you have been mistaken? I doubt that even the earl would be so bold as to abduct you."

"You told me years ago, when we formed our plan, that it was legally impossible for a husband to abduct a wife because he had a right to her."

He had said more than that, and the rest of it hung in the air unspoken. He had explained that it was also legally impossible for a husband to rape a wife.

"Perhaps I was mistaken, but my peace was over. I could not stay there after that. I booked passage and came home."

Instinctively, she parted the drapes and gazed down at the street. It had become a habit, a precaution of the hunted. The way below was silent and empty.

"Are you thinking of returning to him?"

She swirled around, stunned by the question. "Never. I did not return for that reason. In fact, this is only an interlude on my journey. I have decided to go to America. He will never find me there. I will disappear into that vast land and—"

"No." The interruption was abrupt, firm, and resolute.

"I think it is the best course of action. In fact, I can think of no other."

"I do not advise it."

"I do not care what you advise. We are beyond that. Unless you tell me that the law will protect me from him, I am leaving England forever."

He did not respond. He knew better than she that the law would not protect her at all. Quite the opposite. Only the threat of exposure and scandal had kept the earl at bay this long, and evidently he had decided he did not care about that anymore.

"I want you to go to my brother and get me some money so that I can live once I am in America."

"Since you are in London, you can ask him yourself."

"I do not want him to know I am here. If he does, and the earl confronts him, I do not want him to have to lie.

Let him think that I am still in Naples and have asked you to speak for me. Once I have the funds, I will—"

"Laclere is not stupid." He rose and walked toward her. "He will suspect something is wrong. He will demand to know the truth."

"You must not tell him what Anthony is trying to do. Vergil may fight him if he learns of it and it will create a terrible scandal and—"

"I do not think your brother cares overmuch about scandals. His own choices in life have proven that."

"I will not have him facing one for me. I won't have him fighting duels for the sister who made a shambles of her life by marrying an evil man for all the wrong reasons. This is how I want to do it. Just go to him and get the money."

He was near her now, looking down with those unfathomable eyes. His face rarely showed his thoughts, but in his eyes one had glimmers of the mind. Women found that intriguing. There had been much discussion among the ladies regarding Julian Hampton over the years. Did the depths boil and churn, or were they cold as ice?

Looking in his eyes now, she saw something that made her heart sink. "You are not going to help me."

"I am not going to lie to my best friend for you. However, I will help you."

"You know some other way to get the money?"

"You are not going to America."

"I think that decision is mine, sir."

"You will have no family there. No friends. No protection at all."

"I will escape *him* there."

"If the earl is so confident that he has you at a disadvantage, there is a reason. I will find out what it is and remove it."

She half turned from him. "By the time you discover that, he will have found me. I cannot risk that. *I will not return to him.*"

The vehemence of her words echoed around them.

"I will discover how things stand, and then you can make your choices. If you are truly at risk, we will assess what those choices are."

"Then you will help me leave if necessary?"

"I will do whatever is required to make sure that Glasbury never forces you to return. Now, until I learn what he is up to, we must find a safer place for you to hide than Mivert's Hotel."

"There is no safer place. There is no place at all that is safe."

"Yes, there is. For the next few days, you will remain right here."

The suggestion stunned her.

Mr. Hampton left her to her astonishment. Excusing himself, he walked out of the library.

As soon as he came back, she would have to refuse. She could not stay in this house. If anyone found out, if Anthony discovered she had resided here, Mr. Hampton would be ruined.

She should not have to point that out. Normally Mr. Hampton saw all the eventualities and costs. He had the kind of mind that instantly appraised matters and carefully weighed factors.

He returned in a few minutes.

"If I can think of another safe place, we will move you

there," he said, jumping right to the end of the argument. "For tonight, there is none."

"Diane will take me in."

"With her and St. John's brood, and the size of their household, your presence would not remain a secret even one day. I think that St. John would insist that your brothers know, too."

She fingered the edge of her veil. "I can hardly wear this all the time here, either. You, too, have a household."

"Mrs. Tuttle, the housekeeper, will see to your needs. Only she and Batkin will know you are here. There are chambers in this house that are not used, not open for care by the servants. Batkin is preparing one now. You will secretly stay in it until I discover what the earl is doing, and why."

She was torn between embarrassment and a gratitude so deep that she wanted to weep. The latter flooded her, making her realize how tired she was of being afraid, and how good it felt to be here with a friend.

"You will stay here and all will be well." He held out his hand. "Now, please sit and have some tea while we wait for Batkin to finish. Tell me all about Naples."

She did not tell him *all* about Naples. She described the beauty of the bay and hills, and the outings to Capri and Ischia. She spoke of the people who surrounded the king's court and of the opera and balls. She told him a lot, but not everything.

He could tell what she avoided. For example, no man was mentioned more than once. There were no indications that she had favored someone. He only knew that she had because of the careful way she did not indicate it.

Well, she had not told him about Witherby, either. He had learned about that just by watching her moods and manner. He had seen his good friend's addresses bear fruit. He had guessed the very week that they had become lovers.

That affair had been another disappointment for her, maybe worse than the earl. She had been old enough to really fall in love with Witherby. The betrayal, when she learned of it, had been devastating.

"So, you can see why I would have liked to stay," she said by way of conclusion. "The weather, the scenery, and the society were all most congenial."

He had never met another mature woman whose normal expression was so soft and open. She had always been incapable of dissembling or displaying hauteur. Her kind heart would not allow the distance and chill that such strategies demand.

Her face was soft in form, too. A little round, but with high cheekbones that kept it from being too much so. Those bones drew attention to her sparkling blue eyes. Even now they glinted with little stars glowing beneath the night of her hair.

"If you contemplated going to America, it must have wounded you to know that you were leaving Naples for good."

"It was hard to leave, but I always knew I would."

"You never thought to make your life there?"

She gave a little shrug. "I never considered it one way or the other. Eventually I expected to return here, probably before winter came. There are some projects that I began before I left England that are demanding attention."

He really shouldn't press, but he wanted to know. "There was no friend whom you mourned leaving?"

She tried to assume a worldly, bored expression, but could not successfully hide a deeper sadness. "I will never mourn a man again, Mr. Hampton."

Batkin appeared at the door just long enough to cast him a meaningful look.

"The chamber is ready, Countess." Julian offered his hand for her to rise. "I will show you where it is, if you will permit it."

"I confess that I would prefer that you did. It would embarrass me to have your valet escort me, since I am sure that he disapproves."

"He knows you are a lady in distress, as will Mrs. Tuttle. There will be no disapproval. However, we will avoid the embarrassment completely this way."

The wide skirt of her ice-blue twill dress brushed his legs as he escorted her. With its low waist, snug bodice, and full sleeves, it flattered her form. An ecru fichu obscured the upper swells of her breasts from his eyes but not from his mind.

Her lovely blue eyes took everything in as they walked to the staircase. "It is a large house, Mr. Hampton. It surprised everyone when you moved here."

"I found Russell Square convenient to the City, and the Inns of Court."

They began up the stairs. The lamps showed wisps of her dark hair escaping her coiffeur to brush against her snowy cheek. Her face displayed fatigue from her worry and the voyage, but her expression was sweet all the same.

"With a house this size, I think you should marry and start a family," she said.

"Lady Laclere agrees with you, I fear."

She giggled. It was a wonderful sound, one he had loved hearing since he was a boy. Suddenly, despite her worries, she was the Penelope he knew.

"Has Bianca been trying to find you a wife?"

"Once your brother Dante married, I suspect I was doomed. She must have concluded that if he could be induced to wed, any man could."

"Is she waging battle alone? No supporting troops?"

"I think the strategy was devised with the Duchess of Everdon and Mrs. St. John. Dante's wife, I suspect, demurred only because she is with child."

"Oh, dear. Sophia and Diane are after you, too. You may indeed be doomed. Having been part of that army, I know how effective we can be. Be glad that I am not staying in England. If I joined up you would not stand a chance."

"My dear lady, your involvement could only benefit me. In fact, should I ever think to marry, your approval of the match will be essential."

She paused on the stairs. "Truly? You value my opinion that highly?"

"Certainly."

"What a very nice thing to say, Julian."

Julian.

She had not addressed him like that in years. He doubted she realized that she had now.

He remembered the precise day when he had become Mr. Hampton. It was the afternoon when she called on him in chambers to seek advice about the earl. As he heard her sordid tale and watched her embarrassment, he had known that he would never be Julian again. The revelations of that day demanded a certain formality in their subsequent relationship.

He led her to the door of a bedroom on the third level. His own chambers were on the other side of the landing. It went without saying that she could not stay in the best of the closed rooms, the one connected to his, the one that would never be used by a mistress of this house.

He stood aside so she could enter. He stayed on the threshold as she surveyed the room.

"Yellow and green and white," she said with admiration. "It is like being in a garden of jonquils."

Decorating this chamber, and all of the others, had been mercifully easy. When faced with any decision he had simply chosen what he thought Penelope would like.

She strolled around, inspecting the restrained carving of the fruitwood furniture and other appointments. She noticed a garment on the bed. "Your valet must have woken the housekeeper if he found a nightdress for me. I have become a nuisance already."

"You will be no nuisance. They will be happy to serve you. I have sent Batkin for your belongings at the hotel. He will make sure that no one knows where they are going."

Her clear blue eyes appeared a little moist and her brow a little worried. He wanted to soothe her in ways denied him. Instead he just stood at the doorway.

"Thank you for doing this," she said. "It is rashly generous of you."

He was not being generous, but selfish. If she lived here even one night, her presence would remain forever.

He would always sense her in the air and feel her in the spaces.

The part about being rash was true, however. Allowing her to remain here was an unspeakably risky thing to do, for both of them.

"It would be quite scandalous if anyone learned of this," she said, echoing his thoughts.

"Not too scandalous. No worse, for example, than that business in Naples with you and those other ladies and that fishing boat."

A blush rose up her neck and over her face. She grimaced with chagrin. "Oh. You heard about that."

"Although the officers on the ship that rescued you showed the discretion of gentlemen, several of the common sailors, upon their return to England, did not."

"Does everyone know?"

"If *I* do, I expect so."

"I want you to know that was quite innocent. We were victims of villainy. Whoever expected that fishing boat to go off with all our garments on it and leave us stranded in that cove like that?"

By "like that" she meant wearing only their chemises, or so the story went. Wet chemises, since the women had commissioned that fishing boat to take them to the secluded cove so they could bathe in the sea.

—Pen walked out of the cool sea. Droplets on her body and eyelashes sparkled in the sun like tiny diamonds. The soaked garment adhered to her soft curves like a transparent veil, and—

"If you are honest, Mr. Hampton, you will admit that the outing to that cove can at worst be described as a bit reckless, a little headstrong, a tad ill-advised . . ." She groped for more diminutives.

"Slightly naughty?"

"Still, not scandalous, as this will be."

"This will be scandalous only if others find out. We will be sure they do not."

She blushed again and made a little awkward gesture with her hands, as if at a loss how to end the meeting.

He memorized the image of her standing in his home.

"Good night, madame."

"Good night, Mr. Hampton."

"Julian! Sir Julian, save me!"

The cry came from the tower. Julian looked up to see pale skin at the arrow slit, high on the guards' chamber.

"I am up here, Sir Julian. Help me!"

Julian grasped his wooden sword tighter. "I am coming, my lady!"

Above on the battlements of Laclere Park's medieval ruins, Vergil whacked his own sword against Dante's as they fought for control of the castle.

The plan had been for Julian to join Vergil, overpower Dante, and together rescue the damsel imprisoned by her evil guardian, Sir Milton. But Vergil could defeat Dante alone, and the lady was calling to Julian for help.

Julian charged across the bailey yard, jumping stones that had fallen from the decaying fortress. He dodged past little Charlotte, who had been permitted to join them but only if she played Vergil's squire. She stood safely in the bailey holding an invisible horse, shouting treasonous encouragement to Dante up above.

Inside the portal of the guard tower, Julian pressed against the wall and listened.

Above, Lady Penelope called again, her girlish voice gaining maturity in the stones' acoustics. Another sound caught his attention as well. Bootsteps on the stairs. The evil guardian was coming down.

The boots stopped. Preparing himself, hoisting his plank shield, Julian started up the curving stone staircase.

Milton waited halfway down, his own sword and shield at the ready. Julian considered how to attack from his disadvantaged position.

"That is the thing about these curved stairs," Milton said with a smug smile. "The invader cannot use his sword arm unless he exposes his body by turning."

"I will risk the blows."

Milton's dark eyes turned serious. The eldest of the Viscount Laclere's sons, he was also the most handsome, even more so than young Dante. He and Julian had a special affinity, since they were both quiet and more given to observing than participating in the raucous conversations of the others. Milton had made it clear that while Julian visited Laclere Park as Vergil's friend, Milton considered him a kindred soul.

"You should always weigh whether any prize is worth the blows, Julian."

"I do not seek my own prize, but my lady's freedom," Julian said, assuming the bluster of a medieval knight.

Despite the advantage of the stairs, Milton could not defend well. He had never been especially interested in the actual battles of their games, but rather the strategies.

Whacking his way past Milton, Julian rushed up to the guards' chamber. Playing her role with enthusiasm, Penelope ran to his protection.

Her gratitude was interrupted. Milton appeared at the

threshold. Julian thrust Penelope behind him and prepared to fight again.

She cowered closely, her body tucked against his back and her hands on his shoulders. Their contact stunned him and incited a pleasurable warmth. Time froze for a moment while he accommodated the powerful sensation.

He glanced back at Penelope. She had frozen, too. She looked in his eyes with a curious, startled expression.

He forgot about Milton and the sword and the tower itself. He turned slightly, unable to stop looking at her, incapable of breaking the silent, astonishing conversation they were having and for which neither of them knew any words.

Finally, Pen stepped away. She glanced past him. He looked in the same direction to find Milton watching them. Milton's own expression was both unfathomable and comprehending.

"The tower is yours, Julian. The lady is rescued. Well done." Milton looked down at his sword. With a small smile, he let it drop to the floor along with his shield. "I think that I am much too old to play such games anymore."

The memory came to Julian as he lay in his bed, sensing the presence of Penelope as surely as if she slept beside him.

A year before that day neither of them would have noticed that touch. It would have been one of many, as the stories that Julian created played out on the estate.

That moment changed everything. At fourteen he had been aroused before, but not like that, not by a specific female whom he knew and honored.

It had been a turning point in other friendships, too. Milton had never played with them again. It had taken Julian many years to realize that his long look with Penelope was the reason.

Now Milton was dead and Penelope was married and here he was, lying in bed, wanting another man's wife who slept in a nearby chamber.

He weighed the events of the night. Pen had been correct that the law would not protect her. Only the combination of her courage and Julian's own guile had ever done that.

He did not know what waited around the curve in the staircase he had begun climbing. As always, his position in the whole matter would inhibit his sword arm as surely as that wall had in the old tower.

He knew only one thing for certain.

Glasbury would never hurt Penelope again while Julian Hampton lived and breathed.

chapter 3

Anthony, tenth earl of Glasbury, tried to ignore the sound at his dressing room door. He did not like his pleasure disrupted by any distraction, least of all one that heralded complications to his well-calculated plans.

Now just such a disruption had occurred. Caesar would never interrupt with that loud knocking otherwise. Caesar knew better than to incur his master's anger.

Gritting his teeth, swallowing hard, Glasbury stepped away from the pretty round bottom raised for punishment. The most delicious arousal swam in his loins, demanding more stimulation. The submissiveness of the naked body obeying his commands lured him to ignore the interruption.

The loud raps continued on the door. Something had gone wrong. There could be no other explanation for that sound.

He groped through the haze of intoxicating power for some clarity of thought. He gazed at the cane in his hand

and the red welts on his pleasure slave's buttocks. Should he have her stay and wait? She was new, and he had not determined yet that she would be adequate.

"Look at me," he ordered.

Dark hair rose. A face turned. Moist eyes looked back at him. There was enough fear in them to arouse him again. He saw no indication that she had enjoyed this.

Good. He did not want partners who took pleasure. It made the submission less than complete.

He plucked a guinea from his pocket and tossed it on the floor. "Get dressed and leave. Return Thursday and there will be more."

She swept up the guinea as she rose on her knees. There was no question that she understood "more" meant other than just more money.

She appeared unsure that she wanted to return, but he knew she would. She was a whore and the pay was good. It wasn't quite the same when you paid them, of course. The control was compromised if they had a choice, too.

But she would do for a while. He would bring her along slowly, and she would learn well enough.

He turned away. Within moments the woman and the pleasure were out of his mind and body. He left the chamber to find Caesar waiting in the corridor.

Caesar was not in his livery, so he must have been roused from his bed by another servant. A dark mulatto, Caesar obeyed all orders with precision. He showed no fear of reprisal for this interruption, however. He remained expressionless as always, a demeanor that reflected the dull mind in the dark head.

It was also a reflection of the changes twenty years could make in a country's sense of rights and privilege. There had been a time when Caesar would have had good cause for fear, but those days had been slipping away most of Glasbury's life and were over for good now.

More's the pity.

"He came back," Caesar said. "A groom heard him in the garden and came and woke me."

"He is alone?"

"Just him."

Damn.

"Where is he?"

"The library."

"Return to your chamber. I will not need you anymore."

Glasbury returned to his dressing room where his pleasure slave was struggling to close her dress.

He did not aid her. "Go down in a few minutes."

He made his own way through the silent house to the library where the man waited.

The visitor sat on a sofa. He was round faced and bland in countenance, and insignificant in presence and size. One had to look closely to even notice this man existed. The ability to be unseen was one of his great talents.

He looked over with eyes that could reveal a deep cunning if the anonymous mask slipped.

"She was not there," he said simply.

"She had to be. The person who saw her knows her well. Veil or not, the identification was not likely to be wrong."

"I said she was not there when I went for her. I did not say she never was there. I found a night servant who says a lady of her description, always veiled, was a guest there for a few days. But she is gone now, and her trunks were moved just this night. I must have missed that by an hour, no more."

Glasbury barely contained his anger. The little bitch had slipped away again.

He would find her, however. He would no longer tolerate the way she had repudiated his rights. He would no longer bear the humiliation she had heaped on him with her willfulness. He certainly would not stand still while she used his name to promote revolting ideas that directly insulted him.

He no longer needed to.

"Where did the trunks go?"

"The manager said he does not know. He did not like my waking him to ask about it, and he could have been expressing displeasure by not giving me what I wanted. I could try and make him talk if you—"

"No, we can't have you doing that. The police will be involved if you get rough."

"So, what do you want to do?"

"Have your colleague keep a watch on her house, in case it is opened. I will let you know when I need you again."

Glasbury did not expect that house to be opened. If Penelope was no longer at the hotel, he knew where she most likely had gone. She had probably run to hide behind her brother Laclere.

Well, he knew how to handle that. His rights of possession had been compromised in all kinds of ways these last years, but not where she was concerned. It would be more complicated to fight her family, but he would prevail.

After all, he owned her.

chapter 4

Julian was surprised in the morning by a summons to Laclere's house. He left Mrs. Tuttle to see to Penelope's comfort and rode his horse to the one o'clock appointment.

He was shown to the viscount's study. Laclere's dark head rose at once from its contemplation of some documents on the desk when Julian entered.

"I am expecting a caller. I thought I should have you here when he comes," Laclere said without formality. "I wrote to you as soon as I received his letter in the morning post."

"Someone was rude enough to demand to call? It is generous of you to receive him."

"It was Glasbury." Laclere's normally bright blue eyes wore a dulling concern. "I can't imagine what he wants, since he and I have not spoken in years. I assume it is about Pen, of course."

They chatted about the banquet as they waited, carefully avoiding the subject of Lady Laclere's designs where a certain bachelor was concerned.

A visitor soon arrived, but it was not the Earl of Glasbury. Laclere's brother Dante entered the study and greeted Julian.

In face and stature Dante was a more refined version of his brother. Where the viscount's features had a roughly hewn quality, Dante's were smooth and perfect, as if the sculptor's rasp had sought to make all the edges subordinate to the total effect.

Dante raked his fingers through his brown hair in a gesture that spoke befuddlement.

"I received a letter from Glasbury this morning. He said he was meeting with you and suggested I attend."

"The mystery is getting thicker," Laclere said.

"More than you know. I saw Charl's carriage coming as I entered the house."

"If he wants to meet with the whole family, he must be planning a dramatic announcement."

"Maybe he intends to pursue a divorce," Dante said. "Rather late for that, I would say."

Julian did not say a word. Both these men had long ago accepted his silences, and today that was extremely convenient.

Charlotte entered, looking much like her older sister with her dark hair and pale skin and middling height. She had always been more slender than Penelope, and her eyes were more worldly and shrewd. It was not that Charlotte was hard in her appearance and outlook, but that Penelope was so soft.

She explained that she had received a letter similar to Dante's. "I considered ignoring it, since I cannot imagine why he wants me here. Aren't such things supposed to be too important for a woman's participation?"

"The earl almost has me interested in this business," Laclere said.

"Glasbury is many things, dear brother, but interesting is not one of them." She turned her attention to Dante. "How is Fleur?"

Dante smiled the smile that brought women to swoons. "Glowing. Serene. I am the one who will age ten years before this child comes."

"Do not get into a state so soon. There are still many months for that," Laclere said. He glanced at the clock on a shelf behind him. "He is late. No doubt that is Glasbury's way of exercising his precedence."

"I hope it is a divorce," Dante said. "I would like to see Pen completely free of him."

Charlotte's attention slid around the room and came to rest on Julian. "Do you know what this will be about?"

"I agree with your brother that it probably has to do with your sister."

"That is obvious. Do you know just what it has to do with her? Did she write to you from Naples about something that she neglected to tell any of us?"

"If she did, it was a private correspondence, Charl," Laclere said. "You have benefited from Hampton's discretion, so allow Pen to as well. I am sure that none of us wants the whole family knowing all of our legal affairs."

Charl retreated, but not before she cast Julian a very sharp and suspicious glance.

Glasbury arrived just late enough to make his point that others wait for him and not the other way around. He was brought to the study at half past one.

He was not alone. A man of neat but common appearance accompanied him. This other man stayed near the door like a servant and did not advance on the assembled party as the earl did.

Julian barely received the earl's acknowledgment during the greetings. However, he did not miss that the nod in his direction was accompanied by a smug smirk that temporarily twisted the earl's flaccid mouth.

Julian did not allow himself to react, but a small fury swirled in his head. He hated Glasbury, and not only because of Penelope. The man embodied all of the decadence and callousness that inherited privilege could breed when it was visited on the wrong kind of character. He wielded his power irresponsibly and selfishly.

Most recently the earl had been one of the few lords to argue against the bill abolishing slavery in the colonies, because he owned some plantations in the West Indies that would be affected economically. Few men in Parliament had the audacity to stand on the side of selling human beings anymore, but it had not bothered Glasbury to do so at all.

Worse, that smirk had reflected triumph. It was the reflexive expression of a man who knew he had won a game. Julian's concern for Penelope instantly deepened.

Glasbury took a position beside Laclere's chair so he could look down on the dark head of the man sitting in it. Julian considered that it was probably the earl's only opportunity to do so, since Laclere towered over Glasbury when they both stood.

The earl's slender body assumed a military rigidity. With his gray hair and lined face, he appeared a generation older than anyone else in the chamber even though he had only ten years on Laclere.

"I have little time to waste on this business, so I will be

blunt," Glasbury said with all possible pomposity. "I demand to know where she is."

"By she, you must mean our sister. Penelope is in Naples, as you know. You wrote to her there."

"She is not in Naples any longer. She was seen in London yesterday. I have learned that she took a room at Mivert's Hotel upon her return, but she is no longer at the hotel this morning."

"I am sure that whoever saw her is mistaken. If my sister did return to London, she would not have to reside at a hotel, since she has a house. Did you try calling there?"

"The house remains closed. There has been no activity to indicate she is living there."

"Glasbury, forgive me for not being overcome with concern at your pique, but it has been many years since my sister's activities were your business or interest. I assure you that she is in Naples, but if she is not, what do you care?"

"She is my wife."

"In name."

"In *the law*."

"In reality she has not been your wife for over a decade."

"The law is the only reality that matters, as Hampton here can explain to you. I am done indulging her whims on the issue."

"What is that supposed to mean?" Dante asked. "Do you plan to change the legal reality by divorcing her?"

"Indeed not. I have decided that our long estrangement is no longer acceptable. Laclere, I demand that you return her to me."

Laclere's eyes reflected astonishment. Julian could see

the truth sink in, and the dismay that after all these years the earl wanted Penelope back.

"I cannot return what I do not have."

"If you are hiding her—"

"My home is always open to her, and when she visits she does not have to hide. But she is not in this house, or at Laclere Park, or even in England."

"I demand that you prove it. That man by the door is Mr. Lovejoy. He is an inspector with the Metropolitan Police. He will search this house to see if my wife is here."

"The hell he will," Dante said.

Laclere leveled a piercing gaze on Mr. Lovejoy. "You brought the police into my home, Glasbury?"

"It was necessary."

"I doubt Mr. Lovejoy agrees. You are not searching for a criminal. The inspector's authority in such a case is ambiguous at best. Isn't that so, Hampton?"

Julian donned his most severe professional demeanor. "Most ambiguous. I assume, Mr. Lovejoy, that the superintendent is aware of your intentions?"

Mr. Lovejoy mumbled something noncommittal.

"In any case, Laclere's word as a gentlemen is good enough for the police, is it not, sir?"

Another mumble was accompanied by a vague nod.

"There. That is settled," Laclere said, dryly.

Lovejoy, recognizing a dismissal when he heard it, ducked out of the room.

Glasbury's face got red. "When I learn that you are lying, I will—"

"Be careful, Glasbury." Laclere's voice turned steely. "The insult of bringing Lovejoy here cannot be excused, and I do not take well accusations that I am a liar."

The earl turned to include Dante and Charlotte in his final pronouncement. "If any of you take her in, you will deal with me. If I learn that she is living on any of your properties, I will make you regret that you have interfered. Do not doubt that I will bring the full force of my rights and influence to bear on the matter."

He strode from the study.

"Vergil, we must do something," Charlotte said, her expression barely recovering from her shock. "For heaven's sake, he really expects to force her to come back."

"It is the heir," Dante said. "He must be, what, forty-five now. There he is, with no son and no way to get one since he has a wife who has left him. I always thought it odd that he let her go before there was a son."

Laclere darted a glance at Julian. "Yes, well, I expect he had his reasons for such generosity."

Charlotte did not miss the pointed look. "You know what those reasons were, Mr. Hampton. You negotiated that separation. It was a private arrangement, and you were the mediator."

That brought Dante's expectant attention on him, too. Julian tried his usual silence but their expressions indicated it would not work this time.

"Madame, I did as your sister bid me do. We were fortunate that the earl saw the rightness of her preference and did not force her to remain in his home."

"Oh, don't turn into the lawyer on us, Hampton," Dante said. "You procured an allowance and her freedom. There had to be a reason he agreed to it. What was it?"

Julian refused to respond.

Charlotte gave him a critical glare. "Well, if you should have any communication with my sister, please tell her that she is welcome in my home, and that Glasbury can do his worst. That little toad does not frighten *me*. If he brings Mr. Lovejoy to *my* house, I will tell the footmen to throw them both out." Marching like a palace guard, her parasol pumping like a baton, she headed for the door. "If he has not left the street yet, I will tell him so myself. *Insufferable* man."

The study echoed her words, then pulsed with a hollow silence.

Dante laughed. "It appears I have been upstaged by Charlotte. I am left with merely repeating her words. Hampton, if Pen writes to you, tell her she will be safe with us. Glasbury will need an army to get her away."

Dante took his leave. Julian began to follow.

"Not yet, you don't," Laclere said, stopping him.

Laclere still sat at the desk, his gaze on a pen that he handled absently. Julian waited, counting on their long friendship to spare him an interrogation that would get too pointed.

"I did not miss the look Glasbury gave you when he entered," Laclere said.

"Nor did I."

"She is no longer in Naples, is she?"

Julian did not answer.

Laclere leaned back in his chair. "Years ago you told me that you got him to release Pen because he had bigger secrets than most men. Secrets that, I assume, he would not want exposed if he or she sought a divorce."

"Did I say that? How indiscreet of me."

"It appears the years have dulled his appreciation of my sister's consideration for his reputation."

"It would seem that *something* has."

"Yet you were silent while he was here. You did not point out that she holds those aces."

"I try not to threaten men when there are witnesses present."

"I trust that you will find a private way to remind him of the cost if the world knows whatever it is that Pen has on him."

"I will attend to it very soon."

Julian began to leave, so he could attend to it immediately.

Laclere's voice caught him at the door. "If you should have communication with my sister, please tell her that I am always here for her. We all are. She is not to worry that we care a fig for whatever Glasbury threatens or tries. Let her know that the earl really would need an army to take her from us."

"I am sure that she knows all that."

Laclere looked at him. A pause stretched into an eloquent silence. Julian hoped nothing passing between them would be put into words.

"Julian, if for some reason my sister cannot or will not turn to us for aid, I trust that you will do all that you can for her."

"I always have, Vergil."

Mr. Hampton's house was proving a very comfortable sanctuary. Penelope did not mind her seclusion at all. Mrs. Tuttle saw to her comfort in the morning, then appeared every hour or so to inquire if anything was needed. Other than a few books from the library, Pen asked for nothing.

Her trunks had arrived during the night, and she poked through the small one for her letters and papers. Sitting by the window that looked down on a nice garden, she studied a long document that had arrived in Naples before she left.

It was to be a pamphlet criticizing the legal position of married women. She and several other ladies had contributed to this work during the last year. Now, with the recent passage of the bill ending slavery in the colonies, the time was ripe for their treatise to go to print. The country and Parliament were in a mood of reform. It was time to emancipate the last human chattel on British lands.

Married women.

She carefully read this most recent draft, penning in a few changes. They would wait until the new year before publishing it. They wanted the country to digest the recent bill before raising this issue. She had intended to return in late fall and see to its final preparation. Now she could ensure its completion more quickly.

Unless she had to flee the country, of course. She hoped that Mr. Hampton was correct that she would not need to. She wanted very much to see this project through. Her name as an author would give it weight. It was also the only worthwhile thing she had done with her life.

A knock on her door in the afternoon distracted her from her work. She tucked the document away and opened the door to find Mr. Hampton.

"Is there news?" she asked.

"Yes. May I come in? I apologize, but we can hardly go down to the library or drawing room for a conversation."

No, they could not. She bid him enter, and they sat in two green-patterned chairs near the window.

He appeared indifferent to the location of this conversation, but she could not entirely ignore that he was in her bedchamber, with the door closed.

His back was to the bed itself but she could see it plainly behind him, bright and happy with its jonquil drapery. She had slept in that bed last night, and now this man was here. It was a silly reaction to have, but she suddenly remembered the sensation of his hand on hers last night. The sparkling vitality that she had felt when he kissed her through her glove returned and danced all through her.

"The news?" she prompted, forcing herself to look only at him and not see that bed. Except there it was, just looming in the background, provoking some alarming curiosities about Mr. Hampton and how he made love, or whether he ever did at all.

If he did, with whom? And if he did not, what a shame, because she could not deny that there was something exciting about his dark good looks and mysterious silence and—

"Glasbury called on Laclere," he said, interrupting her sudden speculation on what he looked like without his coats and shirt. "He also arranged to have Dante and the Dowager Baroness Mardenford present. He demanded to know which of them had you as a guest. He dared to try and have Laclere's house searched for you."

"Vergil must have been ready to call him out on that. And poor Charlotte. It was very ignoble of him to try and browbeat her."

"I think that Lady Mardenford is well equipped to deal

with the earl, madame. He was fortunate that she did not browbeat *him,* most literally, with her parasol."

She giggled at the image of that. "See, I was correct. They did not have to lie for me, because they do not know I am in England."

"That is true. They did not have to lie."

"Did you?"

"It did not come to that."

"But it will, now that the earl knows I am here. Eventually he will ask you where to find me."

"As your solicitor, I am under no obligation to answer. Quite the opposite."

His tone made her heart heavy. He looked very serious. Too serious. And thoughtful.

The bed disappeared, as did her foolish, wanton musings. "He will find me. If he was so bold as to try and search my brother's house, he will not give up easily. Even if I hide forever in this room, he will eventually learn I am here."

"I called on him to remind him of a few things he seems to have forgotten. He either was not at home or would not receive me. However, I will have that conversation with him very soon. That will end his pursuit."

"It will not make a difference. He has forgotten nothing. He merely does not worry about exposure anymore."

She abruptly got up and turned to the window. She scanned the space below, even though her mind knew that a private garden would not hold any danger for her.

Memories tried to force themselves into her mind. Ugly, old ones that she had learned long ago to deny. Explicit scenes flickered that showed the slide into degradation she had lived the first years of her marriage. She had been so ignorant that she had not even known it was not normal, even if it was shocking.

Then the earl went too far, and she realized the hell she had bargained for. It had not been the pleasure that the earl took in perversity that had gotten her free, however. When she went to Mr. Hampton for advice, he had asked questions that revealed bigger secrets, more damning than anything that Glasbury did with a wife.

Mr. Hampton had been so enigmatic at that meeting. She had turned to him because he was an old friend, and because he knew the law, and because if she had confided in her brothers one of them might have killed Anthony. Mr. Hampton had been all she had hoped, steady and sober and unemotional, but she had not missed the fire in his eyes that spoke his disgust of what he heard.

Fortunately, he had understood the significance of her evidence in ways she had not. He had used that, ruthlessly she suspected, to negotiate with the earl. He had gotten her free.

Now she felt that freedom slipping away. The earl would get her back, and this time there would be no escape. She would be at his mercy, and the anger of the years would drive him this time.

She began shaking inside. The trembles affected her soul and heart and eventually her body. They weakened her so much that her composure broke.

She turned away so that Mr. Hampton would not see her tears. She had given the poor man enough trouble without expecting him to deal with that, too. She fought to calm the panic that threatened to send her raving.

He was suddenly standing right behind her. She could

feel his warmth. His proximity distracted her enough that her emotions did not entirely overwhelm her.

His hands came to rest on her shoulders. That should have astonished her, but instead she savored their strength and the way they steadied her.

He turned her to face him. Barely touching her face, but touching it all the same, he tilted her head up so he looked in her eyes. "I said that I would not permit the earl to force your return. I meant that, dear lady."

The expression in his face mesmerized her. As he looked down and made his promise, she saw the youth she had known years ago. The boy she had played with was talking to the girl she had been. Both of those people had been lost to the world when they matured, as had their easy friendship. Now, for a brief respite, it was all back again, and the reasons for her trust were rawly alive between them.

The realization moved her so much that she could not contain her emotion. She closed her eyes but the tears flowed anyway, snaking down her cheeks.

Did he reach for her, or did she move to him? Suddenly she was in his comforting embrace. She welcomed the intimacy. They were old friends, after all.

It felt wonderful to be held. His arms reassured her as much as his words had.

"The earl has now warned off your family. I expect him to soon turn his attention to me. You may not be safe here. I think that it would be best if you left London," he said, as she nestled against him and drank in his support and warmth. "I have a property on the Essex coast and want to take you there early tomorrow. It is isolated, and I have to warn you that it is also fairly rustic. For a day or two you will have to be alone there, until I can make other arrangements. Do you think that you can bear that, and the lack of servants or comforts?"

She nodded. She could bear anything if it meant not living as though she sensed the earl behind her every moment.

She found her senses, and grew starkly conscious of their touching bodies. Feeling herself flush, she stepped back and out of his arms.

He did not look discomfitted at all, but then Mr. Hampton never did. "I must go to my chambers for a few hours now. I will wake you before dawn so that we can be off. Is that agreeable to you, madame?"

"Yes, Mr. Hampton. That is agreeable."

chapter 5

Rustic described the cottage very well. Heading up a low rise in the land, Julian aimed the curricle for a small, isolated stone house. Nothing but the sky hung behind it, and only some outbuildings and the sound of the surf surrounded it.

They had left Russell Square silently in the dark hours of morning, long before Julian's household had risen. Even Batkin and Mrs. Tuttle were not told she was leaving.

"Do you own this house?" she asked, as he handed her down from the curricle.

"I bought it some years ago when I first established myself."

"Did you seek a retreat from your life in the city and the social obligations forced on you?"

"I only thought of it as having a home on the coast. I have always enjoyed the sea."

"Maybe that is in your blood. After all, one of your uncles was an officer in the navy, and you even thought of a career in it yourself. Do you ever regret not doing that?"

"I do not believe in regrets over the past. They are very pointless. The few that I do harbor have nothing to do with how I employ myself."

The house was simple but appealing. A sitting room and a small, densely stocked library faced the sea, and they entered through a kitchen garden and door. A small dining room and one bedchamber made up the rest of the ground floor.

While Julian went back out to carry in some provisions he had brought, she strolled through rooms with exposed beamed ceilings and whitewashed plastered walls. The furnishings were simple and spare, but not crude.

"It is very charming," she called to him when she heard his step in the kitchen. "Do you never have servants here?"

"No."

"Not even Batkin?"

"Not even Batkin."

He would have silence then. Only the sounds of the sea and the winds would be his company. The house had not been closed, so he did not come here only in the summer. It would not surprise her to learn that he deliberately traveled here when a storm was brewing so he could experience nature at its most primitive.

She retraced her steps to the sitting room where Mr. Hampton was building a fire. As she watched him, she considered why she felt she knew the attraction of this house to him.

It came from the past. She remembered one summer when he was visiting Laclere Park and a terrific storm blew in. She had found him in the library right at the window, watching it, almost entranced. He had abruptly left her there; then, she had seen him walking outside, right into the turbulence as if the excitement of the fury had drawn him into itself.

"That should spare you from the worst of the damp," he said, dusting off his hands as he rose beside the fireplace. "I will make one in the kitchen, too, and a bedchamber once you choose which you prefer. Do you want to sleep down here, or above? The rooms upstairs are much better."

"I expected a hovel, not a choice of chambers. I will go above and see which suits me."

"I will tend to the kitchen fire while you do."

She ascended the narrow stairs to three bedrooms. The one facing the sea was quite large and, she guessed, Mr. Hampton's own. The two others faced the back of the house and overlooked the little kitchen garden tucked inside its low stone wall.

She paused in one of them, surveying its clean coverlet and white, simple curtains and pine wardrobe.

It was a woman's room.

There was something to it, a subtle refinement, that proclaimed it feminine.

Or maybe she inhaled a lingering scent that did so.

She felt her face flushing. Of course. How stupid of her. There was another very good reason for a city man to have an isolated retreat not too far from London. A very practical one. And an excellent reason for not having servants here, too.

She did not know much about Mr. Hampton where women were concerned, except that there was a lot of speculation about him, and many unproductive flirtations which he never seemed to notice.

It seemed those flirtations had not all been in vain after all. Evidently it had been discretion, not abstinence, that kept that part of his life hidden from the world.

She paced around the room and wondered which women had visited this cottage and if she knew any of them.

Perhaps there was currently a lady who used this chamber and considered it her own.

"Do you want this in here?"

Mr. Hampton stood at the threshold with her large trunk in his arms. Her mind saw him entering this chamber for a different purpose. It was an exciting and dangerous image, and an alarmingly easy picture for her mind to paint. Her heart rose to her throat.

When she did not answer he strode in and set the trunk down near the wardrobe.

"Perhaps not," she said.

He bent to lift the trunk again. "The seaside chamber is much more comfortable."

"Yes. I mean, no. Not that one. That is yours, isn't it?"

"When I am here it is, but I will not be here, so it can be yours. You will like it. You can hear the surf so clearly at night it is as if you are sleeping on the waves."

"I do not think I would be comfortable using your chamber, Mr. Hampton."

"As you prefer." He set the trunk down again.

"Actually, I was thinking of the small chamber next door. I would be most comfortable in that one."

He began to bend for the trunk, but stopped. He straightened.

"Why would you find it more comfortable than this one?"

"I think it is very charming and cozy."

Comprehension flickered deep in his eyes. He knew what conclusions she had drawn. Was it her imagination that she saw the smallest hint of a smile, as if he found her discovery amusing?

"I would prefer that you use this chamber, charming though the small one may be." He went to the doorway, leaving the trunk where it sat. "You can see the road from this window. When you are alone you may find it comforting to be able to see that no one approaches."

Julian brought up the smaller trunk and some water, then left Penelope to refresh herself. He strolled out the sitting room door to the little stone terrace that looked over the sea.

The day was not cold, but the brisk breeze carried a salty bite. It whipped around him, echoing the energy of the waves and the swells of the sea.

He had always loved the way the sea's rhythms threw thoughts into his head and provoked a deeper knowing of himself. The contemplations did not always have words, but the conclusions emerged all the same.

He did not only think about Penelope when he visited this cottage. In fact, he almost never did, although she was never completely absent from his soul. He probably would think of her all the time now, however, since she had actually walked these floors and would soon stand on this terrace.

He pictured the woman in the chamber above, settling into the room she had concluded was used by his lovers.

He could not decide if he would welcome her eternal presence in this corner of his life or not.

The day was clear, and he could see far to the south where the masts of ships heading for the Thames poked into the sky. He had been on enough ships to know that he would have enjoyed a life at sea. He had meant what he said to Pen, however. He did not hold regrets about the path he had chosen instead.

He had taken it even though it meant becoming a solicitor. His father had been an impoverished gentleman but a gentleman all the same, and sons of gentlemen who entered the law were supposed to become barristers. Barristers did not work for pay, although indirectly they really did. Still, the world permitted the little lie and pretended barristers did not soil their hands with trade. Solicitors, however, were paid directly, and that made all the difference to most people.

The choice had meant a more secure existence, and, he suspected, a more interesting one. Barristers briefly entered a person's life, then left. Solicitors stood by their clients' sides until the day they died.

He would have been no use at all to Penelope if he had become a barrister.

Had her mother known that? Was that why Lady Laclere had taken him aside that day when he was fifteen and proposed this course to him? She had then told her husband to pay his university fees for two years and later arrange his position as an articled clerk in their old solicitor's chambers.

She had spoken that day only of concerns about her eldest son, Milton, and his need for good counsel and a practical influence when he assumed the title. But she was already casting her lure for the Earl of Glasbury by then. Julian had always wondered if she suspected that her daughter would also need counsel in the years to come.

If so, marrying Pen off to Glasbury had been unforgivable.

"Will you eat before you leave? I have laid out some of the food you brought for me."

He turned at Pen's voice.

She stood at the door. For an instant he saw the woman-child she had been her first season, coming to him on another terrace, excited about her recent engagement to a great title. She had been so happy, so full of sparkling giggles, that he had had to smile even though it was the most desolate day of his life.

She looked even more beautiful today. Her hair's simple chignon made her look very young. Her manner even appeared girlishly awkward.

He returned to the house. Pen had put out ham and bread and cheese on the small table near the sitting room window.

"I thought we could see the sea from here, and the dining room in back is dark," she said.

They sat on either side of the table. Julian sensed distraction and discomfort in her.

"Will you be at ease here alone tonight?" he asked.

"Of course. I am a grown woman. I do not need care like a child."

Her tone was close to a challenge. Not able to imagine what response she expected, he gave none.

"I am thinking that it was unwise to come here. I should have found another solution," she said.

"You needed a sanctuary."

"I do not think this cottage should have been that sanctuary."

"Why not?"

No doubt she thought her expression utterly bland as she cut some ham into tiny pieces, but he knew her too well. Her mind was working hard at something.

"I am concerned for your reputation. If this becomes known, it will be assumed that you are my lover. If Glasbury thinks that, he will ruin you."

She was lying. Oh, she was truly concerned for him, but that was not the reason for this peevish resistance now.

"However," she continued, "contemplating the potential consequences of coming here has made me realize that I have another choice where the earl is concerned, besides running away."

"What is that?"

"I can have an affair and be very indiscreet. I think he would divorce me then. It could work, don't you think? He always said if I did that it would void our agreement, but since he is trying to void it anyway—Are you unwell? You look peculiar. Are you choking or—"

"I am fine."

"What do you think? Would it work?"

He tried to summon professional disinterest. "I do think it would induce him to divorce you. If it was commonly known you were having an affair, it would endanger the succession to his title, and humiliate him as well."

"Do you think he would go to Parliament? I would not want anything less than full freedom."

"He would want to be able to remarry and have his heir, so he would go to Parliament."

"Then it may be a course worth weighing seriously. Don't you agree?"

"It is one solution to your dilemma. I would have proposed it years ago if you had been older and less meticulous in your honesty."

She stopped eating. She set down her fork.

"You contemplated back then that I should give him evidence of adultery so that he could divorce me?"

"I did."

Her lids lowered. "It was not only my youth and honesty that kept you silent, I think." Her tone definitely carried a challenge this time. "You thought that I could never do it, didn't you? That was why you never raised that option."

"You were not willing to consider divorcing him because of the public nature of the proceedings and the revelations that must be made. I assumed you would not want the scandal if he divorced you, either."

"It was not only the scandal, but also the cost of going to Parliament. My family's finances could not support it."

"You could have gone to the church's courts. It did not have to be Parliament."

"The church was a half-measure, and I was spared the humiliation and obtained the same terms with the agreement you suggested we negotiate. Better ones, since I received some support and was not thrust back on my family."

"Not entirely the same terms, madame. Had you gone to the church, you might indeed be divorced now, half-measure or not, and the earl could not touch you."

His own tone had turned firm, but he'd be damned if he would accept responsibility for the course she had taken.

He had advised her to end the marriage. He had come damn close to imploring her to do so.

Her gaze fell and the atmosphere grew heavy. When she looked up again, her eyes held a very determined expression.

"All the same, this option of giving the earl cause to divorce *me* was not among the ones enumerated that day in your chambers. I know the real reason why, and it was not the ones you admit to."

"I assure you that—"

"You assumed that I could never bear being with a man after what happened with Glasbury. You thought I was ruined forever for such intimacies in any way."

She flushed deeply. She looked astonished to hear herself speak of such indelicate matters. Almost as astonished as he felt at hearing such an accusation blurted out.

She made a display of turning her attention to her meal. Her manner denied him a response.

Just as well, because the retort flaring in his brain was not the measured, professional kind she expected from her old friend and solicitor.

"Do you advise divorce now? Either I divorce him, or make him divorce me?" she asked.

"If I cannot dissuade him from his current intentions, it may be the only choice."

"I see others. I can do as I first intended, and run far away."

"He has shadowed your adult life so far. Will you give him the victory of destroying your future?"

"I hear America is very pleasant. Living there is hardly destruction."

"To disappear, you will have to go inland to the frontier, and to a life that makes this cottage look like a palace."

"I think that you exaggerate." She sighed. "Well, that is all of the choices, I suppose. Except killing him, but that will never do."

Julian said nothing to that.

He rose. "There is no need to make any decision until after I speak with Glasbury. I will leave you now, if you are sure that you can manage on your own. I have engagements in London that I should not miss, or it may raise curiosity. I will visit you tomorrow, however."

"That is a lot of riding, Mr. Hampton. You do not need to journey here daily. It will be an inexcusable inconvenience to you. Even on horse, riding cross-country, it will take hours each way."

"I will return tomorrow afternoon, madame."

She accompanied him to the kitchen and stepped out into the garden with him. He did not like leaving her here, isolated and alone. He did not mind solitude, and often sought it, but he knew that he was unusual.

She noticed his hesitation. "I will be fine. Thank you for doing this for me. For helping me. I fear that I sounded very ungrateful while we dined. I am not, and I want you to know that."

"Until tomorrow, then."

He walked to the curricle with her bold accusation still in his head.

Instead of getting in, he pivoted and returned to where she stood.

"I never thought you were ruined. That day I saw that you were frightened and sad and shocked. To have suggested that you have an affair would have been inappropriate at any time, and especially insensitive and cruel then. But I never thought you were ruined forever."

She turned to the door. "Well, I thought I was, even if you did not."

chapter 6

Penelope read a history of the ancient Etruscans in the library after Mr. Hampton left. When the sun moved enough to leave her spot in shadow, she set aside her book and debated how to fill the solitude facing her.

The temptation to seek some evidence in this cottage of Mr. Hampton's lover kept prodding her.

An odd vexation simmered whenever she contemplated the feminine chamber above. She knew that was stupid. It was foolish to assume his life was a blank in the areas she did not know about. If it were, there would have been months, *years,* when he did nothing but practice law and attend clients' parties and occasionally provide advice to the Countess of Glasbury.

None of which made the intrusive speculation and peculiar annoyance go away.

She walked over to the library's writing desk and peered at the drawers that she definitely should not open.

At least if she knew there was no *current* lover, she would not feel so strange here. The notion that an invisible person dined with them had made her peevish in the sitting room. A female person, lovely no doubt, whom Mr. Hampton never saw as ruined for men.

He had lied about that. Or rather he had chosen to hear her words only one way. Perhaps he truly had not thought that she would be incapable of such intimacies again. However, she did not doubt that in his eyes she had indeed been ruined, hopelessly soiled, as far as men were concerned. Of course, every man in the world remained ignorant of those sordid details so it had not mattered much.

Except with Mr. Hampton, who was not ignorant at all. However, since he was just an old friend, it had not really mattered too much with him, either.

She impulsively pulled open a drawer. A stack of papers lay in it. Battling guilt, imagining she heard his step behind her, she lifted the top one and unfolded it.

She read the first two lines and quickly returned it to the drawer and shut it away.

It was a love poem, written in Mr. Hampton's hand. A draft, full of changes, before the final version was sent.

Well, that was that. There had been lovers. There probably was one in London right now.

She slowly paced through the echoing rooms and forced herself to think about the choice they had discussed today. If she committed adultery and showed no discretion, would the earl divorce her?

Her independence had been contingent upon her never having lovers. Should she ever court scandal, or embarrass Glasbury that way, all support would cease and he would seek her return.

Unsaid, but understood, was that if he had evidence of

adultery her own accusations would be compromised and no longer a danger to him.

Now, however, the earl had broken the agreement anyway, so an affair might just force his hand.

She sat at the writing desk and helped herself to a clean sheet of paper. She would make a list of prospects for such a liaison, men who might not mind playing such a role. She wrote the first name.

Colin Burchard.

"He is appealing enough," she said to herself. Her voice sounded loud in the empty house. "He may think the scandal great fun, since he doesn't care much about anything society says. He may even enjoy being named in criminal correspondence. He would dine on the notoriety for years."

Ewan McLean.

The dangerous Scot. Handsome and full of the lure of forbidden fruit. Not at all discreet, either. He had been named already in one divorce, and there was something to be said for experience.

However, there were rumors about the doings in those chambers he had in London.

"He may be too . . . adventurous."

She neatly penned a few more names of men who were possibilities. She gazed at the last one.

Archibold Abernathy.

"Yes, Archie would be more than happy to accommodate me. He has been insinuating as much for years."

Only she did not much care for Archie. She had trouble picturing herself doing adulterous things with any of these men, and least of all with him.

She studied her list of six names, wondering if she had

it in her to throw herself at one of them. She would have to explain the plan, of course. He would have to be told it was an affair of convenience.

She tried to picture how she would propose such a thing.

"Sir, would you be interested in engaging in a sophisticated affair, where physical intimacy existed with affection but not love? You would be under no obligations to me at all, and we would part once sufficient evidence of my adultery was established."

Unfortunately, the woman in her mind as she practiced the overture was much more worldly than the Countess of Glasbury. The adulteress was one of those clever, confident ladies who dangled three men at a time.

Sighing, she dipped her quill again. Its point hovered above the paper, ready to write more names.

Julian Hampton.

She did not actually write it. Her conscience and good sense stopped the impulse. So did a startling surprise at how greedily her instincts grabbed the notion to consider him.

Picturing herself with *him* was not difficult at all. The images and sensations poured through her, provoking warmth and excitement. She actually saw him looking down at her and felt his hands on her, caressing . . .

She abruptly got up and fetched her book. She carried it far from that list, into the dining room where she found some western light. Perched by the window, she tried to continue reading about the Etruscans.

The images of Julian would not leave her. She laughed at herself.

Poor Mr. Hampton, to have to deal with a woman whose

fear and loneliness lured her to such foolish and inappropriate speculations.

Late in the afternoon, Julian called at Glasbury's house in London.

A tall Negro took his card. Julian recognized the servant, despite the years that had passed and the white wig and livery. His name was Caesar, a common slave name on English plantations. He was one of the servants that Glasbury had imported years ago from his estates in the West Indies.

Caesar returned and escorted him to the Earl of Glasbury's drawing room.

Little had changed in the room since Julian had last come here long ago to blackmail the earl into releasing Pen. It had not been real blackmail, not criminal, but the effect had been the same. *Permit her to leave your home and bed, give her an allowance, or face ruin and worse.*

The earl's allowance had not been handsome, but calculated to make sure she felt the privations of her decision. The separation had not been without cost to Penelope in other ways, too. However, Julian knew that even if her fall had been complete, she would have taken it to get away from this man.

Steely gray hair precisely groomed, expensive frock coat and cravat pressed to perfection, the earl sat on a small settee that made him look larger than he was. He bid Julian to a nearby chair.

"I regret that I could not receive you the last time you called," the earl said. "I am glad that you returned."

He smiled. Charlotte had called him a toad in Laclere's

study, and there was something to his lax mouth that reminded one of a frog.

"Your performance at Laclere's house required that I call. Your expectation that the countess should return to your home surprised me."

"Did it? I would have expected her to confide in you that I have changed my mind. After all, she has told you everything else."

"What surprises me is that you think that changing your mind has any significance. I doubt that her feelings have softened, so the situation remains as it was when she left you."

"In my view, the situation has changed considerably. Enough that this estrangement is no longer tolerable. I want you to communicate that to her in the event her brother will not."

"You can write to her and communicate it yourself."

"Since I do not know where she is, I cannot. Do not tell me she is in Naples, since I am sure she has returned to England. You know where she is, too. After all, you are her special confidant. Her servant. Her blackmail-monger. The lady bids and you perform, much like a well-trained dog. She may not have contacted her brothers, but she most certainly contacted you."

Glasbury rose and stiffly paced to the fireplace as if remaining in proximity to his caller was distasteful.

"She was having affairs in Naples. A whole string of them. That negates our agreement, as you well know."

"You have evidence of this?"

"I received enough letters describing her lovers to fill a ship's hold."

"A woman in the company of a man at a public function is not evidence."

"I know that she was playing the whore, damn you. I won't have it. It is intolerable. She is my wife. She *belongs to me.*"

There it was. Glasbury's view of marriage. Of Pen. Property.

The law's view, too, unfortunately.

"Whatever you may think you know, do not forget what she knows," Julian said.

Glasbury pivoted and glared at him. A dangerous gleam entered his eyes. "And what *you* know, too. Only you do not have the stomach to use it, even though you threatened that you did. You backed down once before after I spelled out the cost to you."

Julian greeted this allusion with silence. He knew that years ago someone had tried to blackmail Glasbury for money over these secrets. Glasbury had accused Julian of being that person, and returned his own threats. When the blackmail abruptly ceased, it looked as if Glasbury's interpretation had been validated.

Only it had not been Julian at all.

"The countess *does* have the will to use it, even if you think I do not," he finally said. "I repeat what I said when I first entered: Nothing has changed."

Glasbury strolled back with a confident gait. He eased back down on the settee. "I think much has changed. Time does that. She has a story, but who will believe her now? Who will believe the fantastic accusations of a woman so conceited and spoiled that she broke her marriage vows and refused her husband, a peer no less, his progeny? A woman who flaunts herself all over Europe as if she has no duties here in England? A woman who waits over a decade to reveal the source of her great unhappiness? See it with the world's eyes, Hampton. The years have made her tale of woe very stale. Her behavior has made its veracity very suspicious."

Something despoiling poured off Glasbury as he explained his invulnerability. That aura just got darker and darker, until Julian felt he was seeing the naked soul of this man. It was not a pleasant sight.

An old, recurrent vision intruded into the mutinous corner of Julian's mind. *He faced Glasbury on a meadow in Hampstead, as the sun inched above the tops of the surrounding trees and the beauty of the grass and breeze became so intense it could drench a man's soul.*

Another man joined them and opened a box, revealing two pistols. Silence reigned until a voice cracked it with the call to stations. He paced away and turned to aim—

"She has played you for a fool from the first, Hampton. There is much you do not know."

"I know enough to be disgusted with you."

"Ah, yes. I can see her now, pouring out her unhappiness and your believing every word. No doubt she neglected to mention that she was a willing partner in my games. She enjoyed them."

—the earl's body folded in on itself as his legs gave way and he sank to the ground—

"I will have her back." Glasbury speared Julian with a very confident glare. "And I will *finally* have the son she denied me. I would not get in my way if I were you. Bringing down Laclere would require some effort, but destroying you will be easy."

"I have been threatened by better than you, Glasbury,

so do not expect me to sweat. If your goal is a son, remember that the countess is no longer a girl. She is well past thirty years, and a first child may endanger her at this age."

"So long as the child is born alive, what do I care?"

The flat, callous reply chilled Julian. "And if that child is not a boy?"

"Then I will sire more, as other men do."

And if she does not get with child at all? Julian did not ask the question, but he could not ignore the obvious answers. One of them, the worst one, seemed very possible from the man on the settee.

Julian rose to leave. "As I said, you should write to her with an explanation of your plans. Perhaps she will view your position more kindly than I do. However, do not assume that her story will be disbelieved should she tell it. It is a compellingly sordid one, and time has changed many things, including the tolerance of society for men such as you."

Mist rolled in during the afternoon. The coast became veiled by the kind of weather that heralds rain. The sky hung so low that it appeared to melt right into the sea. Only the whitecaps on the waves seemed to break the bland expanse.

Pen sat at the desk and tried to work on her pamphlet. Her gaze kept drifting to the list of potential adulterers that she had made.

Finally, to distract herself, in late afternoon she fetched her blue cloak and went out to the stone terrace. She gazed out at the eternal expanse, with no horizon marking the edge of sea or sky. The surf sounded muffled, and the snapping wind seemed to pull one right into the soft wash of atmosphere.

She spied stone stairs going down the cliff to the beach. A small boat swayed on the eddies twenty yards from the bottom step.

She walked down the narrow steps and strolled south on the damp, packed sand, taking some air and exercise. When a big wave sent water nibbling at her feet, she slipped off her shoes and continued in her bare feet.

The sand beneath her toes reminded her of Naples. She had walked thus on the coast with young Paolo. The youngest son of a count, Paolo devoted his life to composing mediocre operas and charming foreign ladies. *Feel the sand and its heat, cara. Feel the cool water lapping against your skin and how glorious the contrast is.*

The memory of Paolo made her smile. He spoke frivolous flatteries, and easy words of love that had no truth. They were fun to hear all the same. Naples had been full of men like Paolo. She had been carefree and young in the light and happiness that Naples offered.

A theatrical light. A superficial happiness. She had been playing a role there, much like the ones she took as a girl when she and her brothers acted out Julian's medieval epics on the grounds of Laclere Park.

No. Those childhood games had been more honest. . . .

A wave's edge chilled her feet, and she had to scurry close to the cliff to avoid it. She looked around and realized that she had walked farther than she thought.

Her isolation rang into her awareness like a bell. Not another soul could be seen. The cottage was not even visible.

Another wave heralded the incoming tide. Already there were strips of beach threatening to be submerged.

Turning on her heel, she quickly headed back toward the cottage.

She almost did not see the man. The day was so gray, and he was just a smudge of a figure against the overcast sky. He stood on the cliff path above, his back to her, not moving, as if he watched something.

The cottage was the only thing visible up the coast. It was the only thing for that man to be looking at.

Fear scurried up her back. She told herself that she was being too suspicious. Soon, surely, he would walk on and appear very normal and not the least bit furtive.

Finally, he did move. He simply disappeared.

The fear shivered all through her. Someone just walking from one place to another along that path would not disappear. He would continue on.

She looked up and down the beach. Far to the south she could see the cottages of a fishing village. Perhaps he had come from there, but she did not think so. Smudge though he had been, it seemed to her he had worn a frock coat, not a fisherman's garments.

She moved close to the rocks dotting the inner edge of the beach, away from the surf, so anyone looking down from the cliff path or house might not see her.

She slid along the cliff face toward the cottage. A hundred yards from the cottage it jutted out in a little point. Hiding behind that shallow barrier, she peered around and looked up at her sanctuary.

A movement caught her eyes. A darkness, like a shadow, moved along the edge of the terrace.

Someone was at the cottage.

Her heart pounded so hard she felt it in her ears. Panicked thoughts poured into her head in a jumble.

She and Julian must have been followed this morning. That man was from the earl. He was looking for her, she felt certain of it. Maybe he had entered the house and seen her trunks. Maybe now he was going to use the boat to search the beach.

Cold water sloshed against her ankles. The shock of the sensation restored some of her senses. Hitching up her skirt and petticoats, she turned and ran back down the coast, frantically looking for a place to hide.

She stayed close to the rock face, praying she could not be seen from the terrace.

The wind whipped around her, carrying the evening's cold. It permeated right to her bones, aided by the chill of terror.

Swallowing a bile that threatened to make her sick, she darted her gaze along the rocks as she ran. Two large boulders beckoned.

She squeezed between them. She wrapped her cloak tightly around her and sat on a little bed of sand behind them.

Teeth clenched and heart beating with the dreadful hysteria of a hunted animal, she waited for discovery even as she prayed for salvation.

"You do not favor her, I think."

The soft, feminine voice barely penetrated Julian's thoughts. His body might be at this gathering but his mind was in a cottage on the coast, sitting by the fire with Penelope.

The revelation of her parting words continued repeating in his head.

She had thought she was ruined by Glasbury. For years she had believed it.

But that had changed. Eventually a man had resurrected what the earl had killed. A man who knew nothing of why she left the earl, and who did not have scruples about adultery, and who thought nothing of risking her independence, which was contingent upon no scandal surrounding her.

How did she remember that affair now? Were her memories kind to her lover, despite what had happened?

She probably still loved the man. If she had been reborn in that affair, she could probably forgive Witherby anything.

"Mrs. Morrison. You do not favor her, do you?" Diane St. John repeated.

He turned to his hostess. She had abundant chestnut hair and warm, soulful eyes, and possessed the kind of delicate beauty that grows more interesting with the years. Her natural grace would conquer time no matter how her face fared in the battle, however.

Normally he would have welcomed attending one of the St. Johns' gatherings. This one, however, had become a burden. It would have raised questions if he had begged off so late, however, since there was to be a brief business meeting in the library soon.

"She is very lovely and charming," Julian said. Mrs. Morrison stood nearby. Her mouth kept moving. "Was she your choice, or do I have Lady Laclere to thank for the introduction?"

Diane laughed. "I told them that you would be onto the game very quickly. Were we so obvious?"

"I concluded a month ago that certain ladies have turned their attention to finding me a wife."

"Not necessarily a wife. There is some concern that you may be lonely, that is all."

No, not necessarily a wife. He glanced to a corner of the drawing room where Señora Perez sat on a sofa, surrounded by men who laughed and hovered. Twice now she had caught his eye and favored him with long, smoldering looks.

He did not think she had been included tonight for his sake. Her vivacious personality ensured many invitations because she enlivened any gathering. She had caused a sensation in society, and by the beginning of the season would undoubtedly be a fixture at even the most elite parties.

Diane noticed his attention. "Daniel does not believe she is from Venezuela," she confided lowly. "He says her accent is quite different from Señor Perez's. He thinks she is from Guyana, perhaps."

"Since your husband has spent some time in that area of the world, he is probably correct."

"He also is not convinced that she is the legal wife of Raoul Perez. He does not think Señor Perez would permit a wife the freedom to flirt as this woman does. Also, it is obvious she has very little European ancestry. Raoul is a son of the *criollo* elite and would be meticulous about the bloodlines of his legitimate children."

"A mistress?"

"Possibly. What do you think? Is my husband correct?"

"I think that the parties in London promise to get very

theatrical during the next months if he is, but that the real dramas will play out in private, if we are fortunate."

Diane's gaze did a slow hostess scan of the drawing room, to make sure she was not needed. "Do you think it too intrusive for us to wonder about your happiness, let alone seek to influence it?"

"I am honored. If I do not cooperate, it is not for lack of understanding the kindness intended. I may not seek a wife, but I am grateful to have friends."

"I told Bianca and Sophia that I did not think you would cooperate," she confided. "I told them that I think you are a man who waits for something other than what we can arrange."

Julian had no idea how to respond to that, so he said nothing. Neither did his hostess. She remained beside him, however, as if they continued the conversation. That was one of the things he had noticed about Diane St. John from the start. She did not always feel obliged to fill the silence.

This time, however, he sensed an agitation in her, as if she would like to speak but held back.

Finally, she sidled one step closer. "Charlotte told me about Glasbury. I never liked the man. I remember when I first came to this country and Penelope befriended me. She had recently left him and he did all he could to see that their old circles cut and dropped her. He even insinuated himself among the new friends she made, so that his presence would make hers unacceptable."

"The countess knew that would happen."

"Pen is one of my dearest friends. It would give me great comfort to know that she is safe and unharmed and that Glasbury has not found her."

"I have no reason to believe that she is not safe."

Her expression cleared. "Please come with me, then. I have something to give you."

Julian followed her out of the drawing room and into the expansive quiet of the library. She walked to a writing table and extracted a sealed letter from its drawer.

"Please take this, Mr. Hampton. Daniel owns properties throughout England and Scotland. This letter contains information regarding some of their locations, and instructions to the people who care for them to welcome you in the event you ever visit. These are lovely but isolated houses that you may wish to visit someday."

Julian accepted the letter. "I do not anticipate visiting, but I am grateful for the invitation."

"You may decide that some country air has appeal one day. With that letter you can indulge yourself at once, on an impulse."

"You are too generous."

Just then the library door opened and the master of the house strolled in. Daniel St. John usually appeared either very distracted or very intense. Tonight it was the latter. His sharp dark eyes took in the two of them and his hard mouth smiled in its naturally sardonic way.

A shipper and financier of immense wealth, St. John was French born, although most of the world did not know that. His past was shrouded in mystery to all but his closest friends. One had only to see his attention focus on one like this to hope he would never be an enemy. Even when distracted or indifferent, his slightly cruel countenance warned that he was not a man to trifle with.

Julian suspected St. John's aura of potential ruthlessness ensured his success in business as much as any brilliance with numbers or strategies. Only a fool, upon meeting St. John, would consider engaging him with lies or fraud.

"There you are, Hampton. The others will join us shortly. Please excuse us, Diane. This meeting on Dante and Fleur's Durham project will be brief, I promise. Our guests will be none the wiser."

Diane departed. Julian slid the letter into his coat.

"It is a good thing that I know you to be a good friend, Hampton, and that I trust my wife completely. Another husband would be very curious about that letter and its contents."

"I suspect that I will find your writing should I ever open it, and not hers."

"Yes. Well, she worries about the countess. Now that we have made an attempt to help, she will be less distressed." St. John went to the desk and removed a sealed packet. "She does not know about this, however, so I require your discretion. If she were aware I felt the need to take such a step, she would only worry more."

Julian took the letter. "What is this?"

"A list of my ships, their ports of call in Britain and France, and anticipated dates of sailing. Also a letter from me to be given to any of the captains, with orders that passage be provided to the person who presents it."

Julian fingered the letter's edge thoughtfully. "How much do you know?"

"No more than anyone but you. However, the countess is a woman bred to a sense of duty. If she left Glasbury, it was for good reasons. It is not too difficult to surmise what some of those reasons might be." Steps could be heard approaching the library door. "I trust that you know that I am available, should you ever require my aid in any way."

Julian knew that. It was becoming clear, however, that his closest friends were convinced that Penelope was indeed back in England, and that Julian Hampton was helping her to hide.

Unfortunately, Glasbury had concluded the same thing.

chapter 7

Julian headed back to the coast before dawn the next morning. He rode his horse so he could make good time. The night was rainy, but the weather turned fair once the day broke.

As he approached the cottage he permitted himself a little fantasy, of Pen greeting his return. He pulled his horse up near the stable and surveyed the house.

No face showed at the door or window. No call or wave hailed him.

Of course not. She had more on her mind than the return of the faithful solicitor.

He took care of his horse, then walked to the house. Its silence seemed to grow as he approached. The mood was familiar but out of place this day. Someone dwelled in the cottage now.

As soon as he stepped inside he knew that was no longer true.

She was gone. The chambers echoed with emptiness. He

looked on the terrace, expecting the vacancy he found. He went up the stairs, knowing she would not be there.

Her trunks still were. Their presence chilled him for a moment. Fear that she had been snatched during his absence made his blood prickle.

No, it had not been that. She had walked away. She had tucked her valuables on her person, left the trunks, and disappeared. No other choice guaranteed her freedom, so she was headed into obscurity, where she would feel safe.

Considering his meeting with Glasbury, he wasn't entirely sure she had made a bad decision.

His soul emptied anyway, until it was as vacant as the cottage. He went back down, resenting the house's silence as he never had before.

Not just silent. Lonely. What kind of a man welcomed such a thing?

Out on the terrace, he looked down at the water.

She had left without a word. No warning and no farewell.

The morning tide was in, and the boat swayed in the surf. He stripped off his coats, neckwear, and shirt, and walked down the stone steps. He sloshed through the foam lapping on the sand and climbed into the boat. Taking the oars, he rowed straight out to sea.

The exercise felt good. So did the sun on his skin. It still carried remnants of summer's warmth even if the wind bore a taste of winter's bite. The strain of his arms and back, the battle with the waves as he rose up each one and slid down, relieved some of the turbulence in him.

Maybe she had only made the decision after he departed

yesterday. Perhaps she dared not tell him because she thought he would interfere.

Most likely she had not confided her decision because she felt no need to. He was only her solicitor. Her servant. Her blackmail-monger, as Glasbury had put it.

He pulled harder at the oars. He wished the day were stormy and the waves higher. He wished this exercise would exhaust him, so his mind would be too tired to absorb the desolate truth slicing his soul to shreds.

He would never see her again.

A large wave caught the boat and lifted it high. He stopped rowing and let it bear him forward, tottering on that wall of water, flying. He scanned his high view of the rocks and house.

His gaze halted, and darted back to the left. A spot of blue commanded his attention. Sapphire blue, and not the color of the sea, it draped the rocks below a steep drop from the cliff path.

The wave dumped him down and he turned the boat. He rowed south along the shore with all his strength, praying that the spot of blue did not cover a tragedy.

Pen squinted against the glare of the sea. She thought there had been a boat out there being rowed toward the horizon.

Surely not. That would make no sense. A sane person did not row out to sea.

Unless a person wanted to examine the whole coast, that is.

Had those men waited until now to search? Despite an

exhaustion that had wrung her spirit dry, the old, horrible panic began again.

She glanced back at the plot of sand she had sought last evening. It was submerged during the high tides. Last night she had been forced to climb on this large rock when the tide took her spot. It had been dark then, but it wasn't dark now, and she was visible and vulnerable.

The sea had wanted to claim her perch, but it appeared no longer to be rising. At least the tides turned before there was nothing left above water. In a few hours there should be enough beach to walk back to the cottage, assuming she dared risk it and she was not too numb to move.

The cold spray had soaked her garments and her wet cloak did not offer much comfort. She pulled it tighter anyway, and tried to ignore the chill that had her teeth chattering.

She looked for the boat again. Perhaps she had been mistaken. If not, there was nothing she could do now to escape detection. She was so tired and miserable she was not even sure she would mind being found.

Suddenly the boat came in view, very plainly. Long and dark, it moved parallel to the shore, coming toward her.

The panic surged.

A dark head turned. A shout called out her name.

Her heart took a leap. Tears of relief blurred her eyes.

It was Julian. He had said he would return this afternoon, and here it was early morning and he had already come.

"Julian," she called back. "I am here, Julian. Save me."

The boat came closer. She could see his taut arms pulling the oars and his dark hair blowing in the wind and his strong shoulders glistening from the spray. He appeared so magnificent that she forgot her peril.

He rowed right to her, then set up one oar and let the sea bring him in. Navigating the submerged rocks, he came within ten feet of her. He jumped into water that reached above his waist, tucked the boat between two boulders, and strode toward her.

Half naked like that, he appeared to be an ocean god striding through his domain. The muscles of his shoulders and chest were certainly sculpted well enough for the role.

"How did you get here?"

"There was a man and I did not dare go back and I hid and then the tide came in and I was stuck and—"

He lifted her into his arms, effortlessly. Strong arms, so welcome and so comforting. "Explain later. You are wet and chilled and we need to get you to a fire."

Grasping her closely and holding her high, he bore her to the boat. In those few steps, her body went slack as both her danger and relief sapped the remnants of her spirit. Her head lolled against his shoulder. The warmth of his skin and the security of his strength almost undid her.

He paused and looked down at her, his face mere inches from hers, his expression both severe and gentle.

He placed her in the boat as if she were made of china, then climbed in and pushed them back into the sea. She sat facing him, shivering in her wet cloak, as he rowed toward the cottage.

She admired how dashing he looked with his naked muscles moving to the effort. She should probably avert her eyes to the water or the boat's floor, but his arms and torso mesmerized her.

"Did you row out looking for me when I was not at the cottage?"

"If I had, I would have worn a shirt." It was not a scold, just a statement that said she was looking as she should not and that he knew it. "I like to take the oars for exercise. When I am in London, I often row on the Thames in early morning."

She was too tired to be embarrassed, but she did manage not to look at him so blatantly. "Did you not think it odd I was not there?"

"I assumed you had decided to leave."

That she might have left did not seem to either surprise or dismay him. He had found her gone, and simply returned to the activities that he normally pursued here.

"I am very fortunate that you saw me and realized I was caught by the tide."

"I saw the blue of your cloak. I did not know how it got there."

He did not sound as if he had been very concerned. He had just been rowing, seen the blue, and investigated out of curiosity.

"It was my hope, of course, that I would find it wrapped around a living woman."

A tightness in his voice caught her thoughts up short. She looked in his eyes, and he diverted his attention to his oars.

He had indeed worried, in the worst way. He had

rowed toward her thinking he might find her dead, from the sea or from a fall. Maybe not an accidental fall.

"I will never hurt myself because of him, Julian."

He brought them to the stone stairs, pushed the boat into the shallows and tied it to its post. He carried her to a step above the water.

She wobbled from the stiffness that had claimed her legs and the exhaustion that had robbed her strength. His arms scooped her up again. He carried her up the stairs and into the library.

He sat her in a chair and bent at once to build the fire.

"It has died," she said. "The fire. Perhaps he did not wait here all night after all."

"Who?"

She told him about the man at the cottage. "I dared not return here, lest I find him waiting."

He got the fire going to a pleasant roar, then left her to bake near it. It felt so good that she got drowsy. Sounds vaguely penetrated her stupor as he moved about the house.

A gentle hand on her arm coaxed her out of the gathering fog. "I have made a bath in the kitchen near the fire. A hot one. You will feel better for it."

She really did not want to move. Wet clothes or not, with relief had come deep aches and a relentless chill.

"Come, Pen. I worry for your health."

She sighed. "If you insist, Mr. Hampton."

She forced herself to her feet.

And found her nose an inch from his chest. He had donned a shirt. Pity.

Her gaze moved up to his face. One of his rare smiles greeted her. Not a completely gentle one.

"So, I am Mr. Hampton again. It seems that I am only Julian when you forget yourself."

"I . . . that is . . ."

"We have known each other more than half our lives, Pen."

She had not even noticed what she called him.

"I do not want you to call me Mr. Hampton in private conversation ever again."

He stepped aside. "I brought down some dry garments for you. They are near the bath. If you require anything else, just call for me."

Julian had set the metal tub close to the fire and filled it with hot water that the hearth kept warm. Easing down into the steamy comfort made her groan with pleasure. The heat immediately started to leach the chill out of her.

She could not ignore the fact that a man was very nearby. Knowing he was there gave the languid soaking a naughty titillation. As she dipped low to rinse her hair, she imagined she heard his footsteps coming toward her. An exciting alarm shot through her.

"I found no evidence of intruders in the house."

She startled at his voice and quickly glanced over her shoulder to the door. He did not stand there. He must be right on the other side, however.

"You are sure?" she asked.

"There are also no wheel marks or horse or boot prints outside, other than mine."

"I did not imagine that man, Julian."

"I am not saying that you did. However, it is common

for people using the cliff path to cross the terrace rather than walk around the property. It happens even when I am here."

"Then I imperiled myself for nothing more than an overwrought imagination."

"If you saw someone at the cottage, your caution was sensible. If your fear kept you on the rocks all night, we should have expected it might."

This conversation, held while she bathed naked just ten feet from him, created a seductive intimacy. She kept glancing to the door, expecting to see it move.

"I will control my fear in the future, Julian. I will need to learn to do that, won't I?"

"I think it will be easier to ensure you are not afraid, Pen."

She heard the slightest sound. She closed her eyes and waited for the change in the air that would say he was in the kitchen.

None came. She looked behind her. The door remained resolutely closed. He had probably walked away, back into the library.

Of course he had.

She looked down at her naked body, assessing what a man would see if he did enter while she bathed. Her breasts were full and firm, and her waist narrow enough for the current styles despite an overall soft plumpness that she had never been able to lose.

There was nothing special to her, however. Nothing stunning, physically or otherwise. She had never been the sort of woman whom men lost their voices over. The only thing remarkable about her was that she had walked out on an earl early in marriage, and that was not the kind of thing that provoked admiration.

She finished washing herself, conscious of the man in the next room who could hear every splash.

She was sure he did not even notice. He had probably retreated into that private place where his mind seemed to dwell most of the time. It went without saying that neither Mr. Hampton nor Julian had ever wondered what she looked like without clothes.

Eventually the water began cooling and she had to get out. Stepping onto the floor, toweling off her skin, she blushed at how much she enjoyed the awareness that he heard everything, even if he could not care less. It was the most delicious bath she had ever taken.

She reached for the garments. No stays had been brought down. The dress was one that fit her a bit large now, so it would not be too ridiculous. She slid on the chemise, petticoat, and stockings, and managed to fasten the dress. She walked to the library.

He was not there.

She stood in the empty chamber and laughed. Not only had he not listened and wondered, he had not even remained in the house.

A blanket had been left on the divan. She understood the gesture. He assumed she would want to rest.

She reclined and tucked the blanket around her. He would stay until she woke, she was sure. She was safe.

He heard every movement. Every splash. Every breath.

His mind saw her removing her garments one by one until she was soft and pink and naked. He pictured the fullness of her breasts and the way her curves elegantly stretched as she stepped into the tub.

Standing in the library he saw and heard it all. The arousal of a lifetime claimed him. Gritting his teeth, he forced some control, but the urge to walk into the kitchen almost won over his better sense.

Finally, to spare her from that raging impulse, he left the house. He paced along the lane, looking again for evidence of a visitor last night.

He did not doubt someone had been here. Pen was not the sort of woman whose fear would make her imagine such a thing. It was obvious it was a local person using the cliff path, however. No carriage or horse or boot had approached the house from the road.

He strolled back into the garden. The kitchen window beckoned. The temptation to peer in had his body tightening again.

He laughed at himself. Here he was, a grown man, established and respected, and he wanted to peek in a window at a naked woman, as a schoolboy might.

He did not approach the window, but his mind saw the interior of the kitchen all the same. *Pen soaked in a tub, with her soft shoulders and dark hair and lovely breasts visible. The heat and water had turned her skin glossy and flushed, and the tips of her breasts had hardened from the cool air.*

He tried to fight what the image did to him, but he could not. For years he had battled this hunger. He had learned how to retreat from it, how to control it. Its victories had been private and pointless, and he had always rebuilt the walls that held it safely in place.

He had kept it from owning his life. Now, Pen's danger

made him vulnerable to the most primitive reactions, and he could no longer master them.

Standing by the garden wall, he closed his eyes as a savage fury maddened him. The desire to possess and protect became one violent, senseless urge.

He knew, even as his essence succumbed, that he would never be able to totally contain this passion again.

Which meant that in the future, his life would be hell.

He was reading in a chair near the hearth when she opened her eyes. He had changed into dry trousers and donned his coats. He looked relaxed and comfortable. And very handsome. The fire played over his features, making his eyes appear even deeper set and darker than normal. It sculpted the planes of his face with sharp lights and shadows.

Julian. She was glad he had insisted they drop formalities. She could not remember when they had adopted them.

He set aside the book. "You are feeling better?"

She pushed herself up and set aside the blanket. She noted the shadows in the room. "Yes. I fear I slept too long. It appears to be late afternoon. You should be riding back if you hope to make it before dark."

"It is not my intention to ride back today."

He said it so casually that one would assume it did not imply something improper. Probably because it did not, for him.

"I think it would be best if I remained here until you decide what to do, and we arrange whatever needs to be dealt with," he said. "Otherwise, tonight you may hear something outside and think men have come again and head into the sea to escape."

"I am not that foolish, Julian."

"No, you are not. But you are very afraid. If I am here, I think you will be less frightened."

That was certainly true.

"There is a chamber above the stables. I will use that."

She was sure that her good judgment would speak to her more clearly if he did not look so unbearably handsome sitting there. Instead, proprieties seemed a little silly under the circumstances. They were alone here, and where he slept really would not make any difference should the world find out. Nor did he represent any danger to her virtue.

"I am not a blushing schoolgirl. If you are going to stay, you may as well be comfortable. As for making a decision regarding what to do, I have been contemplating that for a day now, and doubt I will decide by tomorrow."

"Then I will wait until you do. I told my clerk to manage things while I am gone, and arranged for another solicitor to handle any matters that cannot wait."

He rose and returned the book to its shelf. As he walked back, he passed close to the writing desk.

His gaze fell upon its surface. He stopped.

He reached out and straightened the document on the desk.

"What is this?"

"A pamphlet. I have been using the time here to work on it."

He perused the first page. "You are planning to publish a statement regarding the marriage laws?"

"It is long past time for someone to start that discussion."

He lifted the document and read it. "It is well written, Pen."

She glowed at his praise. "It is not all mine. I have been working on it with some other ladies. Mrs. Levanham and some others in similar straits to mine."

"It has your voice, Pen. The same tone as your letters to me. The same music. Do you intend to put your name to this?"

"It will be taken more seriously if I do. A countess's name will give it more influence."

"Does Glasbury know that?"

"I cannot imagine how he would."

"I suspect the project is fairly well known among certain circles of women. It would only take one person to pass along a draft to him."

"Are you implying that my participation on this essay is the reason he has moved against me?"

"Considering some of its language, it could be one reason. Let me see, how did that one sentence go . . . ah, yes, here it is—*Laws intended to protect women become the means for condemning them to lives of miserable slavery, should they discover their husbands are not decent gentlemen but instead vile, violent, wicked spawns of the devil.* A very impressive passage, Pen. Powerful."

"It is not as if I actually called *him* a vile, violent spawn of the devil. It is very clear I was speaking in generalities."

"It is the rationale you give for why women should be able to leave their husbands. You left your husband. Therefore, one assumes it was your rationale. So, you *are* calling him vile and wicked."

She smacked the sofa's cushion in vexation. "Well, he *is* vile and wicked. Do not expect me to temper my words, Julian. Women are slaves in marriage, and it must change."

He gazed at the papers again, but it was not clear he actually read them. "Your experiences have encouraged too harsh a view. Not all women are slaves. Your brothers' wives are very happy."

This was why she never told men about that pamphlet. *They* could never understand. "If a married woman is not like a slave in a marriage, it is only because her owner is benevolent. Her condition is entirely subject to her husband's whim. That pamphlet will be published, dear friend. Whatever else happens with Glasbury, that will not be negotiable."

Without further comment, he turned to replace the document on the desk. As he did so, his attention was distracted to another sheet that had been beneath it.

She inwardly groaned. It was her list of names for her affair of convenience.

He glanced back at her. "It appears that you did not only occupy yourself with a call to arms to free married women from bondage."

"On the chance that I would be staying in England, I began planning a little party."

She did not know why she lied, but something in his eyes provoked the impulse.

"A very interesting party. Male guests only."

This was really very embarrassing. "If you must know, I was considering the choice of an affair. I thought I should weigh whether such a thing was possible or even worth contemplating seriously."

"So this is your list of likely conspirators." He carried the paper over to the fire where there was more light to study it. "Colin Burchard will be honored to learn he made the cut."

"In truth, I do not really think he would be suitable."

He peered at the paper again. "Ewan McLean?"

"Well, actually—"

"Ewan McLean?"

"It was just a—"

"Naples must have been most congenial if you put McLean on your list."

"I do not know why you are so disapproving. You said this was worth consideration."

"I said the idea was worth consideration, not that Ewan McLean was. I will lock you away first, Pen. He is definitely not for you."

"I think it is for me to decide who is for me and who isn't."

"The hell it is."

She had no idea what that was supposed to mean, but his attitude and tone annoyed her. "It is very difficult to compile such a list, I will have you know. Especially since it will be no more than an affair of convenience. I will not want the complications of some man professing great love or, God forbid, wanting to marry after my divorce."

"You appear to have planned it through in minute detail."

"That part, yes. If I get free of this yoke I do not intend to become chattel again. I would be an idiot to remarry. As for that list, it is astonishing how very few names

I could muster, without even subjecting them to due testing."

"Due testing?"

It was the closest thing to a yell that Pen had ever heard from Julian. It caused her shoulders to press in retreat against the back of the sofa.

"Well, not actually testing—"

"Perhaps you should put an advertisement in the papers. You can have it listed under livestock. Stallion sought, something like that."

Now, that was uncalled for, and outright rude. "What a splendid idea," she responded. "Only why play with metaphors? The direct approach is always best. How does this sound? *Gentleman required for a temporary affair of convenience. Unexceptionable references from previous lovers required. Must be willing to be named in criminal corespondence. Should be presentable, experienced, and have a strong back.*"

His glare said he did not find that humorous in the least.

"I do not understand why you are reacting like this, Julian. You agreed an affair was a simple solution. You sounded very encouraging yesterday."

He studied the list further, looking very critical indeed. Angry, actually.

"I notice that my name is not here."

"You are so honorable, of course, and—"

"You worry for my reputation? That is generous of you." He strolled toward her. His dark expression made her heart rise. "However, since I am the only man who has already shown a willingness to risk the cost, that seems an odd reason to omit me."

He was right in front of her now.

"In fact, I have proven myself willing to risk the cost even without the prize of pleasure. If you decide to bestow your favors I think I should at least be in the running, out of courtesy if nothing else."

He looked down. She could not speak.

"I am also the only man who would completely understand what you asked and why, Pen. The only one who would know why you needed this affair of convenience, and what it did and did not mean."

It was not Julian the old friend gazing at her with those stormy eyes, nor was it Mr. Hampton the faithful advisor. A different man stood just inches from her, darkly displeased, projecting an aura that charged the air and made her heart pound.

His hand came to rest on her face. She stared up in silent astonishment. That touch felt very good, however. Masculine and warm and confident.

"Perhaps you did not include me because you did not think I could acquit myself well enough. After all, you have never subjected me to *due testing*."

His hand commanded her head steady. A sensual anticipation scurried through her.

His head lowered and his mouth pressed hers.

It was not a long kiss, but it amazed her. She responded as if a sexual breeze had entered her. The kiss was firm enough and long enough to make explicit it was not intended as one of friendship, or even one of request.

He stopped and straightened. His gaze affected her even more than the kiss had. She could not even blink.

Then he was gone, walking away, heading calmly for the door to the terrace like a man who had thought of something else he should be attending.

chapter 8

If that kiss was any indication, Julian Hampton could acquit himself very well indeed.

That was the first lucid thought that entered Pen's head as she gained some control on her flustered condition.

She sat on the sofa, trying to find some accommodation to this sudden turn in their friendship.

She had no idea what she was supposed to do now.

She stood up and looked out the window. He was not on the terrace.

He might think she was insulted by that kiss, or that she suspected his intentions now. That kiss could change everything about how one saw his help and protection and motivations, if one permitted it to.

She did not want him wondering if that were the case with her.

Her cloak was nowhere in sight, so she grabbed the blanket and wrapped it around her shoulders. She stepped out on the terrace to see where he was.

Julian stood not far from the bottom step of the stone

stairs, on a strip of beach released by the outgoing tide. He cut a handsome image standing there, framed by the sea, his dark frock coat and hair contrasting with its pale tones. His body bore a casual stance, as if he meditated on the elements and allowed nature's forces to flow through him.

He did not look like someone who would welcome an intrusion on his solitude.

She headed down the stairs anyway. She went and stood beside him.

He did not look at her. "You should have stayed in the cottage, Pen."

"I am not going to take ill. I am quite recovered from my ordeal."

"That is not what I meant." He glanced over, then turned his attention back to the sea. "I do not intend to apologize, if that is what you expect."

"There is no need to. It was an impulse. We all on occasion act without thinking."

"Yes, it was an impulse. Or it may have been the most deliberate thing I have ever done in my life. I haven't decided yet."

She did not know what to say to that, but she felt compelled to say something. "I am surprised, that is all. Flattered, too, certainly, but mostly surprised. I had no idea that you ever thought of me that way."

"Why wouldn't I think of you that way? You are an attractive woman, and men have a habit of thinking of women that way in any case."

That certainly gave the episode a commonplace color. It also explained the true reason for that kiss. A very ordinary one that had nothing to do with impulse, or even very much with whether he thought of her that way.

His pride had been wounded, that was all. His masculinity had been insulted that the Countess of Glasbury had not included him on that silly list of potential lovers, no matter which lover she eventually chose.

Well, what did she expect? He may be an old friend, but he was still a man.

"Julian, I meant it when I said you were not on my list because you are honorable, and because of the cost to you of such a scandal. I almost wrote your name, truly. My pen was poised to do so, but consideration of all that stopped me. Of course the notion entered my mind, but under the circumstances it just seemed to be best if I removed you from consideration."

He stepped in front of her, between her and the sea, listening with amusement. He reached out and gently laid two fingers on her lips, stopping her attempts to assuage his pride.

"It is very sweet of you to explain that, Pen. Also a mistake. It would have been better not to tell me."

She took his hand in hers. "I believe it was right to tell you, Julian. I do not want you insulted or hurt because of that stupid list."

His gaze fell to their hands. His hold tightened. Tiny lightning bolts brightened his eyes. "Touching me right now was another mistake, Pen. A very big one."

She moved in a blur as he pulled her into his arms and captured her in an encompassing embrace.

He kissed her again, but it was different this time. Definitely impulsive. Dangerously furious. She might have controlled her reactions to the last kiss if she had truly wanted to. This kiss gave her little choice but submission.

The blanket wrapped her, but his strength encircled her, too. His tight embrace held her so closely that she could feel all of him. His chest pressed her breasts, and his firm grasp held her to the kisses ravishing her mouth and neck.

He paused and gazed down at her. There was no mistaking the way he looked at her. No mistaking the sensual fury in his eyes. Nor could she ignore the way her lips swelled and throbbed from his kisses, and how that pulse beat its way through her cheek and down her neck to her breasts.

That exciting pulse turned her initial surprise and alarm into a seductive entrancement.

Her whole body reacted to his bold gaze. The throbbing became undeniably sexual and beat in her blood and head, and physically in her breasts and belly.

He knew. New lights entered his eyes that showed he did. No matter what shock her face might show, he could tell that her body recklessly dared him to kiss her again.

He did, ruthlessly. He aroused her as if he knew just how to do it. Each kiss was calculated to render her helpless to the escalating pleasure.

Stunning pleasure. A hot wind of it. Sly currents of hunger flowed ruthlessly to swelling pools of desire. Her breasts grew heavy and tender and sensitive. Moisture began slicking her thighs.

She barely noticed their steps back to the dry sand stripping the base of the terrace wall. He lowered her as if lying on the sand were her only choice of where to go.

He peeled apart the blanket to spread on the sand and

shrugged off his coat. She was able to embrace his warmth during the next kiss. It felt so good to hold him, so blissful that it drenched her spirit and left her even more defenseless.

The kisses calmed. They turned sweet and slow and too tender to bear. Her body both relished the slow pleasure and ached for more.

He rose up on one arm and looked down at her, giving substance to the image of him that had flashed in her head for the last day. The wind blew his dark hair and the sleeves of his shirt. His gaze followed the gentle caress of his hand over her face and neck.

"Do you want to go back to the cottage?"

She could not resist touching him, too. She caressed the face looking down at her and the lips that had been kissing her. The sensation of his skin under her fingertips entranced her.

Her intense reactions confused her. Frightened her. The part of her that shuddered with anticipation knew exactly what it wanted, but her conscience chanted that she should leave at once and not risk complicating and ruining this friendship.

"I do not know what I want."

"I do." His caress drifted lower, to her neck. Her skin began sparkling with warmth. "You will stay for a while, Pen, and we will enjoy the sea and each other."

The next kiss told her what would happen and what would not. It promised as much as demanded, and she was filled with the trust she had always had in this friend. She did not know what she wanted, and he would not take advantage of that.

No more confusion, just total absorption in the sensations and changes. When he asked for more she could not refuse. The intimate strokes in her mouth sent stunning shudders all through her, enlivening her body, making her impatient for more closeness.

He caressed down her side and she felt his hand clearly. No stays protected her body or interfered. His hand moved again, over the fullness of her breast, as confidently as if he had touched her like this a hundred times before.

Only he had not, and the unexpected power of the pleasure sent her reeling. She wanted that touch to continue, desperately. Her body instinctively moved to encourage him. Even her breaths sounded a rhythm that begged for more.

What that hand did to her. His fingers found her nipple through the cloth and stroked it, sending streams of luscious excitement shuddering down her essence. She closed her eyes to try to control the madness that threatened to obliterate her composure. She kissed him back, urgently, to relieve the frightening desire building in her.

His hand moved to her shoulder. He gently rolled her on her side, away from him. Her disappointment lasted only a moment before she felt her dress loosening.

He eased her back on the blanket, then lowered her dress and chemise. He slid the fabric down, unveiling her body. She snuck a glance at what he saw. Her breasts rose naked above the rumpled garments. Her body was completely bare from the waist up.

He propped himself up on one elbow, out of her embrace, leaving her to lie there vulnerable to his gaze. The sensation of lying naked and exposed was incredibly erotic.

His hand came to rest on her stomach, dark against her white skin. "You are very lovely, Pen. Very fair and soft."

From beneath her lowered lids, she could see that hand on her. Her breasts grew sensitive because of its proximity. Even the breeze seemed to arouse them.

"Too soft," she muttered. "This dress needs stays and you forgot to bring me some."

He caressed where the stays should be. "I forgot nothing. There is no one here but me. No need to truss yourself unnaturally. You looked beautiful in the dress. You look more beautiful with it half off."

Calmly, almost languidly, he trailed his fingers up between her breasts and around their swells. They hardened in response and an itching anticipation started making her mad again.

He caressed as if he sought nothing more than to do this for a while. She gritted her teeth and tried to contain what was happening inside her.

His fingertips gently grazed one nipple. She barely swallowed a cry. He circled so lightly, so effectively, that she thought she would scream.

"How long has it been, Pen?" He watched his hand make its patterns, and also watched her body react. "How long since you have been touched?"

His thumb rubbed the tip of her nipple. The sensation defeated her control and she moved, arching her back.

"Not so long." It amazed her that she could speak, since she could hardly breathe. "But . . ."

His fingers continued their sweet torture. "But what?"

"I had to be careful, didn't I? Be on my guard. They could not be trusted, not really, so I could not risk losing control."

He absorbed that thoughtfully while he continued the slow arousal of her body. His head dipped and he gently kissed the side of her other breast. "How long since you have made love?"

She could touch him now, and slid her fingers into the hair of his head while he pressed gentle kisses to her breast. "Do you mean completely?"

"Yes. Completely."

"Almost forever. Since I left the earl."

"Not even with Witherby?"

The name released a stream of sadness into her bliss. An old humiliation and disappointment slid through her heart. She was surprised that Julian would mention Witherby now, of all moments. No one ever spoke of that old love to her. Not Julian nor her brothers nor anyone else who knew of it.

"I could not risk having a son. Glasbury could claim him as his own and take him away, and my child would be condemned to that household and that man's power."

He appeared surprised by her answer. He had assumed there had been at least one complete affair. She expected that everyone believed that.

"No, I suppose you would not risk that," he said. "So even when making love incompletely, you could not abandon yourself to it because you could not trust the men." His hand resumed its meandering path. "Do you trust me, Pen?"

Did she? Her body seemed to. Or else it was betraying her in the worst way.

"It appears that I do."

"I am glad." He kissed her breast again. This time on the tip. His tongue flicked at it, making her gasp. "Now, no more talk. I do not want to hear any sounds except the sea and the wind and your crying with pleasure."

He made sure that she cried. He used his mouth and his hand to breach whatever control she still had. Her breasts grew more and more sensitive as he teased each one with his tongue and teeth. Abandon beckoned, closing in on her awareness, fed by pleasures that ached demand for the completeness she could not have but furiously wanted.

She could not fight it, did not want to. She knew in her heart that she did not need to. Not this time. All of her, body and mind, relinquished control. She entered a place where only pure sensation existed, a state of pleasure and desire and wonderful physical responses.

She did not hear the sea or the wind. Only the pulse of need and her own moans and cries entered her head. And his voice, asking once more, "Do you trust me, Pen?"

A new caress explained the question. Lower, to her hips and thighs, pressing through her petticoat. Her body answered for her, rising to that touch, heedless of any risk now, careless of the danger.

He pressed the hot center between her legs and she almost swooned with relief. Nothing else mattered now except being touched there. Every sensation, every excitement collected at that place and moaned for more pressure, more . . . everything.

She felt a new nakedness, vulnerable and wonderful, and a warm palm smoothing over her legs. She opened her eyes to see a rumpled ledge of skirt and petticoat mounded at her waist.

He rose in her embrace and looked at what she could

not see. He caressed her thighs as slowly as he had her breasts.

He turned back to her and she grabbed him close and kissed him madly, giving vent to her sexual fury.

He caressed up until his fingers touched the one single spot where her whole essence focused. A stroke, one slow touch, made her cries catch in her throat. The intensity of the pleasure shocked her.

He kissed her cheek softly. "Do not lose courage now. If you can finally risk abandon, you should know what that can mean."

He touched again, deeper. She grasped him tighter, gripping his back to contain what little sense she had left.

"Spread your legs, Pen."

Her body obeyed. It wanted to. Even the shock was too delicious to deny.

He showered slow kisses on her face and breast while his hand created shivers that quivered up through her blood then down again to that spot. The flesh he caressed pulsed so strongly that it became the rhythm of her whole life.

She heard the waves now, in her head, mixing with the cries she could not contain. Cries of pleasure and frustration. Her body screamed for something. The intensity just kept getting deeper and her madness more engulfing.

Her spirit entered a place that was blind and senseless and dangerous. Still the pleasure increased, narrowed, rising higher until she tottered on the brink of sensation so powerful it was painful.

He kissed her hard as his touch forced the last step. Her scream entered him as the sensation penetrated her womb and exploded.

After the stunning lightning bolt came the most beautiful rain. Pleasure and peace flowed all through her, sparkling in a magical shower.

She was so lovely. His heart almost could not bear it.

Her astonishment appeared to match his, but he was sure it did not.

The beach became a mystical place, separate from his normal world, a spot hanging somewhere between dreams and wakefulness, between heaven and earth. Her sighs and gentle moves timed the pulse of creation and caused the rhythm of the sea's waves and the wind's swells.

He stroked his fingertips over her face, luxuriating in the sensation of her soft skin. He looked at her as he had always wanted, slowly and carefully, so his eyes and memory would be denied no detail.

He touched her, as he had often imagined doing so. Over the fullness of her cheeks; around the firm little bones of her jaw and chin; softly along the vague, tiny lines barely visible at the outside edges of her eyes.

He kissed those lines. Laughter had made them. They symbolized her sweet disposition, her ability to see good and have hope no matter what her own troubles.

They also represented all the time he had wanted her. At parties and at dinners. Alone in his chambers. Wanting her had been a calmly accepted part of his existence, much like being a certain height. It was not something he resented or regretted. It was just there, framing certain decisions in his life whether he wanted it to or not.

Now, finally, he had tasted what he hungered for. He

knew he should not have done it, but he did not give a damn about that now.

She did not say anything as she lay in his arms afterward. The embrace was so serene that he could have stayed there forever. The lowering sun made the wind cold, however, and their sand very shadowed. They could not stay like this.

She let him right her garments and wrap her in the blanket. She did not object when he rested his back against the wall and pulled her into an embrace beside him.

Together they watched the late shadows claim the rocks and sea. His eyes saw it all but the images in his head were different ones, of Pen in her passion.

He would never hear the sea again without also hearing her gentle, lovely cries.

And her admission that there had been no lovers. At least not complete ones.

The man who wanted her had liked hearing that. The friend who knew her disappointments had not. Over the years he had been jealous at the smallest evidence of lovers, but he had not wanted her lonely and unhappy, either.

He turned his mind from that, and to her and the way she nestled against him.

"What are you thinking?" He did not mind her silence, but he wondered what kept her so quiet.

She tucked herself closer and her head lolled on his shoulder. "I am thinking that I really must remember to put you on my list now."

She damn well better.

"We quite lost our heads, didn't we, Julian? It was very

nice, though. I am thinking that intimacy with a good friend is nicer in ways than that with a great love. More trust, for one thing."

It did not surprise him that she was deciding this had been an impulse between two old friends. Perhaps it was for the best.

"I am also thinking that I need to decide if I will make use of that list, or find another way. What if he does not react as we think he will? What if I embarrass him with a public affair, and he does not divorce me?"

"He will not be able to ignore it. This is not a man who will accept such a thing."

"No, but he may decide to deal with it in other ways." Her quiet voice communicated how deeply she had been contemplating this.

Yes, he might. Outrage could lead Glasbury to take the rash step that would lead to that Hampstead meadow and the call to stations.

She eased out of his embrace and got to her feet. She brushed the sand off the blanket. "I need to decide soon. I cannot avoid it now."

No, she could not, and not only because of what had just happened on this sand.

The mood had changed. She had subtly retreated more than physically.

He stayed where he was. "I will sleep above the stable."

In the weakening light she appeared a little sad.

"You are still my friend, aren't you, Julian? We will continue as before, won't we? You will not let what happened here change that, will you?"

"Of course not."

Her stance appeared to relax. "Then you do not have to sleep in the stable."

"I will use the chamber below, then."

She laughed lightly. "Yes, that may be best."

He watched her walk up the stone stairs. Sleeping below was not only best. It was essential. He would never rest if he used the chamber beside hers tonight. He doubted he would be able to stay in his own bed. This was not the night to test his trustworthiness any further.

He looked back at the sea turning black in the nightfall.

He had just lied to her when he said what had happened did not change their friendship.

In fact, it changed absolutely everything.

chapter 9

Pen tossed in her bed. She tried to name what had just happened with Julian.

She knew women who had affairs that were mostly about physical pleasure. Their brief intimacies were fun little games, no more. Her "incomplete" affairs had been like that, except with Witherby. She was well enough experienced in silly diversions based on flirtation and stolen caresses.

There had been nothing silly about tonight, however. This had been different than a dalliance for superficial thrills. Her friendship with Julian made it more than that. Nicer. More intimate. She could trust him, and that had changed everything.

That friendship was confusing her reactions in other ways, she decided. If she had not known him so long, if their history did not stretch back for years, the notion of being kissed by him would not be so startling.

After all, he was a man and she was a woman. As he had said, why wouldn't he think of her that way? Why wouldn't she react to his kiss? If she had not been so stupid, she would have realized that their continued proximity these days might give rise to such a development. Everyone knew that men were inclined to experience sexual impulses given the least provocation.

She turned on her back and listened to the silence. Julian was sleeping below this chamber, directly underneath her. She tried to hear if he snored or moved.

Memories of their embraces crept into her head. They were so vivid that she felt his touch again. The fantasy aroused her. Her body started yearning for those caresses.

No doubt abstinence had played a role tonight, too. Maybe when a woman spends years being titillated by flattery and incomplete affairs she is well disposed to utter abandon if she once drops her guard.

The beauty and peace she had found in that passion had been more seductive than the pleasure, however. She had felt so innocent. Glasbury might have never existed. She had never before so completely forgotten those years.

Julian had been right when he scolded her for not adding his name to that list. She would not have to explain anything if she had an affair with him. He would know why. He would understand the cost.

She could have an affectionate affair with a good friend and not a superficial liaison. It would not be humiliating and cheap. When it was over, they would still be friends.

She pictured the affair, explicitly. She imagined him walking through the door, his chest naked, as it had been in the boat. She felt him lying in this bed and touching her breasts. She saw him braced above her, and her body imagined him entering her.

The fantasy made an intense arousal shudder through her.

She reached for her wrap.

She would go down and he would be awake, waiting for her.

She just knew he was thinking about her as she did about him. The cottage almost moaned from their wanting to complete what had started on the sand.

They would have this affair and the earl would divorce her.

She would be free.

She opened her door.

New images entered her head. They killed her purring anticipation. She froze with her hand on the door latch.

She pictured Julian being discussed in the House of Lords when the bill of divorce was proposed. The accusations in Glasbury's petition would be ruthless and cruel, treating her lover like a scoundrel.

Julian's motives would be impugned. His lack of honor made explicit. The newspapers would print every word, too, and everyone would read it. Everyone. The scandal would be public and the scorn unrelenting.

Many of his clients would abandon him. Other solicitors would refuse to deal with him. Even her brothers' use of his services would be compromised. If he were named by an earl for criminal correspondence with a countess, it could ruin him.

That was a lot to ask of him, no matter what pleasure he received in the bargain.

He was just being noble and kind. That was really what those kisses had been about. He was offering the damsel in distress an easy rescue, even though the dragon would burn him horribly while he saved her.

He was just being a good friend.

She released the door. It softly closed.

This was her problem, not his. Her youthful mistake, and her wasted life. It would be inexcusable to drag him down with her.

She returned to her bed with a sadness in her heart that she did not understand or expect. She tried to contemplate her other, less selfish choices.

"I did not know that you could cook."

Julian turned at the sound of Pen's voice. He had not heard her come down. His eyes had been watching the fish sizzle in the pan, while his head had been imagining how Glasbury would word his divorce petition.

Should it actually come to a divorce. He did not think it would. If Pen had an affair with Julian Hampton, of all men, Glasbury would want to do more than merely ruin his wife's lover.

She looked over his shoulder. Her close presence had his blood burning again. "Did you catch that this morning? You must have risen early."

Very early. He had not slept much at all.

Nor had she.

He had heard her steps on the boards above him in the middle of the night. He had heard her pace toward her bedroom door.

Toward him.

He had silently urged her on, his teeth on edge from the intensity of his desire, his brain exhausted from the battle he waged against the urge to walk up those stairs.

Each of her footfalls above him had sent edgy shards

through his skull and blood. Her long pause had maddened him. He had cursed violently when she retreated.

He slid the fish onto two plates and carried them to the dining room. Pen brought along the tray with tea and bread.

She looked very lovely in the soft light coming through the northern window. Her dress this morning was more fashionable than yesterday's. Green, with ivory lace at the neck and black braiding on the bodice and skirt, it encased her snugly to her narrow waist, then flared into a wide skirt over the feminine hips he had watched rise to his caresses yesterday. Full sleeves tapered to long cuffs tightly closed by long rows of buttons.

She had managed to get into stays and multiple petticoats today. She had felt the need to wear some armor.

When those steps above had stopped at the door, he had guessed that she would.

"I have decided what to do, Julian."

"Have you decided what to do, or what not to do?"

"I do not even know what that question means."

Yes, you do, damn it. "Please, tell me your plan."

She put all her attention on pouring them both tea. "It is not really a plan. I have only decided what my next step should be."

Not making love with Julian Hampton; that much he already knew.

He ate his breakfast, letting her decide when to favor him with an explanation. He greeted this turn of events with silence, because the reaction seething in him had no gentle words.

"I do not like that Glasbury is controlling this," she

said. "He gets a whim and I am left to choose misery or scandal. That is not fair. Not to me and not to . . . whomever I would use to create that scandal."

"The world is not fair. The law on marriage certainly isn't. Resenting that does not solve your dilemma."

"No, but last night it made me angry enough to see another option. He thinks time has made him safe. I do not think it has. He assumes it would be my word against his should the truth come out. It need not be." She looked at him. "Cleo could support my accusations."

He sat back in his chair, surprised. "You would not use me, but you would use that child?"

"She is not a child any longer."

"She was half mad by the time we got her out."

"It has been years. Time heals much. Perhaps it has healed her."

"I am astonished you even consider—"

"She may *want* to do it. She may yearn to denounce him. Have you considered that? I think she remembers those years with a different view now. If I were she, I would hate him, not fear him. I would want some justice."

"Are you going to offer her justice, Pen? Will you sue to divorce him, and bring it all out? Or just use the threat of her testimony to make Glasbury continue the arrangement with you as it has been all these years?"

Her expression said it all. She *had* been thinking that strengthening the threat would make Glasbury retreat.

She had concluded that maintaining the arrangement would be the easiest solution.

Anger flashed in her eyes. "Do you think I like this limbo in which I live? That I welcome it?"

"I am sure you do not. However, I also think if Glasbury

had not made this move, you would have accepted it forever."

"Because I am such a coward?"

"No, because it means that no one gets hurt except you. But I think he will do whatever he can to make sure that he either has you back, or is free to have another wife. So think hard before you take your next step, and be sure you are prepared to stay the course."

She rose to her feet. "My next step does not require me to stay the course, because I will not be choosing it yet. I only want to know if that path is open. I want to know how she fares, and if she could do this, and if she wants to."

She left the room to make sure he could not argue with her anymore.

He let her go because a storm had blown into his head.

Julian paced out into the garden, his blood hot with rage.

She was going to do it again. Retreat to half-measures. It had worked before, after all. She assumed it would again.

He went to the stable and threw himself into work to release the explosive resentment in him. He rarely got this angry. He could count the times he had on one hand. Most of those times directly related to Penelope.

There had been the day he learned she was to marry.

And the day he confronted Witherby.

The worst time, however, had been when she visited him in chambers and confided the truth of her marriage.

He had been very young at the time, just twenty-one

and in the process of taking over for a senior solicitor who had managed the Duclairc family's affairs for decades. Although just three years into his clerkship, with two more to go, he already directed most of the legal work in that office and everyone knew it. His future seemed paved with happy prosperity.

Then, on a late winter day, sweet, good Penelope had entered his chambers, sat down, addressed him as Mr. Hampton, and told her story.

She was embarrassed and frightened and had not looked at him. He was too stunned to do more than listen. He had fought hard to keep his face impassive, but with each sentence he wanted more and more to find Glasbury and thrash him bloody.

Eventually her composure broke. So did his heart. He remembered touching her arm in impotent reassurance, battling the impulse to take her in his arms and swear an oath to provide salvation.

While she cried out her heart, images finally entered his mind, showing what she described and all the details she avoided telling. A terrible fury raged in him. He almost strode from the chamber to find a gun to go kill the bastard.

Instead he had hidden his outrage and enumerated her choices like the damned, logical, dispassionate servant he was supposed to be. He made sure that she understood that doing nothing meant living in hell, however. A hell that would only get worse.

"Now that you know this is not normal, any cooperation will count against you later, should you try to divorce," he explained.

Her eyes widened. "I am sure no court would think any woman would cooperate, Mr. Hampton."

"There are women who enjoy such things, madame."

"There are? You do not think that Anthony would claim that I . . . that I . . ."

"He undoubtedly would."

She almost cried again. Instead a new resolve entered her eyes. "Then I must get away, mustn't I?"

"I think that is clear. Let us consider your choices in that regard."

There were damned few. She could try to divorce him, claiming adultery and cruelty. A divorce through Parliament would leave her free to remarry, but women almost never succeeded in obtaining them. Worse, any parliamentary action would be preceded by two trials: first a church divorce, and then a civil proceeding against Glasbury.

Divorce "a mensa et a thoro" *through the church alone would not permit remarriage for either of them, but she stood a better chance there. The judges were growing more lenient in matters of cruelty. A woman no longer had to prove her husband had done life-threatening violence. But such a divorce would leave an earl without a son, and that detail might badly affect her chances, even though it should not.*

"Either way would be very public," she said. "I have read how the testimony is printed in the papers. All of it, no matter how sordid. Even the Times *loves the spectacle and profits handsomely from it."*

"I think that your circumstances warrant accepting the embarrassment, Countess."

"My family will be caught up in it. No matter what my justification, they will be hurt."

"Your brothers will bear it for you."

"But Charlotte . . . she is still a child. It will badly affect her chances of a good marriage when she comes out. The family finances are not good, and if she is tainted by such a scandal . . ."

He could not lie to her, much as he wanted to. He could not promise that her younger sister would not be hurt.

But his heart yelled in rebellion at the way her objections became steps away from the protection only divorce could bestow.

"To be safe, you must divorce him. If you only leave him, you are at his mercy." He said it more severely than he intended. "At any point he can sue to have his conjugal rights restored. He does not even have to sue. He can force you to return to both his home and his bed and no one will stop him."

"There must be a way to ensure he never does that. There is, isn't there?"

There was.

He had bargained hard when he went to Glasbury. He had pushed the man as far as he dared, then pushed farther. When the meeting was over he had handed Pen the half-victory she had chosen. Not freedom, but sanctuary.

A sanctuary now threatened.

He left the stable, cleaned off his boots, and washed his hands. He strode through the house. Out on the terrace he looked at the beach. A blue dot stood on a strip of sand.

His anger was not entirely altruistic. It was partly, perhaps largely, the frustration of a man who wanted a woman so much he would have her any way he could.

She had lived for a long time in the keep they had built years ago. It had served her well. He could not blame her if she wanted to try and repair its walls, rather than ride out to meet the enemy.

Compared to the safety she had found in that fortress,

the chance to have an affair of convenience with her friend and solicitor would not carry much appeal at all.

He went down to the beach and joined her.

"Cleo is still in Yorkshire with Mrs. Kenworthy," he said. "I will take you to her."

chapter 10

Having decided to make the journey, they prepared for it at once.

Julian rode his horse to the nearest town, Billericay, to hire a gig so he could collect Pen and her trunks. The plan was to secure her a room for the night in a safe place in the town, while he returned to London. There he would find a woman to travel as Pen's companion, to preserve respectability.

They decided to stay in small inns until they reached Yorkshire, and to travel under false names. She would be Mrs. Thompson and Julian would be her cousin, escorting her to a wedding in the Lake District.

After Julian left, Pen walked through the cottage, realizing that she would be a little sad to leave. She had rediscovered an old friendship here, one that had become obscured over the years. Mr. Hampton had become Julian again, and she would always remember this retreat as the place where that had happened.

She collected her treatise from the desk. When she got

to Billericay she would post it to Mrs. Levanham. Then her comments could be compared to the ones others had made, and a final draft prepared. The lessons she had learned from the disaster of her life might make a difference for other women someday.

Up in her chamber, she set about packing her trunks. She was finishing with the large one when she heard Julian return. The sound of wheels came down the lane, then the thump of the kitchen door from below.

She tucked the last few items in her trunk and went to him.

Halfway down the stairs, she halted abruptly. Alarm immobilized her.

She could already see the legs of the man who waited.

The garments were not Julian's.

The boots paced toward her, and the rest of the man came into view. Her stomach sickened.

Glasbury smiled up at her. "Welcome back to England, my dear."

Panic swelled in her head. She half-turned to run and hide, even though she knew there was no place to go.

"Come down, Penelope."

She battled to hide her horror. He enjoyed seeing that too much, and she would not give him the satisfaction of knowing what he did to her.

He stood right at the base of the stairs. He would not move as she descended. That forced her to brush against him as she took her last step and aimed around him.

He grabbed her arm. "No kiss? After all this time?"

"I would prefer not to."

"I would like a kiss, my dear."

She glanced out the window. He had not brought his

state coach. No insignia marked this one. Only the coachman tended it, and he was not in livery. "Ask one of the horses to kiss you. If it refuses, you can enforce your prerogatives with impunity."

"Not only on horses, Penelope. On all that I own." He pulled her closer and pressed a kiss on her lips.

Her stomach heaved. She held in the bile and jerked her arm free. He let her go, but his expression said it was his choice, not hers.

He paced around the kitchen, viewing it with distaste. "So Hampton tucked you away in this hovel. It was annoying to have to track you down. It would have been simpler if he had just told me where to find you."

"I insisted he not do that. How did you find this place?"

"I merely learned what property he owns, and had my people check it. When they reported last night that a woman was living here, I knew it was you." He peered into the next chamber. "Has he been staying here with you?"

"He has been in London. No doubt many people can attest to that."

He went to the garden door and gestured. When the coachman lumbered in, the earl pointed to the stairs. Glasbury strolled into the library while his man went up for her trunks.

Pen followed the earl, desperately glancing around for any evidence that Julian had recently been here, hoping she could hide it before the earl's gaze took it in. She had not been alone with Glasbury since she left him, and she was terrified. A visceral tremor shook all through her.

"This is such a crude place. No servants. No comforts.

You will be much relieved to be back on Grosvenor Square, I am sure."

"I am not going back to Grosvenor Square."

"Of course you are."

"Not willingly."

"Your will does not concern me. Only my rights do. If you show the grace and obedience to which you were bred, I will be kind. If you force me to drag you out by your hair, I will punish you."

Punish. He liked that word. He caressed the sound with his voice as he spoke it. He gazed at her with his slack mouth in a cruel smile. His eyes reflected memories of punishments of the past.

"Why now, Anthony? After all these years, why are you so determined to have me return now?"

"You broke our agreement."

"I did not."

"The world thinks that you did. So do I. Also, I received a letter last spring. An anonymous one. It included a copy of an odd treatise, written by a deranged woman raving against marriage." He looked at her as if she were a stupid child. "Did you really think that I would stand by and allow you, *my wife,* to publicly condemn my right to control my family and household?"

"There is not one word in that document about you."

"Every damn word is about me."

"Force me back and I will still publish it."

"I assure you that you never will."

It sounded like a threat. A chill slid up her spine.

He had gotten harder over the years. Crueler. The attempts at hiding his inclinations seemed to have been abandoned. It had been a mistake to ignore him all this time. In pretending he did not exist, she had lost sight of what he was becoming.

"I refuse to believe that you will risk the scandal I can create simply because you do not want that pamphlet published."

He smiled again. She had never liked his smiles. Even when young and excited over the proposal from an earl, she had not cared for that earl's smiles.

"I do not seek your return only for that reason. It is one of many. Most significantly, my nephew is now on his third wife, and none of these women has borne him a child, nor have any of the plantation slaves. The problem, I think it is safe to say, is not with all those women but with him."

"It must infuriate you to know that the new law means that those slaves will now be freed, and no longer available to test the breeding abilities of the men in your family. You so enjoyed your visits to Jamaica. You managed such a journey last year, didn't you? Perhaps that will sustain you for a while."

"There will be compensations for the situation on the estates. They will not resolve the inadequacies of my nephew, however. When you left, I convinced myself that through him the succession would continue in an acceptable manner. Now it is once more left to me. And to you."

His expression softened. For a moment he appeared beseeching, even sad. "Come back and give me my heir, Penelope. Give me the son that your vows promised."

"I am astonished that you throw vows at me, as if your position is one of moral superiority. I left because you lacked basic human decency. If you want me back, you will indeed have to drag me by the hair. But be prepared that I will let the world know what you are."

He chuckled and shook his head. He sighed. "You are such a stupid cow. As I explained to your blackmail-monger, few will believe you, even if you get a chance to speak of it. No one will care now anyway. All of that is long in the past."

"There are others who know. It will not be my voice alone."

"None of my people will speak against me. My control of them is complete, no matter what new laws are passed."

He walked toward her. She startled, and backed up. He kept coming until she was trapped against the window.

"Your trunks are in the carriage. Come, my dear, it is time to go home."

"No."

He reached for her. She tried to dart away, but he caught her forearm. His grip closed tightly.

"I had hoped we could do this with some dignity, but I see not. It would have been better to deal with this in our home, but this cottage will do. It is private enough."

His fingers clutched so hard that her eyes watered. He appeared indifferent to her pain. Almost bored. She had long ago learned to recognize the signs that said otherwise, however, and she saw them now.

The vague flush on his neck. The heavy lids of his eyes. He enjoyed hurting people.

She gritted her teeth and refused to cry out. His grip got worse and worse until her whole arm was on fire.

"The years have made you rebellious. Too much freedom does that with dull-witted people of inferior nature.

It is easily remedied, however. Your will is a flimsy thing. We both already know how quickly it can be bent and broken."

"For a dull-witted woman who was bent and broken, I still bested *you.*" She spit the words right into his face.

He flushed. "I think that I am glad you have so stupidly resisted. The sooner you learn your place again, the better."

His hold on her arm became a vise. Arrows shot through her veins from the pressure he exerted. Black spots swam in her sight.

"You will kneel in submission now, my dear. You remember how to do that, don't you?"

Tears streamed down her face, but she made no sound. The pain had claimed her whole arm and shoulder. It seemed to be invading her chest, blocking her breath.

Glasbury did not repeat his command. He just kept gripping her arm, increasing the pain, waiting for her to succumb to his demand that she humble herself.

It would be a mistake to submit. She understood what he really wanted. Not mere obedience. He wanted the control that fear breeds. His pleasure in others' debasement was complex and dark.

Her body wanted relief so badly that it begged her to give in. Her soul, however, knew that yielding even once would start her down a path toward helplessness again.

Julian almost did not see the marks on the road. He had driven several hundred yards down the lane to the cottage before the meaning of the long lines penetrated his awareness.

Suddenly they loomed. All thought left his mind. An alertness to danger pounded in him.

He stopped the horse and gazed down at the ruts that periodically showed on muddy patches of the lane.

They were fresh since he had passed this way several hours ago. When he had ridden his horse to Billericay, he had looked yet again for signs that might indicate the man Pen had seen here had arrived by carriage or horse. The lack of such evidence was the only reason he had left her alone.

He knew at once that had been a mistake. Someone had come this way since he had departed.

Cursing himself, he jumped from the gig and tied the horse to a low bush. Beyond the bend in the lane ahead, he could see the roof of the cottage.

Praying he was not too late, hoping Glasbury had not discovered this property, he left the lane and circled to the right. He aimed for the cottage through the scrubby growth and spindly trees that eked out survival in the salty air.

A movement caught his eye as he passed behind the bend in the lane. A man was sitting right inside the road's curve, leaning against a thin tree trunk. His back was to Julian, and he appeared intent on watching the lane.

Julian glanced toward the cottage. He could make out the dark top of a carriage now. Whoever had come was not gone yet. If they had left a guard on the road, Pen was definitely in danger.

Fear and anger owned him for a moment. Fear for Penelope and anger at himself. Then his head cleared, leaving nothing but icy determination. He scanned the ground at his feet, and lifted a good-sized rock.

He walked toward the sitting man.

The horse with the gig whinnied down the lane. His quarry stiffened. The man's hat angled up, as if he sniffed the air like a dog. He rose to his knees, and a pistol appeared in his right hand.

He did not hear Julian until it was too late. He twisted in surprise, and raised the pistol right before the rock landed on his head. He had no time to cry out before he fell facedown in the weeds.

Julian took the pistol. He found another gun tucked in the waist of the man's trousers.

Carrying one in each hand, he returned to the brush and strode toward the cottage.

He noticed indications that another had recently walked through this brush. Several crusted boot prints showed, made when the rain had wet the ground. Weeds had been trampled and branches broken.

Self-recrimination raged in his head. Pen had been right about that man yesterday. There had been no evidence because the intruder had done what he was doing—left the horse or carriage at the end of the lane and approached on foot through the grounds.

No sounds came from the cottage. No screams or yells. The carriage appeared deserted, but he could see Pen's trunks tied to its back.

He crossed the yard to the carriage and looked in. The coachman lounged on the seat, tipping back a little bottle. He was a portly, flush-faced man with sparse pale hair sticking out below his high hat.

He noticed Julian in mid-gulp. At first he merely frowned with curiosity. Then he saw the pistol barrel resting on the window frame, pointed right at his stomach.

His eyes widened in shock. Liquid splashed down his chin as he choked.

"What is your name?" Julian asked.

"Harry... Harry Dardly." It came out a croak. He stared at the pistol.

"Aside from your passenger, are you alone?"

"There was another man, but he stayed back down the lane."

"Who hired this carriage?"

Harry shrugged. "Didn't give a name. He is a man of quality, though. A gentleman. The pay was good."

It sounded as if Glasbury had come himself. Perhaps he had hired this coach anonymously, and not used his own servants and equipage, so there would be no witnesses.

The silence in the cottage ceased to be reassuring.

Julian opened the carriage door. "Come with me."

"Now, sir, there is no need for that. I'll just stay here and mind the horses. You have my word—"

"Out."

Heaving his bulk unsteadily, Harry climbed out. He put some distance between himself and the pistol, and went white when he saw the other one in Julian's left hand.

Julian gestured toward the cottage. Looking like a man headed for the gallows, Harry led the way.

"Harry, your passenger is the Earl of Glasbury."

"Glasbury! Oh, hell. See here, now, if there's to be trouble with an earl, I don't think I want—"

"There is a woman in there as well. If Glasbury has harmed her in any way, I need you as a witness."

"Witness!" Harry dug in his heels. "I won't do it. Nothing but trouble for me to speak against one of them. My wife will kill me if I risk such a thing."

Julian tapped Harry's shoulder with the gun. "I require that you come with me. Courage, man."

Looking more miserable with each step, Harry entered the kitchen.

Not a sound greeted them. When Julian saw that the kitchen and back rooms were vacant, he aimed Harry for the library.

The coachman's bulk entered first and halted right inside the doorway. "Oh, my word," he muttered.

"What are you doing here? I told you to wait unless I called you." The snarling voice was Glasbury's.

Julian pushed Harry forward a few steps and moved into the room.

An explosive fury burst in his head when he saw what was occurring in the library.

The bastard had Pen's arm in a grip so tight that his knuckles had turned white. With his arm extended, Glasbury was trying to force her down to the floor. Pen's body bowed unnaturally, as if she resisted the collapse that would ease her suffering.

And she most certainly was suffering. Her face had drained of all color and her eyes were glazed. She appeared ready to swoon. A grave determination showed in her expression, however. No sounds came from her. No cries or pleas.

She saw Julian first. The earl was too interested in watching his victim to notice that Harry had not entered alone.

Julian aimed his pistol right at Glasbury's heart and

cocked it. He barely found the control not to pull the trigger.

"Release her." His voice sounded unnaturally calm to his own ears. His brain had yelled the command. His soul begged Glasbury to refuse.

Glasbury's gaze snapped over. For a moment he appeared very frightened. Then a sneer formed. "You would not dare."

"I will not only dare, I will succeed. *Release her*."

Glasbury hesitated. Julian's finger caressed the trigger.

With an expression of annoyance and reluctance, Glasbury released his grip. Pen staggered away.

Glasbury glared at the coachman. "This is my wife, and this man is interfering. Remove him."

"Remove him? *Me?*"

"I paid you well. Now earn it."

"He has *two guns,* in case your lordship hasn't noticed."

"He will not use them."

"Damned if I am going to find out about that." Harry crossed his arms over his ample chest to make it clear to everyone he intended no moves.

Julian was watching Penelope. A bit of color had returned, and she appeared more steady. "Countess, there is a carriage outside, with your trunks tied down. Go and wait for me there."

Glasbury's eyes blazed. "If you take her from me, you are interfering with my rights."

"You forsook your rights when you abused them," Pen said quietly.

As she walked past Julian, he handed her one of the pistols. "Take this, in case he brought another man whom I missed."

She paused and gazed down at the weapon in her hand. She glanced back at her husband. An unholy expression entered her eyes that revealed the temptation she felt.

"Wait outside, madame," Julian said firmly.

She collected herself. She pushed past Harry with her left arm hanging limply at her side.

Harry assumed a dolorous expression. "Am I correct, sir, that you intend to make a bad day worse for me by stealing my carriage and the horses?"

"If you are agreeable to my plan, you will have both by evening and also payment for their use."

"Well, now, that paints a different picture."

"This is intolerable," Glasbury said. "I hired that carriage for the day and—"

"I will leave the carriage at the end of the lane. The horses must come with me a bit farther. Say, halfway to Billericay. For the use of your property, I will leave five guineas in the carriage."

"This is robbery," Glasbury drew himself to his strictest posture. "If you take that carriage, I will see that you are hunted down as a thief and—"

"Now, my lord, seems to me it is my place to decide when I've been robbed. Never seen a thief who left me five guineas."

"We will be stranded here, you idiot!"

"Only for a day. Harry should be able to walk to the horses and be back before night." Julian backed out of the room. "Now, gentlemen, do not let me see either of you leave this cottage as I go down the lane. The lady will be keeping watch, and I suspect she is well disposed to use the pistol I gave her. If not, I will not hesitate to use mine."

"Stop him, you worthless fool," Glasbury yelled.

"You stop him. Or are earls only brave when it comes to women?" Harry sneered with disgust. "A fine thing to see. You best be glad my wife wasn't here, I can tell you that—"

Julian left Glasbury to Harry's censure. Pen had managed to get herself up on the driver's box by the time he reached the carriage.

"Are we stealing it?" The notion did not appear to concern her too much.

He climbed up and took the ribbons. "We are borrowing it, with the owner's agreement."

After he turned the carriage and aimed down the lane, he glanced over at her. Her left arm rested inert on her lap. Her expression had become a stoical mask. Her lids hid most of her eyes.

"I am sorry, Pen. I blame myself."

"There is only one man to blame, and it is not you. I thank you for coming when you did. I do not know what might have happened if you had not arrived."

Nothing good. If the earl only wanted to collect his wife, he could have ridden in style with footmen in attendance.

He had not been able to resist the chance to have Pen alone and isolated, however. Glasbury had intended to hurt her in some way from the start.

What that could have meant, how far it could have gone, rolled through Julian's head. The image of her fighting the pain hung over his thoughts like a veil. Fire and ice fought a battle in his body. The urge to turn the carriage and go back and kill the scoundrel kept spiking.

She touched his arm. "I will survive, Julian. But drive

quickly once we reach the road. I would like to put distance between myself and what just happened."

There was no question that they would move quickly now. He not only needed to put distance between Pen and what had happened. He needed to get her far away from the Earl of Glasbury.

chapter II

They moved to the gig when they reached it. Julian unhitched the carriage horses and tied them to the gig, and they left the larger carriage on the lane.

Pen tested her arm. It was no longer numb. The place that Glasbury had gripped throbbed badly, however, and a deep ache possessed the whole limb. She suspected that a huge bruise was hidden by her sleeve.

Julian appeared to have calmed somewhat. She had never seen him as angry as when he entered the library. He had been so dangerous and dark that she had expected him to shoot Glasbury. In her pain and despair, she had actually hoped he would.

When he had placed that gun in her hand, she had been tempted to do so herself.

"Do you still want to see Cleo?" Julian asked.

"Yes."

Oh, yes. Most definitely.

She had bested Glasbury before, and she would again. The world might not believe her, but it would listen to

Cleo's tale. Faced with that possibility, the earl would retreat and never touch her again.

"You cannot stay at Billericay. We will have to do this differently now. I must put you someplace tonight where I am absolutely sure that you will have protection. Until we are well away from Glasbury, you must never be alone again."

"I do not think there is such a place. We are running out of sanctuaries."

"There is one more."

That evening, as the light waned, the gig rolled up a tree-lined lane in Hampstead. They had released the carriage horses halfway to Billericay.

It had been a tiring journey in the gig. The horse had needed rest quite often, and the road had bumped the small carriage along. Only the knowledge that Glasbury was stranded on the coast had kept Pen from getting fearful and impatient with their progress.

They approached an old cross-timbered house nestled picturesquely in a clearing. "Do you think he will agree to this?"

"He will be flattered to be asked. He will also not hesitate to stand against any man who tries to intrude."

"He is a little old for that."

Julian laughed quietly. "His sword arm is still unsurpassed, Pen. He has also relented and learned to use a pistol."

The man they discussed stepped out the front door to observe their approach. Gray-haired and fine-boned, his average stature gave no hint of his wiry strength. Pen had seen him spar with sabre and foil, however, and knew the deadly concentration and precision that he brought to that noble form of combat.

The Chevalier Corbet walked over to the gig. He greeted Pen with a bow. "Countess, I am honored. Julian, have you come to display your skill to the lady? The hour is late, but—"

"This is not a social call, Louis. I have come to leave the countess in your protection until morning. I do not expect any trouble, but there is a chance your skills will be needed."

The chevalier's eyes brightened. He flashed a subtle, smooth smile as he handed Pen down from the gig. "For the lady's sake, I hope not. For my own, I would not mind. It has been too long since I did more than instruct others."

"I trust that no students will be coming for lessons tomorrow morning," Pen said.

"I expect no one. If any should arrive unexpectedly, I will turn them away. Both your person and your reputation are completely safe."

Julian carried her trunks into the house and up to the chamber indicated by Corbet. Pen accepted the offer of some wine, in a room behind the big hall where the chevalier held those lessons for which he was famed.

Louis made her welcome and at ease. She had known him for years. Laclere and Dante had long been among the chevalier's students. Along with Julian and St. John and some others, they still met here to practice with the sword.

When Julian joined them, the chevalier discreetly departed. Julian lifted a lamp and brought it to the table next to her chair.

"He does not appear very curious about this intrusion," she said.

"He will demand no explanation, nor give advice unless asked. He will guard you with his life, however. Do not doubt that."

He lifted her left hand. She thought it was a gesture of reassurance. Instead he gently turned her arm and began unbuttoning her sleeve.

"I am not sure that I want to see this," she said.

"I do." His fingers carefully unfastened the tiny buttons. "You told me Glasbury was not violent in this way."

She winced when he reached the buttons over her bruise. Glasbury's grip had embedded those small bumps into her skin. "He was not, in the past. This was my fault. I refused to pretend. I goaded him, to be honest."

"Never say that again. The blame rests only one place, and it is not with you."

He parted the gaping sleeve to reveal the damage. Her skin showed a bruise darkening in a thick band around her forearm. The images of the earl's fingers were clearly visible.

"The bastard." Julian gazed down at the abuse cradled in his hand. "It must pain you badly."

"Not so badly." That was a lie, although the sensation of his touch distracted her from the ache. A different, more pleasant warmth enlivened the skin resting against his firm palm.

"I will get something to ease the swelling."

"No, Julian, you will start off for London. I can tend to myself, and if I need any help the chevalier will aid me. I daresay he knows more about wounds and injuries than we do."

He appeared reluctant. "I will return in the morning, with what we need for this journey," he said. "Expect me a few hours after dawn at the latest."

"I will be ready."

He gently kissed the ugly bruise.

"Whatever else happens, Pen, I swear to you that he will never hurt you again. *Never.*"

"He caught me unawares. Snuck up from the rear."

"If a solicitor can best you, Jones, what good are you at all?"

Glasbury paced around the ridiculously small chamber he had been given at the inn in Billericay. To be left at that cottage while Dardly retrieved the horses had been intolerable. Then the coachman had insisted they wait until morning to return to London. Now he was stuck in this sty of an inn without his valet or clean garments or—

Jones's eyes became two slits in his moon face. "I'll find her once we return to London. Don't you doubt that. I've a debt to pay Hampton, too." He rubbed the blood-crusted hair on his crown.

"You idiot, do you think he would take her to London now? Hampton is not the most brilliant mind in creation but he is not a total fool."

"If not London, then where?"

"Hell if I know. They also have a day's start because of your negligence, so you can hardly follow, can you?"

Glasbury barely contained his frustration. To have been so close to finally ending this illegal and humiliating estrangement, only to have the incompetence of Jones and that coachman ruin it—

He poured more of the foul wine the inn had sent with his meal. He drank a deep swallow.

The meeting with Penelope had been playing in his head all day, infuriating him. For years he had been helpless against her threats, but no more. She would comprehend that soon enough.

There are others who know. Yes, but none who would speak. The best thing about power and wealth was that one could buy silence with fear and money. Or buy men like Jones if necessary.

"Well, if he is not bringing her to London, we will have to wait until she shows herself," Jones said. "No way I can run her to ground with all the roads and canals and villages in England, now can I?"

Glasbury took another swallow of wine. He pictured Penelope's face in the cottage. Belligerent. Challenging. She had changed over the years. But then, so had he. Weakness no longer appealed to him. There was no victory if your opponent was weak.

Her resistance had been very . . . exciting.

There are others who know. It will not be my voice alone.

He heard her words again. He saw her confident expression as she threatened him.

He set down his glass as her meaning suddenly became clear. *Yes. Of course.* She had not meant his Jamaican slaves or his English servants. Not those still with him, at least.

He chuckled. He no longer cared about the discomforts of a night at the inn.

"I know where they have gone. I know where you will find her. You may even catch her on the road. I will give you instructions tomorrow. You will need another man to go with you. This must be done without incident, without notoriety."

Jones left, and Glasbury sat at the table. The wine was tasting better, and he poured some more.

"When you said a woman would accompany us, I thought you meant one of some maturity," Pen said.

She stood beside Julian in front of the chevalier's house while her trunks were hauled up to the top of the hired coach Julian had brought.

Directing the chevalier and the coachman was a young woman named Catherine Langton. Sandy-haired and fair-skinned, Catherine was sturdy in build and demeanor, and a head taller than Penelope. Her posture and crisp orders bespoke a woman who did not suffer fools gladly.

The chevalier climbed off the carriage and dusted his hands with finality. Catherine's steely blue eyes examined the ties on the chests. Little hollows formed beneath her high cheekbones, as she sucked in her cheeks in disapproval. The chevalier responded with a low-lidded expression that indicated further criticism would carry risks.

"She *is* a mature woman," Julian said.

"You know what I meant. Older. At least as old as I am. She cannot be more than twenty-five."

Catherine marched to the door of the carriage, climbed in, arranged the window curtains to her liking, and waited.

"Where did you find her?"

"I called on your friend Mrs. Levanham last night and asked for a recommendation. Her fame as a woman who abandoned her husband brings other women in similar straits to her attention."

"Like me."

"And like Catherine. I thought that another embattled wife would be glad for the position we had. Since Catherine's husband is a sea captain due back in England any day, the opportunity to take a journey away from London appealed to her."

"She is quite overbearing."

"No doubt that is due to her circumstances. She makes her own way now."

He sounded as if he admired her. For some reason, that made Pen like Catherine even less.

"Does she know who I am?"

"We will use our false names at inns, but could not maintain the ruse all the time with her. She should do splendidly, Pen. She is willing to act as lady's maid, but is educated and well spoken. Mrs. Levanham informed me that she also has a most unusual talent."

"What is that?"

"An expertise with firearms. Catherine is a crack shot."

He guided Pen to the carriage and handed her over to the formidable young woman waiting within.

Catherine immediately shook out a carriage blanket and tucked it around Pen's feet. "Mr. Hampton will be riding above?"

"It appears so."

"Why would that be? There is room enough in here."

"I do not know."

"Don't you now? Is he a stranger to you?"

"I have known Mr. Hampton since I was a girl. He is an old friend. I cannot read his mind, however."

"Not a matter of reading a man's mind to know his habits and preferences." Catherine spoke in the kind of brusque, no-nonsense tone that Pen had always disliked.

"He does enjoy being out-of-doors. Perhaps he wants to see the countryside, and feel the wind. That would be like him."

With farewells to the chevalier, the carriage rolled down the lane and headed northwest. The overcast day held a bitter damp, and Pen was grateful for the blanket wrapping her feet.

She looked down and saw Catherine's serviceable old shoes poking from beneath her skirt and petticoats. She bent and rearranged the blanket so that it covered Catherine's feet and legs, too.

Catherine's expression fell as if the gesture surprised her. Suddenly she appeared very young and not at all severe. With the smattering of freckles dusting her nose and cheeks, she actually looked somewhat girlish.

She leveled her blue eyes on Pen. They had not turned to ice yet, but in a few more years they might.

"I know about you," she said. "Bold of you to leave an earl. Hard to give up that life."

"No harder or bolder than your own decision. Less so, since I had family and resources that you did not."

"Did he punch you?"

The blunt question startled Pen. No one had ever asked before. Not her brothers or friends. Not even Julian when she went to him that day.

She shook her head. The earl had not used his fists on her. Prior to yesterday, he had never hurt her in that way. The blows had been of a different, more wicked sort.

"My Jacob did. He would get drunk and hit me. First

I took it because he was my husband. Then I took it because I had a daughter. Then one day I walked away, even though it meant losing my precious child, because staying was too dangerous."

"You feared for your life?"

"I feared for his. I woke one morning bruised and hurting, with hatred in my heart. I knew that if he thought to hurt me ever again I would kill him first. So I left."

She told her story so calmly that one would think she described an old, vague memory. Her eyes betrayed her true emotions, however. Sadness and anger burned lowly in them, like fires dying but not yet extinguished.

"Have you not seen your daughter since?"

"He sent her north to family of his near Carlisle. He thinks my love for her will make me return, or else he can force me to on his own. I am safe while he is at sea. When his ship comes to England I am not, so I disappear however I can."

"That must make it difficult to keep employment."

"I manage. I haven't had to sell myself at least. Although I could if I had to, I expect. After all, I sold myself to Jacob, didn't I? If I could do that with a man I had grown to fear and hate, I expect it would be possible with a stranger."

Pen knew that she should say something moral about virtue and sin, but she did not have the urge to do so. Who was she to judge this young woman and the choices that might be made? Especially since she herself had written a list of men with whom she might do "that" in order to find a way to be free.

The farms rolled past, gray and bleak like the sky. In a few days they would be in Grossington, and she would see

Cleo. She wondered how the years had passed for her, and what kind of woman that cowed, frightened girl had become.

Was she being cowardly in considering this choice instead of a bolder move? She would love to be truly free. She envied Catherine her greater freedom, even if they both remained bound to their husbands in the law. Catherine could escape Jacob's reach, could disappear within Britain. The Countess of Glasbury never could.

For her, running away and hiding meant leaving all she knew and loved.

And standing and fighting meant hurting family and friends.

"Mr. Hampton is very handsome," Catherine said.

"I think so."

"I guess all women would think so. Quiet, though. I think more men could stand to be quiet more often. Usually they talk a great deal but say little of significance."

"I think Mr. Hampton would agree with you."

Catherine smoothed the top edge of the blanket on her knees. She watched her long fingers play at the binding.

"Are you going on a holiday? Is that the reason for this journey?"

Just like Julian to explain nothing. "I have a visit to make, and Mr. Hampton is escorting me."

"Ah. I see. Odd to be taking different names, then, but it isn't for me to say." Her fingers stroked and smoothed some more. "Will you and I be sharing a chamber at the inns?"

"I expect so."

"Will Mr. Hampton be staying at the inns as well?"

"I think that will be necessary. You do not need to

worry. If Jacob is following you, you will not be without protection."

"I protect myself, my lady. However, having Mr. Hampton nearby may be useful. I sleep very soundly. After a journey it would take a cannon to wake me. Should there be any trouble, it is good to know that Mr. Hampton will be right next door. If anyone were to enter our chamber during the night, I would be completely unaware of it."

Pen realized what Catherine was insinuating. "I am very sure that there will be no entering or leaving during the night."

"Yes, madame. However, should there be, I will certainly sleep right through it. I thought you should know how deeply I sleep." She bent and fished beneath the seat. "Let me get you another blanket, madame. You are looking pale."

It became obvious to Julian that Catherine Langton had concluded several things about her new position.

First, she thought that her presence had been arranged to provide the pretense of respectability to what was in actuality a lovers' tryst.

Second, she had decided that she had no interest in interfering with that tryst.

She possessed an admirable talent for making herself scarce. She arrived late for meals and departed early, so that he and Pen could have time alone. She went down to the carriage before her mistress, and found excuses to leave Pen's chamber at regular intervals in the evening.

Had Julian in fact been conducting an affair with Catherine's lady, he would have been delighted.

Since he wished that he was even though he wasn't, he welcomed the privacy with Penelope anyway.

The third evening, they dined in Pen's room at an inn in York. As soon as she completed her meal, Catherine excused herself.

"I think I will get some air, if that is acceptable to you, madame."

"It is raining, Catherine."

"I do not mind a bit of rain. I have my cloak and will stay under the eaves. I feel the need to take a turn after riding in a carriage all day."

She left the chamber. Julian wondered if she would be carrying her pistol with her.

He looked through the flickering candles at Pen's perfect skin and soft red lips and sweet expression. The urge to reach over and caress her velvet cheek almost triumphed over his better sense.

He loved the gentle softness in her face and body, and the greater one in her heart. The latter had led her to befriend young women in need of a protective wing before, and he could see how she was warming to Catherine now. Pen might never use a gun, but she could be selfless in defending those she cared about.

"I was too quick to judge Catherine. You were correct, and she is a pleasant companion, Mr. Hampton. You chose well."

"I said that you were not to address me formally again. Considering what transpired at the cottage, it would be absurd to take that up again."

She blushed prettily. The candlelight heightened the rosy glow. It also reflected tiny sparks in her eyes that revealed the real reason she had tried to be formal. As her lids lowered, her glance darted around the chamber in awareness that this was her bedroom.

She nervously fingered the handle of the fork near her hand.

He knew he should leave, or say something to put her at ease.

Memories of her body, of her breasts firm and soft under his lips and her hips rising to his caress, had invaded his mind, however. The light from fire and candles, the bed hidden behind its drapes, the mutual memories of what had been—it all created a mood that he had no interest in dispelling.

"Approaching Mrs. Levanham for help was very clever, too. Did she know you were aiding me?"

"I did not say that the lady requiring a companion was the Countess of Glasbury, but I think she assumed as much. After all, I made her acquaintance when you sent her to me for advice on the law."

"If I had known you were visiting her, I would have given you my essay to deliver. I was going to post it from Billericay, and will do so tomorrow before we leave York."

"I would prefer you did not, Pen. It can wait until we are finished with this journey."

"I can see no reason to delay."

Julian looked at her left arm. She still favored it a little. "When you spoke with Glasbury yesterday, did he say anything about that pamphlet?"

"He mentioned it."

"I assume he is displeased."

"Very displeased. I told him I would publish it anyway. He said it was one reason he would make me return, along with the need for an heir, but I do not think this is about either of those things. Not really."

"What do you think it is about?"

Her expression became thoughtful. "I spoke of his estates in Jamaica, and how the new law had taken away his slaves. Something frightening entered his eyes when I said that. An angry, resentful spark."

"The law will have economic consequences. Even with the compensation granted by Parliament, it will cost him dearly."

"I do not think it was the financial effects he reacted to. He liked owning slaves, Julian. He loved owning the rights to human beings and having them subjugated to him. He tried to recreate that world here in England, and after I left he visited Jamaica from time to time so he could enjoy that power again for a while. Now, with the new law, that is over. Legally, he can never know it again."

Except with me. The chamber seemed to whisper the words. He practically heard her thinking the final sentence that she did not speak.

She was right. Glasbury could know something very close to those godlike rights with a wife or children.

All men could, but most did not exploit the power.

She rose and paced away to the window. She glanced through the curtains, as she so often did when Glasbury was discussed.

"Until yesterday, I had not really understood what drove him. I had not comprehended just how wicked he is. I should have, however. In two days we will be facing the evidence that should have enlightened me."

"I sense that you are unsettled about seeing Cleo, Pen."

She tilted her head this way and that, peering through

the darkening world, her breath making little fogs on the windowpane. "It is making me remember, that is all. Not that one ever really forgets."

Her voice was bland but her eyes looked haunted.

She was remembering right now.

He got up and went over to her. He did not want her remembering, ever.

He carefully placed his hands on her shoulders, forcing the gesture to be reassuring and not possessive. He wanted to embrace her, however. He wanted to hold her and banish her worries. He wanted to make love to her. He had been thinking about little else for three days.

"I will speak with Cleo alone, Pen. You do not have to see her at all."

She glanced back at him. He could see her wavering, tempted.

She shook her head. "I was responsible for her. I should have understood sooner. If I am going to stir up the past, I should not shirk from witnessing what it does and what it means to her. I will not know otherwise whether she has the courage to stand beside me if the need arises."

She appeared so troubled and sad. He instinctively reacted and caressed down her arms in an impulse to—what? Comfort? Seduce?

Her body flexed in awareness, then did not move. A lovely flush colored the elegant nape mere inches from his mouth. He waited for a sign, any sign at all, that said she would welcome more. He was indifferent to whether it should or should not be, and so hungry for her that the reasons did not matter.

She did not move. She did not shrug off his hold. Her beautiful neck mesmerized him. He was convincing himself that a seduction would not be dishonorable, when a small commotion interrupted him.

Outside the door a feminine voice called for hot water. Shoes stomped on wood amidst loud muttering about bitter cold, drenching rain, and muddy streets.

Catherine had returned and was ensuring they heard her arrival.

Pen jumped out of his hands, and hurried to the other side of the chamber.

chapter 12

"Will Mr. Hampton be wanting to depart at once?"

Typical of her somewhat nettlesome efficiency, Catherine was busy planning the morning down to the last minute while she and Pen ate breakfast at the table in the chamber they shared.

"I have not spoken to Mr. Hampton since he left us last evening, so I do not know what he intends."

After the awkwardness that had greeted Catherine's return last night, Pen felt some obligation to clarify that she and Julian *were not* having an affair, nor intending to start one.

"Mr. Hampton spoke of a short journey today. Are we near your destination?"

Pen had suffered a restless night and unsettled morning. Her conversation with Julian last evening had provoked reactions that she could not sort out. A wrenching sadness shadowed all the confusion, and not only because of Cleo.

His touch, his closeness, the overwhelming manner in

which her spirit had hoped he would embrace her—her need for comfort and distraction was luring her to abuse their friendship most ignobly.

Catherine's reference to the journey's conclusion made her agitation rumble. "We should arrive today. We will stay a day or two. After that, I do not know where I am going." *Perhaps to America. You can come, too. Even Julian will approve if you are there blazing a path for me through the wilderness.*

They prepared for their journey, only to discover that Catherine's cloak was still heavy with damp from last night's walk in the rain.

"Take my blue one and I will use the brown one," Penelope said. She bent to flip through the garments folded into her smaller trunk.

Catherine smoothed her palm over the superfine bright sapphire wool. "This is a very lovely cloak."

"My brother gave it to me." Not Mr. Hampton, and not the earl, Pen wanted to add. Never the earl. His allowance had not even paid for her house in London without additional help from Laclere. Help that could ill be afforded when she first walked out.

The cloak had been a gift, but there had been other garments less obviously given. After Laclere married and his fortunes improved, his wife Bianca made a habit of inviting Pen to join her on visits to modistes. The bills for Pen's own dresses went to Laclere along with Bianca's, with no accounting ever expected.

I have not been in want, but it has not been easy. I have had to humble myself. I have been reduced to taking charity, no matter what other pretty name it is given.

She was being stupid and she knew it. There was no

competition with Catherine on who had been more miserable. Catherine would win that hands down just because of her daughter. But she wanted to disabuse this self-possessed young woman of any notion that just because a woman was a countess she paid no price at all, and lived in luxury and committed adultery with impunity and attended the best parties in her jewels and silks.

Catherine's presence became intrusive and annoying. For one thing, Pen noticed that the blue cloak looked stunning on her. It made her appear fresh and lovely and brought out peaches in her cheeks.

Julian already thought Catherine was admirably independent. If he saw her now, he would also realize she was gorgeous.

"The other cloak is not here. Please go and ask the servants to bring my large trunk from the carriage."

As Catherine left, her blue eyes glanced to the wall adjoining Julian's chamber.

The glance did not seem conspiratorial on Pen's behalf this time. Pen pictured the man in that chamber the way Catherine saw him, handsome and dark and cool and masterful. If he kissed this young woman the way he had kissed the Countess of Glasbury, he could probably have whatever he wanted. Catherine would ask only for protection in return.

Pen fussed with the mess she had made in her small trunk, fretting all the while with a simmering unhappiness. She did not know its reason, but it was making her sour and nasty this morning.

"Will you be ready to depart within the hour?"

She looked toward the doorway, and the question. Julian stood there. Yes, handsome and dark and cool and—

"Did Catherine leave my door open?" she asked.

"It appears that she did."

"Well, please close it. And go away. I am not fit company for anyone today."

"Why?"

"I do not know why, Julian. I just wish my other trunk would arrive. I want to take a turn in the fresh air. Perhaps then I will feel better." She slammed the lid down on her trunk. "When will we see Cleo?"

He leaned a shoulder against the doorjamb, neither entering nor leaving. "We will arrive in Grossington this afternoon. I thought that we would call on Mrs. Kenworthy tomorrow, unless you would prefer to do it some other way."

"There is no other way. For once, where Cleo is concerned, I should not be a coward." She pushed to her feet. "I will go to my trunk, since the alternative is to wait a year for it to come to me."

For once, where Cleo is concerned, I should not be a coward.

She was remembering things she did not want to remember. She admitted that as she strolled through a kitchen garden tucked behind the inn. Every mile closer to Cleo brought forth more images that engendered more guilt and humiliation.

She had been so ignorant. So unbelievably naive. When she had seen that isolated country house in Wiltshire filled with the dark-skinned servants, she had never suspected that they still lived in England like the slaves they had been in Jamaica.

She had not guessed that Glasbury kept that private estate so that he could indulge himself with those servants in ways no English servant would allow.

His ability to do so had probably protected her for a while. It had been a year before he began treating her like a slave, too.

At first the earl's dictates had been mild, but his scathing anger made her fear displeasing him. He would order her to change her gown for dinner, then dislike her new choice and make her change again and again, each time heaping her with criticism about her inadequacies as a countess.

He found fault with everything, until she dreaded his presence and cringed at his approach. He isolated her from her friends. He said terrible things about her family and went into a rage if she had the temerity to object. When she did not become pregnant, he used that as a lash, too.

Her fear grew and her joy died. He liked what he was doing to her. He fed on the tremor in her voice, on her vain and anxious attempts to please him. For her efforts she received only more criticism, more demands, more rules.

Finally, when he had her cowed and childish and afraid to think, the punishments began.

She halted in her walk and stood there, immobile, as those memories finally broke through the barriers she had built around them.

The physical punishment had been the least of it. The rituals he demanded were what made it thoroughly degrading. He never just hit her. He let her wait, knowing what was coming, like a child preparing for a whipping.

Then he would arrive in her chamber and demand she strip naked and walk to him and lay herself across his lap so he could use his hand on her bottom.

It aroused him. It took her a long time to realize that. And the rituals got more creative, and more sexual. She winced at the memory of the first night he made her crawl to him and turn and raise her bottom to his strap until she was screaming. When he had her begging him to stop he had taken her like the submissive animal he had made her become.

She wiped the images from her mind. She forced them back into the shadows where she kept them. She had gotten off easy compared to little Cleo. Or at least she escaped before he dared go as far with her as he had with that girl.

A blue cloak appeared near the garden gate. Catherine spied her and gestured to indicate the carriage was ready to depart.

Pen marched to the inn's yard, consumed by an unholy anger toward herself. She should not have been so docile. She should have confided in someone, no matter how humiliating the admissions would have been.

She should have seen sooner that she was not the only female in that household who cowered and shrank when his attention lit on her.

The activity of departure distracted her. Focusing on the confusion of carriages in the yard, she was able to block other, darker thoughts from her mind.

They would come, however. She did not doubt that they would. She would not be able to face Cleo and not face the past, too.

• • •

The sun shone all the way to Grossington that afternoon, but it did not lighten Penelope's mood. She had returned from her walk as preoccupied with her thoughts as when she had left. Even above on the box with the driver, Julian could sense her disquiet.

That night he stood by the window of his chamber, looking out on the silence. On the other side of the wall he could hear subtle movements. Floorboards creaked in a regular rhythm as feet trod them, back and forth.

She was remembering things, she had said.

He held the vigil with her, even though she would never know. For two hours he listened to her pace.

He takes pleasure in giving punishment. Those were the words she had used that day while she looked resolutely at a corner in his chambers so that she would not see his reaction.

He guessed that she had spent weeks finding a way to say it without having to actually say much at all. It had been eloquent in its own way, however. She had not said *he beats me when he is drunk*. Her simple statement had alluded to much more.

It seemed the pacing would never stop. Finally he could no longer bear it. He stepped out of his chamber and lightly rapped on the door several feet from his own.

The door opened a crack. Pen stood there in her white nightdress and lace-trimmed cap, with a blue shawl wrapping her shoulders and breasts.

He looked in her eyes and knew that she would pace all night.

He pressed the door wider with his palm. In the

chamber's darkness, he could see Catherine sleeping on a small bed against the wall.

He took Pen's hand and pulled her out of the room and closed the door. Ignoring her resistance, he dragged her into his chamber.

chapter 13

She crossed her arms over the shawl and pressed her back against his door.

"Catherine says that if men accost her, they find her knee where they wear no armor."

"If I accost you, I deserve the same."

He walked away from her because he did want to touch her, very much. She looked lovely and womanly in her nightdress. He imagined plucking the bed cap off her head and her hair falling down.

"You have not been to sleep yet, Pen. The night is half gone."

"You have not been to sleep, either."

"I have been listening to you pace."

"It happens sometimes that I cannot sleep." She still hugged the door with her back, as if she feared him.

"There is a reason this time, however. I will go alone tomorrow."

"You cannot spare me this, Julian. You have no shield that will protect me from this dragon." She moved away from the door. Her expression turned sad as she walked aimlessly about the chamber. "I was the mistress of that house. I was responsible. But I was blind."

"He made sure you were too frightened to see."

"No, Julian, I covered my own eyes because what existed in front of them made no sense, and was so foreign to the world I knew." She shot him a challenging look. "He did not want me unseeing at all. So one night when he punished Cleo, he forced me to witness it. I was horrified. Shocked. Both trembling and numb at the same time. I did not comprehend all of it yet, but I could not lie to myself after that. So I came to you."

He had always guessed that one specific episode had driven her to the confidences in his chambers. There had been an initiation. A night when the earl had shown Pen what his pleasure really required. No doubt he had thought her fully broken by then.

He had been wrong. The soft, innocent bride had proven stronger than the earl expected.

"It was disgusting," she muttered, speaking more to herself than to him. "I thought I had descended into hell."

"You had."

"My heart broke for her. But one thought stayed in my head and would not go away. A selfish one. That could be me, I thought. Someday, it *will* be me."

She turned away. He knew she was crying. His heart clenched. He went to her and laid his hands on her shoulders. "You got her out, Pen."

"*You* got her out, Julian." She turned, but did not pull away from his touch. "You guessed all of it, didn't you? That imagination of yours could see it all, couldn't it?"

Her eyes sparkled with the tears brimming in them. "You always knew what he did with her. And with me."

"I do not dwell on what he did with you." He brushed a tear off her cheek with his thumb. "You were only a victim. A sweet, kind girl who had been grabbed by the devil. I have wanted to kill Glasbury because of it, but it never once changed my thoughts about you."

Her reaction almost broke his heart. She appeared grateful, skeptical, and terribly vulnerable. The old images of meeting Glasbury on a field of honor entered his head.

Thank God she had been strong. Thank God she had found the courage to leave. And thank God her experiences had not indeed ruined her, or left her a shell of a person as they had little Cleo.

His thumb still rested on her soft cheek. Her eyes still held confusion and sadness. The chamber pulsed with a raw intimacy provoked by her emotions.

"I should go," she said.

"Will you sleep now?"

"Most likely not."

"Then stay here. We will await the dawn together."

"I should not."

He could not bear the thought of her returning to her chamber and the memories. "If you are not alone, perhaps the dragon will stay in his lair." He took her hand and kissed it. "Rest here in my arms. You will be back in your chamber before Catherine wakes."

She did not agree, but she did not refuse, either. When he stepped backward toward the bed there was no real resistance in the body that he guided by the hand.

She looked at the bed for a long while.

"If I accost you, you can always follow Catherine's advice about knees and no armor," he said.

She giggled. The musical sound broke through the sadness and lifted the darkness.

She removed her shawl, folded it neatly, and placed it on a chair. The domesticity of the action entranced him.

"You will be sure to get me out before the servants are about?"

"I promise."

She lifted the bedclothes and climbed in. "We keep doing things we should not, but you are right; I do not want to be alone with my thoughts tonight."

There was an implicit trust in her movements as she settled into the bed. He was both flattered and amused. The images romping through his imagination were not at all trustworthy, but he expected he could survive the night. After a life of restraint a few more hours should be manageable.

She looked up from the pillow. "Do you intend to sit by the bed like a nurse?"

"No."

"Do you plan on lying here in coats and collar?"

"No." He slid off his frock coat and went to work on his neckwear.

He extinguished the lamp. The fire was down to embers, but it still gave some heat and hints of light.

"I think that you should remove your shirt."

"Do you now? It might be wise if one of us is not dressed for bed. There are limits to any man's chivalry."

"Yes. Of course. Forgive me. You are always more sensible than I am, Julian."

Sensible, was he?

He removed the damn shirt.

And turned to find her looking at him.

At least she did not appear to be thinking about Glasbury anymore.

He sat on the bed and pulled off his boots. Deciding not to be sensible in the least, he removed his trousers, threw them on the chair, and joined her under the blanket.

His body was already in a condition that would make the night a torture.

"I suppose this is very reckless and dangerous," she said.

"You are in no danger from me." That was not entirely true.

"That is not what I meant." She turned on her side and propped her head on her hand. "This helps, not being alone. I am glad you will be with me tomorrow as well. I do not think I could do it otherwise."

"You can do anything if you decide it is important. You have already proven that."

"I have not, in truth. If you think about it, I have never had to act alone. Someone has always been there to help me. But I do not want to think or talk about that anymore tonight."

"What would you prefer to speak of?"

She rose higher on her elbow. "How magical the firelight is. It makes a little glow along your edges, like one sees in paintings." She reached out and traced a line along his nose, over his lips, and down his chin.

Desire began cutting through him.

Her feathery touch traced over his shoulder and onto the muscles of his chest. The blanket moved down with her hand.

"What are you doing, Pen?"

"You looked at me. I want to look at you. You are much more athletic than I expected. No doubt all that rowing explains it." Her fingers ran over a rough edge on his left side. "What is this scar? It is very long."

"I got it some years ago in Hampstead."

"I did not realize that the swordplay of the Dueling Society was so dangerous."

She referred to the group of Laclere's friends who met at the chevalier's house to practice with swords and pistols. Julian had been a part of that set since he was at university, and still met with them on occasion to continue the old camaraderie.

"We all have a few nicks. Swords will do that."

"This is more than a little nick." Her hand traced down the scar to its end on his hip.

His body reacted, prominently. He moved her hand back up and suppressed the erotic images trying to conquer his mind.

"You are making this dangerous despite my best intentions. Even old friends are not made of stone. I am not completely sensible all the time."

"No, you are not. What an interesting discovery that has been." Her fingers and gaze moved over the top of his abdomen.

He finally clutched her hand, stopping her. "Are you trying to seduce me, Pen?"

"Not completely," she whispered. "I suppose I am putting the dragon back in his lair, Julian. And I am reminding myself that there are good memories and good friends and that I was not ruined for such things."

Good memories, but not with him. And another had

shown her she was not ruined, long before Julian Hampton ever kissed her.

He knew how to make all the dragons retreat. He weighed whether he dared do so, and if he had it in him to show the restraint she would expect.

He did not want incomplete sensual games. Their lovemaking on the beach had been precious, but he did not want to be one of the men who had stolen kisses and caresses over the years. Men who could be easily forgotten, and quickly relegated to a list of frivolous, playful flirtations with no consequences and no meaning.

If she had just lain there quietly, he might have followed his better sense. But she turned slightly and her warm breath flowed over his chest, and suddenly he wanted whatever he could have.

Sensual anticipation drenched the silence between them. Her hand still rested on his skin beneath his own. He lifted it and kissed her palm and pulse. "We will put the dragons to sleep for the night if you want."

She turned her head and looked up at him. "It is not fair to you, is it? As you said, even old friends are not made of stone."

"It will not be all that I want. I will not lie about that. But it will be enough."

He lifted her and moved her, so that she was the one in the dying fire's glow, lying on her back. He slid her bed cap off and her hair poured down. He tried to remember when he had last seen it falling free. Ages ago, when she was a girl, he was sure. Yet he often saw her this way in his mind.

He swept her tresses up so they fanned her head on the pillow. He pulled the ties of the little bows that held her nightdress together. She watched his fingers from beneath the thick lashes of her lowered lids.

"You take my breath away, Julian, and you have not even kissed me yet."

"Then you should be too breathless to object when I remove this."

"Completely?"

"Yes." This at least would be complete tonight.

He lifted her shoulders so he could slide the garment off and watch the fabric inch down her body. Her scent told him that the disrobing aroused her, but then her expression was already that of a woman halfway to ecstasy.

She had been right about the fire. It did make a glowing line along the edges of her body. He traced it as she had, down her face and neck, then along her chest and up the swell of her breast. Her rosy nipple tightened more as his fingertips neared, and her back subtly arched. Her breathlessness was audible now.

He gently circled her nipple with his fingers. "You are very beautiful, Pen. I cannot imagine passion more lovely than yours."

Her hand pressed his nape until his face was close to hers. "The dragon does not only sleep when we do this, Julian. He dies for a while. It is as if I am a girl again, at Laclere Park, and nothing ugly or sad has happened yet."

Her words touched him. "Then we will go back to Laclere Park, Pen. To when you were a girl and I was a youth." He kissed her cheek. "It is spring, and I have taken a turn near the lake and found you there alone, sitting amidst the flowers."

She giggled softly and closed her eyes. "Yes, spring. It is a warm day with a blue sky and big, white clouds.

There are jonquils under a tree. The oak leaves are not out yet, though. Where are my brothers? Why are you alone?"

"They have left with the steward to buy a horse. I chose to stay behind."

"To get me alone?"

"Perhaps. If you like."

"I think it should be an accident. An impulse. We are very young, after all. I do not think it would speak well of you if it was a calculated seduction."

"Actually, in my story you were going to seduce me."

She reacted with shock, but it melted into a little grin. "How very naughty of me."

"Well, nothing new there. When I find you, you are removing your hose so you can wade into the lake and try to catch fish with your hands, the way you did that one summer when Vergil and I came upon you."

"My governess will make me stay in the house for a week when I go home with muddy feet. If I lift my skirt to enter the lake, you will see a lot of my legs, won't you?"

He slid the blanket over so that her whole left side was visible, down to her toes. He watched as he caressed her silky skin along her side to her knee. "Quite a lot. Very beautiful legs. I am entranced."

"So, after playing in the lake, we kiss," she whispered. "It is my first real kiss, ever."

He kissed her. The purity of the pleasure saturated him.

She looked up and smoothed her fingertips over his face. "And you? Is it your first real kiss, Julian?"

"Yes, Pen. You are my first."

"I am glad. Kiss me again, Julian."

He was no longer so young, but he might have been.

She was not really his first, but as he caressed her it was as if his hand had touched no other woman.

The difference was in his heart. Every kiss was new and perfect, a revelation of emotions buried too long. There might be no future but there was also no past. She only wanted to kill the dragons for a night, but his soul shook from what was happening.

His body roared with impatience, but his heart wanted an eternity to pass. He controlled the hunger and kissed her slowly, listening to every breath she took and every response she gave. Nips on her ear made her shiver. Kisses on her neck made her gasp. During a long, deep kiss she joined him, venturing her own little invasion into his mouth, letting him know that she would not be passive.

He kissed one breast and caressed the other, entranced by their softness. He memorized the sensation of her skin beneath his fingers and mouth, and the song of her increasing madness. Dreamy ecstasy marked her expression, and breathless encouragement flowed to his ear.

He rose up so he could see her face and remember it forever. He stroked her hard, erotic nipples while he watched her joy in the pleasure.

She opened her eyes. She appeared embarrassed that he watched her reactions, but it passed. A warmth entered her eyes.

"Do you like seeing what you do to me?"

"Yes."

Her gaze moved slowly over his chest. "Then you will not mind if I play, too. Fair is fair."

Her childish words reminded him of the fantasy they had begun. It was no girl whose hand moved down from his shoulder to caress his body, however.

Her touch had him gritting his teeth. Flames crackled through his blood and burned in his head.

She ventured lower and his head began splitting. She touched his phallus through his smallclothes, then slipped her hands beneath to caress it. They got rid of the impediment and she began to drive him insane.

His arousal became savage and dangerous, but hers remained lyrical and luxurious. He dipped his head and licked and sucked her tight velvet nipples. He claimed her whole body with his hand, caressing her fluid curves, deliberately seducing her to abandon.

She bit her lower lip and a powerful tension flexed through her, as if she relinquished control of her reactions. "Perhaps... perhaps it does not have to be merely enough tonight. Just this once. Maybe..."

He looked in her eyes, barely daring to breathe, let alone speak. His body did not remain silent, however. It shouted with chaotic hungers breaking loose of their tenuous bonds.

"Maybe, if we are careful at the end... it need not be so unfair," she said.

A good friend would not let her decide this now, here, while he exploited pleasure's lure. An honorable man would not allow her to abandon the caution of a lifetime, especially on a night when the memories had made her vulnerable.

His own desire had pushed him far past good and honorable, however.

"I can make sure we are careful." Somehow he would find the strength to make good on that promise. "You are sure, Pen?"

"I think that I will die if we do not."

He was beyond thought, beyond judgment. He drowned her in pleasure so she could not change her mind. Her cries grew more frantic. When he stroked up between her thighs and touched her intimately, she joined him in a state of passion where nothing was careful or slow or contained. They shared and traded grasping holds and biting kisses and erotic touches. "Yes," she whispered again and again, until it became a desperate melody of assent and desire.

He moved on top of her. Another "yes" flowed on her breath, but her embrace suddenly turned awkward, as if she did not know what to do now. A different note sounded on her sighs.

He wanted her so much he could hardly think, but her subtle hesitation restored a spot of calm amidst his fury.

With their bodies pressed together, heart to heart, he looked down at her. In her eyes, beyond the desire, he saw the vulnerability he had almost forgotten in the heat.

"Are you frightened, Pen?"

She just looked at him.

"There is no need to be. I would never hurt you."

He gently coaxed her legs apart. He entered slowly, as if she were really the virgin in the little fantasy that had started this.

She reacted as if she were, with surprise and initial discomfort. Then her body relaxed and she accepted him deeply.

It was his turn to be surprised. The sensuality was the least of it. A profound contentment permeated his essence, awing him.

He closed his eyes and savored all the sensations, not moving. He had never before been so totally alive to a moment of existence.

When his lids rose, Pen was looking at him with a worried expression that touched his heart.

"I am fine now," she whispered. "It had been so long that I . . . do not think that you cannot . . ."

"I am not so good as that. I was just enjoying the feel of you."

"Oh. Like the eye of the storm, you mean."

"I expect so." He knew so. Already the winds were beginning to howl again.

He held off the madness as long as he could. He withdrew and thrust slowly, enjoying the delicious sensation and the soft sighs of her responses. He bent her knees high and rose up on his arms so he could see her face and her body and look down at how they joined.

His body would not let it go on like that. The urge for completeness forced its demands. Balancing his weight on one arm, he reached down and slid his finger high in her cleft to caress her clitoris.

It was her storm that guided the rest. Her groans as the pleasure unhinged her. Her moves as the need moved lower and her body tightened to grip him. Her hips rose and fell and shifted as she anxiously sought relief. His own passion turned hard and wild in response and began rising to a peak.

He straightened her legs and pressed them together beneath him. "Do not move." When he thrust the next time her fingers clawed his shoulders as the pressure stroked more effectively.

"Yes," she whispered, beginning her entrancing song again.

She moaned with astonished pleasure the next time. Then little assents exhaled on each breath. Their rise told him how close she was, and he found the control to continue. When she was muffling screams against his shoulder and shuddering with her finish, he finally gave in to his body's demands.

Even at the climax, he never forgot it was Pen that he held. Her presence drenched that bliss just as it had every touch and every pleasure. Somehow, in that glorious cataclysm of being, he managed to keep his promise and relinquish their physical unity.

chapter 14

The dragons stayed in their lair all night. Even when Pen left Julian's arms and sneaked back to her own chamber, they did not threaten her.

They only began stirring when the dawn woke her. Even then, the past remained vague and distant. The bad memories could not penetrate her thoughts of the night.

Putting on her cloak reminded her, however. Walking down the stairs to join Julian at the carriage lifted her out of her daze.

In an hour she would see Cleo, and would relive much that she had tried to forget.

She was a little embarrassed when she saw Julian in the light of day. His greeting was formal and proper, but his eyes showed warmth and a hint of playful conspiracy.

He joined her in the carriage, and it rolled out of the town. He sat across from her, saying nothing, as was his way. She was the one who felt compelled to speak of last night.

"I do not know how to behave with you now, Julian. It is all I can do not to giggle."

"I have always thought that was a lovely sound."

"I am astonished with myself. It appears I am more sophisticated than I thought. I suppose my long abstinence accounts for my losing my head last night."

"One does not need a long drought to enjoy a summer rain."

"I was not implying that it had nothing to do with how much . . . with the rain. Still, I am having difficulty accommodating how bold I was. Are you? Have you ever had a . . . sophisticated liaison before?"

"I have had nothing else except sophisticated liaisons, Pen."

"Good. At least one of us knows what to do and what to say the next day."

She waited. After a five count, a slightly bewildered expression passed over his face. Then an amused one, as he seemed to realize she was demanding guidance.

"Well, Pen, normally, at some point in the days ahead, some expression of gratitude is made."

"Of course. I see. Well, then, thank you, Julian."

He scratched his temple while a smile twitched the corners of his mouth.

"I am supposed to express the gratitude, Pen, not you."

"I assumed we both—"

"Not normally."

That did not help *her* situation much.

She was sure there were expectations of the woman, too. She probably should be clarifying matters, and reassuring him that there would be no scenes. She had known women who misunderstood and built huge expectations on what men thought were casual affairs.

"Julian, I want you to know that I will not become childish and demanding and insist on continued attendance. I will not start convincing myself it was other than it was."

His subdued smile did not change, but his eyes assumed penetrating lights.

"And what was it, Pen?"

The question startled her, but he was right; it definitely needed clarification. She sifted through what she had experienced in that passion, and before and after. She set some of those reactions aside, because they were not very sophisticated at all.

"I think it was one very special night of sharing between two friends, Julian. A momentary abandon to an intimacy that was safe and unfettered so I could ignore the past a while longer. I suspect that such a thing is a rare occurrence between men and women, and only possible because of our long history."

He reached over, lifted her by the waist, and moved her onto his lap. "Extremely rare. But not so momentary that I do not want to embrace you today and enjoy the remnants of that sharing for a little longer."

He held her almost all the way to their destination. She was grateful to be in his safe and caring arms. Their quiet contentment soothed her agitation about the meeting that waited.

When the carriage turned off a road and followed a lane through some chestnuts, he slid her off his lap.

They stopped in front of a modest house surrounded by extensive plantings.

"What lovely gardens these must be in season," Pen said.

Julian handed her down from the carriage. "Mrs. Kenworthy tends them herself. That and books have been her great passions."

"A bluestocking?"

"She was a friend of my uncle, the vicar, and could converse with him on any topic as an equal."

"Is that why you thought she would take in Cleo?"

There, it was said. The reason they were here. It could not be ignored any longer.

Her heart started beating in a discomforting patter.

"I knew her to be a kindhearted woman, and thought she could help the girl."

The maid accepted Julian's card, then returned to lead them to the gardens in back. They found Mrs. Kenworthy bending to cut the dead stalks of a herbaceous garden. She wore a man's straw hat atop a simple cap, and a loose, green dress with no stays.

As they approached she straightened carefully, as if her body rebelled against her activity.

"Now this is a wonderful surprise." Her pale eyes gave Julian a warm inspection much as an old nurse might. "You are rarely in these parts, Julian. It must be eight years now since your uncle passed."

"If you are saying that I have been neglectful of old friends, I stand admonished."

He introduced Pen. Mrs. Kenworthy's curiosity was obviously piqued.

"The countess would like to speak with Cleo," Julian explained.

Mrs. Kenworthy's brow knit. "Did you not receive my letter?"

"The one in January? Yes, and I replied."

"But not the next one? Four months ago?"

"I did not, madame."

Mrs. Kenworthy suddenly did not appear very stiff and old at all. A vivid clarity entered her eyes.

"Come inside. We must talk. If you did not receive that letter, something suspicious is afoot."

"What did the letter say?"

"Cleo is dead, Julian. She hung herself."

"We always knew it was a danger, of course." Mrs. Kenworthy handed Pen a cup of coffee. They sat in a cube of a library stuffed with books and pamphlets. "She was never quite right after she came. She possessed a deeply melancholy nature. Even with me, after all these years, she acted like a dog that was kicked often as a puppy."

Pen remembered that manner. It was as if Cleo tried to make herself small and invisible. She could see her in the earl's Wiltshire house, slinking out of a chamber, head bowed and shoulders hunched.

The news that Cleo was dead had numbed her. "How did it happen?"

"She simply walked away from this property, found a tree, that big old chestnut at the next crossroads, tied a rope, and jumped off a stump. I wrote you about the sad event, Julian. I sent the letter to you through your agent, as you requested. Now I am wondering if he was your agent at all."

"He was not. I have no agent who would have contacted you."

Mrs. Kenworthy sighed deeply. "Oh, dear. I have been most negligent. I fear that poor woman's death is my fault."

"You have been nothing but generous to her, and no fault in this is yours. Please tell me about this agent of mine, however."

"He visited last spring. He said that he served you and that your duties kept you very busy, so you had asked him to handle certain matters in your name. Matters such as this. You had sent him to speak with Cleo, he claimed, to see how she fared. He said that you would continue sending money for her board, but that it would be easier if I directed any requests or news to him in the future."

Pen had not realized that Julian supported Cleo. He had told her that Mrs. Kenworthy had taken Cleo into service here.

"Did he meet with her?" Julian asked.

Mrs. Kenworthy turned fretful. "Yes. I allowed them to speak alone. She was a mature woman, and this was a personal matter. I could see them in the garden from this window, of course. She showed no particular reaction to whatever he said."

"Your judgment cannot be faulted," Julian said.

"I fear you are wrong. It was the next week that she killed herself. I wonder now if that man said something that drove her to it."

An ominous feeling spread through Pen. She dreaded that Mrs. Kenworthy was correct.

That man had come from Glasbury. There was no

other explanation. Cleo might well seek sanctuary in death if she feared falling into Glasbury's hands again.

"I would like to see where she was found," Pen said.

Julian shook his head and raised a halting hand in an imperious gesture. "No, madame. It will only distress you."

"I *demand* to see where it occurred, Mr. Hampton."

She stood under the old tree, picturing Cleo older now but still childlike in her dress and grooming. She empathized too much with the despair that had resulted in this act.

Her horrible suspicions crystallized. "Glasbury knew she could support my accusations, Julian. He wrote that letter to me in Naples saying the arrangement was over right after this happened. *He* knew she was a threat before I realized it, and comprehended how her death untied his hands."

Julian appeared lost in his thoughts. He did not examine the tree the way she did. He looked at nothing at all.

"My God, Julian, we thought we had defeated him, and he was watching her the whole time. Since she left. Since *I* left."

Mr. Hampton the solicitor stood there, but she knew he was not dispassionate about this. His reserve hid contemplations she did not see, but she knew he was not unmoved by this tragedy.

She could not be so silent. Her heart was crying with anger and frustration. "That man told her she would have to go back, and she was too ignorant to really understand that Glasbury had no power to make her do so. That is what drove her to this. He guessed it would. He counted on it. She was born a slave and she thought as a slave. After tasting freedom and safety she would have died before accepting the chains again. I would have, too."

"I do not think that is how it happened."

His tone made her turn to him. He appeared angry now. Dangerously furious.

"That man did not tell her he came from Glasbury, Pen. He said he came from *me*. He had to, otherwise the inconsistency might come out when Cleo spoke with Mrs. Kenworthy. Whatever he said to her, he said in my name."

She feared he was correct. If Julian had sent Cleo a message saying she had to go back, she would have no hope.

Unless . . . she looked at the tree. *That big chestnut at the next crossroads.* Not just any tree. A big old one, known to the folk who lived in the region.

Why would Cleo have chosen this tree?

A shiver slid up Pen's spine.

Cleo had not come here to kill herself, but to meet Mr. Hampton's agent, who would spirit her away to another place of safety. That was why Mrs. Kenworthy had seen no distress as she watched that conversation.

She had been wrong in her assumptions. Glasbury had not been watching Cleo all these years.

He had been looking for her, however.

And last spring he had finally found her.

Pen thought about what she knew of Glasbury's character. She saw that country house with its servant-slaves. She saw his expression while he hurt her in the cottage.

Could he have done it? Arranged someone's murder?

Her mind wanted to reject the idea, but her heart knew the truth.

"Julian, when you negotiated with Glasbury to get me free, what did you say to him?"

"I spoke of his misuse of you and the servants, especially the girl. I said that if he did not release you that you would divorce him and that it would all come out, what occurred there and the crimes he had committed."

"Did you specify what those crimes were, besides his use of Cleo?"

"It was not necessary. He understood. He knew that a man cannot have slaves in Britain, either in the law or in practice. He knew that he would be publicly scorned if that little plantation he had created in Wiltshire became known."

Would that have been enough? What if there had been other crimes, bigger ones, that would bring down more than scandal and scorn if known? What if Cleo had seen far more than the Countess of Glasbury had?

She walked away so Julian would not see the horror her thoughts were provoking.

Glasbury had killed Cleo. She was sure of it. He may have been looking for her for years, since it all started, so that he could. Cleo had been lured here in Julian's name and murdered.

Pen felt horribly vulnerable suddenly, in a way even Julian's presence could not shield. She experienced no panic, however. No terror. With a calm certainty, she realized what she faced now.

Either Glasbury would succeed in forcing her back, or he would kill her, too. There would be no continuation of the agreement. She would win no divorce on her story.

As for provoking him to divorce her—

She looked back at Julian. A visceral fear clutched her. If Glasbury discovered what had happened last night . . .

What would it be? A fall from the cliff walk while Julian visited the cottage? A riding accident when he galloped out to Hampstead?

She had been concerned for Julian's reputation and livelihood.

She should have been worrying for his life.

chapter 15

"I have made my decision, Julian. I know what I should do."

She found the courage to broach the subject back in Grossington, after their supper in the inn's private dining room.

Catherine had eaten quickly, then retired, claiming a headache. Pen suspected that her companion did not sleep soundly at all, and knew about the leaving and entering last night. She now wanted to give the lovers some time alone.

Julian made a gesture dismissing the servant who waited to see to their comfort. When they were alone he took her hand. "What decision is that?"

There was no expectation in his manner, but she sensed it anyway. Her heart swelled with sad longing. This morning she had been sure that last night had not been a mistake, but now she realized that it had.

Not only because of the danger to Julian from Glasbury. She had not realized how close to him she would feel, and how hard it would be to deny what they had shared.

"I must go away, Julian. As I first planned. If Glasbury was so diabolic with Cleo, if he drove her to her death, he will not be fair with me. We are not dealing with a man who acts or thinks in the normal way, or whose honor and conscience create the normal restraints."

She expected an argument. Instead he just looked at her hand while his thumb gently stroked its back. That touch contained everything they had ever known. She focused on it so she would never forget the sensation. Every minute of their friendship was emblazoned in that discreet caress.

"Bianca has spoken of friends in Baltimore. I will go there and ask for their help until Laclere can arrange something for me."

"I will not allow you to do this on the hope of charity from people you do not know."

"It is not for you to allow or not allow, Julian," she said softly.

She saw a flicker of anger in his eyes. A slight possessive pressure changed his touch, as if saying he had no rights was an insult.

That was another reason why last night had been a mistake. She did not think men could give honest advice to women who were their lovers, even if the union had been framed by friendship instead of romantic love.

"Pen, if what happened with Cleo has made you fear Glasbury more, that is understandable. I said I will never allow him to hurt you, however, and I meant it."

"I know that, Julian. I still think it would be better to go away." *Because you would protect me, even if it imperiled you. Not only because of last night, but because of all the years of friendship and the duty you think they created. Because of those afternoons when we were children at Laclere Park.*

And if Julian Hampton stood against the Earl of Glasbury now, the earl would remove the nuisance.

"If you are resolved, then that is how it must be. However, you will not go penniless. On this I must stand firm. Tomorrow I will hire a post chaise and ride to London. I will bring you back enough to live on until formal arrangements can be made. I must insist on this, Pen. It will delay you only a few days."

He had promised to let her make the decision, and he was doing so. Her heart wished he would not accept it so calmly, however. She wished he would try and dissuade her, even if he could not.

She held in the confusing disappointment that was muddling her emotions. At most, there might have been an affair of convenience if she were not leaving. A temporary illusion, to force the earl's hand. If it ended after one night instead of twenty, that really made no difference.

Only she would have gladly had the twenty. The apprehension in her soul said that leaving would be hard in many ways, but especially because it meant not seeing this dear friend ever again.

"A few days should not make a difference, I suppose."

"You can remain here, or stay with Mrs. Kenworthy, whichever you prefer. I think that you will be safe either way."

"I would like to visit with Mrs. Kenworthy if she will have us."

• • •

Catherine's breaths timed the passing seconds and minutes as Pen lay in bed that night.

She was remembering again. Not about Cleo or Glasbury. That dragon lurked in deep shadows tonight. Knowing she would sail far from its lair lessened the sense that it waited to devour her.

Tonight's thoughts were different ones. Beautiful and sad ones. Memories of Julian from years ago and from last night. The sight of him at a party when she would face society's scorn, lending reassurance with his quiet strength. Standing in the library at Laclere Park, as familiar to her surroundings as a vase or chair.

Looking down at her with his face transformed by passion, so masculine and severe and gentle and warm all at once.

He had said and done nothing to suggest that they should repeat last night's indiscretion. He had allowed her to retire without any special comment or look. He had accepted that last night had been what she offered and no more, one night to comfort and distract her.

In the morning he would leave for London and not even know that it was their final farewell.

She sat up in bed. The silence of the sleeping inn hung around her. Catherine's breathing remained steady and deep.

Last night had been a mistake for many reasons, and should not be repeated. She knew that. But her heart grieved so badly that she had to at least be in his presence tonight.

She slipped from the chamber and took the few steps to Julian's door.

The faintest light leaked out in a thin line all around three sides. It was slightly ajar.

She pushed the door a bit wider.

He stood near the fireplace, arms taut as he braced them against the mantel and looked down into the low flames. Their light made reflected patterns of gold on his shirt.

He appeared very romantic, and so handsome and unsensible without his coats and cravat, his dark hair mussed and his eyes dangerously intense.

She entered and closed the door. The small sound made him straighten. His arms fell from the mantel.

He turned and looked at her.

"I did not think you were coming."

"I wasn't sure that you wanted me to."

"I will always want you to."

He did not approach her. He just stood there, looking so wonderful that her heart pounded.

"I am not so afraid tonight." She spoke to fill the silence that had begun pulsing with a demand for . . . *something*. "Making a decision has freed me more than I thought."

"I am glad. Did you come to tell me that?"

"I do not know why I came."

"Don't you?"

Yes, she did, even though it would only make tomorrow harder.

He held out his hand.

She took the few steps to place her hand in his. As soon as they touched, his cool restraint cracked. He pulled her to him and wrapped her with possessive arms.

There was little of last night's gentle care in his passion. His kisses did not lure, but demanded. His caresses claimed her body in a way that permitted no denial. His heat blazed into her. Within moments she was gasping, first from astonishment and then from the savage arousal that burst in her.

No words. No requests. No illusions like last night. They were not young, tasting this for the first time. They were a man and a woman overwhelming each other.

She abandoned herself to the delicious pleasure. She welcomed the consuming kisses on her neck and mouth and the confident strokes of his hands over her body. She swam within the primitive fury, secure that she was safe despite the danger.

She wanted him badly. Almost viciously. She used her mouth and tongue and hands to tell him so, which only intensified their fervor. She pulled at his shirt, anxious to remove it so she could feel him. Somehow he got it off in the midst of their clutching holds and biting kisses. She pressed her palms to his chest, and then her lips, too, and let their heat brand the taste and feel of his skin on her memory.

He held her, looking down at what she was doing. The power did not diminish in that interlude. She felt it in him, thundering, crashing, making him grasp her against him.

He slid off her nightdress and kicked off his garments until they were both naked in front of the fire. She reached between their bodies to touch the tip of his arousal. As if that had been a challenge, he caressed to where she throbbed and made that hungry pulse tremble through her whole body.

She became crazed and desperate and lost hold of the world. She wanted him inside her, nothing more and nothing else. In her madness she must have whispered that, but she did not hear herself speak.

"Soon," he murmured.

She expected him to move her to the bed. Instead he turned her so that she faced the warm glow of the dying fire. He embraced her from behind while he pressed hot kisses to her neck, provoking incredible shivers that made her arch her bottom against him and languidly writhe within his arms.

He caressed her freely, wonderfully. His hands moved in slow, sweeping strokes over her breasts and stomach, her hips and thighs. Luxurious pleasure lapped through her in delicious waves. It felt so good she almost could not bear it. It increased her impatience, even as she never wanted it to end.

He lifted her hands to the mantel and pushed her hair over her shoulder. She realized what he was going to do. Her astonishment was eclipsed by a deeply erotic excitement that had her body trembling.

He caressed down her back and over her bottom. "You are so beautiful. You make my heart stop." His hands grasped her hips.

He entered slightly and paused, barely joined, creating a tantalizing fullness that teased her until she was crazed. She closed her eyes as that taste of fulfillment became the only reality. She felt him so distinctly. Her flesh throbbed from the exquisite torture. The sensation became too powerful to bear.

Finally he thrust, deeply. The perfection made her moan. He reached around her body to where her breasts tingled, sensitive to the air and fire's warmth. He lightly caressed the tips, sending intense pleasure down to where they were joined.

She could not contain what it did to her. Clutching the mantel, arching her back, she submitted totally to the crescendo of sensations carrying her to the bliss of pure pleasure.

She snuggled against him in the bed. He had carried her here some time ago, but the daze of their passion had only now lifted.

She drew little lines with her fingertips on the arm that wrapped her. "How many sophisticated affairs have there been before me, Julian?"

He thought it an odd question. Perhaps she wanted to fill in the big gaps in her knowledge from when he was Mr. Hampton.

"I suppose some men keep a count, but I did not. There was none who truly mattered to me, nor I to her, however."

The devil of it was that he had tried to make it matter. As a young man he had even convinced himself there were great passions. Eventually, too soon, he would admit in his soul that he was lying to his lover, and to himself.

It was during moments like this that the emotional vacancy of those affairs could not be denied. There was an essential dishonor in taking a woman and then having as your first clear thought that you wished it had been someone else.

"You had frivolous affairs, then, not only sophisticated ones," she said. "We have something in common."

"Not entirely."

"True. I did not really have affairs."

That was not what he meant.

"Is that why you never married? Because none truly mattered to you?"

He was not sure he wanted to have this conversation with her. "After your brother wed, I considered marrying. It seemed it was time and I was established. My interest could not be sustained long enough to do the deed. I concluded that I was not made for marriage."

It was true, every word. Just incomplete.

"I do not remember you on the marriage mart. I never saw you surveying the girls. Nor did you have your friends make any introductions."

"It happened, only not in your society. Solicitors seek their brides in other circles." Lower circles. The daughters of viscounts were not for them. That was so accepted, so well known, that it never had to be said.

Nor did Pen question it now.

She occupied herself with her finger tracings, as if the patterns distracted her. Eventually those soft pads found their way to the scar on his side again.

"Did my brother do this? I would have thought he would be more careful."

"It was another member of our set."

Her touch brought back the images from the day he received that long wound. He had arranged to meet Witherby at Corbet's fencing academy on a day when he knew even the chevalier would not be there. He did not ride to that meeting with any intention in mind except a blunt conversation about his suspicions.

His companion had been waiting, already prepared. Julian walked into that large hall and saw Witherby practicing his steps and moves, sabre in hand. He guessed at once that Witherby had his own reasons for agreeing to come.

"That was quite a drama here with Glasbury last week," Witherby said as they began their mock contest. "He appeared to be accusing you of something."

"He was wrong in his suspicions about me. However, he has evidence that someone knows things they should not."

Witherby's sword made an elegant block of Julian's own. "Well, secrets eventually become known."

"Only if someone speaks of them. In this case, I think that someone spoke of them to you."

Witherby paced away. A hard expression masked his face when he turned back. His eyes held a coldness Julian had never seen before.

"Be plain, man. What are you saying?"

"What you expected me to say. Only two people know the earl's secrets. Me and the countess. I have spoken to no one. That means she has. She told you."

Witherby laughed. He swiped his sword at the air, then took his position again. They engaged once more. "Why would she tell me? More likely she confided in a friend."

"She told you because you have seduced her." Putting it into words darkened his mood and sharpened his skill. "She confided in you as her lover. Only you saw a way to enrich yourself by threatening the earl with exposure. There is no other explanation, Witherby. Nor is there any excuse for such a dishonorable violation of her trust."

Witherby's smile turned into a sneer. "You cannot prove it."

"I need only to ask her if she told you."

"And I only need to tell her to keep silent, and she will. Which of us do you think has her first loyalty?" Witherby's sword in-

stantly became more aggressive. "Stay out of it, Hampton. You have no standing to interfere."

A storm broke in Julian's head and his sword acted accordingly. They no longer sparred for sport but in a duel.

Clanging steel rang through the empty hall. The exertions of their fighting linked them in an increasingly deadly dance. Julian's sword grazed Witherby's arm: First blood was drawn.

Julian stepped back and stared at the red oozing in a thin line. Sanity returned.

Witherby stared at his wound in astonishment.

Julian lowered his sword. "Retreat from any contact with the earl and I will speak to no one about this."

"Are you trying to protect yourself from his suspicions, or that pig from his crimes?"

"I only seek to protect the countess. I do not want her to discover that you used her so badly."

He turned to walk away. Suddenly a hot pain slashed his side. He staggered and pivoted and saw Witherby's crazed eyes and red face.

Somehow he found the strength to fend off the deadly challenge that ensued. He let his own fury loose and it kept the pain at bay. With a relentless attack he backed Witherby up against the wall until there was no room to move.

Witherby dropped his sword and tried to sink into the stone. Julian placed the tip of his sword against his neck and battled the primitive urge to kill him. For a few moments only their deep breaths sounded.

The blood lust mostly passed, but not entirely. He could not resist pricking Witherby's skin so that a bit more red showed. Then he lowered his sword and swung his left fist right into Witherby's body. His opponent crumbled to the floor.

The fight had not left the scoundrel. He grinned up from where he doubled over his gut. "I have never seen you so impassioned, Julian. And here I thought you were made of ice. Did you expect her to live her entire life alone, like you, so that you could watch from afar with the contentment that no man had her?"

Julian walked away. "If you hurt her, I will make you regret it. If you betray her further, I will kill you."

That warning had stopped Witherby. The earl had received no more anonymous demands for money. But Witherby's dishonor had all come out anyway, and Pen had indeed been hurt.

"Another caused this scar?" Pen asked, making him realize he had only been lost in the past for a few seconds. "Not St. John or Adrian Burchard, surely. They are too skilled for such carelessness."

She suddenly went very still, as if her process of elimination had led to a stunning conclusion. Or maybe she had heard his thoughts as he relived that day in Hampstead.

"Oh, dear God. He did this because you guessed what he was doing. He could have killed you."

"He could have, but he did not."

No, he did not. Pen considered that while she touched the scar once again. Julian made it sound like it had been generosity on Witherby's part, but she did not think it had happened that way. She did not think Witherby had won that sword fight.

She embraced the man who had confronted her betrayer all those years ago. She wrapped her arms around him and pressed her cheek to his chest.

It was sinful that she had lived all this time not knowing how he had tried to protect her.

The passing time suddenly pressed on her. She felt the minutes and hours flying past, and with it this sweet intimacy. She dreaded the dawn and his departure for London. She inhaled deeply so she would remember his scent. She pressed her lips to his skin and memorized its taste.

He touched her head, and turned it so he could kiss her.

His passion was not savage this time, but slow and heartrending. He moved her atop him, straddling his hips, and sat her up so he could look at her while he caressed her body. She looked down and touched every inch of his muscular shoulders and chest, while his strong, masculine hands fondled her breasts.

Her arousal built poignantly. Perfectly. He did not hurry it. Her complete awareness of him drenched every pleasure, every touch. It was so beautiful and sad that she wanted to weep.

He lifted her hips and then lowered her so they were together. She leaned forward to kiss him, then spoke as she nuzzled the crook of his neck.

"Julian, you said that lovemaking had not truly mattered to you or your lovers."

"Yes."

"I want you to know it does this time. It truly matters to me that we have shared this."

He lifted her enough that he could see her face. "As it does for me, Pen."

"I am glad, Julian. I am thankful that we are each other's firsts in this way. It is very special to have that with a good friend whom you trust."

An odd little smile passed over his mouth. "Yes, a good friend."

He eased her forward so she hovered over him. His tongue flicked at one nipple and his fingers played with the other. "Now cry for me, darling, so I hear nothing else all the way to London."

chapter 16

"Are you going to tell me where we are going now, madame?"

Catherine made the demand as soon as they left Mrs. Kenworthy's house two mornings later. Catherine had not been pleased by Pen's sudden change in plans. She had not liked the notion of continuing the journey with little rest.

The carriage that had brought them from Hampstead made a turn at the crossroad where the big chestnut grew. The view of its branches reinforced Pen's wobbling security that she was doing the right thing.

That could be me. One day it will be me.

"I am going to Liverpool, Catherine. After that, I am going to America."

"America! That is certainly a change in direction. No one told me I was expected to go to America."

"You may come as far as you like, or you can depart at the first coaching inn. Mr. Hampton will see to your wages in the latter case. If you embark with me, I can promise nothing except freedom and adventure and economic uncertainty until I contact my brother."

"Madame, really... America? If you had a disagreement with Mr. Hampton, could we not just visit Bath? Your displeasure will be expressed. I daresay he will be very contrite."

"America it must be. Be assured this is no impulse. Nor is this the result of some quarrel. I have been thinking about it for some time now. Months."

"If he gave you no clear cause for your decision, that is worse. Mr. Hampton will be heartbroken."

"I expect he will quickly recover, Catherine. You have misunderstood this journey from its start, and now you are misunderstanding its conclusion."

Pen was not sure of much about this decision, but she was quite secure that Julian would not be heartbroken. She had learned long ago that passion and love were not the same thing, especially for men. His affection for her was precious, but her departure would not leave him feeling betrayed.

Maybe he would even be relieved. Her disappearance would spare him from facing the dragon he could not vanquish, and from getting embroiled in an affair that would destroy his security.

She was the one who would remember this brief tryst forever. She was the one whose heart had been touched to new depths. It still ached from the intensity of last night, and hurt so badly she wanted to weep.

"The offer to accompany you is generous, and tempting," Catherine said. "However, I do not think I could be so permanently parted from my child. I will accompany you to Liverpool, madame. Then, since we will be so close to Carlisle, I will travel on and find a way to see my Beth."

Pen had guessed this would be Catherine's answer. She had known she would be sailing to America completely alone.

The coaching inn at Blackburn was a busy place, with carriages and horses filling its yard, and footmen and coachmen crowding its public rooms. Ladies in fur-trimmed carriage mantles mingled with passengers who rode atop mail coaches. Servers dispensed ale and mulled wine to anyone with the coin.

As she had since leaving Hampstead, and as she had the last night in Skipton, Pen used a false name when she secured a tiny chamber for herself and Catherine. While she shook out a few garments for the night and the next day, Catherine left to take a turn, as was her habit in the evening.

Domestic duties finished, Pen was left with her thoughts.

Early tomorrow they would reach Liverpool, and she would find a berth on a ship. Very soon she would leave England forever.

She kept seeing her brothers and sister as she last saw them, images that would never change or grow older. She pictured her nieces and nephews, forever young in her mind even as they matured and found their lives.

It would be the same for them, too. She would be the aunt who was swallowed by America. In ten years it would be as if she had never existed.

If thoughts of her old world filled her with nostalgia, those of the waiting one left her anxious. She saw herself as America would see her, a countess who had left her own people, a woman who had abandoned her husband.

The latter point would keep many people of quality from associating with her, just as it had in Britain. There would be men who did not want their wives to have her as a friend, and women who would only speak of her in whispers of gossip. She would have to travel far from the cities and society in order to escape from her shaded history.

She would have to in order to escape the earl, too. Julian had been right about that.

Julian.

She refused to picture him when he found her gone. She did not want to speculate on his expression then, or his response. None of the ones that flashed through her head lifted her melancholy. All of them, whether those of sadness or relief or acceptance, clawed at her heart.

She heard steps on the boards in the inn's corridor. She hoped they heralded Catherine's return. She would find some other subject to speak of with Catherine, and distract herself from these sad thoughts.

The steps stopped outside her door. A drop of curiosity dripped into her awareness. A tiny shiver of anticipation danced in her heart.

One step had sounded heavy. Perhaps Julian had—

The door opened abruptly. Shock obliterated her budding excitement.

Catherine flew in, trying to keep her balance as her body lunged forward, hurtled by a rough push. Two men followed and closed the door behind them.

"No screaming, now," one man commanded. "No yelling. No reason for either of you to get hurt, then."

Pen darted over to steady Catherine. "Oh, dear. Did Jacob somehow have you followed? I am so sorry—"

"It was not Jacob who had us followed, madame." Catherine said. "They are Glasbury's men."

Julian found Laclere at home, sitting in the library with the viscountess. It did not surprise him to find them together. Laclere and his wife Bianca often spent time together, as if this mansion did not have forty chambers and they lived in a cottage where one had to share every space.

It was not the first grand house that Julian had visited today as he hurried around London, but it would be the last.

"I am glad you have called, Hampton," Laclere said. "You have been making yourself scarce of late, and there are matters that require your attention."

Bianca untucked her feet from under her rump on the sofa and assumed a more decorous seat. Laclere's wife had never conformed to expectations of normal behavior for her station. An American heiress, she was a handsome woman with golden hair, large blue eyes, and a heart-shaped face, but not a great beauty.

That concerned her as little as the gossip in drawing rooms. She had given Laclere four children, then shocked society by going onstage as an opera singer. Her success at that career, and her obvious devotion to her family, only partly absolved her of the usual taint such an occupation carried. The general opinion was that Laclere must be a little mad to have permitted such a thing.

"Yes, you have been missed. We are all very worried about Penelope, now that Glasbury has made his intentions clear," she said. "Some reassurance from you would have been consoling."

"I have had responsibilities that required I remove myself from town. As it happens, I must leave again shortly and do not expect to return for several days."

Bianca raised an eyebrow. "Can I be of any assistance in these other responsibilities that you have?"

"No, madame, but your husband can."

"I will leave him to do so, then. I trust that after you attend to these other matters, you will give Glasbury your full attention and make sure that Penelope is never obligated to return to him."

Julian had long ago made the vow that Pen would never be obligated to return. Now he needed to make sure that with freedom came safety.

"How can I assist you?" Laclere asked, after Bianca had left the library.

"I have some debts that must be paid immediately. I thought that you would agree to cover them for me."

"You have been gambling, Julian? It is not like you to lose big."

"I misjudged my opponent. He held aces I did not expect. I have brought some papers for you to sign." Julian removed them from his coat and set them on the writing desk.

Laclere perused them. "Let us drop the dissembling.

This is about my sister, is it not? You will sign this bank draft over to her."

"It is made out to me. You will record it as payment for services rendered. By the time the bank actually receives it back, it will not matter who used it."

Laclere's expression turned sad. "She is running, then. To where?"

"Vergil, you are not a man who would easily lie before the law. Do not ask me to put you in a position where you have to do so in order to protect your sister."

Laclere dipped a pen and signed the bank draft. "I had hoped there was another solution. How badly have we misjudged your gambling opponent?"

"Very badly. I should have realized years ago what the man was capable of. The evidence was in front of me. It was my bad judgment, not yours or hers."

"You are wrong there. It was my family's, for ever allowing her to marry him. Without you, she would have been trapped in his power forever." He held the draft lightly in his fingers. "Tell her that once she is settled I will arrange for a regular allowance. On second thought, I will go to her with you. I cannot bear the thought of her leaving us like this, without a word of parting."

"She wants to move quickly. Invisibly. She cannot be anonymous if the Viscount Laclere accompanies her."

"At least take my coach and six. If she wants to move quickly, that is as fast as it can be."

"I have already arranged such transport, from another source. One whose coach does not bear a peer's coat of arms."

"Yes. Of course." Laclere handed over the draft. "I am not accustomed to leaving important matters to others, as you know. There are few men I would trust with my sister's safety. I know that your judgment is sound, however, and probably more sensible than mine would be under the circumstances."

Julian wondered if Laclere would assume such sound and sensible judgment if he knew his faithful solicitor had slept with the sister in question.

He looked at his lifelong friend, and images poured out of the private corner of his mind. He saw Vergil as a youth, swinging his wooden sword while they played at the old keep . . . as a very young man, while they watched St. John pace off in a duel, and then together for the first time they saw a man die . . . as the new Viscount Laclere, hair blowing on the French coast, taking his own station in another duel, sabre in hand.

Vergil's blue eyes looked deeply into his. "A bank draft for five hundred pounds is not very much under the circumstances."

"There are other resources, and other payments of services rendered."

"I suddenly have a feeling, Julian, that my world will lose more than the presence of a sister in the days ahead. If you intend what I think, it is too much to ask of a family solicitor and I will not have it. We will find another guardian to do this."

"There is no other. It may be too much to ask of a solicitor, but not too much to expect of a friend."

Laclere's jaw tightened. "I have often thanked God for that friendship, but never more than at this moment."

He accompanied Julian to the door. "How soon can I expect your return?"

Julian stepped across the threshold of the home that had always been open to him, and walked away from the only real family he had ever had.

"I do not know, Vergil."

chapter 17

St. John's coach and six could make very good time when required. Two days later it rattled up the lane to Mrs. Kenworthy's cottage.

Its owner was out in front, pruning back some rosebushes that lined the path. She unbent her body and watched the equipage roll to a stop. Julian hopped out.

"Impressive, Julian. You have done very well for yourself these last years. I had no idea."

"It is not mine. I trust all is well here, and that the countess accommodated herself."

"All is not well, I fear. Nor will you find the countess and her companion here. She departed almost immediately. The next morning. I discouraged her to no avail."

Julian gazed at the cottage while his heart absorbed the blow. His brain did not accept it so quickly. Thunder rolled on the edges of his mind.

She had done it. Just walked away from everything.

From him.

She had come to him that last night knowing she would.

"Do not be too angry, Julian. I do not believe the choice was an easy one for her. She was very subdued the day she was here. Quite wistful, in fact."

"She has no money. A few jewels and a few guineas, nothing more. She is unprotected." Hell, she barely had enough for sea passage and food. She would arrive in America almost destitute.

Mrs. Kenworthy peered at him from under the rim of her straw hat. "She spoke of being safe forever. I think that she suspects that Cleo's death was no suicide, as I do. I worry that she fears for her own life."

Possibly. Probably. He should have known that she would see it all. He should not have tried to protect her from fear by hiding his own conclusions from her.

"She did not have to leave so quickly even so," he said, holding his fury at bay with rational words. "She could have awaited my return."

"She could have. However, it appears she did not want to."

The storm broke and anger rained down on his other emotions.

No, she had not wanted to.

Well, he'd be damned before he let her go like this.

"I must leave you now, Mrs. Kenworthy. Thank you for your generosity and kindness. If anyone should arrive here asking after the countess, I beg that you pretend you have never met her."

"That should not be hard, Julian. I am an eccentric old woman with a very bad memory."

• • •

The coach approached the inn in Blackburn in late afternoon. Julian had instructed the coachman to make all possible speed as he followed Pen's path to the coast. His expectation that she was headed for Liverpool had been confirmed when he questioned the innkeeper at the stop she had made her first night in Skipton.

Now, as his coach entered the inn's yard, he spied the hired coach that had taken them from Hampstead. His heart rose in triumph, but foreboding instantly quelled his relief.

She should have gotten farther than Blackburn by now. If she had stopped here the second night, she should be in Liverpool already. Perhaps she had thought better of her plan?

He entered the building and questioned the innkeeper.

"Mrs. Monley, who came in that carriage, is gone," the innkeeper said. "The other is above, waiting the magistrate's pleasure."

"You mean her companion is still here? The lady departed on her own?"

"Slipped out, she did. Left the one above to face the law. Quite a drama we had here two nights ago. Not what one expects from women, let alone a lady of quality."

"I must speak with the young woman."

"Suit yourself. Chamber above, on the left."

He took the stairs in haste and knocked at the chamber door.

It opened. When he saw Catherine, his breath left him for a moment.

Two large bruises marked her face. One had caused swelling that almost closed her right eye. Her careful posture suggested there had been other blows to her body.

She managed a distorted smile and gestured for him to enter the tiny chamber. "I knew you would come, sir. She thought you would not follow, but I knew differently. I have been waiting for you."

"Tell me what happened."

She eased herself down on a chair. "Glasbury's men have been following. They caught me as I took a turn and then brought me here. They have abducted her. We were headed for Liverpool, but I do not think she is going there now."

"And your bruises?"

Her blue eyes turned to crystals. "Don't be worrying about me. If you explain to the innkeeper what has happened, the magistrate will let me be. You should be on your way soon, to find her."

"Was she hurt as well?"

"Just me. When they said we were to go with them, I knew what it meant for her. So while we packed, I got hold of my pistol. I always load it with dry powder, every night. I thought the noise would bring help. Only they stopped me before I could shoot, and took her away. Still had time to pound me a bit, though. Now, you be going, sir. They have almost a two-day start on you."

"I will not leave until I am assured that you will not suffer more for this. I will speak with the innkeeper, and wait for the magistrate if necessary." He fished in his pockets and produced ten guineas. "Here are your wages, and something more for trying to protect her."

She took the money and slid it into her valise.

"What will you do after you leave here?"

"I am going to Carlisle, to see my daughter. I will find

a way to get her alone, somehow. I wish I could have her with me forever, but just seeing her will help us both."

Julian looked at this brave young woman who had taken a beating to try to save Penelope.

He excused himself, went back to the coach, and returned with more money.

"Take this, so that you can live for a while. It will also pay for your use of the carriage that brought us from London."

She tucked the money away, wincing as she did so. "You go find her now, sir. I will handle the magistrate. As for these bruises, they won't stop me. They never did before. Oh, there is something else you should know."

"What is that?"

"She got hold of my pistol as they scuffled with me. She fired and hit one of them in the leg. That may have slowed them down some."

Penelope eyed Mr. Jones, who eyed her back. They sat opposite each other in the small sitting room on the outskirts of Manchester. The only light in the chamber came from an iron candelabra that burned five tallow candles.

Muffled growls of pain penetrated the door that separated them from the kitchen. The surgeon who lived in this cottage was digging the pistol ball out of Mr. Henley's thigh.

"He will be unable to travel," she said. "It will keep bleeding if he is on a saddle. It may become corrupted."

"Not my problem if it does. We have a job to do. He knows how it is."

If her abductors had procured a carriage, they might

have gotten her back to the earl before this procedure was needed. But Mr. Jones had insisted they all ride horses, and that had only aggravated Mr. Henley's wound. It had slowed them so much that they had not even made it out of Lancashire yet.

Mr. Jones did not appear at all disconcerted by his companion's misery. No doubt he would insist that Mr. Henley get back on the horse come morning.

For all of his gleaming gaze, his attention was not really on her. She sensed that he listened for something. This man was always alert, always checking the road and fields, always on guard. She suspected this was not the first criminal act he had performed.

It was Mr. Jones who had beaten Catherine.

Seeing that, watching helplessly, had sent her reeling back into the old nightmare.

She was still afraid, but her wits had returned and she was no longer numb. A seething indignation had been brewing for most of the day.

A loud yell of pain rang from the kitchen.

"I trust you are being paid well, if this job may cost him a leg or his life."

"Handsomely, thank you."

"Have you been in Glasbury's employment long?"

He did not answer.

"If you followed me, you guessed where I was staying when I left the inn at Grossington. You are familiar with those parts, then. You have been there before. You know why I was there, I think."

His lids lowered.

She knew then that her suspicions were correct. This

was the man who had visited Mrs. Kenworthy claiming to be Julian's agent.

This was the man who had killed Cleo.

Terror breathed on her nape. She had assumed they were taking her to the earl, but what if—

Mr. Jones suddenly shifted his gaze to the door. His body stiffened and his concentration sharpened.

She tried to hear what had raised his caution. The only sounds reaching her were the guttural moans from the kitchen.

"You did not answer me. Have you been to Grossington before?"

"Be quiet." He sat up straight, slightly cocking his head.

"And if I will not be quiet? What will you do? Do not forget that I am not a woman alone in this world. My brother is a viscount, and I also have powerful friends who will demand answers and an accounting if anything happens to me."

"Be silent."

He rose and took several steps toward the front of the house. He stood very still, listening, then moved the candles far from the window and lifted the curtain to peer into the darkness.

The kitchen door opened.

"Done here," the surgeon announced. He was a young man with receding blond hair and a portly body. Fresh blood stained his apron. "He cannot ride. You can all stay here if you like. The sum is five pounds a night."

Mr. Jones glanced back at the surgeon. "A hotel of the first rank you must have here."

"If I am sought out in the dark by strangers, at my home, I know the value of my skill and silence."

"Just patch him up. We are leaving."

The surgeon retreated to the kitchen. Mr. Jones continued studying the dark outside the window. Making a decision, he snuffed out the candles, leaving the sitting room dark, too. After moving around a little, he opened the door.

His body formed a silhouette on the threshold. In the dim moonlight Pen could see that his right hand held a pistol.

He just stood there, waiting and looking.

With his back to her, as if she represented no danger at all while he held that gun.

Her indignation crackled. His certainty that fear would make her docile was suddenly the biggest insult she had ever received.

She quietly rose. She lifted the candelabra from the table.

She took four quick strides, raised the iron with both hands, and crashed it down on him.

He staggered forward but did not fall. Hunched like a wounded animal, he swerved around with a vicious hiss and raised the pistol.

"Bitch!"

She backed up in shock, staring at the weapon aimed at her.

Then suddenly the gun was gone, and so was Mr. Jones. In a flash, he simply flew away.

Another figure stood in his place. One she recognized.

The sweetest relief flooded her.

Julian had found her.

• • •

Julian was not alone.

Two other men entered the cottage after him, carrying an unconscious Mr. Jones.

"Quite a blow you gave him, sir," the elder of the two strangers said. A middle-aged man with longish gray hair under his felt hat, he peered down at Mr. Jones. "Found them like you said. Smart to check the surgeons in the county as you suggested. A man can't ride far or fast with a hole in his thigh."

This particular surgeon stood at the kitchen door, flushed and dismayed. "Are they criminals? I had no idea."

"You can be explaining later, sir, but an honest man would have wondered about that leg in there and this woman out here," the man said.

"This is Mr. Fletcher and his son," Julian said, introducing his companions. "Mr. Fletcher is a county justice of the peace."

Mr. Fletcher and his son had come well armed. Each had two pistols belted to his chest under his frock coat. The son, about twenty years of age, appeared disappointed that the night's hunt had ended without the chance to discharge his firearms.

"We'll be needing your carriage to get them to gaol," Mr. Fletcher said to Julian.

"A secure gaol, I hope," Pen said.

"Oh, he'll be secure. We'll hold him until the quarter session. You will be needing to come and swear evidence against him, madame. The other woman, too."

Pen opened her mouth to object.

"Of course she will do her duty," Julian said.

It took them an hour to transport her abductors to the

gaol, and another one for Julian to deal with formalities and legalities. Dawn was breaking when he climbed into the coach and they rode away.

She embraced him in gratitude and relief.

"Thank God you are safe," he muttered between kisses.

He closed the curtains and kept his arm around her.

He did not speak for a few miles. She did not pretend it was his normal silence. Despite their embrace, she sensed his disquiet. The air inside the coach trembled.

"Thank you," she said.

"Thank you for hitting him on the head. It made quick work of it for us."

"Catherine?"

"She is on her way to her daughter."

"Will I really have to return to testify? I do not see how I can."

"Fletcher saw enough to put Jones and Henley on a ship to New South Wales. If you testify, it would only complicate things, since the innkeeper and Fletcher think you are Mrs. Monley. You will have to write to Dante and explain that you used his wife's late mother's name, I expect."

"It was the first one that came to my head at the first inn. Yes, I should probably explain that."

Their conversation did nothing to clear the air. He still sat there darkly displeased, the depths churning.

"Are you going to scold me?" she asked. "You do not have to. I already know what you want to say. That I was reckless, and it was dangerous, and that—"

"You cannot even begin to know what I want to say, madame."

She expected him to remove his embracing arm. When

he did not, she waited for the brittle vehemance of his comment to pass. After a few more miles, the silent turmoil seemed to ease.

"Do you think Jones has been our shadow the whole way, Julian?"

"Unfortunately, yes. Glasbury must have guessed that you would seek out Cleo to have someone to support your accusations."

"He has not only been following me, then. He has been one step ahead of me all along. For years." A larger worry instantly occupied her. "If Mr. Jones followed, Glasbury knows that you have been with me since we left the cottage."

"Mr. Jones probably sent him reports by mail. That is the least of our concerns, however."

She did not agree. Her relief at being saved was instantly drowned by the worry that had sent her off to Liverpool. Not for her own safety, but for Julian's.

If Mr. Jones had sent reports, the earl may have assumed the truth about those nights at the inns.

Mr. Jones might be in gaol, but there would be others taking his place. Glasbury was rich, and such men could always find those who would do their bidding for the right pay.

She fell asleep in the coach. When she woke it was late afternoon, and they were stopping in a small village in front of an inn.

"We will stay here in Bruton tonight," Julian said. "With equipage like this we will be noticed wherever we go, but there are fewer here to do the noticing."

He took two rooms for them. As soon as their trunks were deposited and the second level of the inn was quiet, he came into her chamber.

The expression on his face made her swallow hard.

"I knew it was too much to hope that you would not scold eventually."

"You have made it clear that I do not have the right to that, or anything else. You are also smart enough to know the risks of your plan. You did it anyway. I just want to know why."

"I already told you. I cannot beat him. He will win, one way or the other. I decided that my first plan was my best one."

"That does not explain why you left before I returned."

"I chose not to delay."

"Why?"

"I am not going to be questioned like a criminal. Tell me I was stupid if you want, but do not interrogate me."

"I am not interrogating you. I am not speaking as your solicitor, damn it. I am a man to whom you gave yourself, and I want to know why you chose to flee without so much as a word of farewell."

She had never seen his expression so dark and hard. It affected his whole being and the entire chamber. She half expected lightning bolts to fly from his head.

"I do not think Cleo killed herself. That changes everything, Julian. I looked in my heart and admitted Glasbury could do that. To her. To me. To . . ." She busied herself unpacking toiletries in order to hide how the last thought distressed her.

"To me," he said.

"I did not know we were being followed. I thought if I just left, disappeared, that . . ."

She felt him behind her.

"You thought that I would not be harmed."

"If you are now, I will never forgive myself."

He turned her around and gazed in her eyes. He still looked angry, but no longer hard. "All of your life you have done this, Pen, and you must stop it."

"I realize I have not always been a paragon of good judgment, Julian, but you are not being fair. I did not think this little journey would be dangerous. Not yet."

"I do not speak of the danger, or of your judgment over the years, but of how you sacrifice your own security and happiness to protect others. To spare your family, you did not divorce. You even married Glasbury so that others would not be hurt."

The last accusation shocked her. "I did not marry him for that reason."

"Didn't you? Did your mother never explain the large sum that Glasbury gave her? It kept things afloat for several more years when the family finances were a disaster."

"She explained no such thing. She *did* no such thing. I married him because I was young and stupid. He was an earl, and such things matter to ignorant girls."

"Your mother threw you at him. Even your brothers did not like it."

She had to take deep breaths to contain a spinning indignation. "You are lying. You are—"

"I have seen the accounts, Pen. Nor do I think you were completely ignorant."

"What a horrid thing to say. How dare you accuse my mother of . . . of . . ."

She came close to smacking him.

Instead she grabbed a shawl and ran from the room.

She flew down the stairs and out of the inn, mind red with resentment. She strode down the street, impatient to find some privacy where she could curse Julian for impugning her family. Shops and homes blurred past as she mentally put a certain man in his place, and castigated him for such bold and unfair accusations.

She found her way to the churchyard where the village eyes would not see her. She paced out her anger amidst the grave markers and along a little garden's paths.

Slowly the fury abated. A miserable fact kept blunting her righteous denials.

Julian *would* have seen the accounts. As family solicitor, he would have access to all the financial records, even the ones from when she got engaged to Glasbury.

She sank down on a bench beside a bed of dying plants. Confusion replaced her anger, and sadness her indignation.

A shadow fell on the ground in front of her. Julian had followed her.

She glanced to where he stood at the other end of the bench.

"Mama did speak well of Glasbury. She encouraged the match even before I came out," she admitted. "When I suggested that I would perhaps like to wait until my second season to decide, she said we could not afford that. I knew how much my presentation cost, and my season. She often spoke of my father's impracticality, and how we lived on credit."

"And your duty. I am sure she often spoke of that, too."

"Yes. Often." She looked over at him. "I will admit

that I ignored my misgivings because of all that. If what you say is true, about the money, it is not so unusual. She did not know what he was, Julian. She could not have suspected."

"I am sure she did not suspect. It was not your mother's motivations that I spoke of, but yours. Now, once more, you have taken a path to protect others. Your family. Me. It is a sign of your good heart, Pen, but I am very angry. I will decide for myself what I will risk and what cost I will pay."

He reached in his coat and withdrew a stack of folded papers. He set them down on the bench.

"What are those?"

"Your future, if you want it. Bank drafts and letters of introduction. You can go to America, but not destitute. It is all there, even the means of passage."

She opened the documents. The bank drafts and letters were signed by her brothers and her dearest friends. There was more than enough to live comfortably for years. She need only go to Liverpool and sail away to find herself safe, at least for a while. One sheet was a letter from St. John giving her free passage on any of his ships.

She unfolded the final letter.

"What is this, Julian?"

"A letter of transfer."

"Your bank and your account? So much? I do not need it, dear friend. Not with the other—"

"That one is not for you, but for me."

His response stunned her.

"I cannot permit this, Julian. I do not need the protection you think to give. I am not helpless in any case, and especially not with these drafts and letters."

"It is not your choice to make, but mine."

"I truly do not need your protection on the voyage, especially if it is with one of St. John's captains. You must not remove yourself from London for so long, just to see me established in America safely. You would be gone for months."

"Longer, I expect. Unless Glasbury dies."

The calm resolve of his voice delayed her comprehension of what he was saying. The implications of his words astonished her.

He did not intend merely to see her safely to America.

He planned to stay there, too.

"This is foolhardy, Julian. What will you do in America? Their laws may derive from ours, but I doubt they are the same. Will you become a clerk again, and start over?"

"I will do what I have to do. I will become a fisherman or farmer if necessary."

"You are not being very sensible at all."

"I am being most sensible."

"No, you are not. You are being honorable in the same way that honor leads men to duels. You feel responsible for me now, because of what has happened. The result is that the ruin I feared you would face here will follow you to America, and be worse there."

"I told you that it is my decision whether to pay the cost."

"We will both pay. Do you think to continue an affair? If I use these letters, everyone will know who I am. I will still be a married woman. We will be seen as adulterers. I doubt that is more acceptable in America than here. Less so, to hear Bianca speak of their mores."

"I am not doing this so that we can continue an affair.

You can ignore me on the crossing. You can refuse to receive me in America. You can never speak to me again."

"I do not want you to do this," she said firmly. It was a lie. Her heart grabbed at the notion that she would not be alone, that he would be there with her.

He did not see her thoughts, but he heard her words. His expression sharpened. His isolating reserve fell like a barrier.

"I am still coming."

"I can take care of myself."

"Normally, I would agree. However, your situation is far from normal, and I will be watching your back now."

His voice was calm. Too steady.

Suddenly she understood.

He was not joining her because of the passion of the last few days, but because of the friendship of many years. Not because of obligations created in bed, but because of a chivalry learned as a boy.

She gazed down at the letter of transfer in her hand. He was going to throw over his whole life. Walk away from it.

There was only one reason he would take such a rash, irrevocable step.

"You, too, think he had Cleo killed, don't you?" she said.

"Yes."

"You do not believe I will be safe in America, either. You once said Glasbury could follow me there, and that is what you think will happen."

"I expect he never forgave the humiliation of your leaving. Also, he wants his heir. Such men always do. I think he will do whatever is necessary to have one."

Whatever is necessary. Force his countess to return, or find a way to have a new countess.

"When did you conclude he was capable of this, Julian?"

"After I met with him in London."

Before that first kiss, then.

"Julian, I want to ask Mr. Hampton something. Can you be him again, for just a short while? I need his advice, and I want to know that it will be objective, and the advice he would give any woman in my situation."

"I will do my best, madame."

He smiled as he donned his professional tone. However, that smile gave his eyes a warmth that had her thinking about things she had never thought about with Mr. Hampton.

"Then, tell me, Mr. Hampton: What do you think is my best course of action?"

"I first must know what resolution you seek."

She had to look in her soul, past the confusion of the last weeks, to find the answer.

"I want to stop living like this, being free but not free. I want to never think of him again, nor have to. And I want to be done with this fear that I have now, that he will harm me or those I care about if he cannot get his way."

"You will have none of that if you go to America."

No, she would not. Even with Julian there shielding her, she would not.

"How do I get what I want, Mr. Hampton?"

"You discovered the answer yourself, before I became Julian to you again."

"You mean that I force his hand, and give him easy cause to divorce me."

"He will then have what he wants, which is the ability to remarry and sire a son. You will have what you want. As always, of course, the greater cost will be to you as the woman. However, it does offer a solution to him that has few risks."

"Few risks for him, not for me. What if he is not amenable to this solution?"

"You are safer in London than anywhere. You have friends and family and a household to protect you. You need never be alone. If the world knows you are involved with another man, suspicion will fall on Glasbury if you are harmed. He would have to be very stupid to hurt you instead of taking the easy way out, and he is not a stupid man."

She listened while Mr. Hampton laid out the logic of his thoughts. Something in his eyes left her wondering if Julian would have given the same advice.

"However, madame, I must add that if you do this, it must be immediately, and very publicly. I also need to say that there is no path that guarantees what you want. None that absolutely secures your safety. If there were, I would demand you take it instead of leaving the decision to you. Of the two facing you now, however, I think this is more likely to achieve what you seek."

"And my good friend Julian. What does he advise?"

He did not answer at once. His silence held a moody turbulence, as if his soul fought a battle over the answer.

"Julian hopes that for once in your life you will choose what is best for you, and not for him or anyone else."

That did not tell her much. His eyes hinted at words not spoken, and even appeared a little sad.

Nor could she make this choice as selfishly as he requested. Either path affected him. Both would cost him dearly.

She looked down at the letter of transfer. Both would cost him dearly, but one would cost him everything.

Suddenly the danger of staying in England did not frighten her so much. She knew what she had to do.

She would follow Mr. Hampton's advice. She would take this battle to Glasbury and fight it on ground she knew.

Then she would hand the earl an easy victory.

She rose and walked around the bench to him. "Mr. Hampton, it appears that I am in need of a lover for an affair of convenience."

"I think that is a wise decision." He paused. "Alas, there really is not sufficient time for you to conduct due testing on all the likely prospects."

His reference to her silly list made her laugh. That made him become Julian again. He took her hand in his and regarded her warmly.

"May I offer myself, Pen? It does not have to be an affair in reality, if you prefer not."

It would take a stronger person than she to resist indulging in the crime, especially since she was going to reap the scandal anyway. Despite his words, his gaze and aura were already shamelessly seducing her. His touch might appear discreet, but he managed to make her heart flutter with anticipation.

No, passion and undying love were not the same things. But temporary passion with warm affection could be very nice.

"Are you certain that you have assessed the cost, Julian? Are you very sure that you want the role?"

He raised her hand to his lips. His breath and kiss sent glorious shivers of excitement up her arm. "I would be honored."

chapter 18

Pen and Julian instructed St. John's coachman to make a leisurely pace to London.

They did not hide their identities. They stayed in large towns at the best accommodations. Julian always took two rooms, but the servants would not miss that the lady had no woman servant, and that her gentleman companion was too familiar with her. On two occasions Julian did not use his bed at all, a point the maids would notice.

Two days out of London, they saw the first indication that their behavior had become known. Julian procured a copy of the *Times.* On the back page, amidst the news of the counties, they found a short notice from "an occasional correspondent."

A certain lady of high station was seen in Warwick, staying at the King's Royal Arms. Her only companion was a gentleman highly esteemed at Chancery whose reputation has been unexceptionable. On last hearing the lady's husband, a peer, was residing at his home in London, long anticipating his wife's rejoining him there.

"*Rejoining him.* That last sentence points a fairly direct finger," Pen said.

"The *Times* correspondents pride themselves in choosing their words carefully and economically." Julian set aside the paper.

"Do you think we will be met at the city's edge by the bishop and barred from entering?"

"I doubt it will be so dramatic."

"Once we are in the city, how bold must we be?"

"Bold enough that your servants know more than a discreet woman would want. Are you ready for the scandal, Pen?"

"I confess that if we could put off facing it for another week or so, I would not object."

He took her hand in his. "Nor would I. Not because I will mind the scandal itself, but because these last days have been precious and I would not mind having more of them."

They *had* been precious. Cheerful and carefree and full of a lovely peace. He had treasured them all the more because he knew what was coming.

Soon things would change. The affair would continue, but under the glare of thousands of eyes. The notices in the papers would be less circumspect.

He allowed his mind to dwell on this interlude instead. It might be a sophisticated affair of convenience to Pen, but it was much more to him. He would treasure the memories forever. The friendship and the pleasure. The days filled with conversation or exquisite silence. The nights filled with ecstasy.

They were not met by the bishop, but they were met all the same. Several miles outside London, the coach unexpectedly began slowing. It stopped right on the road. A few moments later the coachman's head appeared at the window. "Best you see this, sir. Ahead, on the left."

Julian opened the door and angled his body out.

"What is it?" Pen asked.

"Carriages. Three of them." He sat and closed the door. "One is Glasbury's. I can see the coat of arms from here."

"What do we do?"

"We continue on. He cannot stop six horses."

"If he brought enough men to fill three carriages, maybe he can."

He called for the coach to continue. As it moved forward he took one of the pistols from its holder on the back wall.

"What are you doing?"

"I am making sure the powder is dry."

"You don't think to use that, do you?"

"I want to be prepared, that is all."

The coach slowed and stopped again.

"The earl's coach has moved onto the road in front of us," their coachman called down. "It is blocking the way."

The color drained from Pen's face.

"He will not remove you from this carriage," Julian said. "I promise you that will not happen."

Horses whinnied outside. Their coachman called for the earl's carriage to pull aside. The response he received was inaudible. Sounds of an argument poured in the window.

Pen's eyes widened. "That sounds like Laclere."

"So it does."

Even while the argument continued up ahead, the viscount in question appeared at the coach window. "Welcome home, Pen."

Laclere's expression was all warmth as he addressed his sister. "You had best come out, Pen. Glasbury will not move his coach until he sees you."

Laclere handed Pen down. As he did so, he gave Julian a quizzical and critical look. Julian read its message. *Is this how you protect my sister, old friend? By subjecting her to scandal and her husband's wrath?*

Julian stepped out of the coach.

Dante walked up to join his brother and sister.

"What are you doing here?" Pen asked her brothers after reunion embraces were exchanged.

"Your progress to London has been well documented. We thought that Glasbury might try to meet you on the road. We decided to make sure he had our company," Dante said.

"All of this drama because of a letter to the *Times*?"

"The *Times* was the least of it. Similar letters have been appearing in less discreet papers all week," Laclere said.

Julian looked ahead on the road. The earl stood behind his coach, as straight as if someone had welded an iron rod to his spine. He was not alone. Several strapping footmen flanked him.

Laclere and Dante were not alone, either. Standing aside, near their own carriages, were Daniel St. John and Adrian Burchard.

"Burchard had a man watching Glasbury's house for any departure so we could follow," Laclere explained. "I think St. John came to make sure his coach was not damaged. He will be grateful that you did not try to run the blockade."

"It appears we may still have to," Pen said.

A shout caught their attention. Another carriage approached behind theirs. The coachman waved his arm to tell them to move forward or pull aside.

"We will eventually have carriages lined all of the way through Middlesex," Dante said.

"Glasbury will have to move eventually, so he may as well do so at once. I will go explain that to him," Julian said. He took a step to do just that.

Laclere caught his arm. "If you address him, it will only throw oil on the fire. You should stay right here. And you should return that pistol that you have under your coat to the carriage."

Julian ignored the last suggestion.

Up ahead, Adrian Burchard walked over and spoke with the earl. He then headed toward them.

Adrian's black eyes and Mediterranean features had branded him a bastard long before his nominal father, the Earl of Dincaster, had unofficially repudiated him. Beneath his urbane charm there lived a deep streak of danger. Astute persons sensed that, even if they did not know the events when that streak had done its worst. Julian wondered if Glasbury had shown enough sense not to insult Burchard.

It did not surprise Julian that the Duchess of Everdon's consort had been the one to have Glasbury's house watched. In his less domesticated days, Burchard had performed missions for the government that engendered expertise in watching and following people.

Adrian greeted Penelope, then glanced back at Glasbury. "He says he wants his wife, and added a few words about Julian that do not need to be repeated."

"She does not go with him," Julian said.

"I told him that, and pointed out that at best he has a stalemate here, and at worst a defeat. He then threatened to call Julian out here and now, but I dissuaded him from that."

"If he wants to meet, that is fine with me."

For a few moments no one spoke or moved. Pen looked at him with astonishment.

"It is not fine with *me*," she said.

"He thought better of it," Adrian said. "He insists, however, that he will not move his carriage until he speaks with his wife."

His wife. That alone had Julian almost reaching for the pistol. "She does not have to speak to him. He can stand there until hell swallows him but he *will not* require anything of her that she does not want."

The men donned expressions of careful blandness in reaction to his vehemence.

Penelope kept looking down the road at Glasbury.

"I will speak with him," she said.

"He cannot demand it. You should—"

"I will speak with him, Julian. Mr. Burchard, will you escort me, please. Tell him that we will talk over there, in that little field, away from his coach and footmen."

Adrian offered his arm. Pen took it and walked down the road. St. John came forward to meet them halfway.

That left Julian alone with Dante and Vergil. They all watched Pen's progress toward Glasbury, and Glasbury's building agitation.

"He is understandably angry," Laclere said. "The whole town awaits the arrival of the two lovers. I assume this notoriety was planned."

"Yes, it was planned. It is good to know we succeeded."

"You definitely did that. This was published yesterday, and has sold quite well." Laclere pulled a document out of his coat, fanned it open, and handed it over.

It was an engraving such as publishing houses made to exploit scandals and political controversies. It showed a caricature of the earl with big horns protruding from his head. He listened while another figure, this time a drawing of Julian, read from a long scroll full of legal writing. Beside Julian was a pretty image of the countess. Julian's arm was behind the countess and, despite his professional pose, his hand was resting on her bare bottom, which was exposed by the way she hiked her skirt in back.

"The artist captured your sister's likeness quite well."

"Her face, yes. I wouldn't know about the rest," Laclere said dryly.

"I thought she was running away," Dante said.

"She changed her mind about that."

"So now she is goading him into divorcing her?"

"That is her hope."

The two brothers shifted their weight. Julian could practically hear them assessing how to interpret this new development.

Laclere would never ask, but—

"So, is it a ruse, this affair? Or are you really Pen's lover?"

Laclere sighed. *"Dante."*

"Hell, if the two of them are going to hang, it seems to me they might as well—"

"Yes, yes, I'm sure it seems that way to *you,*" Laclere said. "Julian, your willingness to accompany and protect her on her flight was chivalrous enough, but pretending to be her lover, and sacrificing your reputation to procure a divorce for her, is foolhardy. The scandal that waits in the city is insurmountable."

Julian was still watching Pen. She and Burchard had stopped on the road, and St. John now spoke with Glasbury. Glasbury began walking toward the field on the left.

Pen stepped away from Burchard and followed Glasbury. Burchard and St. John took up positions along the road's edge, blocking the footmen from reaching the field.

Pen approached her husband.

Her husband. Julian's head almost split from holding in his resentment at that old bond. He hated everything it implied. Glasbury had rights he had abused, and claims he did not deserve. Julian Hampton had none under the law. None at all.

But he now had rights besides those given by the law. Rights of possession.

"I am not pretending to be her lover, Vergil, so I must decline the praise for my great sacrifice."

Dante gave his arm a roguish little punch of approval.

Vergil coughed as if his breath had caught in his throat.

Pen could not lie to herself. The earl frightened her.

Their last meeting at the cottage had sharpened her sense of danger. The recent revelations about Cleo only made it worse. She could not hide her hatred of him anymore, either, now that she comprehended the true depths of his depravity.

He tried to smile, but his mouth could not manage it. His eyes revealed his rage.

"I will crush him."

"I have known for years that you are cruel, Anthony. I never realized that you are stupid, too. You demanded to speak to me, and here I am. If you only want to issue threats, our conversation will be a very short one."

"This outrage is not to be borne. How dare you so publicly flaunt your immorality and adultery."

"It is laughable for you to speak of immorality. Besides, if this outrage is not to be borne, then do as other men do and free yourself of the burden."

His expression relaxed but his eyes still burned. "So that is your game—to have me divorce you."

"I am merely aware that under the circumstances you will have no trouble doing so."

"You speak as if there is no price to be paid if I do."

"I cannot see where there is."

"You are a countess now. If we divorce you will be nothing. Less than nothing."

"Oh, you are talking about *my* paying a price. I have already paid most of it. The fall that waits is a very small one compared to what happened when I first left. With the passing years, such matters have grown insignificant to me anyway. So do not worry for me, my dear. Divorce me with a free conscience. I am sure there are many women who will gladly pay whatever it costs to be the Countess of Glasbury, but I decided *that* price was too high a long time ago."

His flaccid mouth found some firmness. His frown deepened until his eyebrows met. He looked past her to where her brothers stood with Julian.

"This was his idea. He seduced you with this nonsense, and cajoled you—"

"Believe me when I tell you this was *my* idea. Also believe me when I say that I am not returning to you. A wise man would avail himself of the simple remedy."

His gaze sharpened on Julian. "I can think of several simple remedies."

The threat toward Julian was unmistakable. A flurry of panic tried to overwhelm her, but she beat it back. "Do not let your pride lead you to folly. Do not think for a minute that defeating him means victory. He is only my distraction of the moment. There will be others."

"Not if you are back with me."

"Even if I am."

His attention swung back to her. He appeared surprised. Then his anger melted and a leer brightened his eyes. "But of course. I should have realized that your experiences playing the whore would make a difference. Have you learned how to like it, my dear? Does the notion of fidelity to one bed bore you, now that you have enjoyed such variety? No doubt if the man is handsome enough you will even welcome with him what you resisted with me."

She felt her face warming.

He tipped his head toward her. "Return and give me my heir. After that you can have as many others as you desire, any way you want. You can retain your title and live in luxury as you liberally distribute your favors."

She felt soiled by his presence. She turned on her heel and aimed toward her brothers. "Arrange to have another woman give you an heir. If you force me to return, I will make sure that you never know for certain if any child I bear is yours."

chapter 19

They entered London as if in parade. Glasbury led a long procession of coaches and carriages extended by the jam that had built behind their blockade.

The earl's coach pulled out of line near Grosvenor Square, but the Dueling Society's carriages rolled on to Laclere's house. There they joined another collection of equipages that indicated the viscountess was not alone.

Julian recognized every vehicle and horse. The women who had thought to find him a wife had congregated.

Pen walked beside him to the door.

"I expect they all will be wanting some explanation," she said. "This turn of events, and such an indiscreet one at that, must have surprised them. I daresay the fact that it is you has left them quite astonished."

"No more astonished than it has left Laclere."

"Do you think so? Well, he can hardly disapprove. After all, he—" she caught herself and snuck a glance back at her brother. "I am very sure he will accommodate himself to the development."

They found the women in the library. Diane St. John sat beside Dante's wife, Fleur. The viscountess and Sophia, the Duchess of Everdon, were chatting with Pen's sister, Charlotte.

"Well, Julian, if I have to fight scandal's battle, I could do worse than having such formidable troops on my side," Pen whispered.

"And such experienced ones." Of the women assembled, only Charlotte had been spared society's cruel glare.

The most formidable presence was that of Adrian's wife, Sophia. A duchess in her own right, she had tried to repudiate the role. Having finally accepted her position, however, she was not above using it.

She had forced society to accept Adrian as her husband, and wielded the power of her station to protect her friends. There were some very select circles that did not entirely accept her, but even they dared not leave her out completely.

And yet, Julian knew that when Sophia left certain drawing rooms, the tattle turned to how she was not entirely appropriate to her position, and too lax in her choice of friends, and careless to her duty and bloodline in her choice of husband.

All eyes had turned to the door after the footman opened it. Julian stood beside Penelope, with their entourage close behind. Laclere broke the awkward silence that ensued by telling the footman to send down orders for refreshments.

The ladies continued giving Julian a very curious inspection.

Diane St. John came over to embrace Pen. "My dearest friend, it is such a joy to see you again. I am relieved that you have returned to us, and thankful that Mr. Hampton has seen to your safety."

The others found their wits. The ladies descended upon Pen and absorbed her in their welcomes and kisses.

Laclere offered brandy to the men, and they circled and chatted, too.

Julian could see the viscountess eyeing him from across the library while the ladies continued their talk.

My dear Lady Laclere,

I apologize for the surprise. I hope you are not too disappointed that your efforts on my behalf have suddenly been made irrelevant, since good society will never again consider me a suitable marriage prospect. If you wonder why I court such ruin, perhaps you should consult with Mrs. St. John. I have reason to think she is the only person in this chamber who has suspected the whole of it. Or you might ask your own husband, who I have cause to believe risked as much or worse at one time, and for a similar reason.

Your devoted servant,

Julian—

"It seems to me that we have some decisions to make," Laclere said, interrupting both Julian's thoughts and Dante's description of some horse race.

His voice carried enough that the ladies heard. The chamber hushed. All attention turned to the matter at hand.

"We? Do you expect the decisions to be collective ones?" Julian said.

A murmur of "of course nots" and "we would never intrudes" hummed through the library.

"It would help us, however, to know what the decisions will be," Sophia said. "Should we try to blunt the scandal? Deny the allegations? Explain away the gossip? I have received more cards from callers in the last two days than in the last two weeks, often from ladies who normally do not court my company. I am sure they only call in the hopes of hearing the particulars, since they know I am Penelope's friend."

"According to Laclere, everything has been published. One paper even included the meals we ate as we journeyed to London," Julian said. "What further particulars could these ladies want to know?"

"Trust me, sir, you do *not* want an answer to your question," Charlotte said.

"The point is that we are all relying on the two of you to direct us," Sophia said. "If we all put our efforts to it, I think this could still be managed."

"It is not my intention to be discreet," Pen said. "I do not want any of you managing anything. We will let the winds blow as they must."

"It is as we thought, then. You and Mr. Hampton have devised this strategy to invite Glasbury to divorce you," Charlotte said. "I expect it will be a relief to finally end this for good."

"If the rest of you want to have a purpose, let it be protecting Penelope," Julian said. "Glasbury must not have the opportunity to meet with her alone, or find her without friends or family by her side."

"She cannot live in her house if she requires such protection," St. John said. "Her servants could never stand against Glasbury."

"She will reside here," Laclere replied. "I will brook no argument from anyone on that point." He gave Julian a severe glance that said whom he meant by "anyone."

"I think I would prefer to return to my own house," Pen said, proving that her brother had misjudged the source of resistance.

Bianca reached over and patted her hand. "You will stay with us so Laclere can bar the door with his sword. As for your scandal and its intended conclusion, have no fear. If so ordered, our servants can be as indiscreet as yours."

The other guests left, but Julian stayed. When Bianca invited Pen to go up and choose her bedroom, he was left alone with Laclere.

"Let us go out to the garden," Laclere said.

They strolled between boxwood-framed rose beds and ivy-covered tree trunks.

Laclere appeared very thoughtful, but eventually a wry smile broke on his face. "Since Penelope is a woman well past thirty, I realize that there is absolutely nothing I can say to you without being ridiculous."

"Perhaps you should say it anyway."

They walked a bit more.

"This is not the first time one of my best friends took up with her, of course."

"I am not Witherby, Vergil."

"No. He was all talk and wit and charm. One assumed one knew what one had, but in fact saw nothing of the soul. You are the opposite. He was a long, rambling, self-indulgent novel with no moral theme. You are a slim book of poetry."

On the one hand Julian was flattered by the comparison. On the other he knew that novels were more popular, and easier to comprehend.

"Pen is getting the worst of it," Laclere said. "The talk paints her as some Jezebel who had a string of lovers before you. Gossip came back from Naples that is now being freely circulated."

"She had no lovers in Naples. Flirtations, but no affairs."

"That will not matter now, will it? And you, well, you are being painted as her dupe, a man who led a life without incident only to now be seduced to madness by the scarlet woman."

"I am insulted."

"Serves you right for being so inscrutable and discreet over the years."

"I can arrange to let past liaisons be known, I suppose. I could probably find at least one woman who will testify that I am perfectly capable of seduction."

Laclere laughed, and they continued their slow stroll. "Since Bianca all but announced that you are free to continue the drama while Pen resides here, I have nothing to say to that. Except, of course, to ask that you be discreet where the children are concerned."

They walked some more. Julian knew Laclere very well, and could tell that he struggled with something and debated how to broach it.

"You do realize, of course, that divorce is not the earl's only option. No one knows how good he is with a pistol. Inquiries have been made on that, to no avail."

"If he calls me out, we will find out."

"The notion does not appear to bother you at all."

Julian listened to the pleasant crunching their boots made on the fallen leaves.

The pair beside his suddenly stopped. Laclere's gaze

pierced into him. "You all but invited it back there on the road. It is what you expect, isn't it?"

"From a man like Glasbury, yes."

"Does Pen realize that you see this being resolved by a duel?"

"No."

"And if you lose?"

"Then you will have to use that sword to bar the door, as your wife described. I trust you can do so. However, I do not expect to lose."

"I cannot countenance this, Julian."

"If it happens, believe me when I say that Glasbury has done things in his life that would get another man hung. And also believe me when I say that only his death will truly protect her. You may not countenance it, Vergil, but I will welcome it."

"To punish him, or to free her?"

There it was, the question that had been shadowing this whole conversation. "Are you asking me if my intentions are honorable?"

"Damn it, I suppose that I am."

"Regarding my motives in a duel, or those with your sister?"

"Hell, Julian—"

"Should the opportunity arise, because of divorce or otherwise, I would of course do the right thing in light of my role in the scandal that has engulfed her. However, I think that it is unlikely that she will remarry if she is free. The state of matrimony has not served her well, has it?"

Laclere sighed deeply. The little furrows between his eyebrows deepened. "No, it has not." He aimed back to the house. "Let us join the ladies. I think they have had enough time for Bianca to get all the particulars, as Sophia put it."

"You don't suppose that by particulars, she meant ladies are asking whether I am a good lover, do you?"

Laclere actually blushed. "God only knows."

Where the hell were Jones and Henley?

Glasbury smacked his stack of mail against the tabletop in frustration. No letter bearing the tiny square letters that Jones used was among them.

Even if Penelope had given them the slip, they should have written by now. And if the whole of Britain knew which roads she took and which inns she visited, how could Jones not have known?

The lowlife had probably taken the pay and disappeared.

His valet held up his frock coat, and he slipped it on.

"Will you be needing me when you return, sir?"

"No. Caesar will see to things tonight."

"Very good, sir."

Glasbury glanced sharply at his valet's reflection in the mirror. There had been a note . . . a flicker . . . Did this man dare to imply disapproval? There had been a time when such audacity would have meant . . .

He suppressed his rancor. The valet's face displayed nothing at all, let alone disapproval. He was letting the meeting with Penelope anger him more than it should.

He completed his dressing for the dinner party. He hoped the other guests were more agreeable than those at the one he had attended early last week. That Perez had been present at that one, along with his lowborn wife.

The woman had been so bold as to ask him his thoughts about the new law on slavery. Her mixed blood was obvious, and her presence in good society an abomination. She clearly did not understand that she was merely an exotic curiosity of the moment and that nothing had really changed. Her pointed query had implied she was stupid enough to think that the whole country approved of the outrageous infringement on rights that the recent law represented.

He had seen the smirks and glances directed at him when she raised the subject. They did not embarrass him at all. However, he had put her in her place anyway. He had privately let her know that he suspected she was not Perez's wife, but his whore.

That had made her retreat. He had not missed the delicious fear of exposure in her eyes when she looked at him then. He had been unable to resist pressing his advantage once he saw that expression.

He went down to his coach. It was early for the party, but he had other matters to attend to first tonight. Jones and Henley had disappeared, but their work was not completed.

He directed his coachman to take him to the rookery near Newgate. He needed the service of the kind of men who loitered there.

The next night, Pen flaunted her affair in front of the world. She attended the Adelphi Theatre in the company of Sophia and Adrian Burchard, and sat in Everdon's very visible box, where she could not be missed.

Julian joined them, carrying his hat and a walking

stick with an ivory handle. He appeared very handsome and dashing.

As he moved to take his seat beside her, he bowed and kissed her briefly on the cheek. It was no more than something an old friend might do in greeting, but under the circumstances it gave the gossips grist for their mill.

It was not Julian the lover who sat beside her, however. The theater saw the Mr. Hampton they knew, cool in his silence and mysterious in his reserve. The only difference was that he did not leave her side. They greeted the world as two halves of a whole, and no one missed the implications.

"You are very subdued tonight," she said.

"If I act drunk with passion, it will only convince them I have gone mad."

So, he had heard how the gossip was describing the affair.

"They are getting an eyeful in any case," he added. "That is the goal, is it not?"

That was certainly true. From her spot at the front of the box she could not miss the looks in her direction, nor the comments conveyed behind open fans.

His tone in pointing that out had been less than pleasant. She sensed a storm brewing in him.

"It could be worse," she said to mollify him. "I expected to get the direct cut, and no one has done that. There has been some coolness, but nothing truly insulting."

"We are still a novelty. Curiosity is more compelling than righteousness. In your case, I expect the cuts will wait until you are divorced."

"And in your case? It has happened already, hasn't it?"

"It was nothing of significance."

Maybe not, but it had happened. That probably explained his mood. And it would occur again and again. Her heart twisted, that he should be facing that scorn before she did. It really was not fair.

Friends came to visit with Sophia and to welcome Pen home. None of them said a word about the scandal. The words and expression directed at Pen and Julian were carefully chosen. The curiosity shone through, however, and on occasion a touch of the righteousness. Within the first hour, Pen identified two women from her circle who would most likely never call on her again.

Not only old friends stopped by. New ones did, too. When the box was crowded already, Señor Perez, an emissary from Venezuela, arrived with his exotic wife on his arm.

In the low light of the theater, all Pen noticed about Señora Perez's face were her dark, fiery eyes and wide, sensual mouth. The rest of the package was more visible. Her deep scarlet gown was very fashionable in its cut, and very revealing in its décolleté.

There was nothing really improper in her attire, and nothing truly bold in her vivacious manner. However, her arrival immediately made all the other woman look like virginal schoolgirls. Pen suddenly felt awkward and pale and bland.

Several men in the box subtly shifted until they were closer to this exotic flower. It seemed they had no control over their movements, much as iron is drawn to a magnet. Soon she was the center of their attention, even if they spoke with someone else.

It turned out she knew Julian. When he did not join

her admirers, she cast him a smoldering glance that he acknowledged with a slight dip of his head. A smile of amusement broke on her face and she walked toward them.

Pen barely resisted the impulse to throw herself between Julian and this seductress.

Señora Perez accepted the introduction to Pen with a long gaze of assessment. She did not appear very impressed by what she saw. Then she turned her magnetism on Julian.

"What a pleasure to have you back among us, Mr. Hampton. Your absence made life much duller."

"I doubt my absence was even noticed."

"It certainly was. I missed your quiet, deep waters. Within days, I felt completely parched." Her throaty voice made the metaphor heavy with innuendo.

Pen felt her smile thinning. She took some satisfaction in the firm line that had formed on Señor Perez's mouth, too. The husband had noticed his wife's conversation.

Señora Perez's attention followed Pen's gaze, and she saw her husband's glare. She turned back to Julian with a velvety laugh. "It appears that suddenly you are considered dangerous, Mr. Hampton. What a shock for the men to discover what the women have always known."

"Perhaps you should reassure him that I present no danger at all to him," Julian said.

"I do not think that a wife's assurance will console any husband where you are concerned now. Nor am I in the habit of lying to Raoul. Besides, a little jealousy is good for a man."

With that quiet, blatant invitation, she retreated and insinuated herself into a nearby group.

"What a bold woman," Pen said.

"She was only vexed that one bee did not buzz over."

Pen was grateful that her bee had not, but his expression during the exchange had not been entirely indifferent. He may not have rushed to attend on Señora Perez, but she thought he had done some buzzing in the past all the same.

Her jealousy was unwarranted. She had no right to it, either. Admitting that did not quell the urge to smack that woman's face.

"I suppose I should expect such things to happen in the future." She fought a petulance that tightened her voice. "Every unhappy wife will now consider you a potential paramour."

"We knew my reputation would be affected."

"It appears there will be compensations."

He had not appeared at all dismayed by the recent overture. She suspected that the first notes had been played some time ago, and Señora Perez was only continuing a flirtation begun in the past.

"Will there be others, Julian?"

"Others?"

"Other woman casting their lures into the quiet, deep lake? Women not at all discouraged by our affair of convenience." *Women who have been your lovers and will try to get you back?*

"Recently there was Mrs. Morrison, but since she was fishing for a respectable husband I expect she will pull in her line and cast elsewhere."

Good heavens, he was actually telling her the name of his last lover. She now had a name to go with the vague feminine scent in that cottage chamber, and would soon have a face.

"You appear vexed, Pen."

"Señora Perez surprised me, that is all."

"I expect we will both find ourselves treated differently now, with more boldness."

"I expected to be treated differently, Julian. I knew I would be cut and insulted. I expected insinuations about my morals. I anticipated all of that, and I am prepared. I just had not expected women to openly challenge me over *you.* I think you should have discouraged her more directly."

He took her arm and eased her toward Sophia. "I was very direct with her. A woman like that hears what is said even if words are not used. Now, smile, Pen, or the world will think we are having our first row."

chapter 20

In the crush outside after the performance, Pen entered Julian's carriage and not Everdon's. Although she pretended to be quick and subtle, she made sure that at least some ladies noticed.

The arrival of that carriage at Laclere's house, and the departure of it without its owner shortly thereafter, no doubt would also be noted.

Laclere and Bianca had retired early, making it easy for Julian to accompany Pen up to her chamber. The footman who admitted them had not left the reception hall when they began walking up the grand staircase. The maid who waited to attend on Pen accepted her immediate dismissal without blinking an eye.

"I expect that Glasbury will get a lot of mail in the morning," Pen said as she removed her plumes.

Julian set down his walking stick. He strolled around the room, examining the appointments. He checked the bindings on the two books on the table, and ran his fingers along the carved edge of the upholstered chair. His gaze swept over the mahogany bed and its white curtains and coverlet.

"I am sure that he will get many letters, Pen. The affair of convenience has done its job. The indiscretions of tonight will verify all gossip and suspicions."

Something in his tone made her pause with her head-dress in her hands.

"The world will make the assumptions we require, no matter what actually happens between us now."

"What are you saying, Julian?"

"I am saying that accompanying you to this chamber was enough. The plan does not require anything else."

He did not speak unkindly, but the cool distance he had shown all night had intensified. His manner raised a dreadful apprehension in her. Her soul sensed something terrible was about to happen.

"Of course, I would not want you to think you are obligated to play this role longer than necessary, Julian."

"I am not speaking of my sense of obligation, but yours."

"Is that what you think we have been sharing? I assure you, I am not nearly as *obliging* as you seem to think."

"You misunderstand me."

"Then explain, please. You are clearly displeased with something. Was it my little pique over Señora Perez? I am not accustomed to having such gauntlets thrown. I will be more sophisticated in the future."

"It has nothing to do with that woman, I assure you."

"Then what is the reason for your mood?"

He did not reply at once. She sensed him framing his thoughts into words. "I sat in the theater, watching the drama on stage, and I realized we played another in the box. I do not mind that, I promise you. However, once this door closed behind us, the curtain fell. The audience has been satisfied, and our actual affair means we need not lie to a judge. There is no reason for this affair of convenience to actually continue."

"This did not start as an affair of convenience, Julian."

"No, it started as two friends killing the dragon for a night. Glasbury has never been far from any of it, has he?"

Sorrow churned her stomach. Her heart beat painfully, swollen by the sickening heaviness caused by the anticipation of loss.

"Are you throwing me over, Julian?"

She thought she would die when he did not answer right away.

He walked over to her. He reached out and touched her cheek, his fingertips just lying there in faint contact.

"Pen, you have accepted me as the old friend helping to fight the bad memories, and as your partner in the affair of convenience. I am explaining that if we make love again, there will be no good excuse left, except that I want you and you want me. If we do not make love, it will not affect our plan. It would not matter at all."

Except to her. If this tender touch on her face should be the last touch of all, her heart would break. A vitality flowed to her through that gentle contact. It soothed her distress and stimulated her senses. It seduced her as a more blatant touch never could.

He stood an arm's length from her, still contained and complete. His eyes hinted that the deepest currents were not so calm, however.

"Do you want me that way, Pen? With no good excuses?"

She wanted him any way she could have him. She would grieve if he never held her again.

Admitting that increased her vulnerability to him tenfold. It made her both euphoric and afraid.

"Yes. I want you in that way, with no excuses. Very much."

"Then when we are here alone, and the curtain descends, it must be something apart from the public drama. I do not want him here with us. We will tend to all that by day, but at night it must be only you and me."

He began undressing her. His slow, deliberate hands released her from her garments one by one. His manner was subtly different, as if he declared a new right to her as each item fell away. By the time he slid the lacings down her stays, she was thoroughly aroused.

She learned that no excuses meant no defenses. Everything was different. The way he looked at her when her chemise dropped to the floor. The way he lifted her in his arms and carried her to the bed. The way he commanded her passion after he undressed and joined her there.

She almost resisted the way it affected her. Her heart would not allow that. In admitting she could not lose him, she had exposed herself to a wondrous power. His warmth, his scent, his skin, his breath—her consciousness completely filled with his presence and reality, so much that even the pleasure was drenched with it.

She wanted him inside her long before she attained abandon. She longed for the intimacy more than she craved the ecstasy.

She touched his face and pressed his shoulder to let him know. He moved on top of her. It seemed that their bodies fit perfectly tonight, as his strength nestled into her softness.

She trembled when he entered her. The fullness moved her so much she wanted to weep. She pulled him down against her breast and held him tightly, savoring the powerful emotion.

"It is different when there are no excuses," she whispered.

He rose enough to look in her eyes. "Yes."

"There may be no excuses, but there are good reasons. Happiness is a very good reason. So are desire and affection."

He kissed her gently. "Those are excellent reasons."

So is love. Her heart forced the words into her mind before she comprehended what she was admitting.

Not the love for an old friend. One did not want to die at the mere thought of losing the touch of a friend. Only a heart that was in love would fear such loneliness and misery.

"This is really very astonishing, Julian."

"We can be astonished together."

She did not realize just how astonished. She had not guessed how admitting her love would change everything even more. Each touch and kiss and move became another bond, until she felt as linked to his soul as to her own.

He even dominated her abandon. Her cries carried his name. She submitted to the emotions that saturated her climax, so that moment of blind intensity was transformed. Afterward, as they lay entwined and exhausted, she did not move lest she disturb the beauty.

Eventually she had to relinquish him. A few hours later, he rose and began dressing.

She resented that this precious night had to end like this, with Julian sneaking out in the darkest hour. She wanted him to stay with her so they could greet the new day together.

He sat on the bed and angled down for a last kiss. She could not see his face in the dark that had claimed the chamber with the fire's extinction, but that tender kiss revealed more than any expression or word could.

She touched his face. "I wish . . ."

He turned his head to kiss her palm. "What do you wish, my lady? I am yours to command."

Her heart glowed at the playful allusion to their childhood games. Tonight had revised those old memories. They now were deep strong roots that supported this special love.

"It is a terrible thing to think, but . . . I wish he were gone, Julian. God help me, but I do. I wish we did not have to play out any long dramas on the world's stage."

His head hovered, close to hers. "He will be gone soon. It will be over very quickly, Pen. Now I must go, even if I would give up a year of my life to stay even one more hour."

He rose and walked away, melting into the dark.

It was only much later, as her drowsy mind filled with the night's memories, that she understood the other implications of her love.

The stakes in her battle with Glasbury had just been raised.

Julian slipped out the door of the vacant kitchen and passed through the garden.

Considering his euphoric peace, it was hard to believe the night had begun with such inner turbulence.

Sitting in the theater box, he had not minded the curious eyes turned on him, but he had resented like hell the ones that examined Pen. Señora Perez's boldness, and Pen's jealous pique, had only added to the feeling that he had a role in a farce.

His mind had turned stormy at how their game with Glasbury made their affair frivolous and cheap, and more a sham of reality than the play unfolding on the stage below. Their affair had been pleasurable and fun, sensual and friendly, but always a means to an end.

He had walked up those stairs to her chamber knowing he would not continue like that. He would see it all through for her, but he would not hold her again merely as part of a drama played out for society's sake. He would not lie to himself that there was more, if in fact there was not.

She had amazed and awed him. Her words, her touch, the look in her eyes had left him with no defenses at all.

He had loved her for years, as much as his heart could love, but tonight had deepened that love so much that it shook his essence and preoccupied his consciousness.

Suddenly the real world crashed into his tranquil solitude. His instincts shouted a warning.

The dark had shifted. Two figures had emerged from the shadows to block his path in the alley. They did not approach. They merely waited for him to come to them.

He looked behind and saw another figure blocking his retreat.

Laclere had been right. The earl had other options besides divorce.

As Julian walked forward, he removed his gloves so his grasp on his walking stick would be firm.

"Have you been waiting for me all night in the damp? The earl is not very considerate of his servants." He strode right up to them. One backed up a few paces, as if shocked by his boldness. "You are not his smartest men, however, nor very shrewd criminals. I have only to yell, and you will be in prison by daybreak."

"They got to catch us first," the braver one growled.

Julian sensed the arm swinging more than saw it. He ducked and swung his walking stick at the man's knees.

An iron rod falling on paving stones makes its own sound. So does a bone cracking. The weapon clanged and the man sank. A barely swallowed howl sounded down the alley.

Bootsteps heralded the quick approach of the third man. Not waiting for another attack, Julian swung his stick again and sent the second man sprawling.

Julian stepped over both men and faced their final comrade. His companions' moans caught him up short.

"Get them out of here, and bring them to the scoundrel who sent you," Julian said. "Give Glasbury a message from me. Tell him I said it will not happen this way, in a dark alley. If he wants to see me dead, he will have to do it himself on the field of honor."

The last man bent to help his crippled friend up on his good leg. Julian left them to find their way back to their master.

He tapped his stick on the paving stones as he walked down the silent street. At least tonight he had not been forced to use the sword hidden within it.

It was fortunate that Pen's abductors were in gaol back in Lancashire. The earl had been forced to resort to more clumsy and cowardly criminals.

If Mr. Jones and Mr. Henley had been waiting in that alley, someone would probably be dead now.

chapter 21

"Women talk about men's talents all the time," Dante said.

He spoke with great authority to the other members of the Dueling Society, who had gathered at White's at Adrian Burchard's invitation.

It was past time for one of their nights of cards and drink. However, Julian knew that this particular meeting had been arranged for a purpose. The men at this card table sought to show the world that a certain solicitor would not be cut or dropped by some of his influential friends and clients.

Others had not been so generous. Three days after returning to London, Julian arrived at his chambers to find the first letter from a patron explaining he was moving his legal affairs to another solicitor. In the past week, three more such letters had arrived.

"I am sure you are wrong, Dante," Laclere said. "Ladies do not speak of such indelicate matters."

Charlotte's warning about "particulars" had come up

in the conversation. Dante had now obliged them with the least welcome explanation of what that meant.

Dante took a long puff on his cigar. "Believe what you want, but Fleur told me such things are discussed all the time. Openly. Even unmarried women hear it."

"Fleur told you this? *Fleur?*" Laclere asked incredulously.

"That is astonishing," St. John said.

"I was shocked, let me tell you. She told me this well before we married, by the way."

"She was just goading you, Dante. Taunting you because of your amorous reputation," Laclere said.

"I do not think she was only doing that. My impression was that she knew of what she spoke."

"I regret to say that I have some reason to believe that Dante is correct, even with regard to unmarried women, although only those of some maturity," Adrian said. "Before I married . . . well, let us just say that I had some evidence that I had been so discussed."

A thoughtful silence fell on the group.

"Not that any man here has any concerns regarding his reputation in those matters," St. John said.

"Indeed not."

"Of course."

Another pensive silence.

"Gentlemen, let us at least put each other's minds at ease. Can we agree that in the unlikely event that Dante is correct, the ladies keep such indiscreet confidences among themselves?" Laclere said. "Do we all acknowledge that our wives have never reported to us any such gossip about another man?"

"My brother means another man seated at this table, I

think." With an expression that revealed complete confidence in his own reputation, Dante flicked more ash off his cigar.

Adrian's hand went over his heart. "Sophia has never, ever, in any way indicated, even by innuendo, that she has heard that any man sitting here is wanting in that department, I so swear."

St. John appeared very bored. "I am sure that Diane does not participate in such talk."

"Don't all look at *me,*" Dante protested. "Fleur told me they talk about it. She did not tell me what they said."

"I am sure such conversations are not common, and that women talk about many other things when they are together," Julian said.

"Certainly."

"Gowns, children, politics . . ."

"This topic probably does not occupy more than, oh, a half to three quarters of their time," Julian said.

They all laughed, and St. John started dealing the cards. His gaze rose as his hands moved. His expression hardened, and a focused intensity entered his eyes. He glanced sharply to Laclere and continued dealing.

Laclere turned his head for a second. "Glasbury just walked in. Someone must have sent word to him that Adrian invited Julian here tonight."

Julian picked up his cards. He barely noticed their numbers. Most of his awareness was on the unseen earl behind him. He felt that man as if Glasbury were a cold spectre in the card room.

The mutinous corner of his mind had been full of Pen the last ten days. She dwelled there all the time, a beautiful voice and face that calmed and soothed. Her embraces made all the cuts and smirks insignificant.

Now she retreated, and older, harsher emotions stirred. A ruthless anger chilled his blood.

He looked up from the cards to find St. John examining him.

"You are not carrying a weapon, are you, Hampton?"

The other men at the table turned their surprised attention on him.

"To repeat what you once said to me, would you swing for this?" St. John asked. "He is watching us and will come over here soon. I am sure it is not your intention to harm him, but let us be sure you are not tempted. Pass the pistol to Adrian under the table."

The command did not come only from St. John. The expressions of the three others demanded he do it, too.

Exhaling between his teeth, Julian slipped the small pistol from under his coat and placed it in Adrian's invisible, waiting hand.

Glasbury took his time, but eventually he approached their table. He acted as if Adrian Burchard were the only person sitting at it.

"Burchard, I think the membership needs to address the matter of inappropriate guests being invited to the club, don't you?"

"I see no need. We leave it to each member to make that decision himself."

"Normally, yes. One assumes, however, that gentlemen will exercise discretion, and know better than to invite someone who is the subject of notoriety and scandal. If a member's judgment fails him, the other members have cause to complain."

Adrian looked Glasbury directly in the eye. "The thing about scandal is it is often just gossip. If we barred men from these chambers for that alone, we would lose half our members. Now, should you be speaking of a guest who has been officially made notorious, through evidence, I might agree with you. For example, if a man were named in criminal correspondence with a peer's wife, other members might feel obliged to consider that peer's insult, especially if that peer was also a member. Barring that, however, such matters are of no account to this club except as topics of conversation."

Glasbury's spine stiffened. "I see that you are no better than your company. I have some influence at the palace, you know. A few ears that always listen to me."

"What does he mean by that?" St. John asked, simply ignoring how Glasbury hovered by his shoulder.

"They are thinking of giving me a title," Adrian said. "For two years they have been debating it. My marriage to Sophia presents a conundrum. On the one hand, they disapprove and do not want to look to be sanctioning it. On the other, a duchess with a husband who is not titled—well, it doesn't fit right, does it?"

St. John shrugged. "You never fit right."

"They could do it for services rendered to the Crown prior to his marriage, thus ostensibly ignoring the marriage itself," Laclere said. "Only that would require admitting what those services were, which the Foreign Secretary refuses to do. So, the conundrum deepens."

Glasbury did not miss that his presence had become irrelevant. He might have been an extra empty chair at the table.

His face reddened. His steely glare lit on Julian.

"You are a scoundrel. It is not to be borne that Laclere and Burchard bring you here. But then I should have expected it from men who have courted scandal themselves."

"I trust that you are not going to get into high dudgeon of moral indignation, Glasbury. That would be both hypocritical and ridiculous," Julian said.

"I know your game, Hampton. Penelope told me what you expect. It won't happen. I will never let her go."

"Then we have a stalemate, don't we?"

"The hell we do."

"I assume that means you received the message I sent back with those men you employed, and that you came here to challenge me."

Glasbury's mouth slackened in surprise that Julian had lured him to a very uncomfortable place.

"Not a challenge? Just bluster, then. Pity."

Glasbury managed to find his sneer again. "I do not duel over whores."

Five men were on their feet in an instant. Adrian swung out his arm to block Julian and Laclere from grabbing the earl, while St. John held back Dante. Every eye in the card room turned to the disturbance.

"Apologize, Glasbury," Adrian warned. "Explain that your anger got the better of you, or you will leave with three challenges to face."

"On what standing? She is *my* wife."

"I don't give a damn that she is," Julian snarled. "If you insult her, I demand satisfaction."

Glasbury maintained his pose for a few seconds more. Then he took one step back. "I admit it is tempting, Hampton, but I have other plans. I want you to know that today I initiated a petition to the courts demanding the return of my conjugal rights. As for the rest of you, I will be organizing votes against the Parliamentary charter for that Durham project in which you are partners."

Silent astonishment fell on the table. Julian tried to shrug off the hands holding him so he could strangle the bastard.

Glasbury smiled in smug satisfaction at the reaction to his surprise. "My anger got the better of me, gentlemen. I apologize for calling your sister a whore no matter what appellation her behavior deserves."

He turned on his heel and walked away. Julian clawed his way back to sanity.

"Coward," he muttered.

Not a word was said about Glasbury's announcements, but it had subdued them all. They sat down to return to their cards.

Everyone except St. John. He placed his palms on the table and leaned forward to focus an intense inspection on Julian. "He *is* a coward, and you are becoming an idiot. He was right. *You* have no standing. He can challenge you, but you cannot challenge him. A man cannot arrange to kill his lover's husband in a duel and get away with it. What has happened to you? Have you lost your mind?"

Julian glared back at him, but his returning rationality admitted the truth.

Love was what had happened to him, and he *had* lost his mind.

"I think that I will retire now," Bianca said. "I doubt that the gentlemen will be home for many hours."

While the Dueling Society had gathered at White's, their ladies had congregated at Laclere's house. Now that the guests were gone, Penelope and Bianca strolled to the staircase.

Pen mounted the steps with her friend. She wondered if Julian would join her tonight. Perhaps it would be too awkward for him to just come up these stairs alongside Laclere.

Men could be very peculiar about such things. Of course, Julian did not know that Laclere and Bianca had an affair before they married.

She trusted he would visit anyway, so she did not go to bed. She busied herself at her writing desk. Mrs. Levanham had sent her the final draft of the essay on the marriage laws to review. Under the circumstances, the accompanying letter had explained, Pen's name would no longer be included as an author.

She told herself she did not mind, although in her heart she really did. Still, the goal was to begin some social discussion of the matter, not to take credit for the pamphlet.

"The kind of divorce I will have will add nothing to the debate," she said aloud as she read the opening paragraph. "My adultery will be the only issue, and not Glasbury's behavior. My name will contribute nothing to this essay's reputation, and will only hurt it now."

She read the paragraphs that were her own, but which she could never claim. Halfway through the essay, she was distracted by a low rapping on her door.

She knew it was not Julian. He no longer requested permission to enter.

She opened the door to find one of the servants. The young woman appeared a little furtive.

"I am sorry, madame. Someone has come asking for you."

"The earl?"

"No, madame. We know not to admit him. This is a woman. She has been in the kitchen several hours, waiting until the other ladies left. Cook took pity on her and let her stay and told me to come tell you now. We hope that you will not be displeased we did this."

Curious, Pen followed the girl down to the kitchen.

A figure rose from a stool near the pine worktable.

"Catherine!"

"It is good to see you, madame." Catherine tapped a little shoulder, and a young blond girl of about five years stood, too. "This is my Beth. Darling, this is the Countess of Glasbury."

The child's eyes widened. She made a curtsey.

Catherine's manner requested privacy before they spoke further. Pen had the servant take Beth to the other end of the kitchen to play, then sat down with Catherine.

"How is it that you have your daughter with you?"

"I stole her," Catherine said in her blunt way. "I saw how she was being treated, and I had to take her away. She was dirty, and not even sleeping in a bed. They are her family, but they treated her like the worst servant. Look at how thin she is. Do not tell me I have no right. I am her mother, and I have every right."

"I am the last woman to preach to you about your lack of rights. So you just took her?"

"Their own neglect permitted it. No one paid attention to where she was and what she was doing. She could have fallen into a river for all they would know. Getting her away was easy."

"What will you do now?"

"I've decided to leave and take her with me. Go to America, the way you had planned. I hear it is a big country. Bigger than we in Britain can even imagine."

"Yes. Very big."

"A woman and a child could probably disappear there. I must leave quickly, however. Jacob will soon know what I have done, if he doesn't already. Beth said he was due to visit her, and he may be looking for us already. I dare not delay."

"Do you need some money?"

Catherine's blue eyes moistened. "I have no right to ask, I know. Mr. Hampton was very generous when he left me in Blackburn, but I did not expect to be leaving the country then. If it were just me, I would take any berth, but Beth—I do not want her getting sick on the voyage and—"

"Of course I will help you. I will give you what money I have, but I know a way to help with more than money. Wait here until I return."

Pen walked through the sleeping house, back to her chamber. She extracted the pile of documents waiting for her flight, should she ever need them.

Sitting down at her desk, she made some quick changes on three of the papers, then grabbed her brown cloak and hurried back to the kitchen.

"How did you get here, Catherine?"

"We walked."

"Well, we cannot walk now." Pen sent the serving girl to call the night footman from above. She then ordered him to procure a hackney cab. "Be very sure that no one follows," she said. "Be alert to anyone watching the house or alley."

Catherine eyed the cloak in Pen's arms. "What are you doing?"

Pen held up the documents. "One of these is a bank draft from my brother. It has now been signed over to you. I hope it still is accepted. This one is a letter of introduction from him to his wife's aunt in Baltimore. I have added a note that I trust will be understood by her."

She waved the final one. "This is a letter from Daniel St. John to all of his captains. It will get you a berth on any of his ships. One is in harbor here now, due to sail to Marseilles tomorrow morning. I will take you there, explain that you are to have the berth, and also explain to the captain that he is to write another letter to be given to any of St. John's captains so that you can transfer. It will be a roundabout way to make the voyage, but it will remove you from England at once, and eventually you will get to America."

When the cab arrived, Pen hurried Catherine and Beth into it. She gave the footman instructions to follow them for a while, to check that no one had noticed their departure or appeared to be following.

She gave the coachman directions to head for the docks, then settled in. She had taken every precaution possible, and did not expect any interference.

She would be gone only a few hours, and in this anonymous cab would not attract attention. Glasbury would have to be God himself to know how to find her.

She was very sure that she would be safe.

Quite positive.

"Catherine, just out of curiosity, do you still carry your pistol?"

"Certainly, madame. I would not think to travel without it."

Pen sensed Julian in her chamber. His presence roused her out of the deep sleep that had claimed her once she returned from the docks.

It had taken longer than a couple of hours to attend to Catherine and her child. The captain had accepted St. John's letter without question, but required some persuasion to understand that he needed to make sure that the privilege of passage was transferrable. Pen had decided that she wanted him to write it out once he agreed, so that Catherine would have the letter in her possession.

Julian had not been waiting when she returned, which she decided was just as well since he would scold her for leaving. As she had prepared for bed she thought that she heard indications that Laclere had come home, but Julian did not come up the stairs with him.

Now he was here, hours later.

"Did you pretend to go home so that my brother would not be embarrassed?" she asked as he joined her in bed.

"I felt the need to walk for a while."

"To clear your head? Too much drink?"

"To clear my head, but not because of drink. Go back to sleep, darling. I will be here only a short while. I must return to my house soon so you can prepare for your journey."

"Journey?"

"Your brother has decreed that you are all going down to Laclere Park."

"Has he now? That is a sudden decision, since Bianca knew nothing of it several hours ago."

"You are all to leave tomorrow."

"She has done nothing to prepare, and will be displeased by Laclere's whim."

"All the same, you will be off, and I will accompany you. I believe St. John and Burchard intend to bring their families the next day as well."

She rose up on her elbow. "Why are we abruptly forming this house party?"

"Vergil interferes too much. It is an old habit of his and does not improve with the years. Now go to sleep."

She sank back to her pillow and nestled up against his side. She was flattered that he had come when it could only be for an hour or so, but these sudden new plans were very odd.

"Julian, did something happen tonight to raise my brothers' caution?"

"Glasbury was at the club. That is all." He spoke with a finality that ended the conversation.

She doubted that was all. It was clear Julian was not going to tell her what had happened, however.

She would just have to wait and get the details from Bianca.

Pen left London the next afternoon as she had entered it, in a parade of carriages. Transporting Laclere's family to the country was not a simple affair. Children, nurses, governesses, and tutors filled several equipages.

Dante and Fleur rode with Pen and Julian. Pen had been in Naples when Dante and Fleur married, and had only heard the full story of their romance upon her recent arrival back in London. She was grateful for this opportunity to spend some hours with them.

Fleur was expecting, and had just begun showing. Dante treated his wife with a solicitation and care that Pen thought was adorable.

"I really do not need another blanket, darling," Fleur said when her devoted husband tried to tuck a second one around her.

"I think it has gotten colder now that we are in the country. You must not catch a chill, Fleur."

"A woman in my condition is rarely chilled, my love. Quite the opposite."

"Perhaps you should let Fleur guide you on how to see to her comfort, Dante," Pen said. "She will not put herself at risk."

That checked him. "Of course. You are right."

Fleur gave Pen an appreciative glance.

Pen returned one of her own. It was a joy to see the change in Dante, and his unabashed love for his bride. She felt a new closeness to him because of it, since she now comprehended that emotion as she never had before.

Her own lover was very silent on the journey.

She looked at his perfect profile, with the landscape moving behind it through the window. He sensed her attention and looked at her.

He took her hand in his and glanced meaningfully to their companions. Dante and Fleur were head to head in a private gaze, lost to the world.

"And to think I advised against that marriage," Julian whispered.

"Is that why you are brooding? Is the solicitor counting his mistakes?"

"I am not brooding. I was admiring their peace, their contentment in their love, and their joy in the child that is coming."

She did not think he had only been admiring them. She wondered if he had also been envying them.

Her contemplation of that was suddenly interrupted. For some reason the carriage began slowing.

The change startled Dante out of his private world. "Another blockade? Glasbury must know we will not permit highway robbery."

Julian stuck his head out the window. The carriage rolled to a stop, but the sounds of carriages and horse hooves continued in the distance. "We are being followed and hailed, but I do not think it is Glasbury. A coach and four is approaching, and two horsemen."

One of those horsemen galloped past on a bay steed. Julian opened the carriage door and stepped out to get a better view. "He is speaking with Laclere."

"I wonder what this is about," Fleur said. "Do you recognize the man?"

Julian looked back on the road. "Unfortunately, I recognize one of the men stepping out of the carriage that just arrived. His name is Lovejoy, and he is an inspector with the Metropolitan Police."

Dante muttered a curse. "He is also Glasbury's puppet." He jumped out to join Julian.

An old, familiar panic beat in Pen's heart. It was the sensation she used to have when she thought the earl was stalking her, before Julian's protection had made her feel safe.

Suddenly she did not feel safe at all. Even with her brothers and Julian here, even with Laclere's footmen and servants forming an army to shield her, all the vulnerability returned.

A hand touched hers. She looked down to see Fleur's glove covering hers in comfort.

Boots and low voices approached. Julian's expression hardened. Suddenly Laclere was standing alongside the carriage with two men she had never seen before.

Laclere appeared concerned. He stared the strangers down until they retreated a few steps. He then said something to Julian.

They both came to the open door of the carriage.

"We must all return to London at once," Laclere said.

"What is happening, Vergil?"

"Pen, Glasbury was found dead this morning. Someone killed him."

chapter 22

Laclere forestalled the police by pleading his sister's shock and grief. He gave his word as a gentleman that the Countess of Glasbury would return to London immediately to attend to her husband's funeral preparations.

No one in the carriage spoke on the ride back to the city. Julian held Pen in his arms the whole way. Although his voice was quiet, his heart was not.

The earl was dead.

Penelope was free and safe.

His soul yearned to speculate on what that could mean. *Pen resting her gray hair on his shoulder, warming him through winter after a magnificent summer.*

He dared not release the emotions straining to burst in him. He worried about the circumstances of Glasbury's demise.

When they arrived back at Laclere's house, Julian jumped out and cornered Vergil as soon as the carriages stopped.

"I am taking Pen to your study. No one is to join us, not

even you. Send a message at once to Nathanial Knightridge and ask him to come here. Send him to the study as soon as he arrives."

"Knightridge? Surely you don't think—"

"Just do it, Vergil."

Julian fetched Pen from the carriage and quickly escorted her to Laclere's study. She was in such a daze that he had to physically lead her to a chair and press her into it.

He found Vergil's supply of brandy and poured her some. "You have had a shock, darling. Drink a little of this."

She obeyed. Some color returned to her face. "I find myself in a very strange state, Julian. Almost numb. I do not think I have even begun to accommodate the news."

"That reaction is normal. Just rest quietly for now."

"I have wanted this. God forgive me, I have sometimes wished he would die."

It was admissions like that, made while in shock, that he did not want others to hear. "We cannot always control our thoughts. You should not feel guilty for them now."

She made a valiant effort to collect herself. He could see her pulling the pieces back together.

"Julian, those men. The police. Why did they follow us to bring me this news?"

When he did not answer, her head cocked thoughtfully. A startled realization entered her eyes.

"They think I may have had a hand in this, don't they?"

"They will want to ask you some questions. Once it is clear that you have not had any contact with Glasbury since you arrived in London, once they are shown that you have not even been out of this house alone, they will be satisfied. It will end there."

"Except that I have been. Out alone, that is."

"Excuse me?"

"I have left the house alone. Not really alone, but without Bianca or any servants."

Hell.

"When was this, darling?"

"Last night."

Jesus.

"Catherine sought me out. She had her daughter, and knew her husband would be looking for them. So I took her to St. John's ship and gave her some of my documents."

She described the events of the night. The solicitor in him heard them the way a court would hear them. He saw at once the holes that made her terribly vulnerable.

"Who knows that you did this, besides Catherine and the ship's captain?"

"A scullery maid, and the footman who hired the cab. And the driver, of course."

More than one, which meant far too many. One could be bought off, hidden, sent away.

She still appeared dazed. Nothing in her expression indicated that she comprehended her danger.

He lifted her up and sat down in her chair. He pulled her into his lap and embrace. "I am waiting for a man to come, so you can speak with him before anyone else. Until he does, let us think about better things. What will you do now, Pen? Your goal was to be free of him, and suddenly you are."

She looked at him with an odd, blank astonishment.

"That is what I cannot accommodate. I realize that I have no idea what I want to do with that freedom. I never dared to plan or dream how to live afterward."

He kissed her temple. His heart twisted.

If she had never planned or dreamed, it meant that she never really believed it would happen.

"Thank you, Countess. I think that I have a clear understanding of the facts now."

Pen rose to leave the study. Nathanial Knightridge gave her a reassuring smile. Julian escorted her to the door and handed her over to Laclere, who had been waiting outside.

Julian closed the door before Laclere could think of entering.

Knightridge had made himself comfortable at Laclere's desk. He jotted a few more notes onto the sheet he had used, put down the quill, and lounged back in the chair.

He was a tall, athletic young man with a compelling presence. His dark golden hair framed a face with dark eyes that could hold a crowd's attention with ease.

Those physical details, along with a tendency for flamboyance and an undeniable brilliance, had made him very successful at the Old Bailey. At only twenty-six years of age, Knightridge had become famous for his defenses. He possessed a remarkable talent for exploiting the few moves and strategies permitted to defense counsel in criminal trials.

"I will speak frankly, Hampton. The word in chambers is that it was a caustic poison. He was found in his dressing room, and there was blood that indicated intestinal bleeding. There were two glasses and a bottle of wine still there. The remains of one glass smelled of more than the grape. So, he had a guest, and the guest poisoned him. That is the police's thinking."

"Do they suspect the countess?"

"The pursuit of her on the road shows that they do. She could easily gain entry to the house, for one thing. They probably envision that she met with him, pretending to reconcile, and then did the deed. If she were not a countess, and her brother not a peer, I expect she would be in prison already."

"You certainly do speak bluntly."

"If you want me to lie and offer false hope, I will oblige. That will not help her, however."

No, it would not.

Julian stared out the window, seeing nothing.

He should have forced Pen to take that ship to America.

He should have gotten down on his knees and begged her to flee into obscurity with him and find a new world for themselves. He should have asked her to be his lover with no excuses when she weighed her choices in the Bruton churchyard.

Would she have done it? Would the protection he offered have been enough to sway her? Would she have decided she cared for him enough to sustain a lifelong affair of convenience?

"Do you think she did it?" Knightridge spoke as blandly as if they discussed some waif accused of being a pickpocket.

"Hell, of course I don't."

"Then keep your mind clear, or you will be worthless to her. I can think of several ways to defend her that will at least spare her from the worst and open a door to a successful appeal to the King's Bench. However, if she tries to flee and she is caught doing so, that alone will be the noose that hangs her."

Knightridge eyed him sharply, as if seeking reassurance that his warning had been heard. Julian accepted the rebuke with silence. He had in fact begun debating how to aid her escape.

"Should she need your services, will you speak for her?"

"I could not resist this one. Not only because of your friendship, but because it promises to be so dramatic. The sales of the proceedings should be astounding."

"I would never deny you your drama or fame, but I remind you that we are speaking of a woman's life."

"I never forget that, my friend. We are also speaking of your lover's life, are we not? To continue being blunt, you are her motive. If you cannot trust me to do well by her, you had better recommend another man."

"No. It must be you. I will tell her that."

Knightridge folded his page of notes and rose. "Tell her family to put off the police as long as possible. Let her swoon five times a day or whatever it is women do when they are distraught. Have Laclere send someone to Marseilles at once, to see if Mrs. Langton can be brought back. With luck she will not have transferred to another ship before we find her."

"She may refuse to return. She has stolen her daughter, and will not risk being forced to give the child back."

"She must be made to return. I will put an advertisement in the papers in the meantime, hoping to locate the driver of that hackney cab the countess used last night. I think that her only hope of avoiding arrest is if he comes forward."

"Yes, of course, that is a good first step. Do people normally do that? Come forward?"

"Regretfully, if they sniff any attachment to a crime, they almost never do. But we will hope for the best."

"I cannot stay."

They were the first words Julian had spoken in the last hour. Pen's heart sank, and she nestled deeper into his embrace.

His quiet statement had just told her that this would be their last time alone together for a long while.

Maybe forever.

"My brother is very worried."

"Laclere is always worried when those he loves are in trouble."

"I am in more trouble than any of us has been before, aren't I? Even Dante never got embroiled in a disaster like this."

They had all tried to put the best face on her precarious situation after Nathanial Knightridge left. As Julian explained matters to Laclere and Bianca, they had all laughed at how preposterous any suspicions would be.

She might have been reassured if she had not known them so well. But she saw through her brother's forced indifference, and recognized the deep lights of concern in Bianca's eyes.

And Julian had been so very careful with her these last hours. Very gentle and protective. Extremely kind, but in the manner one uses with someone on her deathbed.

"All will be well, Pen." He kissed her as though he might never get to again. That tore her heart.

"If you will not stay tonight, you are not sure all will be well," she whispered. "You think there could be a trial, and that evidence that I took my lover to my bed right after Glasbury's death will sound like I danced on his grave."

"I do not think there will be a trial. The police have been told you are too distraught to speak with them, however. You can hardly entertain me and claim that."

"So I must pretend to mourn him?"

"You should retreat from society completely. If that is interpreted as mourning, so be it."

He was not being honest. She suspected he did worry there would be a trial.

She certainly did. She had no trouble seeing how her absence last night looked. If that hackney cab was not found, she would never be able to prove where she had gone.

She held him tighter and closed her eyes so nothing existed except him. She barred her mind and heart from everything else, and dwelled in the blissful security of his care.

The sweetness was touched by the uncertainty facing them. She was able to block the world out, but it waited right outside their unity, shadowing it. The intimacy was drenched with poignancy, and with her fear that they might never share this again.

"Will you not even be able to visit during the day?"

"I am your family's solicitor. I can visit for short periods."

At least she would see him. They could not be alone, but he would not disappear.

That notion did not help much. She wanted him holding her like this during the days ahead. She did not know how she would survive the nights, and the lonely hours of imagining the worst, without him lying next to her.

Suddenly the full implications of her vulnerability flooded her. If she were tried and found guilty . . .

Even Julian's embrace could not keep the terror from building in her. "At least they do not burn wives who kill their husbands anymore. Or is it different if he is an earl? Is it treason then?"

"Pen, do not—"

"Maybe they would allow me to have the mercy of garroting first, the way it was done with that poor woman up north when I was a girl."

"Darling, you should not dwell on such things."

She could not stop herself from thinking about it. Envisioning it. A trembling shook through her. "I want to know what I am facing. Maybe they will just hang me. Perhaps my status means I will get a silken rope."

He turned so that he could look in her eyes. "You are not to frighten yourself with such speculations. I will not allow your life to be in danger. You will not see a trial."

The trembling conquered her composure. She gazed back at him through a film of tears.

He pulled her into a tight embrace. "Pen, I promise you that you will not be hurt. I swear it. This is one dragon I will definitely slay."

She swallowed the burning tears so that he would think she believed him. "I do not expect you to slay this dragon, Julian. But I am miserable because you will not be able to help me make it sleep in its lair during the nights."

He kissed her tenderly. She could not let him stop. She

needed that kiss to continue. She could not bear the thought of it ending.

He understood. He gently broke her clutching embrace. Leaving her arms, he walked over and locked the library doors. He returned to her, and held out his hand to help her to rise.

He led her over to a padded bench. Sitting down, he loosened his garments, then lifted her skirt and petticoats.

"Like this," he said. He showed her where to put her legs when he guided her down on his lap. With her petticoats crushed against her breast, she straddled him and let her legs dangle down the back of the bench.

He lifted her hips and moved her until they were joined. The connection was very close and deep. They sat face to face, not moving, just sharing the sensation of how he filled her.

She memorized the expression on his face. She branded her mind with the deep warmth in his eyes, and the exciting severity of his desire. In that gaze she understood all his mysteries. She absorbed it all, not knowing what names to give what she saw, astonished anew that this man contained such hidden passions.

He looked at her the whole time they made love. As they moved his gaze demanded she believe he would protect her. His whole aura said he would never allow his lady to come to harm.

She submitted. She allowed herself to believe for a little longer. As their passion turned furious, she gave up her fears.

For one last time she was free and safe in a place where only she and Julian existed, and their intimacy created a shield against the ugly things in the world.

• • •

The advertisements were published in the papers.

Not a single driver of a hackney cab came forward.

Laclere spread the word that he was offering a reward.

Sixty-four drivers of hackney cabs came forward.

"All of them said they took the lady from Laclere's house the night the earl died," Knightridge explained to Julian four days later. "Half of them say she had another woman with her."

"That is a predictable guess, since ladies do not go out alone."

"Unfortunately, yes. Worse, at least twenty say they brought the countess to Glasbury's house. Lacking any imagination in their lies, and even knowing it is her brother offering the reward, they give a story that fits the rumors. There is no telling if our man is even among them, but I will continue with my questions to try and determine that."

"The footman?"

"One hackney cab looks the same as another in the dark."

They had met at a tavern in Smithfield, far from the Inns of Court. Knightridge wore a blue riding coat of surprisingly simple cut, so Julian assumed he had interrupted a day of leisure for the meeting.

"I am confident something will turn up soon," Knightridge said soothingly.

Julian did not miss the tone. He had used it himself often enough. "I thought you were going to spare me lies and false hopes."

"I am trying to be sympathetic."

"I need you to be honest."

"As you wish. I expect that tomorrow or the next day they will demand to speak with her. I also expect that she will be arrested."

"Surely Glasbury's own staff know who visited the house."

"If they do, they are not saying. That does not help the countess, of course. It is assumed they try to protect her. One of them, an old cook, did say that the earl on occasion had visitors none of them saw. It seems Glasbury would arrange it so he himself let the person in. There is no indication that happened, of course, but I will use it to our benefit."

Knightridge was already planning his performance in court, it seemed.

"How do you assess things at this point?" Julian asked, quite sure he did not want to hear the answer.

"Cases like this are very public. Already the papers speculate, and already minds are being decided. Your recent discretion was wise, but I fear it was too late. I see difficulties arising. The opinions of the world carry too much weight in such notorious trials. Juries are swayed, and judges play to the audience, too. Then, of course, they are watching this very closely at St. James."

"In other words, you are concerned."

"If she were some nameless woman of low birth, I think I could get an acquittal because there is no hard evidence. However, your public affair makes it clear she yearned to be free, and that will affect matters. Unless something new develops, I will tell you that I am not optimistic."

Julian had entered this tavern with a weight lodged in his chest. He had hoped against all rational sense that Knightridge would display supreme confidence and put his own growing fears to rest. Instead, Knightridge had only confirmed them.

He imagined Pen sitting in Laclere's house. He saw her facing the questions and then being led away. He pictured her in prison.

He felt her fear as if they shared one soul.

"I am sorry, Hampton. I feel as though I should quote you some poetry to soothe your distress. The problem with poetry is that it doesn't solve real problems, does it?"

A sarcastic response formed in Julian's mind, but it died before it reached his lips. Another reaction obliterated it.

He sorted through an idea that had presented itself.

Actually, in this case, poetry might solve the problem completely.

chapter 23

Laclere entered Julian's study on Russell Square the next night. Without saying a word he poured himself some port. He positioned himself near Julian's chair by the fireplace while he sipped it.

He looked terrible. Drawn and tired. The creases between his eyebrows appeared permanently etched now.

"The police are asses," he muttered. "I question whether it was wise to form the institution when such stupid men are drawn to the duty. That Lovejoy is offensive. I think the earl's death means he is out some private employment, the way he impugns my sister."

"How is Pen faring?"

"She is very brave. Braver than I am, I will tell you that. I am sickened by the whole matter. I see a dreadful future unfolding for her, and I can do nothing to spare her."

Julian set aside the book he had been reading. "Actually, perhaps you can."

"Is that why you asked me to call? If there is a perhaps, explain it to me and I will make it for certain."

"It will require that you do something somewhat dishonorable, and admit to it."

"To hell with honor. We are speaking of my sister's life. Be plain, Hampton. I am in no mood for subtlety."

"The surest way to spare Pen from arrest is to offer someone else to the police instead."

"Yes, but who? Even Knightridge has no theories on who really killed Glasbury."

"I did not go home that night after we parted outside the club, Vergil. I did not go to Penelope, either. I was not anywhere that anyone saw me. For two hours I was about in the city, alone. I later visited your sister, and the night footman can attest to when I entered your house."

Laclere's expression fell. He looked to the fire. "I cannot permit this. I will not have you sacrifice yourself."

"Are you positive that is what I am doing?"

Laclere's gaze snapped back to him.

Julian assumed his coolest reserve so that his friend's questioning eyes would find no answer. The air in the study got very thick.

"There are incriminating papers, written in my hand," Julian said. "They are in a drawer in that desk over there. If you had the slightest cause to suspect me, you might be excused for taking an opportunity to look through that desk to see if there was anything that might save your sister." He rose from his chair.

"Hell, you don't expect me to—"

"I do expect it."

"It is—"

"Dishonorable? To hell with honor, you just said."

"That is different. You are innocent, and you are a friend."

"You do not know I am innocent. As for our friendship, if that is what stops you, I will end it before I leave this chamber."

They faced each other in silence.

Hearing no more protests, Julian strode to the door.

An hour later, Julian returned to the study.

Laclere sat at the desk reading a sheet of paper. Other papers were piled on the desktop. Several had been set aside in their own special stack.

He looked up when Julian entered. He dropped the paper, sank back in the chair, and gestured to the pile.

"Some of these are very old."

"Yes."

"I found the ones where you plot about killing Glasbury, of course." He glanced to the separate little group. "Duels and whatnot. Not really murder."

"They will be enough. I think that you should take them all, however. The history will establish my motive better. It will convince them I am not just trying to be chivalrous by substituting myself for her."

Laclere lifted the paper he had been reading. "You must have been, what, sixteen when you wrote this poem to her. And the letters—I had no idea, Julian."

"Didn't you?"

Laclere let the paper fall. "Perhaps, back then. Milton said something . . . I assumed it passed, as youthful *tendres* do. I never suspected—" he gestured to the stack again, with bewildered amazement.

"I thought it would pass, too. I counted on it. Waited

for it. Made every attempt to encourage it. But it did not pass. Do you think I am a fool?"

"*Hell,* no. God, no. I am stunned, that is all. By your loyalty and your love. Actually, I am more than a little in awe."

"Tie them up and take them. It will be all they need—those, and the reports of that argument in the club, and my hours alone that night. The police will be relieved to know it is me and not a countess. It will make things easier for them."

Laclere hesitated, then began stacking the papers neatly. "I did not realize you had such a talent with the pen, either. Your words are quite moving. The stories, the verse—to think my sister spent all these years surrounding herself with writers, and unknown to her the finest one was standing in front of her, totally silent about his abilities. I should have guessed, I suppose, considering those little epics of yours that enthralled us when we were young."

"These were private, and never intended for the public eye."

"They will not be private soon. Can you bear that?"

"Yes." He could bear anything for her.

Laclere tied the papers into a bundle. He stared at them for a while, then rose. "I will sleep on this and decide what to do."

Julian knew Laclere would want to contemplate the choice, but they both knew what the decision had to be.

Laclere opened the door. With his hand on the latch, he turned back. "I know why you are doing this. I would do the same for Bianca. But there is no need for a lie between us. You can admit to me that you did not kill him."

Julian turned his back on Laclere. Moments later he heard the door close behind his friend.

Pen sat in the garden on a bench beneath a tree. The sun was shining. That raised her spirits a little. It did not completely dispel the clouds in her, however. Ominous dark ones hovered. They made her churn like the sea when a storm approaches.

She kept the panic contained, but it was always there, threatening to conquer her. Maintaining her composure was easier when she was alone. Seeing her brothers worry, watching the dullness that had claimed her friends' moods, only made it harder.

Waiting was the worst part. It reminded her of when she lived with the earl and she knew he would be coming to punish her. He was dead now, but here she was, living again with the sickening anticipation of pain and humiliation that she had experienced back then. The waiting was worse than the reality.

Soon the waiting would end.

Last night Laclere had been so quiet, so brooding, that her sense of danger had spiked. Then Dante had visited, and he and Vergil had disappeared into the study. When Dante emerged, he looked so dismayed that she had wanted to comfort him.

A funereal mood had claimed the house this morning. Everyone knew that the police were coming to speak with her today.

She would not be able to exonerate herself. They would put her in prison.

She might never sit in the sunshine amidst a garden again.

Her eyes misted. She held onto her sense by a thin thread. She groped her way back to some control.

The thud of the garden door made her jump. Steps sounded on the path. Her heart began beating so hard she felt the throbbing in her temples.

The police must be here. Laclere was coming to bring her to them.

She closed her eyes and gathered her dignity. She would not embarrass herself or her family. She would behave with the decorum appropriate to her station.

The steps stopped in front of her. Bracing herself, she opened her eyes.

"Julian!"

He smiled and sat down beside her. "The day is unseasonably fair."

She looked up the garden path. "No chaperones?"

His arm circled her and he drew her near. "No chaperones."

They had not been alone in over a week, since that dreadful day. He had not touched her since they made love in the library. "I have missed you terribly."

"My love is always with you, even if I am not."

It was the first time he had used the word. It made her heart glow to hear it. She was glad that he also thought what they shared was love. He did not mean it the way she felt it, but just the word made it more special than friendship or passion or affection.

"I know that. But it is good to have you with me, too, now. Especially since . . ." She bit back the words. She did not want to ruin the tiny oasis of peace that had just formed.

He caressed her shoulder and pressed a kiss to her hair. "I am sorry that you had to suffer such fear, darling. You no longer do. You will still be questioned, I expect, but not today. You are no longer suspected."

"I am not? What has happened?"

"They have turned their attention elsewhere."

Her heart skipped a beat, then broke in the best way. A glorious relief sparkled through her. She threw her arms around his neck and gave him a happy kiss.

They both smiled at the same time and their teeth knocked. She giggled and looked up at him. His mood matched her own. She could not remember seeing him so happy, so clearly light of heart. Almost boyish.

"I cannot believe it. Just last night my brothers appeared to be preparing for my wake. Even this morning—"

"Knightridge just sent the word to Laclere and me. Believe it, Pen. You are safe now."

"As you promised I would be." She nuzzled the crook of his neck and inhaled deeply. She would not have to cling to memories of his scent and strength now. She would actually have him in her arms.

"Once this has passed, can we go back to the cottage, Julian? I would love that. Just you and me. I want to make love in that chamber of yours that overlooks the sea. You said that the sounds of the surf are so clear it is as if you are lying on the waves."

He tucked her closer and buried his face in her hair. He just held her like that for a precious, perfect minute.

"We will go there as soon as we can."

She could hardly contain how wonderful she felt. "I

keep giggling like a fool, but it is as if I am rawly alive. The sun is warmer and the breeze fresher. Oh, Julian, this is the grandest day. To be truly free of fear—to be out of all the shadows, old and new—I hardly know what to do with myself."

He laughed. "What do you think you want to do?"

"I want to spend the entire day with you. I want to go somewhere and run in a meadow and get ruddy cheeks and play like a child." She jumped up and tugged on his hand. "Let us go down to Laclere Park. We can forget all of this trouble for a few days."

He tugged back and she fell into his lap. "I cannot go to Laclere Park. There is something I must do late today. We can go to Hampstead, however. The chevalier's property has a meadow and a woods. Would that be good enough?"

She hooked her arm around his neck and pecked a kiss on his nose. "Anyplace is good enough, Julian, now that I know we can be together."

The Chevalier Corbet welcomed them. He fed them a simple meal, chatted amiably, then quietly vacated the premises.

Once she and Julian were alone, Pen strolled into the large hall where Laclere and his friends had practiced their dueling skills since back when they were in university.

"I have no trouble picturing you all here," she said as she examined the sabres hung on the wall. "After all, I once saw it."

"That was very naughty of you."

"It was, wasn't it. I did not expect to be discovered." She laughed at the memory. "Oh, how Laclere scolded. He was not much more than a boy, and he puffed up with authority like a parent. Thank God Bianca saved him, that is all I can say."

The empty chamber echoed with their steps. She saw the young men of the Dueling Society as she had that day, their sabres clashing, their naked torsos gleaming with the sweat of their exercise.

Most of them hurried to put on shirts when they realized she and Diane were watching. One of them gave her a mesmerizing, seductive smile as he did so.

Not Julian.

Witherby's ghost suddenly stood beside her, exuding the charm that had made him so attractive. His memory no longer made her sad. She looked back on that episode now with astonishing indifference.

She glanced at Julian and guessed that he was reading her thoughts. "I do not mourn him any longer, Julian."

"I am glad."

"My only regret is that . . . I suppose I regret that it was not you back then. I wish that you had been the one to pursue me, and not him."

"Would you have noticed if I had?"

"I do not know. Perhaps not. I may have been too young to understand. Too young to appreciate you. I am a little nostalgic, however. And jealous, for no reason. I suppose that I wish you had wanted me back then, and thought of me that way."

"Actually, I did think of you that way back then."

She laughed. "Well, perhaps you did on occasion. As you told me, men have a habit of thinking of women that way in any case." She grabbed his hand and dragged him to the doorway. "Now, let us go out to the meadow while the sun is still high."

It was a perfect day, the best in her life, full of laughter and games and shining with the bright future she envisioned. Her shoes got muddy and her gown soiled as they played some of the games of their childhood. They enjoyed long kisses and caresses between adventures, and twice made love in the dry grass, oblivious to the chill in the air and ground.

When the sun started fading, they rode back to London in Julian's carriage.

"We look dreadful," Pen said, picking a burr off her ruined skirt. She brushed at some grass on Julian's shoulder.

"I would not trade the day for the cleanest garments in the world," he said.

"Nor would I. I wish we had some wine. I would toast to many more days like this."

The city was dark when they arrived back at Laclere's house. Julian helped Pen down from the curricle.

"Julian, that carriage there looks familiar." She gestured to a carriage nearby. "Isn't that the one that stopped us on our way to Laclere Park? The police must have come to speak with me today, after all. Why would they wait if I was not here?"

Julian looked to the house, then the police carriage, and finally at her. "When we go inside, I want you to immediately retire to your bedroom, darling."

The day's joy disappeared in a snap. The last week's fears returned like a cold wave had broken against her heart.

"Julian, did you lie to me this morning when you said

I was safe? Did you just want me to have a last day of freedom, without fear?"

He took her face in his hands and looked down at her. "I did not lie. Now, go to your bedroom. Promise me that you will remember what I said in the garden: My love is with you even if I am not."

"Why would you not be with me? First you say they have not come for me, then you say—"

"They are not here for you, Pen. They are waiting for me."

chapter 24

She did it the way Julian asked. She retired at once to her bedroom.

Then she ran to another chamber that looked down on the street.

For a horrible half hour she waited.

Light spilled into the darkness as the door below opened. Julian walked over to the police carriage, accompanied by two men. They got in and the carriage rolled away.

She saw nothing after that except an ocean of tears. She cried so hard it hurt. She sank to the floor. Holding herself, gasping for breath, she succumbed to all the dread she had been holding in during the last ten days.

The presence of another person broke through her misery. She looked up and saw Vergil standing ten feet from her, holding a lamp. He put it on a table and came over and sat on the floor with her. His embrace only made her cry harder.

Finally the worst passed, but only because she was

exhausted. The return of composure did not make her truly calm.

"You knew," she whispered into his shoulder.

"Yes."

"You let him take me away today and pretend all was well, and you knew what would be waiting when we returned."

"It was how he wanted to do it."

"He acted so happy with me. I never guessed. Not for an instant."

"Perhaps because he truly *was* happy with you."

She inhaled deeply and wiped her eyes. She eased away so she could see her brother's face.

"You must not allow him to do this. You must go and tell him that I won't have it."

Vergil stretched out his legs and rested his back against the wall. "I think it is out of our hands now, Pen."

"He did something to let them think it was he in order to spare me. He is just trying to protect me."

"If so, he will not listen to my pleas that he not do it. Nor will I make such a plea."

She couldn't believe her ears. "Are you saying that you condone such a lie?"

"You are my sister. I will condone anything that saves you, I expect."

"Even the conviction of an innocent man? Your friend, at that?"

He did not answer. Nor did his eyes meet hers. He appeared terribly beleaguered.

"Vergil, we do agree that this is an elaborate deception on his part, don't we? You do agree that Julian is innocent, don't you?"

To her astonishment, he did not reply at once. He actually appeared to be weighing the evidence.

"He refused to tell me that he is innocent, Pen. I asked, and all I got was his damned silence. But, yes, I do believe he is. Not because he is my friend, nor because I think he is too good. In truth, I have concluded that if he believed you were in danger he would not hesitate to kill."

"I trust you did not give such a strange testimonial of his character to the police."

"Pen, he was hoping there would be a duel. Whatever reason he gave you for returning to London, that was how he really expected this all to end. He counted on your affair to force Glasbury into a challenge."

A duel. A furious rebellion swelled in her. Her mind started forming a scathing response to her brother's accusation.

But memories came to her, of Julian promising protection. Even that first night in his library he had sworn Glasbury would never force her to return. *I will do whatever is necessary.* How often had he made that promise with such firm confidence?

She had always assumed he was just reassuring her.

"Vergil, if you think he is capable of this, why do you believe he did not do it?"

"It was poison. Julian would never use such a sly and cowardly method. If he had killed Glasbury, he would have thrust a sword into the scoundrel's heart."

"You do not intend to help me at all, do you?"

Knightridge posed the question with considerable irritation as he paced around the cell.

Not that it permitted decent pacing. It was a tiny, damp chamber, but Julian knew it was one of Newgate's best. His friends had bribed the warden to ensure the new inmate received the best treatment the prison could afford, such as it was. His status as a gentleman's son and a solicitor had gotten him a bit of deference as well.

"This is the trouble with men like you," Knightridge snapped. "When you finally fall in love you suddenly become stupid. I am personally insulted that you had so little confidence in me that you thought up this ridiculous—what statements did you make to the coroner's jury?"

"I said almost nothing. I could not deny that I was not home that night. I admitted I could not prove my movements in the city. I refused to answer questions regarding my relationship with the countess—"

"Lot of good that will do, man. The whole country knows about that."

"All the same, as a gentleman I refused to discuss it."

"Did you at least deny that you killed him, damn it?"

"Of course. Doesn't everyone deny it?"

"Don't get flippant with me, Hampton. *Jesus.*" Knightridge stared at the floor. "Fine. Let me make sure I understand. Your movements are suspect, and you cannot prove you were not at Glasbury's. You have been having a very indiscreet affair with the countess, but the earl had made no moves toward the divorce you hoped for. Worse, he initiated a petition for restoration of his conjugal rights. He threatened to intefere with a project in which you are invested, and you are the partner least likely to survive the financial blow if he succeeded. There was a public argument that evening and you had to be restrained and announced you would have satisfaction."

The litany left Knightridge scowling more deeply and shaking his head with dismay.

"They also have some papers of mine, it appears."

"Papers?"

Julian described them. "In a few, while in deep melancholies, I fantasized about killing Glasbury."

"Wonderful." Knightridge paced some more. "I intend to find out how they came into possession of your papers. That may lead somewhere."

"I would prefer you not do that."

Knightridge crossed his arms over his chest. "If it is your goal to hang—"

"It is not my goal to hang. However, you are to do nothing that will shift suspicion back on the countess. *Nothing.* You are to keep her as removed from this as possible."

"Damned little is possible here, let alone that. She is in the thick of it. I will do what I can for you, Hampton. I am relieved you do not care to hear false hopes, however, since I cannot even offer those at this point."

As if losing Julian was not bad enough, Pen was forced to abandon him for three days. Her brothers tucked her into a coach and brought her to Glasbury's country seat in Cambridgeshire for his funeral.

There she had to play the widow in a public ritual and procession, when everyone present blamed her for the earl's death. Her brothers stood by her side, their faces carved in stone, staring down anyone who looked her way too long.

After the burial, after the polite condolences, after she had borne more glances and seen more whispers than she ever thought to endure, she retired to the library with Laclere and Dante. She tried to restore herself before she had to continue the display by playing hostess to the lords who had served as pallbearers.

She felt like a stranger in this huge house. It had never been her home. Glasbury preferred that obscure, isolated house in Wiltshire when he went to the country. No guests ever visited there. No house parties were held. When they retreated from town life, it was for privacy that permitted Glasbury to indulge in a very special kind of sport.

Dante and Vergil just sat with her. None of them spoke. She spent the minutes wondering how Julian was faring, picturing the horrors of prison. She kept biting back the questions that it would pain her brothers to have to answer.

The door of the library opened and a white-haired gentleman let himself in. It was Mr. Rumford, Glasbury's solicitor.

"I am wondering if there is anything that you require of me, madame. If not, I will return to town." He spoke in a clipped tone, as if he struggled to hide his dislike of having to address her.

"Have you arranged for all the servants to stay on at the various properties?"

"It is all dealt with. I have also informed those who received bequests of their legacies, and made arrangements for any bills to come to me for payment, if that is satisfactory to you."

She really did not care. Mr. Rumford was well respected. She was sure he would manage everything wonderfully.

"I assume the heir has been contacted," Laclere said.

"I wrote to the nephew. Since he is in Jamaica, I expect it will be some time before he learns of the sad event. There may be some delay in his return as well. The estates there are in a bit of a turmoil, as adjustments are made to the emancipation of the slaves. Until he arrives back, of course, the countess has full use of the properties."

If she is so bold, his voice seemed to imply.

Mr. Rumford took his leave.

"His tone bordered on impertinent, no matter how correct his words," Dante muttered.

"He does not know me at all, Dante. I think I met him once before. He also assumes I am responsible, if not actually an accomplice."

"That will pass," Laclere said. "It is the kind of gossip that grows old fast."

That was not true. She might not be the first topic of the day for long, but she would be tainted forever. The little place she had carved for herself in society would shrink even more, she did not doubt.

None of that was of account now. All that mattered was the man sitting in a fetid prison cell.

"I want to see Julian when we return to London," she said. "Bribe whom you must, but get me in there."

• • •

In the hour before dawn, Pen entered Newgate Prison in the company of Charlotte and Mr. Knightridge.

"The warden has the discretion to permit this," Knightridge said.

Evidently that discretion could be influenced by gifts and considerations. Pen wondered what this had cost Laclere.

"Usually such visits are only permitted just prior to execution," Knightridge continued.

"You sound as if you do not think my sister should be allowed to see him," Charlotte said.

Despite the gauze of her black veil and the vague light of the torches, Pen recognized her sister's expression of pique. But then Charlotte's tone had conveyed it well enough.

"I have seen innocent men hang after being denied the comfort of friends and family, madame. I do not regret your sister's privilege. I merely am aware it is unfair."

"Then put your efforts into reform, sir. My sister is distraught enough and does not need your lectures."

"It was not a lecture. Only an observation."

Charlotte's eyes narrowed. She opened her mouth to respond.

Pen placed a restraining hand on her arm. "It seems that the two of you never have a civil exchange. Whether it was an observation or a lecture, Mr. Knightridge, I do not mind. I am grateful that you have arranged this."

Charlotte's mouth closed firmly but her eyes continued sparking.

He led them through a dreary reception room, to an old heavy door, and into a dark office.

The man inside merely nodded when he saw them. Mr.

Knightridge introduced him as the prison's assistant warden.

The warden left. The minutes dragged slowly. Pen had noticed how her emotions were distorting time. Some hours flashed by, but others stretched forever. The ones during the nights seemed never to end.

"He may appear changed when you see him," Knightridge said. "He has been in prison six days now, and it affects a man quickly."

Charlotte took her hand to comfort her. Pen let her, but she found more comfort in her own heart. Her desolation had cleared somewhat these last days. Beneath the horrible foreboding, growing through the sickening fear, a new emotion had emerged. Anger.

The warden led in his prisoner. Charlotte's breath caught. Pen barely hid her own shock.

Julian was in chains.

He stood tall and proud, exuding the same reserve he showed at parties. He had been shaved, no doubt another privilege bought with a sly coin. He acted as if he did not notice how the shackles impeded his walk and restricted his arms.

"Leave us," Knightridge said to the warden.

"I don't think as how—"

"The prisoner is restrained, the women are widows of peers, and I am a gentleman. You can have no concerns. Leave."

The warden left, but not happily.

Once the door closed, Julian turned to Pen. "You should not have come."

"Mr. Knightridge sees no danger in my visiting you."

"That is true, Hampton. I think that the countess's

devotion to a friend will be well received by society. How callous if she simply ignored you now."

"It may be misinterpreted," Julian said. "I told you to do nothing that might—"

"Is a solicitor going to tutor me on criminal trials now? Mind your wills and entailments, and let me tend to saving your neck."

"I trust that you do not intend to save his neck by risking my sister's," Charlotte said.

Mr. Knightridge sighed with strained forbearance, as if suddenly reminded that a certain nuisance existed from which he could not be spared. "My dear baroness, you agreed that if I permitted you to join your sister, you would not interfere. In the future I will request that Lady Laclere be her companion."

"You did not *permit* anything, sir. I remind you that—"

"Please, Charlotte. Upbraid him when we leave if you must, but do not waste what little time I have with Julian in this manner," Pen said. "If this visit is misunderstood or misinterpreted, I do not care, Julian. If some think it implies I am an accomplice, so be it. When I am allowed to see you during this ordeal, I will do so."

With a smug expression of victory that did nothing to extinguish Charlotte's fire, Mr. Knightridge went to the door. "Madame, if you will join me, perhaps we can permit the countess a few moments alone with Mr. Hampton. I am sure that I can intimidate the warden for a short while."

His glance as he left warned it would be very short indeed. As soon as the door closed, Pen went to Julian and embraced him.

"Do not scold. Do not. Just let me hold you."

He could not embrace her back, but he pressed a kiss to her head. "I am too grateful to scold."

"You are not chained all the time, are you? I could not bear it if—"

"The assistant warden fears a dramatic escape, so he put them on me when he brought me here."

That was a relief. She did not want to picture him shackled day and night.

"I know you did not do this, Julian. I wish you had not created this deception."

"There is no deception. Every bit of evidence they have is true. I created nothing."

"Then you must deny it."

"I have. They think they have enough, however."

Yes, they did. That was all that would matter. Content they had their killer, they would not look further. Wasn't that what had happened with her? Julian had saved her simply by giving them someone else to take her place.

"Julian, you did not do this. And I did not do this. But someone did."

"I doubt that you and I are the only ones who knew what he was, Pen. There may have been dozens of people who wanted him dead."

Dozens who wanted it, but not dozens who could do it.

The anger that had been growing formed into a cold determination in her heart.

Somewhere a man was sleeping in his bed while Julian languished in prison. The real murderer walked the streets freely, secure that another would take his place on the gallows.

She embraced Julian tighter, soaking in the human

warmth that would have to sustain her for days. Her contentment did not only come from hearing his heart beat and feeling him breathe, however. A very calm and firm resolve had claimed her.

She knew what she had to do. It was time for her to be the one to lift sword and shield.

chapter 25

"I am asking all of you to help me," Pen said.

She sat in her drawing room, wearing the dull black gown required by her mourning. She had finally returned to her own house the day before, after leaving Julian.

Her dearest friends circled her.

"Tell us what is required," Sophia said. "We are at your command."

"It is not a pleasant duty, I am afraid. You may choose to refuse."

"I doubt that," Fleur said.

"If you do refuse, I will understand. The earl is gone, after all. He cannot defend himself. I only consider this because of Julian."

"He could not defend such things even if he lived, so stop being so kind," Charlotte said. She alone already knew the purpose of the meeting.

Pen had discussed it with her yesterday once they were alone. Charlotte's reaction had been extreme, loud, and full of the kind of language a lady was never supposed to utter.

"I think it would help Julian if it were known why I left Glasbury. Mr. Knightridge agrees," Pen explained. "When ladies intimate they would like the particulars, perhaps all of you should satisfy them. Especially you, Sophia. The very best ears visit you."

"If a duchess's gossip can help you, I will fill those ears. Just tell me what to say."

That was the hard part. It had helped to practice with Charlotte. Still, describing those terrible experiences, admitting her cowardice about Cleo, would be hard. Her heart shrank from the idea of the whole world knowing.

These were her friends, however. She had no need to worry about their reaction. And if it would help Julian—

"I learned within the first year of my marriage that Glasbury had expectations of a wife that were not normal or honorable."

She told them what she meant. She revealed more than she had ever told Julian. For fifteen minutes she gave words to memories that could still make her cringe.

Fleur's mouth fell open by the third sentence and never closed again. Sophia appeared in shock and Diane close to tears. Bianca's expression turned to stone.

She did not have to spell out her suspicions about Cleo's death. She could see them jump to the same conclusions as soon as they heard about it. Bianca noted aloud how that death matched the timing of the earl's attempts to make her return.

Charlotte noted their reactions with furious satisfaction. "It is a wonder you *did not* kill him, Pen."

Bianca tapped her fingers thoughtfully on the rose damask cloth covering the sofa where she sat. "If this is known, there will be many who think Julian should have killed him, too. I assume Mr. Knightridge anticipates that."

"I think he does," Pen said.

"So there will be two trials. One in the courtroom, and one in London's drawing rooms and coffee shops," Fleur said. "My own experience is that the latter can influence the former."

"Was it Mr. Knightridge's idea to reveal this, Pen?" Diane asked. "If so, he is quite brilliant in comprehending the ways of the world."

"It was Pen's own idea," Charl said. "And Knightridge's brilliance is much shadowed by his arrogance, if you ask me."

Bianca chuckled. "And if anyone doesn't ask, you will tell them anyway."

"Will you do it?" Pen asked. "Can you? It is so sordid and dreadful that—"

"Of course we can," Bianca said. "Each in her own way. Not all of the particulars need to be given. Imaginations will fill in the gaps. I daresay there are those who suspected his tastes in such things, and who will now remember their misgivings. Discretion will be thrown to the winds, especially among the men when they are alone."

Pen gazed down at her hands. "I am not without my own misgivings, I will confess."

"You sacrificed yourself to discretion for years, dear

friend," Diane said. "You protected his reputation during his life, at great cost to yourself. After what you have said about that child he misused, I for one do not care if his name is ruined now."

"We are going to do this whether you give permission or not," Charl said. "I certainly am."

"Chin high, Pen."

Laclere muttered the reminder as he handed her out of the coach in Hyde Park.

She smoothed the black bombazine over her petticoats and stiffened her spine. Already heads were turning in her direction. A carriage slowed as it passed so its occupants could stare.

Dante offered her his arm. Laclere flanked her other side. The light wind fluttered the ribbons of her bonnet around her face as they strolled.

It had been only two days since she met with her friends, but she suspected that many of the people who noticed her arrival in the park had already heard about her marriage.

Her brothers obviously had. She could tell they knew. Savage fires burned in their eyes whenever Glasbury was mentioned.

"I have been the topic of gossip before, of course," she said. "It is a bit different to be outright notorious, but not too disconcerting."

Dante patted her arm. "This is hardest the first time, darling. But you cannot hide, and must brave it out. It is the only way."

She had never intended on hiding. If her brothers had not come for her today, she would have sent for them.

"Adrian has ridden to Blackburn," Laclere said. "Sophia told him about that abduction. He intends to see if he can bring Jones back to London."

"I doubt Mr. Jones will admit to killing Cleo."

"In the least, Adrian will clarify that it was you who was abducted, at the earl's command."

"That may only convince the judge that Julian had more cause to kill Glasbury," Pen said.

"We will let Knightridge decide whether or how to use it. I fear the judge may already have sufficient cause to condemn Julian. If it can be cast as defense of a woman imperiled, it may be worth the risk."

"Will you be going to the trial, Pen?" Dante asked.

The schedule had been posted. Julian would be tried in two days. Time had become distorted again, this time running fast, with frightening speed. Running out.

"Of course I am going. It is too late to pretend he is not my lover. We will face this together."

Crowds milled in the streets outside the Old Bailey. Hawkers congregated to profit from the trial's notoriety.

As Dante's carriage rolled to a stop, a boy rushed up to offer a broadside containing a lurid description of the crime. Dante's reaction was so icy that the child blushed and ran off to find other customers.

Pen stepped out. Dante's carriage had not been recognized, but her mourning attire drew attention. The crowd jelled into one mass that began closing on them.

"Quickly, Pen." Dante took her arm and hurried her into the building.

The courtroom was packed. Her arrival in the gallery caused a great stir. The gaping faces struck her as so many challenges. On impulse, she reached up and folded the veil back from her face.

"They all know who I am," she said to Dante. "This veil is ridiculous. Let them look and enjoy the entertainment for all it is worth."

Dante had sent servants ahead to save seats. He squeezed Pen through the crowd and got her to them. Soon other bodies were leaving and being replaced around her. Laclere came with Bianca and Fleur, and the St. Johns and Charlotte followed.

A new commotion drew attention away from their group. Pen turned. A little aisle formed, and a short woman of regal stature walked along it, wearing a stunning apple green dress, a yellow shawl, and a flamboyant hat with two huge plumes.

The Duchess of Everdon had come, and was making sure everyone knew it.

Sophia took a place right next to Pen and smiled impishly. "Do you think the wags will report that I am overdressed for a trial?"

"Of course not. Your taste is always above reproach."

Sophia's smile indicated she knew her taste was not celebrated. "I thought I would give them a good show. The hat will also make it easier for Julian to find us. Before Adrian went to Blackburn, he told me to be sure to sit beside you today."

The true show was that a duchess had come at all. The glaring eyes and buzzing whispers had not touched Pen's composure, but the kindness of her friends now did.

"I doubt the accused has ever had such impressive supporters," Pen said.

"I think there have been a few cases of treason where we were surpassed," Sophia said. "It appears they are preparing to begin his trial." She took Pen's hand. "Courage, now."

Pen had to admit that Mr. Knightridge made an impressive counsel. With his commanding height and spotless wig and gown, he made the judge appear shrunken and old. With cool wit and insinuating tones, he questioned the witnesses in ways that entertained the crowd and also revealed ambiguities in their information.

Julian proved unhelpful to his own case. His reserve looked arrogant today, even cold. His lack of emotion as he gave his story had mouths pursing.

Pen's heart broke as she watched him holding onto his dignity despite being an animal on display. She imagined what a torture it must be for him to be pilloried in this public arena. He did not even proclaim his innocence very forcefully.

She knew why. He did not want them looking elsewhere. He did not want them turning back to her.

He had noticed her as soon as he entered, but he never looked at her after that. She sat through it all, face stoic but heart bleeding. She watched the evidence laid down against him, and felt him slipping from her embrace forever.

The prosecutor walked toward Julian with some papers in his hand. "You hated the earl, didn't you, sir? You wished him dead, in fact. This document is in your hand.

In it you plan Glasbury's death. There are several of these, written over the years. Let me read them for you."

He read them. They sounded like diary entries. In each one Julian revealed his darker passions and anger, and described the earl's death at his hand.

The courtroom hushed. Pen's heart pounded. Julian remained expressionless. She glanced at the faces in the gallery and saw how they looked at him. They saw a sinister man, not a good and quiet one.

Even her friends appeared astonished by the storm that thundered within the words being read. Laclere in particular turned ashen-faced, as if he knew that those pages would seal Julian's fate.

Satisfied with the effect he had produced, the prosecutor left the stage.

Knightridge rose with a deep frown. He reached out his hand for the pages and the prosecutor gave them over.

"They are dated. The dates' ink appears the same as that of the prose, so we can assume they were dated when written. Two of these are ten years old, and a third five years. And wait, this one here is—excuse me, it is hard to read—it looks like it was the first, and was written *fifteen* years ago." He struck a dramatic pose with his hands on his hips. "Sir, for a man bent on murder, you damn well take your time getting around to it."

Laughter broke out.

Even Julian smiled. "Perhaps I do not plot as well as I plod."

The audience roared.

"Indeed, perhaps you do not. I suggest that you do not

plot at all." He waved the pages and his voice boomed. "These are the words of a man incensed. Furious. I suggest that they are the outpourings of a soul that was tortured by a secret that burned, and the release of these writings was all that the bonds of honor permitted you. Indeed, sir, I do not think you have told this jury all there is to know about this case."

Julian said nothing.

"Honor still binds you. I put some questions to you, however, that do not require any dishonor, I assure you. You have served these years as the solicitor of the Viscount Laclere's family, have you not?"

"Yes."

"When the Countess of Glasbury separated from her husband, did she seek you out for your advice?"

Julian said nothing.

"I think we can assume she did. I think we can also assume that she confided why she wanted to take such a rash step, one that would affect her position and fortune so drastically. I believe we can assume, sir, that all these years you knew the particulars of her marriage in ways no one else does."

A buzz moved like a swell through the crowd. Pen felt the glances her way. Knightridge was lying, of course. The particulars were now well known, and he was aware of it.

Julian was not, however. He glared at Knightridge. "You assume a lot."

"Perhaps I do. Maybe the mere knowledge of a good woman's mistreatment is not enough to account for these . . . fantasies regarding his death."

With a display of deep thoughtfulness, he strolled in front of the jury. He passed near the prosecutor.

He paused and cocked his head. "I say, that is quite a pile you have there. Are all of those papers Mr. Hampton's? More plots?"

To his adversary's consternation, Knightridge plucked a large handful away and retreated. With great flourish he opened each one and scanned it. "Oh, my . . . well, well . . . I think the jury needs to be aware of these. In the interest of justice, I regret to say they should be read. They speak to Mr. Hampton's character, and perhaps even his intentions."

"What does he have there?" Sophia whispered.

"I have no idea," Pen replied.

"If he *regrets* they should be read, why not ignore them instead? He is supposed to be *helping*."

Knightridge held one page high, at arm's length, ready to start.

"Let me see, this letter is dated the sixteenth of April, 1816. You were new to law then, I believe. Just out of your two years at university, I would guess. Since this was in your possession, I assume it was never sent." He cleared his throat and began reading. "*'My incomparable beloved . . .'*"

It was a letter. A love letter. A beautiful, sweet letter of gentle longing, written by a young man to a woman he could not have.

Pen could not take her eyes off Julian as she heard it. She had no trouble picturing him back then, full of promise. She could hear him saying these words, and saw him sitting at a desk as he wrote them.

She had no idea he had harbored a secret love back

then. She wondered if the girl had hurt him badly. Perhaps that was why he had never married.

Knightridge finished. He looked at Julian. Julian looked away. Pen's heart twisted. How hard this must be for such a private person.

Knightridge opened another paper. The chamber had fallen so quiet that the crackle of the paper could be heard. "The twenty-first of January, 1822. *'My incomparable beloved . . .'* "

It was another love letter. Pen listened to the lyrical words. This letter was a little bitter.

Partway through, her heart skipped. A quiet ringing entered her ears. Her gaze sharpened in surprise.

One line had jumped out at her. One reference. *Unlike the legendary woman who bore your name, your husband is no Odysseus, deserving of a wife's undying loyalty.*

A small commotion trembled through the chamber as a few others recognized the allusion.

The wife of the ancient Greek hero Odysseus was named Penelope.

The letter was written to *her*.

She could only stare at Julian in amazement. As if feeling her attention, he turned his gaze directly on her.

Knightridge read on and on. More letters. Poems. Expressions of unquenched desire and unrequited love. There were verses that praised her as perfect and beautiful and full of grace. Others seethed with the fury of a man imprisoned by a hopeless devotion.

The world fell away, became hazy and distant. She vaguely heard the reactions around her. She dimly grew aware that everyone had figured out who the woman was.

She did not care, could not care. Julian just looked at her, nowhere else. Knightridge continued reading, but it was as if Julian spoke the words himself, and looked in her eyes as he revealed the hidden depths of his heart to her.

chapter 26

"I was magnificent, if I do say so myself." Knightridge preened as he pushed the door closed and rested his weight against it, blocking out the guards waiting to take Julian back to his cell.

Julian folded his arms and kept his distance. If this gaol under the courtroom had a window, he would smash it. "Did you have to read *all* of them?"

"Of course. The men were enthralled. The women were weeping. You heard the roar when the judge tried to interrupt. Besides, by reading them all I have delayed the completion of the trial until morning."

"The prosecutor had the courtesy *not* to read out those papers, even though it would support his argument against me by showing a stronger motive. It took *my* counsel to lay down that evidence."

"You know very well that criminal trials are not only about the law. They are theatrical shows. There is just a chance that I will save your neck despite your miserable performance as the leading man in this one. Couldn't you have smiled more?"

"All you did was embarrass her."

"She did not look embarrassed to *me.* Laclere is bringing her here and you can ask her yourself, if I can hold off the guards that long."

Julian was not sure that he wanted to ask her anything. He had no idea what he could say. She had not actually looked embarrassed, just thoroughly stunned.

"Why did you want the trial to continue tomorrow?"

"Use your imagination for something besides love poetry—it was very well written, by the way; I am impressed—I want the word to spread. I want the city to hear of it. The ladies and peers, the merchants and their daughters, the scullery maids and beggars. If I am right, and I am rarely wrong, tomorrow the crowds will be shouting for your release."

"Wonderful. When I hang the city will drink to me, then go about its business."

"Do not be so sure. About the hanging, that is. Between the evidence of your long, chaste love and protection, and the common knowledge now of how Glasbury mistreated her, I expect—"

"What?"

Knightridge stopped with his mouth open. He flashed a cautious smile. "Um, yes, you do not know about that yet. I would have told you, but—"

"Enlighten me."

"It is all around. The business with Glasbury."

"The facts of her marriage, you mean. Now I understand why you pointedly alluded to that in the trial. If

I am spared the noose over Glasbury, I may hang for killing *you.*"

"It was her idea, I swear it. *Hers.* I did not guess how damning to Glasbury the story would be when she asked me if it would help to let the truth be known. I was astonished when the particulars finally reached my own ears. If you want to yell at someone for those revelations, yell at her, not me."

"It appears you are not sorry she did it."

"It changes everything, Hampton. You walked into prison a scoundrel, but between that and those papers, you are now a knight in armor. Hell, yes, I am glad she spoke of it. Damned brave of her. Most of the ladies I know would have regretfully let you swing rather than admit to such things."

Julian closed his eyes and fought to contain his temper. She was still doing it. Still sacrificing herself for others. She had spent years in that marriage rather than let the world know the truth, but now she had spread the story to try and save him.

His mind's eye saw her in the courtroom while Knightridge read those poems. She had appeared so unbelieving. So amazed. Not unwelcoming, but incredibly perplexed, as if suddenly the world contained colors she had never seen before.

For some reason, that only fed his threatening temper. His love had not been without its resentments and angers, and they now churned in his head.

Voices sounded outside the door. Laclere's demands came through the oak clearly. The viscount was speaking in his most intimidating tone, one that dripped with the expectation of privilege that his title permitted.

He entered with Pen and Bianca, and closed the door on two skeptical but cowed guards. "They will only remain docile a short while, and Knightridge must remain with us."

Pen accepted the lack of privacy with equanimity. Julian fought for some accommodation himself. Hell, the papers would be printing those letters tomorrow, so the presence of a few people in this chamber was a small thing in comparison.

Laclere, Bianca, and Knightridge congregated in one corner of the chamber and pretended to chat. Julian faced Pen.

She no longer appeared shocked or perplexed. A melting warmth entered her eyes. She came over and took one of his hands between her small, soft palms.

She lifted his hand and kissed it. "Julian, I have never been more honored. No woman has."

Suddenly no one else was in the chamber. Only Pen, holding his hand with a touch that brought spring's light and breeze into this space. There could be no storm now. There never could be when she smiled at him.

"I had no idea," she said. "You never . . . Of course not. You are an honorable man, so you would not pursue me."

"I often regretted that honor. I came close to casting it aside. Only the cost to you restrained me."

"I have been a great fool, my love. Not only in the past, but even in recent weeks. You told me in Hampstead, and I did not even understand what you were really saying."

"I did not expect you to understand. I just needed to say it before we parted."

She looked up at him with deeply burning lights in her eyes. Her expression provoked every memory he had of seeing her face. She was so beautiful that his heart wanted to burst.

He drew her into his arms. She rested against him, fitting perfectly and comfortably.

"I sat there while Mr. Knightridge read your papers, seeing you through the years, remembering the ways you protected me. I was so stupid, Julian. So blind. Please tell me that I have not wasted the best of your love. Some of the letters—you sounded so angry, close to hating me. I could not blame you if—"

He tipped her head up and kissed her. "I never hated you. My anger was never with you, but with the little hell my heart had put me in. The anger always passed. I never regretted loving you. If I had gone to my grave never kissing you or touching you, I still would not have thought it a wasted love."

She looked up at his reference to the grave. A sadness passed over her expression, but one of determination quickly banished it. "I am very glad that you did kiss me. You will again, often. I am sure of this in my heart."

He kissed her again. A long, sweet kiss. Right now, holding her, he believed there would be many more embraces. The resplendent emotions she stirred in him obscured any danger.

A loud cough broke through the peace. Pen turned her head and Julian looked up. A fist was pounding on the door. Laclere approached, looking apologetic.

He and the others had heard everything, of course. Their bland expressions said they had. Julian did not care.

He released Pen and gently set her away from him. Tears brimmed in her eyes, and he almost pulled her back. Laclere waited.

"I love you with all my heart, Julian," Pen whispered.

Julian handed her over to her brother. "Remember that my love is with you, darling, even when I am not."

My love is with you, even when I am not. Pen heard those words all the way to her house. They echoed in the library while Charlotte sat with her, trying to fill the evening with distracting talk.

She barely heard her sister. She kept seeing Julian while he said that today. There had been sadness in his eyes, as if he expected she would have only his love, and not him, in the future.

Julian did not expect to ever hold her again.

That was unthinkable. She could not allow it to happen.

She rose from the sofa. "Charlotte, I am grateful that you are keeping watch over me, but I must ask you to leave. I need to go out."

"You are in full mourning."

"I am not going to a party. I am going to Glasbury's house. Until his nephew arrives from Jamaica, it is still my home in the law."

"Pen, it will only stir bad memories if you go there. What can you hope to achieve?"

"I want to see that dressing room. I will talk to the servants."

"Darling, Mr. Knightridge spoke with them. They could offer no information that would aid Julian. Knightridge is a conceited, arrogant—well, he is what he is, but I do not doubt he obtained whatever could be gained from such inquiries."

"There may be a difference between inquiries made by

him and by me. I am the Countess of Glasbury. For years I refused to think of myself as such, but for a while longer maybe I should embrace the position. If I am the countess, right now they are still *my* servants."

"If you are determined to do this, I am coming with you. I will not have you near that toad's ghost while you are alone."

chapter 27

Pen's carriage stopped in front of the house on Grosvenor Square. She peered through the night at its facade.

She had not set foot on this property since she left Glasbury. She had been twenty-one then.

"When I left, it was from this house," she said to Charlotte. "The earl watched me go. He permitted me to take only the personal property that I had brought to the marriage, nothing else. No money. Not the jewels he had given me, nor the dresses he had bought."

"He wanted you to suffer. He thought you would be bought off in time."

"I would have left with the clothes on my back, if necessary. I did not want anything he had given me, either. He never understood that."

The footman handed them down. Pen walked up to the door. She turned and relived the moment she had stepped out this door all those years ago.

It had been raining, but the sun had suddenly shone in

her heart. A heady euphoria had spilled from her soul when she left the shadow of this place.

She had almost run to the carriage that would take her to Laclere Park. Julian had been standing there, waiting to escort her so he could explain to her brothers what little could be told about her shocking decision.

"We were both so young then. Julian took a big risk standing against Glasbury for me," she said. "I did not realize how much was at stake."

Charlotte rang the bell pull by the door.

A bewigged and liveried black servant opened the door. Pen recognized him. When he stepped back and bowed, it was clear he recognized her, too.

"Caesar, it is good to see you," she said, as she entered the reception hall. Caesar was one of the servants Glasbury had brought over from his plantation in Jamaica. He and his brother Marcus had served as footmen for years, following the earl from property to property.

"Thank you, madame." He offered his hands to take her and Charlotte's cloaks.

"Is it known yet when the new earl will return to England?"

"We have no word so far."

Caesar spoke with the same formality he had always used. His face showed no expression, and his eyes revealed nothing. The enigmatic blandness was not unusual for servants, but in Caesar and the other islanders it had always been very severe and closed, as if they knew the eyes were windows to the soul and they deliberately kept their panes covered with film.

"I will be here a few hours," Pen explained. "Before I leave,

I will want to talk to you further. Right now, tell me who else is here whom I know. Your brother?"

"My brother took another situation in the city. Other than me, I think that only Cook is from your time with us."

"Julia? She is here now?"

"Down below, madame. She moved here from Wiltshire some years ago, when the earl began spending more time in the city."

"I must see her. Do not send for her. I will go below."

She brought Charlotte to the stairs. As they made their way down, Charlotte plucked at her sleeve.

"Is he one of the slaves you spoke of? Like Cleo?"

"Yes, but Caesar and his brother did not seem to mind so much. They were very devoted, and seemed to accept the situation. They were probably the only ones Glasbury truly trusted. He took them everywhere with him, while the others stayed in Wiltshire."

"If he did, they should have known he could not hold onto them here in England. They must have learned the truth."

"After I left, Julian forced Glasbury to tell all the islanders that they were free in Britain, but before that, unless other servants spoke of the law in front of them, how would they know?"

"If I were a slave and even sniffed the odor of freedom, I would like to think I would know what it was that I smelled."

"If they did, they chose to remain. He gave Caesar and Marcus a degree of privilege and authority. It was a secure position. Perhaps that makes the shackles less noticeable."

"Do you think Caesar knew about Cleo?"

"I fear in my heart that everyone at the manor in Wiltshire knew about her."

"Cowards."

Pen stopped and turned to her sister. "Yes. As I was a coward. You have never lived in fear, Charl. You have never known how that breaks one's spirit. You cannot understand, and I pray that you never do."

The kitchen was not vacant. Two young women scoured pots in a corner. An old mulatto sat near the hearth, eyes closed but back straight. White frizz escaped her red kerchief in front. She held a bunched apron on the lap of her simple brown dress.

"Julia?"

Julia turned her head slowly. She gestured to the two other women. They put down their pots and hurried from the kitchen.

Julia began to rise. She pressed her palms against her knees and pushed.

"Do not. Please do not. I will come and sit with you." Pen brought a stool to the hearth and sat.

Blank eyes looked at her. Blank like Caesar's. Like Cleo's. Slaves learned young how to hide their thoughts. Survival depended on it.

Charlotte stood nearby, just out of Julia's view. Pen introduced her. Julia acknowledged her properly, but without interest.

"Now that he is dead, you can come back," Julia said with surprising bluntness. " 'Til the next master comes, that is." A nuance in her tone suggested she did not expect the next master to be an improvement on the last.

"I have not come back. I am here tonight to see to a few matters, that is all."

"What matters be those?"

"His death, for one. I am told the servants saw nothing, know nothing. I do not believe that is possible."

Julia scratched the skin under one eye. "We were asleep."

"Surely his valet knows who visited."

"Master had guests sometimes he did not want known. That night, he sent his valet away."

"Who saw to him? I do not believe Glasbury would stoop to doing for himself."

Julia did not reply at once. "Caesar would have done for him, but gone to bed before any visitor came."

Pen looked in Julia's eyes. She looked hard and long. She searched for the lights beneath the film, for the thoughts hidden by the blankness.

"I also came to tell you something, Julia. Cleo is dead. I learned just last month."

Julia turned her dull gaze to the hearth. "The child is in heaven, then. A better place, and the good Lord's embracing her."

She reached for a poker and bent to spread the fuel. As the low fire glowed over her face, Pen saw something reflected from deep in those eyes. Something unexpected and confusing.

Contentment.

A deep satisfaction burned within this old slave.

"She knows something. I am sure of it," Pen said to Charlotte when they were alone in Glasbury's chambers.

"She does not care that he has died, that much is obvious. I cannot say I blame her."

Pen surveyed the bedroom. Like the rest of the house, it was old fashioned in decor, full of the bombé lines and gilding of the last century. Glasbury had refused to allow her to change anything. He trusted no one's judgment or taste but his own.

The bed loomed. And the bench. And the carpet on which she had cowered one night. She turned away and caught Charlotte's expression of concern.

"It was another world, and another woman," Pen said as she headed toward the dressing room. "Do not watch me as though I were going to start raving at you."

The dressing room was as large as the bedroom, and contained sofas and chairs along with wardrobes and drawers. It had been built in the days when people entertained in their dressing rooms.

Pen could tell at once that it had been thoroughly cleaned. Nothing remained of the events of that night. She paced around it anyway, hoping that some clue would present itself.

"Do you think the servants could have done it?" Charlotte asked. "If he ate a meal, the poison could have been in the food, not the wine he had later."

"Why now, after all these years? And there was still a visitor, and that will go against Julian. Two wineglasses. Glasbury would never share wine with a servant. Someone else was here."

"Someone who will never admit to it, I daresay. If a visitor comes in the dead of night and is admitted by the earl himself, if the valet is sent away, there is a reason."

"That reason will prevent the man from coming forward, even if he did not kill him."

"Unfortunately, you are probably right." Charl nonchalantly opened a drawer of the toilet table. "I imagine the house has been searched for letters or notes."

"Mr. Knightridge saw to it."

"Of course he did." Charl strolled to the large wardrobe against the far wall. She opened its doors and examined the earl's garments.

She pushed aside some morning coats and froze. She quickly slid the coats back.

Pen noticed. "What is wrong? You look quite pale." She went to the wardrobe. Charl was smoothing the coats.

"It is nothing. Truly."

Pen pushed the coats aside. Hanging on the back of the wardrobe were Glasbury's whips and ropes, his straps and restraints.

"Knightridge did not search very thoroughly, it appears," Charlotte said.

"He was not looking for such as this."

"Perhaps he should have been."

Pen closed the wardrobe. "I think I know who was here that night. I know who the secret visitors were. He hardly stopped once Cleo and I were gone, and came to prefer London after that. Women came to him here, prostitutes, so that he could indulge himself."

Charlotte closed her eyes, then opened them. "Oh, Pen, you are too good to ever see the truth."

"What do you mean?"

"It may still have been a man, and it need not have been a prostitute. I have received gossip these last few days, just as I have given it out. I have learned that Glasbury did not restrict himself to women in his games."

Pen faced Caesar in the library. She had left Charlotte in the drawing room. This interview needed to be held alone.

He stood tall and straight, impressive in his livery. The earl had interpreted Caesar's manner as deferential and submissive, but she had always recognized the underlying pride in his face and posture.

She had no idea how old he was. Forty? Fifty? Did the wig hide gray hair? The people of the islands did not show their age on their faces the way the English did. Julia, who actually looked old now, was probably ancient.

"I do not intend to ask you any questions, because I know you will not answer them," she said.

"Whatever is your preference, madame."

"My preference is that you listen to me, and take my words to heart. I think that you know who visited the earl that night. Perhaps you will not say because you fear being seen as an accomplice. You may want to protect Glasbury's name, or that of someone else. Whatever the reason, I believe that both you and Julia, in the least, know what happened but are not saying."

"We have not lied."

"You have not told the whole truth, either." She walked over to him. "A man is being tried for this death, and he is innocent. Mr. Hampton had no hand in it, and you know it. Will you let him hang?"

Caesar's unflinching pose seemed to respond that if one more Englishman died it was of no concern to him.

"Do you remember Cleo, Caesar?"

That got a reaction. It flexed through his face before he resumed his impassivity.

"Julian Hampton took her away from the earl. Did you know that? Even before I left, he made Glasbury give her up, and made sure the earl dared not do such things with a servant again. He forced the earl to tell all of you that you became free when you stepped foot in England. That is why things changed back then. Because of Mr. Hampton. He brought Cleo to a woman who cared for her, and he paid for her keep all these years. The man you would let hang saw to Cleo's safety and the others' freedom when no one else would."

He looked away. It was as if maintaining his stance now required that he look at plaster instead of her.

She was certain then. This man knew something that could help Julian. He need only speak of it, and the danger would be gone.

"You must save him. Do it however you need to, to protect yourself. Include or leave out what you wish, but you must go to Mr. Knightridge and tell him what happened here that night."

He turned his gaze back to her. He looked right through her. He offered nothing but more silence.

Her inability to reach him maddened her. She thought she would scream or weep. The answer to saving Julian was standing right in front of her, and she could not obtain it. Out of fear or pride or hatred, Caesar and Julia would ignore her pleas.

If things went against Julian tomorrow, she would never forgive herself, or this man.

Livid beyond good sense, biting back her outrage, she marched to the door. "If Mr. Hampton hangs because you remained silent, I will not rest until I find out why. I will fill my empty days and nights with pursuing the *whole* truth."

chapter 28

The next morning, the hawkers near the Old Bailey sold new broadsides that described the dramatic revelations of the day before. Some of Julian's letters and poems were printed, too. The spectators entered the courtroom buzzing with anticipation. They carried newspapers whose stories reflected the city's sympathy for the romantic prisoner.

When Sophia arrived this time, her husband accompanied her. Adrian Burchard had returned to London the previous evening, with a letter from Mr. Jones admitting he abducted the countess at Glasbury's command. That word had spread fast, even if it had not been in the papers yet.

"The general opinion seems to be that Julian at best should be convicted of manslaughter, not murder," Sophia whispered as soon as she sat next to Pen. "I attended a party last night where several very vocal ladies insisted that it was no worse than self-defense."

Adrian tipped his head. "At White's last night, more

than a few men commented that a scoundrel needs killing no matter what his title or how it is done."

Their reassurances did not soothe Pen. Turbulent emotions raged in her.

She did not know if she could bear being here today. She did not expect all these opinions in the city to matter at all. An earl had been killed, and someone would have to pay.

Knowing that the people who could save Julian now sat in Glasbury's house almost made her insane. She had spent the night trying to think of the argument or promises that would encourage Caesar to come forward. Dawn had brought a terrible dread into her heart that she could not control.

The judge and jury arrived. Julian came in. The prosecutor took his position.

The defense counsel was nowhere to be seen.

"Mr. Knightridge seems to have exhausted himself with yesterday's recitations," the judge said sarcastically. "How unfortunate."

He called for the trial to continue.

There was nothing much left except the summation of the facts. The prosecutor proceeded to lay them out again. Knightridge would not have been allowed to refute them anyway, so his absence could not affect the outcome now.

Pen's dread increased anyway. It was as if Knightridge did not want to be present when his friend was condemned, and had let Julian stand alone up there against these accusations.

As the summation wound down, a rumble of voices

interrupted. It began in the back of the courtroom and billowed forward until it drowned out the prosecutor.

The judge called for silence, to no avail. He glared at the source of the disturbance. His mouth pursed and his lids lowered.

Knightridge was squeezing through the court functionaries. He strode to the judge. "I must ask your indulgence, but important matters delayed me."

"Your presence was not missed, sir. You may think you are essential to all you engage, but we are capable of completing the trial without your help."

"Of course. However, the trial is not completed. A person came to me this morning and expressed the desire to lay down information. It is a story that must be heard."

"We have all that we need already."

Knightridge looked affronted. Wounded. Perplexed. "Would you deny sworn testimony that could shed further light on the events? If you require precedents before allowing such late developments, I can give them to you."

The judge peered at him with extreme displeasure. Knightridge responded with a mixture of innocence and hauteur.

It was the spectators who made a difference. Shouts called out for the new evidence to be heard. Other voices agreed. The din grew.

Faced with exercising his prerogatives or retreating from the threat of pandemonium, the judge chose the latter.

Knightridge turned to face the door of the chamber. He gestured to someone. Every head turned.

A woman walked into the courtroom.

Señora Perez.

"My goodness, what is this?" Sophia whispered.

Pen had no idea. She was as stunned as everyone else.

Señora Perez walked down to the judge. Her demure ivory dress contrasted with her almond skin. Her hat was very sedate. Only her shawl appeared exotic. Long and silken, dark blue with a green pattern, it flowed over her like water, and its rivulets hinted at the curves obscured by garments.

The light from a window illuminated her face. Pen's breath caught. In the theater she had not been able to clearly distinguish this woman's features, but now the morning light revealed her unusual and alluring beauty.

With great skepticism, the judge addressed her. "You have information regarding this crime, madame?"

"I have information that should be heard. I know nothing of the crime."

"Really, this is a waste—"

"I know that Mr. Hampton could not have been with the earl that night," she continued. "You see, he was with me."

Pen's breath left her. So did Sophia's and Dante's. So did everyone's. After a five count, the entire courtroom audibly inhaled.

Pen stared at the woman facing the judge. There was something about her expression... something in the manner she had donned for this role...

"Indeed, madame? Are you saying that you are Mr. Hampton's mistress? One wonders how many the man requires." The judge seemed delighted with his little joke. No one laughed.

"He is not my lover. He came to advise me. My husband

was about to embark on an investment that worried me as potentially ruinous. I asked Mr. Hampton to visit when I knew Raoul would not be home, so that I could consult with him and my husband would not know. He arrived at midnight and left two hours later."

"And were you satisfied with his *advice?*" the judge asked with a smirk. "Contented with his *services?*"

The audience did not pick up the cue. The drama was more compelling than the judge's insinuating attempts at wit.

Señora Perez pretended not to notice the double meanings. She assumed the demeanor of a virtuous woman incapable of understanding such things. "His advice was most welcome and sound, thank you. I was able to convince my husband to retreat from this risky business affair."

"Why did you not come forward before?" the prosecutor snapped. "This looks most suspicious to me. Perhaps he is your lover, and now you lie to save him."

"I did not speak, because I feared my husband would misunderstand that meeting. However, Raoul saw my growing distress and, upon learning the secret I had, insisted I seek out Mr. Knightridge." She lowered her eyes submissively, as if a husband's command was law with her.

"You husband actually believed the innocence of this midnight assignation?"

"My maid and a manservant were able to attest to my innocence. They were in the drawing room the whole time. I would never meet with a man alone, even on a matter of business. Where I come from, that is not done by ladies." She turned to the judge. "If you want to speak with the servants, they will explain how it was."

"Oh, yes, I am *sure* they will." The prosecutor threw up his hands to express his exasperation and disbelief.

"I do not think that this new evidence is worth weighing heavily," the judge said to the jury. "Someone killed the Earl of Glasbury, and the woman's very delayed story does not tell us who did or did not."

Julian's face had turned to stone. Pen knew the reason for his anger. If Señora Perez's story was believed and Julian was exonerated, the police had another person they could accuse very easily.

"If I may speak," Mr. Knightridge said very politely.

"I think we have heard you speak enough already, sir."

"Please, indulge me. The lady has indeed told us who did not kill the earl, and I may be able to shed some light on who did."

That certainly got everyone's attention. Julian's frown deepened.

Center stage again, Knightridge spoke lowly, as if confiding to the judge. His words carried to most of the spectators, however. Pen certainly heard them.

"Sir, very early this morning, before dawn, I accompanied members of the Metropolitan Police back to Glasbury's house. I had been told that a more thorough search of his chambers might prove interesting."

He paused and glanced up at the spectators. He gave the judge a meaningful look that indicated continuing could be very awkward.

The judge eyed him like a man who knew the game, but had no choice but to be the pawn. "Go on."

"Well, in his wardrobe, hidden by garments, we found

certain . . . uh, objects that suggest that his secret visitors came to, um . . . shall we say they came at his bidding and to do his bidding, as it were." He looked positively distraught that his duty required he broach the indelicate subject.

The judge's face reddened with embarrassment. And anger.

"The police have those objects in their possession now. Perhaps you should request they be brought forth, so that you can ascertain whether—"

"That will *not* be necessary."

"No? Do we agree, then, that their existence indicates that the earl's murderer should be sought in less elevated circles than heretofore?"

"Oh, my, he is *good* at this," Sophia whispered.

Yes, he was. Very good.

The judge looked like a man who had been backed into a corner. Having gotten him there, Knightridge pressed forward. "Do we agree that this lady's testimony exonerates Mr. Hampton, and that the earl's visitor was a person unknown to the police and not associated with Mr. Hampton?"

This cue was not missed. Spectators yelled their agreement and called for an answer. The judge's cheeks puffed as he debated.

Finally he exhaled, and nodded.

The gallery went wild.

Pen looked at Julian while the din swelled around her. She wanted to grab him and embrace him and cry with relief.

He looked back. His comportment did not change,

but fires burned in his eyes. Lights of life and hope blazed in them.

Others did, too. Private fires, that only she would recognize.

The love and passion of a lifetime now waited for her, if she was brave enough to accept it.

chapter 29

"You told Mr. Knightridge about the wardrobe," Pen said.

She stood with Charlotte outside the Old Bailey, waiting for Julian. The crowds had dispersed, but some people still milled around. Down the street she could hear a new yell, as a boy offered fresh broadsides describing the suspenseful conclusion of the trial.

The judge had recommended the jury to vote to acquit, and they had quickly done so. Formalities were being attended to, but Julian would come through the door soon.

She could not wait to see him. Hold him. There were other people she needed to see, too, but that would come later, after she had Julian back.

"Of course I told him. When they first examined those chambers they were not looking for evidence of Glasbury's character. Your revelations came after that. Now, with the particulars of your marriage well known, I realized Knightridge needed only to allude to them to open other possibilities in the jury's mind."

"You are as brilliant as he is, Charlotte. You must admit that he played it out perfectly. He left the judge nowhere to turn."

Charl snickered. "I suspect the judges all dislike him as much as I do, if he always makes them look like fools when he wins."

The door opened. A robe appeared.

"Here he comes. I hope that you will be gracious and congratulate him as he deserves."

"Without you, me, and Señora Perez, he would have failed. How surprising to find her joining our army. Thank goodness her husband was so understanding and honorable, that is all I can say."

Pen had rather more to say about Señora Perez, and *to* her, but that was for another day.

Today was for joy. Julian stepped across the threshold behind Knightridge. The sight of him had her lightheaded and wobbly.

He paused and looked up to the sky. Then he closed his eyes, as if composing himself against the onslaught of a powerful emotion.

When he opened them again, he was the Mr. Hampton the world knew. Contained. Cool. Removed.

Until he saw her.

A burning intensity entered his eyes. It revealed everything he hid in his soul. She saw the agonizing fear he had battled in prison when he assumed he would hang, and also the exhilaration incited by his unexpected salvation.

In that moment, she also comprehended as never before his resolve to protect her at all costs, even that of his life.

Ignoring whatever Knightridge was saying to him,

unmindful of the eyes that still watched in hopes of more spectacle, Julian strode toward her, opening his arms.

She ran to his waiting embrace.

She brought him to her house. He was incapable of refusing.

He had not entirely absorbed the astonishing turn things had taken. The reprieve left him intoxicated with relief. The trial had also rendered him more tired than he realized.

Pen took him in hand. She ordered some brandy be brought, and then gave instructions that a bath be prepared.

When the brandy arrived, she poured him a good measure, then splashed a bit in another glass. "Promise not to tell," she said. "I feel some need of fortification myself."

The spirits warmed him. They helped tilt the world back upright.

Pen sat on a sofa and sipped. She appeared very contented and happy.

He hoped he did not have to say it, but he thought he should anyway. "I never visited Señora Perez, least of all that night."

"I know that."

"I cannot imagine why she did this. She owes me nothing, let alone a lie under oath."

"Perhaps she is in love with you, and could not bear to see you hang." Pen set down her glass, got up, and came over to him. "Whatever her reason, I am grateful. Tomorrow we will go and thank her. For now, come with me."

She took his hand and led him out of the room.

"Where are we going?"

"Someplace where I can take care of you. Do not object or tell me it is too indiscreet. I am thoroughly notorious now so I get to be as naughty as I like."

"That is one of the benefits of scandal, isn't it?"

"Oh, yes. I learned that early on."

She brought him up to her chamber. Indiscreet was an understatement for doing so at midday with the servants' full knowledge. He would remind her about that later. Today there were no rules he was inclined to obey.

The bath had been prepared near the fire in her bedroom. A steaming tub waited on a large oilcloth that protected the carpet.

"My dressing room is not large enough," she explained. "I thought you would want to wash the last week away."

He still smelled the prison on him, and she probably did, too. He was not sure that a bath would completely spare him from smelling the odor. It was in his head, along with the misery and despair that permeate such a place.

He sat down and removed his boots.

The latch clicked. He turned his head. Pen had not left. She had only closed and locked the door.

She came up behind him and slid her hands down the front of his coat. "I said I wanted to take care of you. Did you think that meant like a mother?"

"I hoped more than the bath waited up here."

"Yes, much more. But first I will take care of you in other ways." She slid his frock coat down his shoulders and off his arms and cast it aside. Her fingers sought the knot in his cravat.

He closed his eyes and rested his head back against her breasts. Her circling arms and deft touch aroused him. Desire burst like a torch.

He turned his head and kissed the swell of her breast. With a soft smile, she went to work on his waistcoat.

Every small touch inflamed him more. He began thinking that the bath could wait.

She moved in front of him to loosen his cuffs and collar. She slowly lifted his shirt over his head. She paused.

He looked up at her heavy-lidded expression. Sensual lights sparkled in her eyes. She was enjoying this.

She caught him noticing her looking. A pretty flush reddened her cheeks. "You will have to stand now. Otherwise, I cannot . . ."

Desire still roared in him, fueled by the heady liberation the day had brought. This undressing had become erotic, however, and he did not mind the delay.

He stood. She turned her attention to working the buttons of his trousers. He turned his attention to the way the light from the window made her dark hair shine.

Her hand kept brushing against his erection. Her face flushed more, and she had trouble finishing the task.

"Do you want some help, Pen?"

"No. I can do this." It sounded more like a statement of resolve than of competence. "I have dreamt for days what I would do if I got you back, and these buttons are not going to defeat me."

She managed it. The trousers loosened. She paused again.

"No help at all?"

She laughed. "You could kiss me. That would help enormously. This is harder than I thought. I expected to feel dangerous and seductive, and instead I feel silly and awkward."

He slid his hand behind her neck and drew her toward him. "You are very dangerous, and I am thoroughly seduced." His kiss revealed just how thoroughly. He barely kept from devouring her. As his tongue swept the moist velvet of her mouth, he imagined other velvet depths and fought the urge to pick her up and carry her to the bed.

He did not succumb, in part because he could not walk. During the kiss Pen had pushed down his lower garments, and they bunched around his ankles.

Eyes bright with her own desire, she kissed his neck, and down to his chest. The warm press of her lips created spots of delicious fire.

She eased away. "If there is going to be a bath at all, it should be soon."

She lowered herself to her knees to extricate his ankles and feet from the garments. He looked down at her as she knelt to tend to him. Like a servant to a master. Or a lady to her lord.

It moved him that she would even consider such a pose of submission. She was the daughter of a viscount and widow of an earl. She had probably never knelt willingly to any person except the king. She had not been educated to humble herself in the care of anyone.

He touched her head. "I am honored, my lady."

She looked up and her eyes misted. She turned her head and softly kissed his leg. Then his thigh. Then she kissed him in a way that made his teeth clench.

He held out his hand and helped her to her feet. He walked to the tub and stepped in.

"Is it still hot?" she asked.

"If it isn't, I am, and my body will warm it fast enough."

He began washing, wondering if she even knew what that last kiss had implied.

She knelt beside the tub, no doubt to help him.

"You will get your dress wet."

"I do not think some soap and water will ruin it."

"There is no reason to take the chance." He rinsed his hand and reached behind her. He began unfastening her dress. "If you are going to be dangerous, Pen, you may as well do it right."

She twisted so he could reach better. He sat up in order to deal with her stays.

He gestured to the chair where his garments were lying. "If you take them off over there, they won't get wet."

He also would be able to watch. She realized that as soon as she stepped out of her dress.

She looked quite demure as she set aside the dress. Less so while she released her petticoats. A sensual smile softened her mouth as she let the stays fall.

"I like the way you are looking at me, Julian. I feel very seductive and dangerous now. I want to see if I can be devastating and wicked, too. You must stay there while I finish."

"Trust me, I am incapable of moving."

She deliberately took a long time to remove her chemise. She teased him with a slow unveiling. The fabric inched down the full, creamy breasts he had dreamed of kissing, over the lovely curve of her waist, around her hips, and over the dark hair below. Finally she stood naked except for her hose, a perfect feminine vision, all white and pink and soft.

Her gaze never left him. Her expression revealed her arousal, and other things, too. Triumph at what she was doing to both of them gave her a very worldly air.

She walked over to the tub. She appeared incredibly erotic like that, nude except for the white silk covering her from thighs to toes. The effects of this disrobing collected in him with a ruthless fury. When she got within reach he grabbed her arm and pulled her down so he could kiss her.

She joined him as if it was the first kiss in years. Her response was shy and tentative at first, then impassioned and aggressive. She bent over the tub, hands on its edges, arms flanking his shoulders.

Her breasts hung inches from his face. He kissed each one, then moved his tongue over one tight nipple and his fingers over the other. Her breath quickened the way he loved, then escaped in little gasps. She moved slightly to make it easier. He knew that her breasts were more sensitive when she straddled him or sat, and he caressed and drew gently, the way that gave her the most pleasure.

"That feels so good," she whispered between deep sighs. "At night I would remember making love with you, and I could not sleep." She touched his face, stopping him, and raised it so she could kiss him. "I could have you do that forever, Julian, but I am taking care of you today, remember?"

She straightened and looked down at him. "I haven't finished undressing."

She raised one foot and propped it on the edge of the tub right near his shoulder. With slow, deft hands, she began rolling down her stocking.

There was no reason for that to make him impatient,

but it did. He was halfway to madness already, and the descent of that stocking made another restraint break. He circled her hips with his arm and kissed her flank and the outside of her thigh. A glorious passion started breaking in him. A magnificent turmoil of hunger and pleasure and unspeakable need.

She switched legs, raising the other, turning slightly within his arm to keep her balance. This position exposed her as the last had not. He had to clench his jaw to control the sexual lightning that flashed through his mind and body.

He became aware that her hands had stopped at her knee. He looked up at her face. Her expression said that she had noticed he was not watching the stocking at all.

"You are very good at being devastating and wicked, Pen."

"You are quite devastating yourself, my love. And right now you look extremely dangerous, in the most thrilling way." She glanced down to the curls and pink flesh he had been looking at. "Do you want to kiss me there?"

"Yes. Does that shock you?"

"A little. It is not something I have done before." She bit her lower lip and suddenly appeared very young and innocent. "I think that I would like to do things with you that I never did before, Julian."

He finished removing her stocking, and used the time to force some control. He put her foot down and rose out of the water. Not bothering to use the towel, he lifted her in his arms and carried her to the bed.

He reclined beside her, braced up on one arm so he could see how beautiful she was in the soft light streaming through a nearby window. He smoothed his hand over her, marveling anew at how soft her skin was, how silken and warm.

She reached and pulled him down into her embrace, the first happy embrace since that day in Hampstead. Holding her quietly and completely, feeling her skin against his, made his heart ache beautifully. Another sentiment, poignant and exquisite and grateful, joined the powerful chaos that possessed him.

It did not remain quiet long. Demonstrating her new aggression, determined to be devastating, Pen pushed him on his back and kissed him hard. She used her tongue as he had, flicking it over his chest, teasing his skin until his mind was blank to everything except the sensation of her mouth and hands and the sounds of her increasing abandon. Desire urged him to take her, but the hunger for a different possession spoke louder.

He flipped her onto her back. He parted her legs and knelt between her knees. Lids heavy and eyes glazed, she looked up at him.

He bent down and kissed her stomach, and then her thigh. When he raised his head, she was still watching him.

He caressed her thighs. "I have never done this before either, Pen. It is not something I have shared with another."

"I like that," she whispered. "I am glad."

He lay between her legs and immediately entered a sexual daze. He kissed the soft flesh of her inner thighs and then the astonishing softness of her mound and silky curls. She instinctively spread her legs wider. He caressed the moist, pink folds exposed to him, and she relaxed and responded to this familiar touch. Her escalating cries filled his ears and her scent filled his head. Primitive, almost violent pleasure stirred his essence.

He kissed her, gently tasting. Her breath audibly caught. He kissed again, using his tongue, letting her cries guide him, finding the best pleasures. She bent her knees and raised her hips, inviting more. Lost now, absorbed by the mysteries, mindless of everything except the powerful desire and pleasure wracking his body and the begging lilt of her frantic cries, he explored deeper, then higher, circling the sensitive flesh with his tongue.

Her climax engulfed him. It rang in his ear and shuddered through her hips and pulsed at his mouth. While her throaty scream echoed, he knelt and lifted her legs so they rose straight up his body. Supporting her hips with his hands, he entered the sweet warmth he had been kissing.

She absorbed him. She tremored around him and sighed with desperate contentment. He thrust hard and fast and long. She began crying again, joining him in the sublime fury until they shared the cataclysm together.

Pen woke in Julian's arms in the soft light of dawn. She drifted in a cloud of languid contentment while she listened to him breathe. She treasured the cozy warmth of his chest beneath her cheek and the subtle pulse of his heartbeat on her ear.

There had been many firsts with Julian, and the bold acts of last night only had meaning as metaphors for the rest. There had been her first day of complete freedom when they went to Hampstead. And last night, the first lovemaking when both of them had escaped all the dangers.

Last night had also been the first lovemaking after she had truly comprehended his love.

It humbled her that he had cared for her so long, so silently. Other men might have sent those letters, or pursued her for a heartbreaking and dangerous affair. Others might have played the lovesick poet on a public stage. Some men would have let the world know about their hopeless passion. Julian's quiet, dignified love had been much more romantic.

He would have declared himself to a different woman. She did not doubt that. He had remained silent to protect her from Glasbury.

A beam of the new day's light moved to Julian's face and he stirred. His arm tightened around her, as if his first instinct was to make sure she was still there.

She remained pressed against him even after she knew he was fully awake. She sensed his eyes were open, then felt the kiss on her head.

"What do you want to do now, Pen?"

There were several things to do today, but they could wait. Right now she wanted to dwell in this lovely contentment.

She knew what the question really meant, however. He was not only asking about this day, but also about the ones ahead. He was asking what she wanted to do with her freedom.

"Today I want to thank the woman who saved you," she said. "Then, very soon, I want to go with you to the cottage again. Right now, however, I want to make love in this incredible light and glorious peace."

They did, slowly, sweetly, perfectly. Afterward, they sent a message to Batkin to send some fresh clothes for

Julian. By noon they were in the breakfast room, drinking coffee and reading the post and papers.

One letter had come from France.

"Julian, here is a letter from Catherine. She wrote from Marseilles, right before sailing again. She thanks me for my help that night very explicitly."

He read it. "Laclere's man must have missed her. You should save this. I am sure that Knightridge's handling of the judge means that you will be safe from suspicion, but should the police get ambitious, this should be enough."

Another letter waited her attention. It had actually arrived two days ago, but on recognizing the hand she had not opened it. She did now.

"It appears that I need to meet with Mr. Rumford, Glasbury's solicitor, soon," she said as she perused the formal and abrupt request that she call at the sender's chambers. "It must regard the property due me as his widow. A manor in Northumberland, I believe. I have never seen it."

"At the time of your marriage, it could support a country life in considerable style."

As the family solicitor, he would know all that. He would have seen the settlement. He would know more than she did. "In other words, it could not support a city life in addition."

"I do not think so."

"It appears that Glasbury's generosity to my family upon our marriage was balanced out by a small settlement on me in the event of his death." She set the letter aside. "I do not mind. Considering how briefly I was truly his wife, I would feel guilty accepting more."

"I am sure that Laclere will continue to help you, if you want to maintain your London house."

"I do not want Vergil to continue. I am tired of being dependent on him. Actually, having shed myself of Glasbury's reach, I am not inclined to be beholden to any man for my keep."

Julian returned his attention to his paper. "Then I will not be so foolish as to offer to help you myself. However, I can afford it, and it is always yours if you ever want it."

Silence settled on the breakfast room. Rather more needed to be said on this topic, and it waited the saying. Pen did not want to broach the whole subject now, however.

She wanted to be done with the past before they spoke of their future. There were still some questions about the events of the last week that needed answering, for example.

As if guessing her thoughts, Julian set down the *Gazette* and tapped it. "This report of the trial's conclusion insinuates that too many questions remain."

"Some people will always wonder, won't they? Whether one of us murdered him?"

"I expect so. They will more likely wonder about me, however. We will let Catherine's letter be known. That will end speculation about you."

How like him to conclude that was all that mattered.

"Do you wonder, Pen?"

The calm question, thrown out as if he queried about the weather, shocked her. "Not at all. I am very sure you did not kill him, and I know that I did not."

"You cannot be completely sure."

"You are wrong. I am indeed completely sure you could not have done it."

"You have more faith in me than I have in myself,

then. I am not completely sure I could not have done it. I wanted to often enough."

"That is another matter entirely, isn't it?" She suspected Vergil had been correct when he concluded that Julian would kill to protect her. But, like the knights of old, it would have been in individual combat, not in murder.

Julian did not challenge her confidence, but she wondered if he would always wonder if she wondered. That was far too much wondering for her taste.

Fortunately, it would not last long. Eventually, he would understand that her love was so complete that she could never doubt him. He would also realize that even without that love, she would never question his innocence.

Why should she? After all, she knew who was really guilty.

chapter 30

Julian stopped the carriage at the handsome but modest house in Piccadilly. A servant came down to attend to the equipage, and Julian escorted Pen to the door.

A dark-skinned servant took their card. He wore no livery or wig, but the resemblance to another Negro servant was unmistakable.

Pen handed over her short mantle. "It is good to see you, Marcus. Caesar said that you took another situation."

Marcus accepted both the greeting and the recognition with a countenance so bland one would think he was deaf. Pen did not care about this servant's actions and reactions, however. Her attention immediately focused on the voice of the person she wanted to speak with.

Sounds of busy activity poured down the staircase. Amidst the calls and scurrying above, a feminine voice dominated, cracking through the confusion like a whip with her Spanish commands.

Marcus left to present their cards. Pen trusted they

would be received. She counted on this woman to want to preen a little about her great performance.

Marcus returned and ushered them to a library. The bindings lining the shelves looked like the kind that might be bought by the box at auction, to fill the libraries of houses to let.

Señora Perez waited for them. She no longer wore virginal white but a vibrant violet. She no longer acted submissive and demure but exuded her magnetic vitality. She greeted them with a wide, coconspirator's smile.

She accepted Julian's expression of gratitude, offered coffee, then engaged them in polite banter. All the while, she wore an expression that suggested she thought their call and the whole direction of their conversation a great joke.

Julian gestured to an open trunk near the writing desk. "Your household is very busy today. Are you leaving the city?"

"England is too cold for me. Already the damp affects my health. I will return home, where winter is not bitter."

"Society will mourn your decision. I trust that you will come back in the spring, and that we can expect your return in time for the Season," Pen said.

"I may return. However, I cannot guarantee that I will see my English friends again." She turned a warm smile on Julian. "Therefore, if there is anything that requires discussion, it would not be advisable to put it off."

"Other than thanking you again for your timely testimony, and bidding you a safe sailing, I have nothing else I feel bound to say," Julian replied.

"Englishwomen must be very accommodating of their

lovers, Mr. Hampton. I assumed that you came today to ask me to reassure the countess that you were not with me that night."

"I do not require any reassurance," Pen said. "And as a gentleman, Mr. Hampton would never request that you admit openly that you are a liar and perjurer."

Señora Perez's eyes flared at the insults.

Pen sipped her coffee, then set down the cup. "I, however, am not nearly as constrained as Mr. Hampton. While I am grateful for your lie, even more than he is, I do wonder what compelled you to tell it."

"He was in danger. I do not believe him capable of such things. What a shame if he were to hang. So . . ." She shrugged.

"You are truly a woman with a generous heart," Pen said.

"Yes," Julian said. "Of course, in giving me that alibi, you also gave one to yourself. Should the countess or I ever have cause to think you had a hand in Glasbury's death, we could not now voice our suspicions to the police without also destroying the testimony that ensured my freedom."

This little speech surprised Pen. She had not realized that Julian suspected—

"Nicely done, señora," Julian said. "Very neat."

Señora Perez began to pout with affront, but thought better of it. She glanced from Pen to Julian, and then back to Pen again. Those dark eyes locked on hers as if concluding where the danger lay. "As your lover says, Countess, to speak of it also puts him at risk."

"You worried I would work it all out, didn't you? That is why you testified. I told Caesar that I would find out the truth if Julian hanged. So you saw to it that he did not hang."

"I did not care if you learned the truth. Glasbury's death was no grief to you. If your lover died, however, you might seek revenge."

"Madame, the countess may know all, but I do not. I came to the conclusion that you killed Glasbury only because of your odd choice to speak for me. I can think of no reason why you wanted the earl dead."

"I do not admit to this crime, sir. I merely protected myself from the countess should she want to accuse me of it."

"Why would she think to?"

"Look at her, Julian," Pen said. "The eyes, and the shape of face. She so dazzled me in the theater that I missed the details. But in the courtroom, the demure and modest witness was very familiar to me. Not only her features, but her manner. So submissive, as if all her personality was drawn behind a wall. It reminded me of Caesar and Julia and all the others. It was a slave's manner."

Julian examined their hostess with new curiosity. Señora Perez began building that wall that Pen knew so well.

"You are related to Cleo, are you not?" Pen said. "The resemblance is there."

"You last saw her when she was a young girl, many years ago. You probably do not remember what she looked like. Most likely you never did. She was a slave who served you, and nothing more."

"If you know how long it was, you have an interest in that household and its servants. You have even taken one into your employment. Nor is my memory faulty. I have seen Cleo's face in my mind and my conscience often over the years."

The wall simply would not stay in place. It crumbled, and Señora Perez sat there like a volcano threatening to erupt.

"Is the countess correct? Are you Cleo's relative?" Julian asked.

Señora Perez glared at him. "She was my half-sister."

With that one statement, Pen knew she had been right in surmising the solution to the mystery of Glasbury's death.

"The earl visited his island estates twenty years ago," Señora Perez said, her tone drenched with disgust. "He had lived there when his father was alive, just as his heir has managed them these last years. He had enjoyed his life there, loved being a god on that land, with slaves who could be bent and broken and beaten. So he came back. No one was glad he had come."

"You still lived there then?" Pen asked.

"Only later did I leave. A visitor took a fancy to me and bought me for too much money. When he died, I walked away. I made my way to Venezuela. I created a history. There are so many like me that it was accepted. I became the mistress of men of influence. I eventually found one who would one day bring me here, so I could see my sister again." She rose and paced around them, her bitter words raining on their heads. "She was a child when Glasbury visited. She was one of several slaves he decided to bring to England. To freedom, I thought. I knew he wanted her. I believed she would be his mistress when she got older. A better life than what she had. All of us thought her very fortunate that the master favored her."

"You did not know his tastes?"

"I only learned of that when I arrived here. I looked for my sister, expecting to find her living in luxury, with servants of her own. Instead she was gone. The others left in his household told me everything. They knew I was one of them."

"How did you learn she had died?" Julian asked. "Even I did not know for months."

"Caesar learned of it. The earl was too careless around Caesar. Familiarity breeds that, and we know how to use it. Caesar had learned to read, and he saw the letter that told Glasbury of the girl's death. He believed the earl had had her killed, and I believe it, too."

"So you killed him for revenge," Julian said.

"For *justice*. It was easy to catch his eye. I already knew he favored dark women. I knew his preferences in *all* things." She paced away, but Pen glimpsed the expression that she tried to hide. Saw it and recognized it. Señora Perez had paid a price as she lured Glasbury to his death.

"If you speak of this, it will do no good," she said, turning abruptly to challenge them. "His servants will never betray me. They are glad he is gone, happy he has paid for his sins with my sister and others. Talk to them if you doubt me. They know of great crimes, of slaves brought here who spoke to the others of freedom under English law, and who then disappeared."

"I am sure the others will not betray you. They aided you and are your accomplices," Julian said. "Did Glasbury never guess who you were?"

"Never. To him I was just another slave for the night, bought with a jeweled necklace that he called a gift." Her lids lowered. "I told him at the end. After he drank the wine. I made sure he knew before he died."

"Of course," Julian said. "You would want to be sure that he knew."

"You sound disapproving. Perhaps you think I should have said prayers for my sister and been contented. Or asked these police of yours for help, with nothing more than a sad story as evidence."

"I believe that murder is wrong, madame. Does Raoul know of this? Is that why he is sending you away as quickly as possible?"

"I choose to leave, but yes, Raoul knows. He is an educated man, Mr. Hampton. He knows all about the moral laws taught by the philosophers. But he also understands there are higher laws than those. If I had been a man, I could have challenged Glasbury. I could have met him fairly with honor. That is denied women. Either we have a man who will do it for us, or we must find other ways. I found another way."

"A way that endangered an innocent woman," Julian snapped. "Do not speak to me of honor if you contemplated letting another pay in your place. You had to know that suspicion would fall on the countess."

Señora Perez looked a little chagrined. "You were not to be in danger," she said to Pen. "I expected you to remain in Naples until it was finished. The authorities were supposed to assume it was a whore, some wretch who gave Glasbury what he wanted for pay, a woman who would never be found."

"But I was not in Naples when this was done. You knew that."

"I could not delay longer. I did not think a countess

would ever face severe punishment, even if suspected. I believed that the aristocracy takes care of its own, if only to silence any scandal."

"You believed wrong," Julian said tersely.

"You did not seem to mind that Mr. Hampton was in the dock instead of you, either," Pen said.

"Your role in the earl's sins was misunderstood, Mr. Hampton. For that I apologize. I thought Glasbury had simply arranged for Cleo to be sold to you, illegally. I thought you were no better than the earl. After the countess explained to Caesar what really happened, I sought to win your release."

"And did so," Pen said. "For that I am grateful."

Señora Perez gave her a woman-to-woman look. Men can make their laws and rules, her eyes said, but we know how life really is.

Julian offered Pen his hand to help her rise, and to signal this call was over.

"As I said, señora, to voice my suspicions against you would necessitate destroying my own alibi. If I mourned the earl at all, I might be in a severe moral quandary. As it is, I think it is well that you are leaving Britain before my conscience mulls this too long. Whether your acts can be accepted as those required for justice, we will leave for God to decide."

chapter 31

"I have been talking too much, haven't I?"

Pen whispered the words while stretching to peck Julian's ear with a kiss.

"Not at all. I never tire of your voice."

Actually, she had been talking most of the way from London. With anyone else in the world, it would have been too much after a mile. This was Pen, however, and she never bored him. Social gossip and descriptions of new fashions enthralled him, if she spoke about them.

"It is because I am excited, Julian. I cannot believe how I look forward to these next days, with absolutely no one near me except you. Goodness, I wonder how we will fill all the hours?" She grinned impishly.

"Well, for one thing, I will teach you . . ."

She hugged his arm. "Teach me what, you rogue?"

"How to cook."

"Cook?"

"With no servants, someone has to cook. If I have a woman around, you do not expect me to do it, I hope."

"We might both live longer if you did. If I am a very good student and learn to cook, will you teach me other things, too?"

"If you promise to be a very good student in those lessons as well."

"I intend to be the very best student, Julian." Her teeth gently closed on the outer edge of his ear. "Worldly and wicked and shameless."

The cottage came in sight in the distance. Giggling, Pen nestled against him and continued a naughty torture of his burning ear.

"Keep that up and I will stop and ravish you right here on the road."

"I would call your dare, except that it appears a storm is blowing in. You enjoy storms, don't you, Julian?"

"I would not say I enjoy them. They awe me, however."

"You mean you are impressed by all that energy. By the terrible forces unleashed. You are moved by how quiescent nature is so suddenly thrust into turmoil, and by how the cool rationality of man is swept aside by primeval powers that will outlast our lives on this earth. Is that what you mean when you say they awe you?"

He looked over at her. She caught his eye and smiled softly. "That is how you explained it to me years ago, when we were very young. It came back to me one night while you were in prison, and the wind and rain were beating on my window. I could hear you saying every word. I confess that I never really understood it until we made love. Great passion has the same power, doesn't it?"

"With the right person it does."

He got them to the cottage before the storm arrived. In the gusting wind, he unpacked the carriage and took care of the horses.

The sky had grown heavy with dark, low clouds when he returned to the house. He looked for Pen and found her out on the terrace, wrapped in her blue cloak, the wind making a riot of her hair.

He embraced her from behind. Together, they watched the sea rise in choppy waves that churned black and green and white.

She was right. He enjoyed a good storm. The dynamics stirred the most human part of him. The emotions that gave a person a heart and soul were more alive in the face of such unrestrained nature.

Pen rested back against him. "My face is getting ruddy. Yours never does, no matter how fierce the cold or wind. That is not fair."

"I have always thought that you look lovely with a rosy face."

She looked down at where his arms crossed her over the cloak. "Is it terrible that I will not wear mourning for him unless I am in public? It seems so pointless, but perhaps it does not speak well of me."

"You said you would never mourn a man again, Pen, and he would have deserved it least of all. You do not have to pretend."

"I would have mourned you, Julian. I would have grieved the rest of my life."

That touched him profoundly. He closed his eyes and rubbed his face against her crown.

"I wanted to come here so we could make love by the sea," she said. "Also so we could be totally alone. But I also hoped that being here would help me make an important choice again, as it did the last time. I need to decide what to do with my freedom, don't I?"

"There is only one choice that I truly want, Pen, but I will live with any you make."

She turned in his arms and looked up at him. "What choice is it that you want?"

"The one that gives me the right to take care of you. I have accepted that you do not want that, however. Having waited so long for your independence—"

"Are you proposing, Julian?"

"Although my position has been affected by the scandal, I still serve as solicitor to many important families. You will never want, Pen. I also have some investments that have done very well, and others that promise to do even better, in particular in Dante and Fleur's Durham project. We will not live in the style of Laclere or the earl, but you will not have to count pennies."

"I do not need to live in the style of my brother. This is a proposal then?"

"I will, of course, accept whatever you prefer. I can see how marriage has little to recommend it, darling. I understand if the entire notion leaves you cold."

She giggled. "Goodness, you do talk a lot, Mr. Hampton. I agree that marriage has little to recommend it, however. There could be no excuse good enough for me to marry again."

"Yes. Of course. I see."

The wind caught her cloak and it flew up and out. It became a billowing cape that made her appear weightless, like an angel touching foot to earth after flight.

"There are no good excuses, but there may be some good reasons," she said.

"I can give you many." He kissed her. "That is one, and there are thousands more like it. Passion is another, and friendship. And being in love, Pen. That is one of the best reasons of all for marriage, and I am hopelessly in love with you."

"Another reason is loving a man who is worthy of love. That changes everything, I have discovered. Are you proposing, Julian? Because if you are, I am almost convinced."

"I am, and will press my case the only way left to me." He kissed her long and hard, and let his heart and soul release their winds of desire and passion and reveal his eternal storm of longing and love.

She emerged breathless and flushed. Her lids rose. "I think I would be a great fool to refuse you, my love. I would be an idiot to risk your changing your mind."

"I will never change my mind. I am yours however you will have me. I will have you any way I can."

"As a husband, Julian. I would be proud to be your wife."

He kissed her again, with profound gratitude. Joy drenched every inch of him, an emotion perfect and pure, and touched by disbelief.

She stepped back, out of his embrace. "I will go inside now. You are to stay here for a while. I want you to know that you do not have to be with me every minute in this love we share. You are not required to give up your silences or solitude completely. I am not jealous of those private moments, and have no desire to steal them from you."

She returned to the house. He faced the sea.

The storm was coming fast. It would not be a long one. Already, far in the distance he could see a glow of divine luminescence streaming down through the clouds.

The water below had become a chaos. Waves heaved and crashed. High ones broke against the sea wall of the terrace, right beneath him. The rain began, first with large droplets, then in driving sheets of spray.

It was a glorious storm with a dramatic wind. It blew right into him, stirring his heart and soul and blood. It awed him as few storms had, and merged with his own emotions the way great tempests did in his youth.

He remained silent, but another's voice spoke in his head. Pen whispered her love. He remained alone on the terrace, but she was in his heart more surely than she was in the house, her essence rising with him into the glory. A rare moment came to him, an instant of transcendence in which his consciousness seemed to join with the natural power of the world.

He had known that only a few times before, and always at the depths of melancholy. This time it was pure joy and beauty that saturated him. This time love unified his soul with the elements.

"Julian."

He turned and looked up. A window to his chamber was open. Pen stood near it, looking down at him. She had removed all her garments and let down her hair. The dark locks flowed over her ivory breasts. She looked so beautiful and perfect that his breath caught.

"I am up here, Sir Julian. Come and sing me a *chanson* or read me a poem, brave knight. Protect me during this fierce storm."

He walked toward the castle tower, shedding his armor. "I am coming, my lady."

ABOUT THE AUTHOR

Madeline Hunter's first novel was published in June 2000. Since then she has seen seventeen historical romances and one novella published, and her books have been translated into nine languages. She is a six-time RITA finalist and won twice for historical romance. Sixteen of her books have been on the *USA Today* bestseller list, and she has also had titles on the bestseller lists of the *New York Times* and *Publishers Weekly*. Madeline has a Ph.D. in art history, which she teaches at an eastern university. She currently lives in Pennsylvania with her husband and two sons.

Be sure to join

Madeline Hunter

in her next tale of seduction

and scandal

Available now

from Bantam

Read on for a preview . . .

Lord of Sin

The Earl of Lyndale was dying.

Again.

He lay shriveled and frail in his bed, cheeks sunken and skin wan. His right hand rested over his heart as if he were waiting to feel its last pulse. He presented a pitiable image of an old man facing the end.

Ewan McLean was not impressed. His Uncle Duncan pretended to lie at death's door at least once a year. Each imminent departure from the earthly realm summoned his sons and nephew so they could ease his passing. While on his deathbed he issued demands and extracted promises of outrageous presumption. Then he would "recover" and use those promises like a whip to get all the cattle lined up in the direction he had decided they should go.

"I fear the end will come tonight." The earl spoke it like a line in a stage drama. Which, for all intents and purposes, it was. "I need to set matters in order before I go."

He held out a trembling hand.

Ewan took it and smiled indulgently. *Here it comes,* he thought. He had been here for four days, waiting for the earl to decide when to finish the game.

"Since Hamish is not here, I must confide in you," the earl said, referring to his heir.

Ewan was all too aware that Hamish was not here. Right now Hamish and his younger brother were enjoying fresh air and sunshine on the continent and not sitting in this drafty old castle in a room hung with heavy green drapes. The same faded fabric framed the earl's body on the big bed, falling in dolorous swags like stage curtains.

The interruption of Ewan's visit to London by the summons had been irritating enough, but the discovery that his cousins, the earl's own sons, had escaped the call by taking off for Switzerland really grated.

"I will confess that I am glad it is you, my boy. Hamish would not have understood the matter that weighs on me. You know how he is."

"I certainly do." All too well. Hamish had grown into one of those purse-lipped, morality-spewing, judgmental Scots. When the earl eventually died, which Ewan expected would not happen for another decade or so, Ewan fully anticipated that Hamish would try to reform his cousin by threatening the handsome allowance that augmented Ewan's income from his modest property.

His uncle had never been so intrusive in his private life, but then his uncle had a history that did not permit umbrage over bad behavior without considerable hypocrisy. The current Earl of Lyndale had been a rake in his youth and a roué in his maturity. Ewan suspected that the fair-haired woman floating about the castle today was the current mistress. In short, the earl had more in common with his nephew than with his sons. If he had chosen to play at dying when only Ewan was available, that meant that his demands for promises this time probably had to do with matters that only another rake would take in stride.

"There is a letter that explains it all." The earl pointed his trembling hand toward a small writing table. Ewan watched the arm and finger stretch out while the earl rose on one shaky arm. His pose imitated that of a dying father in a painting by Greuze. An engraving that reproduced the painting was in Uncle Duncan's extensive fine print collection, its theatrical sentimentality obviously appreciated often by its current owner.

"You must give the letter to Hamish. You must swear that you will see that he carries out my wishes, which are contained in it."

"I will be in no position to do so. He will be the earl. I will remain a dependent relative and can demand nothing of him."

"Tell him you are bound by your promise to me."

"That will be of no account to him. You are asking that I harass a man for the rest of my life. That I pound my head against a stone wall. It isn't fair to make demands that I cannot fulfill."

"You can make him see that it must be done if you put your mind to it. You are far more clever than he is."

Ewan was losing his patience. Being blackmailed into his own promises was one thing. Being forced to ensure that others acted in compliance with Uncle Duncan's whims was another.

"What is this vitally important matter, Uncle?" Attending the next sheep shearing? Escorting some cast-off mistress to a ball? The earl's demands were never dreadful, just damned inconvenient and often boring.

"I did a grievous offense to a man in my youth. The next earl must right this wrong."

"What kind of wrong?" Most likely his uncle had bedded a friend's wife. For all of his envy of the last century's ribald behavior, seducing a friend's wife was something Ewan himself would never do. Once, when he and Uncle Duncan had gotten foxed together, he had tried to explain to the old goat how that was dishonorable. Uncle had simply been unable to grasp the nuances.

"I was vengeful and went too far. It has preyed on my conscience ever since. I had intended to right matters, but now . . ." His hand went to his heart again.

"Well, if it is something that the Earl of Lyndale should do, then you can still make it right yourself. When you are better."

"I will never be better. I tell you I am dying." Uncle Duncan spoke emphatically, with powerful strength of voice. His dark eyes glared out from under his bed cap's edge and his color rose to a nice healthy pink.

Ewan experienced profound annoyance. This entire drama had been so unnecessary. There had been no reason for Uncle Duncan to pretend he was dying. There had been no justification in dragging Ewan from London and from the delicious pursuit of pretty Lady Norton.

"Swear it," the earl demanded. He sat upright, looking fit and hale and ready to ride for twenty miles. "Would you allow me to go to my grave with this unfinished, with no assurance that this sin will be mitigated? Ungrateful wretch! I will make a codicile to my will at once and cut you out without a penny. I will—"

Here it came, the blackmail. The threats. Really,

Uncle Duncan should hire a writer to devise a new set of lines.

"—leave a letter for Hamish telling him to cut off your allowance. I will—"

"Fine, I swear," Ewan snapped. "I swear that I will do all within my power to see that the next earl fixes the problem that you created but never bothered to fix yourself."

It was a toothless promise to make. There would not be a "next earl" for quite some time. Swearing to do all within his own power meant little, since he would have no power at all.

Uncle Duncan did not see the huge holes. His ire receded. He sank back into his pillow. He arranged for his body to go limp and for his cheeks to appear gray.

The earl vaguely waved Ewan away. Still annoyed but also amused by the theatrics, Ewan played his role to the end. He got up, leaned over, and kissed Uncle Duncan's head affectionately before leaving.

That night the earl surprised everyone by actually dying. He passed quietly in his sleep.

Ewan was stunned by the unexpected turn of events, but he suspected his amazement was more than matched by that of the earl himself.

Two weeks later Ewan lay on a sofa in his chambers in London.

If life were fair he would not be reclining alone. Lady Norton would be here with him, receiving the lesson in love that he had long anticipated giving her. Right now he would be plucking at the laces of a corset, preparing to unveil her abundantly luscious beauty.

But life was not fair. He'd had to beg off on their assignation. He could not move, let alone seduce a woman tonight. He could barely think.

He lifted a limp arm and raised the letter. He read the first line again and groaned. It was unbelievable. Incomprehensible. Just a month ago he was happy and innocent and going about his business, which was easy to do because he made sure his business only dealt with pleasure, and now—

His manservant entered carrying a fresh bottle of wine to replace the one that Ewan had just finished. Swigged, to tell the truth. Gulped down as if it were rum and he were a sailor.

Another man came in too. Ewan glanced up from beneath the arm draped over his forehead to see Dante Duclairc gazing down at him. Dante's limpid brown eyes showed more amusement than concern and a smile wanted to break out on his angelically handsome face.

"Duclairc. Good of you to come."

His friend's presence touched him, and a pang of nostalgia sounded in his heart. Dante Duclairc had not been in these chambers since he married Fleur Monley last spring. The parties that occurred in this apartment were a lot less fun now that Dante had been domesticated. Only a calamity such as had visited Ewan today would get Duclairc here now.

"Your message seemed desperate. Are you unwell? You look like someone in a bad Greuze painting."

"Disaster has struck. Complete and total catastrophe. Once you learn of it you will understand why it has laid me low." He lifted the letter.

Duclairc took it and sat down on another sofa to read. He did not even notice the little bronze statue on the table beside his seat. The latest addition to Ewan's renowned collection of fine art erotica, it was a Renaissance work displaying a nymph servicing Pan. Ewan had been proud of the acquisition yesterday, but his friend's indifference seemed appropriate to today's solemnity.

"Jesus," Dante said after peering at the letter for a few minutes.

"I knew you would appreciate how outrageous this is."

"It is certainly unexpected. And amazing. I do not know whether to congratulate you or help you mourn."

"I'll be damned if I'm going to mourn. It was very inconsiderate of them. Hugely so. There should have been a law against both of them putting themselves in danger at the same time. Where was Hamish's sense? If he wants to climb a damned mountain and die in a damned avalanche, let him go, I say, but to drag his younger brother on the adventure and risk their both dying in the same damned avalanche—" He closed his eyes. It was all too much.

"Pity that they both dallied in marrying."

"Pity? *Pity?* Irresponsible! Look where their negligence has left me."

"It appears that it has left you the Earl of Lyndale."

Indeed it had.

Hell.

Ewan swung his legs and sat up. "Make yourself comfortable. I plan to get drunk and need company. I trust you told your pretty wife that you will not be home soon."

"Fleur assumed you were in horrible trouble after reading the dramatic message you sent me. She insisted I come. She had no idea that the terrible news was that you have inherited a title and a significant fortune."

"Do not get sardonic on me, Duclairc. A man has a

right to some warning on such a thing. There I was, assuming there were two strapping men between the title and me. What were the odds they would both die before one produced a son? Negligible. Damned near impossible or at least reassuringly unlikely. And now . . ." He waved the letter that had come from Switzerland, then let it drop to the floor.

He looked down at it. Something nibbled at his dazed mind. Something just as unpleasant as that letter had been. He tried not to acknowledge its intrusion, but it nudged and poked until it had his stomach sinking.

"Oh, hell."

"Your shock is understandable, McLean, but you will be a fine earl. You will rise to the position. It will not disrupt your life as much as you think."

"Yes it will, but this 'oh, hell' was about something else." He got up, walked around the assortment of sofas and chaise longues that dotted the chamber, ducked past the swing hanging from the ceiling, and went to a writing table in a dark corner.

"Uncle Duncan gave me something to give to Hamish should Uncle Duncan die, which I never expected him to do. I brought it down here so that I could fulfill his final wish by handing it over to Hamish as soon as he returned to England." He pawed through a drawer for the infernal letter.

He brought it back to the sofa and stared at its seal. He gulped down another glass of wine.

I swear that I will do all within my power to see that the next earl fixes the problem that you created but never bothered to fix yourself.

"Duclairc, let me pose a philosophical question to you. Suppose a dying man extracted a promise from you, but you did not really believe he was a dying man, nor, for that matter, did he. Let us say further that both of you thought the ultimate responsibility would fall to someone else but that a freakish coincidence meant that instead it fell to you. With all those peculiarities, wouldn't you say that—"

"No."

Ewan looked up to see Dante regarding him severely.

"Yes. Of course. You are right."

Well, hell and damnation.

"Perhaps you should read it. Maybe it is something very minor."

Sighing, Ewan broke the seal.

"Well?" Dante asked.

"It appears that my uncle wronged a man named Cameron many years ago. Ruined him. He wants me to see that this Cameron and his family are cared for, that they do not want for anything. That is deucedly ambiguous. What if they want a coach and four? What if they want twenty thousand a year?"

"I think you would be safe to use your own judgment of what is adequate to be sure they are suitably cared for. I do not think your uncle means you have to hand them whatever their hearts desire."

"Good point. I knew having you here would be helpful. That is why I called for you and not one of the other lads. Marriage has made you so . . . sensible."

"There is no need to get insulting."

"My apologies." Ewan peered at the letter. "It seems this Angus Cameron lives far north of Glasgow. I get to haul myself back up to Scotland and brave the cold and early snows of the Highlands."

"*Angus* Cameron? My father knew an Angus Cameron.

Spoke of him on occasion. They held a lively correspondence."

"Do you remember anything that was said about him? Uncle claimed this letter explained all, but in fact he neglected to include just how he wronged this man."

"I only remember my father referring to Cameron as eccentric. Father found him very amusing."

"That is not encouraging, Duclairc. Your father was more than a tad eccentric himself. If *he* used that word to describe Cameron, I could be facing a raving lunatic."

"I do not think it is as bad as that. I vaguely remember Father speaking of Cameron's erudition on ancient Celtic culture. Druids and whatnot. Unlike my father, who merely had a historical interest in such things, Cameron became more involved. There were some odd doings, but the fellow is only colorful, not mad."

"You are not making me feel better." Ewan poured more wine. "I should have started with whisky. It would have done the job quicker. You must stay. I promise no women are coming. This entire matter has left me cold for such pleasures."

"You are indeed distraught enough to need my company if that is the case. I never thought I would hear such words from you."

Hell, yes, he was distraught. In shock, and barely controlling his temper. He did not want to be the earl and this business with Cameron was only one example of why. Everywhere he turned now people would probably be using boring words like "duty" and "responsibility" and "obligations."

"You probably should attend on that responsibility soon," Dante said, gesturing to the letter about Cameron, which had joined the other on the floor. "The duty will only get more onerous if you put it off. With winter coming, a journey to the Highlands should be made at once. After you fulfill your obligations at court, of course."

Ewan wanted to punch Duclairc in the nose.

It was all too much.

"That should be it down there," Ewan said to Michael, his manservant.

"Lord be praised."

Ewan and Michael sat on their horses at the top of the hill and gazed into the glen where the home of Angus Cameron sat. Highland vistas like this—with the treeless rolling hills and valley, with a sky so blue it blinded your eyes and air so crisp and clean it hurt your chest—inspired poetry.

The mutterings moving through Ewan's mind were not pretty verses, however.

After a hellish journey, most of it on horseback through icy rain and bitter fog and more than enough mud to fill this glen, here he finally was.

I hope that you are enjoying this, Uncle Duncan.

"Do not praise Providence yet, Michael. I do not expect the conclusion of this journey to improve our lot. Angus Cameron probably has six burly, red-haired sons who wear tartan kilts and hurl tree trunks for fun. No doubt the evening meal will be haggis."

"You do not have very kind words for your countrymen, sir."

"I may be a Scot, but I am not fond of Highlanders. Highlanders assume they are purer Scots than anyone else. They imply with their cocky grins and insinuations that a Scot from the south is more English than Scot, in blood as well as loyalty. There are many Scots who never reconciled to the Grand Union into Great Britain, and lots of them live in godforsaken glens like this, on the edge of the world, being whipped by brutal weather that any sane person would flee."

He led Michael down into the valley, anticipating little welcome when he intruded. He had not written or contacted Cameron because that would give the man a chance to rebuff him. The last thing Ewan wanted was a recalcitrant victim prolonging the "making right" that needed doing.

Duty. Duty. He had been practicing that chant for two weeks now, ever since the ceremony with the king. Nothing like donning a coronet and an ermine-trimmed robe to drive the desolate message home. He was no longer Ewan McLean, man-about-town, gambler and drinker, lover extraordinaire, and host of some of London's finest orgies.

Now he was a peer, a member of the House of Lords, paterfamilias to a passel of relatives whose names he had made it a point never to know, and laird of a branch of a Scottish clan with ancient roots.

Worse, what had recently been an unremarkable life had now become notorious. Society had long ago ceased to notice his behavior, but suddenly it was grist for the rumor mill again. He had heard that already some unimaginative wag had dubbed him the "Lord of Sindale."

What a ludicrous development it had all been. The only good thing about this journey, and it was small consolation, was that it removed him from London, where several mothers of eligible daughters had sent him invitations to parties at houses that had never before received him. He might be notorious, but now he was a notorious *earl*. Ladies who should know better apparently had no qualms about throwing their virginal daughters in the Lord of Sindale's path.

"I thought you said it would be a hovel. A dark, drafty, ancient cottage." Michael glanced back with resentment at the packhorse he had been dragging. "You made me bring good linens and soap, but it looks to be a house that will have its own."

It did look to be such a house. Uncle Duncan had said he ruined Cameron, but this house was the nicest one they had passed in many miles. It was not some thatched, wattle-and-daub cottage huddled in a township of others like it. This house was situated on its own, of good size, built of stone, with rather attractive plantings all around it. A large stable stood to the north and a handsome carriage waited out in front.

Perhaps the family hung on to their pride through the property. Maybe they were one of those families that ate nothing but soup in order to keep up appearances.

"I say, sir, what is happening down there? Those people upstream?"

Ewan looked past the house to the congregation of dots about two hundred yards behind it. He hoped to heaven that he had not arrived on some festival day, or in the middle of a party or celebration. He really was not in the mood.

Since it appeared the household was busy by the stream, he and Michael passed the house and headed for the dots. They took on forms as they neared. A little crowd was watching something transpiring among three men.

Two of the men began walking away in opposite directions. Ewan was impressed by the determined expression of the blond-haired one heading his way. Then he noticed the pistols.

It was a duel.

The man coming toward him was much too young to be Angus Cameron. He looked to be no more than about eighteen. Ewan examined the other figure, the one heading in the other direction.

Cameron was dressed bizarrely, like someone in a Restoration costume drama. Boots, pantaloons and a red doublet covered his body. He was tall and wiry, and his spry step implied the years had not taken much toll.

He wore a flamboyant brown hat with a broad brim and big red plume. It appeared this old man wore his ancestor's garments and had never purchased any of his own. Definitely eccentric, as Duclairc's father had said. Or too poor to hire a tailor. Well, it could have been worse. He could have been wearing Druid's robes.

The pacing stopped. The red plume swished the air as Cameron turned. Ewan saw the face under the upturned right brim of the hat.

This was definitely not Angus Cameron.

It was a woman.